Private Listing

Bind Me

C.S. Berry

Author Note

Dear Reader,

Welcome back! If you haven't read book one, please be aware that this is a serial. There is no book one recap and if you haven't read book one, you will likely be lost unless you're looking for that one scene in Chapter 68 Double Entry. Enjoy!

Everyone else, I hope you're ready for this. Private Listing started out as just an idea for a serial and it built itself into a four book series. These books are meant to be read in order and there will be cliffhangers. Fair warning.

Don't worry. There is plenty of group spice, but beyond sex, she develops personal relationships with each of her guys.

PRIVATE LISTING is very much about consensual play.

While I tried to be as conscious of proper play within BDSM, please remember this is a fantasy. While everything might be possible, always go to a more trusted source for information than my book.

I love connecting with my readers. You can find me at my Facebook group is C.S. Berry's Spicy Executive Suite. You can also follow me on Instagram, but I generally post about the stories that are ongoing on Kindle Vella (which may contain spoilers).

While there are new scenes in the ebook, you can always continue in the Vella, in case you need to know now and can't wait for the next book to release. The chapter numbers coordinate with the episode numbers.

For a list of content warnings or to join my newsletter, please visit my website csberry.com.

XOXOXO,
C.S. Berry

Prologue

Coop

"One more fucking year in college." I hold up my glass to Seth and Blake. We're at the bar on campus. I'm going into my fifth year to get my master's while the others are cranking through to have theirs in four. "And to being free men."

"With the exception of Noah." Seth shakes his head but clinks our glasses together. Noah's girlfriend is getting on all of our last nerves. Yeah, it's great that he's found a girl, but she basically wants all of his time. I miss my geeky friend.

"Isn't he supposed to be here?" Blake stares at the door like he can make Noah materialize.

When I glance at the door, I take a drink of my whiskey. A girl with a tight ass and great tits walks in. She's got dark hair and long legs. I could hit that tonight and kick her out in the morning. I blow out a breath.

"Not interested?" Seth asks. He's always been the most observant of us. His gaze holds mine.

I shrug. "Maybe."

Things have been off between us since his girlfriend decided she wanted me more. That pissed off my girlfriend, which made her demand that I choose between being friends with Seth or her. Fuck her. I didn't really want her anyway. Like everything in my life she was a transaction between my parents and hers. Mom was more upset about the breakup than I was.

Seth's gaze turns thoughtful.

"Hey." Noah takes the extra seat at the table and raises his finger to the server. He runs a hand through his blond hair that might look nice if he used product, though I suppose the way it flops in his eyes works for him.

"Kelsey making you earn it?" Smirking, I take a drink. She's like the only chick who looked at me and didn't immediately change tactics. So I figured she'd be good for Noah.

Noah orders a whiskey and turns back to the table. "Fuck her. We broke up."

"What happened?" Seth asks, leaning his elbows on the table.

Noah pushes his hand through his hair again. His gaze goes to each of us. "She wanted me to move in with her and said I needed to choose between her and you guys."

"You chose us over pussy?" I laugh, but we've all had to do the same thing.

"Like you would have done different." Noah smiles at the server as she hands him his drink.

"So we're all single for the next year." I raise my glass.

"These girls." Blake shakes his head. "We need to focus on building our business and reputation. Not trying to appease girlfriends who think they should own us."

Noah nods.

"I mean, I do like getting fucked though." I lean back in my chair and toss a flirty smile at the brunette. Her smile grows and she looks away coyly.

"Yeah, it's great for you." Blake tosses back his whiskey and narrows his eyes at me. "You don't have to share a wall with fuckathon."

I grin. "I mean you can fuckathon all you want, Blake. I wouldn't mind listening to the sweet sounds of moans and spanking coming from your room."

Noah just shakes his head and sips his drink. We've been protective of him since grade school. Maybe I just didn't like injustice or maybe that day I'd been berated too many times by my mother, but when those kids started in on Noah, I broke. Mostly their noses.

My parents made sure I didn't get suspended.

But I let everyone know that if they messed with Noah, they were messing with me. Seth and Blake were already my friends even though they were a grade younger. They took Noah under their wing and the bullies backed off.

There was only one year we weren't all together. I started college a year before they did. I made a few friends, but nothing like these guys. What we have may not be normal, but we're a team.

"Those girls would just be moaning hoping you'd join in." Blake shakes his head. "It would be a hell of a lot easier if you weren't wealthy *and* handsome."

I smirk. "Aw, Blake, you flatter me."

"Not my type, fuckboy."

"It's a shame none of us are gay or bi." Noah blows out a breath. "It would make this a whole lot easier."

I laugh, because yeah, I like a woman's soft body and curves every day of the week.

Seth sets his glass down. "Maybe there's another solution."

"Yeah, I'm not turning gay for any of you fuckers." I shake my head, grinning. "I'd need a prettier group to tempt me."

Seth chuckles. "No one needs to turn gay, but all of us seem to have issues with women. They either want us and someone else or they want us all to themselves."

"That's kind of the definition of having a girlfriend." Noah raises an eyebrow.

"But does it have to be?" Seth asks. The brains of our operation.

Always thinking outside the box. "What do we need to do to have a successful business?"

Noah and Blake lean forward, more engaged in this conversation. I lean back and give the brunette an encouraging wink. I need to get fucked. It doesn't really matter who the woman is as long as she likes to experiment.

I bet that girl will let me take her ass.

"You gonna eye fuck that girl or join our conversation?" Seth's tone is low, but he's using that command in his voice.

"Fuck, boss, that voice must make the chicks drip for you."

Seth's eyes soften and his lips pull into a cocky grin for a moment before he gets serious. "First thing we need is a great idea."

"Which is why I've taken years of computer science." I tap my finger against my glass. "You and Blake studied business management while Noah took accounting. We've got that part down. Cybersecurity for businesses."

Seth nods. "The next thing we need is a plan."

"Which we've spent years perfecting." Blake motions to the server for another round. "Are you going to get to your point?"

"We grow our nest egg. Graduate college. Start our business." I gesture for Seth to continue. Where is he going with this? But I've learned that Seth is brilliant, and when he has an idea, you should sit down, shut up, and let him weave his story.

"The next step?" Seth takes a drink and looks at all of us. When his eyes meet mine, I give him a flirty wink because why the fuck not?

"Funding and surrounding yourself with the right people." Noah leans back. "Which we have."

Blake ruffles Noah's hair. "Thanks to you. Fuck, maybe we should just make Noah the business. He can spin gold from straw."

Noah ducks, but grins. He's a brilliant fucker too.

"We've got each other." I lean my elbows on the table. "So we've got the makings of a great company, but I'm not going to fuck any of you, even if I enjoy fucking ass."

"No one's asking you to." Blake narrows his eyes and leans back in his chair. "I'm not spanking your ass either."

"Focus, assholes." Seth leans forward. "We need each other, but we also need to have sex. These next few years are going to be rough. All our time will be spent building our business. We've already learned that girlfriends don't appreciate the amount of time we spend together. It's only going to get worse when we get our business going."

"If you're going to say we should just have one-night stands, that doesn't work for the trust I need." Blake leans forward on the table his arms bulging. "To truly do scenes properly, I need someone who gives me her trust completely."

"What conclusion are you trying to get us to, Seth? We've either had too much to drink or not enough to get to where you're trying to herd us." I lean back in my chair and sip at my whiskey.

"What happens when we get into relationships with women?" Seth sets his drink down.

"They want someone else within our group or get annoyed with the time we spend together." Noah seems to be following where Seth is leading us, which means he hasn't had enough to drink yet.

"So what if they don't get to choose?" Seth's eyes are calculating.

"Excuse me?" Blake leans in.

"Not in a bad way. What if we ask someone to be with all of us? No competing, no unnecessary drama. You fuck one of us. You fuck all of us." Seth picks up his drink and downs it.

"Together?" Noah asks. "Like at the same time?"

Blake chuckles. "That would never work."

"Why not?" Seth leans in. "I like to watch and give commands. You like to dominate a woman and punish her when she misbehaves. Noah likes to tie girls up and make them beg for release. And Coop—"

"I like to fuck." I lean in and clink my glass against Seth's. "I might have a mild exhibitionist streak and enjoy fun and games in the bedroom. But why can't we just grab some strange once in a while to curb our needs?"

"Most women aren't up for me tying them up on the first night." Noah runs his finger down his glass before lifting his gaze to mine. "I have to work them up to it."

"Same." Blake leans on his elbows. "College girls are experimental but even they have limits."

"If we find a woman that would work for all of us, why not play with her? Together or apart. It doesn't really matter." Seth's eyes burn with the fire of his idea.

"No woman is going to agree to that." Blake shakes his head.

I smirk. "Challenge accepted."

"What the fuck, fuckboy?" Blake leans back in his chair.

"I'm going to go get that hottie I've been eye fucking all night." I stand and straighten my clothes before combing a hand through my hair. "Let's see how experimental this girl might be."

Seth nods. I turn to Noah.

"Fuck, you're going to do it no matter what I say, but fine." Noah shrugs. "I got nothing to lose."

"Blake?" I arch an eyebrow at him and wrap my arm around his shoulder to turn him to see the brunette I mean. "Look at that ass. I bet she'll let me fuck that while you take her pussy for a ride. Isn't college about experimenting?"

"Only if she's sober and consenting." Blake takes a drink. "He's a fucking lawsuit waiting to happen."

I flash him a grin. "Give me a minute."

I walk over to the brunette as she's taking a sip of whatever fruity concoction she has. "Hey."

She smiles and lowers her drink. "Hi."

"Didn't we have economics together two years ago?" I study her face like I'm trying to remember. I mean she could have been in that class.

She sighs. "No, but I wish I did."

"You would have made a boring class so much better." I give her my devastating smile.

"I'm Amy." She holds out her hand.

"Cooper." I take her hand and lift her knuckles to my lips, pressing a kiss to them. "You can call me Coop."

She steps in closer. "It's nice to meet you, Coop."

I keep her hand in mine and tease her fingers.

Her dark eyes darken more.

"Can I buy you a drink, Amy? My friends and I are having a discussion that we definitely need a woman's view on. Care to join us?"

She bites her lip and looks toward our table. Her eyes widen a little, but not in fear. She glances at her friends who have moved closer to the dance area. "I could bring my friends?"

Doubt is in her voice.

I step in closer. "You don't have to. We just want to talk to you."

Her cheeks flush, but she draws back a step. "Just a minute."

She walks over to her friends and gets a girl's attention. She talks with her hands, and when the friend looks at me, I wave to her friendly-like. The girl's eyes get big and she leans into her friend. I'm sure that girl actually knows who I am.

It can't be helped. I'm wealthy and single and very open to exploring new territories. Word gets around. After a very animated conversation, Amy walks back to me.

"I'm good to go."

I bet you are. I offer my arm and she takes it as I lead her back to our table. I grab another chair and hold it out for her. When I sit down, I draw in a breath.

"Guys, this is Amy." I smile and point out my friends. "This is Seth. Noah. And the grouchy one is Blake."

She smiles and nods. "It's nice to meet all of you."

I stop the server as Noah asks what her major is. After ordering her drink, I turn back to the table.

Her smile is bright when she turns to me.

I reach out and brush her hair behind her ear. She gives a little shiver. Good.

"We were just talking about how hard it is to date in college." I glance at Seth. "Girls keep trying to tear us apart."

"Really?" Amy leans into me, showing me she's interested.

"They date Seth but then decide later they want me. Or they think we hang out too much." I brush my thigh against hers below the table.

"That's terrible."

The server stops and hands Amy her drink. Amy thanks her and takes a sip before setting it on the table, giving me her full attention.

"We were contemplating changing the way we do things." I lean back and meet Seth's gaze.

She follows my eyeline and her gaze collides with Seth's. Each of us is an attractive man in our own right. It's just that some women prefer wealth and status, and that's why they come to me.

"I had an idea." Seth leans forward and she leans in too. "Instead of letting a woman come between us, we all share her."

Amy straightens and looks at each of us for longer than a cursory glance. "Like fuck all of you?"

"That's what we're trying to figure out." I brush my arm against hers and she shivers. "We're very busy men and don't have the time to actually date four separate girls. We also wouldn't be able to give four girls enough of our attention, but with one girl . . ."

Her eyes widen. "So you would *date* this girl?"

"Obviously, we'd have an arrangement in place." Blake sets his glass on the table. "Like if we're fucking her, we aren't fucking anyone else."

She swallows as she loses herself in Blake's green eyes. "But she'd fuck all of you? Together?"

"We haven't figured out that part yet." Noah draws her attention. "Each of us likes things a certain way, but there's definitely some intersection with our play."

"But we also would want alone time with the girl." Seth runs his finger along the rim of his glass. "She would be our sole focus."

She swallows and reaches for her drink, taking a sip from the straw.

"It might take us a little time to perfect our technique, since we're used to fucking alone." I touch my lip and hers part. "But do you think a girl like that could exist for us?"

Her hands tremble so she sets her glass down. "As a woman, I want to explore my sexuality while I'm young. I don't think there's anything wrong with what you're proposing as long as everyone is a consenting adult."

I graze my fingers over hers. "What about you, Amy? Are you a consenting adult?"

Her eyebrow arches and she looks at Noah, Seth, Blake, and then her gaze returns to mine. "Tonight?"

"Tonight. The week. Maybe the month. Maybe even the whole year. We haven't really locked that down yet." I smile. "We could consider tonight the interview for the position?"

She drags in a breath and laughs. "Are you guys joking with me?"

"No, Amy, we're not." Seth draws her gaze. "We just know the next year is going to be difficult. We're seniors finishing up grad school. Having someone we can blow off steam with would be useful. What we aren't offering you is an actual relationship, but whatever you need, we'll help you out with. Even if that's a date to your sorority functions."

"So sex with no strings, except you won't fuck anyone else—"

"And neither will you." Blake captures her eyes again.

"Is it like a booty call thing?" Amy sips her drink and looks around the table. "Like I scratch your itch, you scratch mine?"

"It's whatever we make of it." Noah shrugs. "If we decide to go forward, we keep the lines of communication open. We talk about things. If something comes up and you want out, you're free to leave. If we decide it isn't working, we can end things. No hurt feelings."

"What do you say, Amy?" I take her hand and look into her eyes. "Want to interview for the position?"

She wets her lips and looks at everyone else. "Fuck it. Yeah."

Chapter 35

In the Moment

Blake

This day is a fucking mess. It's only Thursday but I'm so fucking done with this week. Between finding that shit on Madison's phone and dealing with the police, I can't fucking concentrate. Whoever that fucker is sent another fucking image of Madison naked when I went to download everything. Whoever is doing this to her is a creep that needs to be found.

I downloaded a copy of all the information off the phone before my buddy on the force and his partner came to pick it up. They spoke to all of us while Madison sat in a chair at the conference table with her arms wrapped around herself, looking pale and small.

So fucking fragile.

They haven't tracked down Valerie or her boyfriend Jeff yet. They promise to let us know what they find out from the texts and pictures. We don't have the resources to investigate cell information. If it had been to our company phone, we would've had someone look into it.

There's not much we can do, unfortunately.

I slam my drawer shut and glare at my office door. Fuck it. I can't stay here any longer. I need to go see if I can find that camera and get anything off it.

Standing, I grab my phone and head into the outer office. Madison stares off into space at her desk. Apparently, work isn't helping her either.

"Come on." I stop beside her and hold out my hand.

She eyes it warily before she stands and slips her hand into mine. "Where are we going?"

"Your apartment."

"No." She freezes and tries to pull her hand away.

I step into her and look down my nose into her blue eyes. "I need to find that camera, and you said you're missing stuff."

She glances at the other doors.

"You'll be safe with me, tiger." I jerk her into my arms and hold her close. "I won't let anyone have you."

Her eyes search mine before she sighs and relaxes into my arms. "Fine."

When I release her and take her hand, she clings to mine like it's her lifeline. I lead her to Seth's office and knock. I enter without waiting for a reply.

"We'll be in touch." Seth looks up with his finger held out to say *one minute*. "Yes. We're aware. Tomorrow."

I close the door, and Madison leans into my side like I'm the only thing keeping her upright. I resist the urge to wrap my arm around her.

She draws comfort from me and I want to do the same. The two of us keep creeping closer to the other, but that's not what's supposed to happen with our arrangement. Strictly sex and work. A contract, not a relationship.

It keeps us focused and makes sure no female can tear us apart.

But I'm having trouble fighting this protective instinct and the need to bundle her away and keep her from everyone else.

Seth puts his phone down. "What's happening?"

"Field trip." I lean against the wall.

He arches his eyebrow at me, and then his gaze softens when it falls on Madison. I'm not the only one having difficulty keeping things separate. This damsel in distress means one thing to all of us. Trouble.

"To?" he asks.

"Her old apartment. Most people won't be home from work, and she's missing stuff."

"And?" His expression is knowing. Seth could always read me.

I grunt to acknowledge his insight. "That camera might still be transmitting."

Madison stiffens next to me, but she doesn't pull away. A camera wifi signal I can trace.

"Fine. Don't take any unnecessary risks." His gaze goes to Madison. "Either of you."

She nods. "Of course."

We make our way down to the car. Traffic is light this time of day, and we make good time to her old apartment building. As we're climbing the stairs, Madison stops.

"I don't have my keys." Her eyes meet mine with a hint of frustration.

I tug her forward. "We changed the locks when we fixed the door. I have a set."

She falls in line with me, but with every step closer, she gets slower and stiffer.

I take her hand. "You're safe. I've got you. I won't let anything or anyone hurt you ever again."

Her wide blue eyes look up into mine.

Ever again. Fuck. Can I even keep that promise? We aren't going steady. We aren't even technically dating. We fuck and sleep together. And I save her from asshole roommates.

"I trust you." Her words scald me to the bone. I'm not sure I deserve that trust yet.

I guide her to the apartment door and unlock it. My gaze searches the hallway for anyone trying to watch us, but the doors are all closed and no shadows move below them.

When we cross the threshold into the apartment, I take a moment to check the doors in her hallway again before shutting and locking the front door.

Madison stands frozen in place, her hand on the front of her throat, staring at the chair still on the ground.

I forgot about her nightmares, being trapped in here all over again with Valerie and her dick boyfriend. And Hunter. Fuck.

"To your bedroom, now." My voice demands to be obeyed. It breaks her out of whatever loop she's in, and she hurries to submit to my order.

I follow her, shutting the door behind me. Except for the bare furniture, nothing remains in here. We had her packed up in an hour. I pull out my bug/camera detector and walk the entire room. Madison stands next to the door with her arms wrapped around her waist. She's stiff as a board.

Fuck. She can't seem to get out of her head.

When I'm sure her room is clean of listening or recording devices, I sit on the edge of her full-sized bed. She needs to be jolted out of it, but I'll use my method of shaking things up.

"Madison."

Her head shoots up, and she meets my gaze. Her eyes are haunted, and I know she's not really here in this moment but trapped somewhere in her nightmares.

I gesture for her to come closer. She stops directly in front of me.

"Across my lap. Ass up."

She lifts her gaze to me in surprise and takes a half step back. "Here?"

"Here."

She stares into the corners. "Is it safe?"

"Now, tiger."

She blows out a breath and lies across my legs. I flip her skirt up and pull her panties down to her knees.

"I don't think this is a good—"

Madison lets out a startled yelp when I cut her off with three spanks. Not hard enough to bruise, but just enough sting to pull her out of what's holding her down today. All those texts and pictures. The memories lingering in this place. I rub her ass cheeks, and she clutches my pant leg.

"You need to be present, tiger. Aware of everything around you. Not caught in a daze." I rub my hand close to her pussy and she tenses a little.

I spank her another three times.

"I'm here," she says defiantly when I rub her ass again. I chuckle lightly at her tone.

"What's weighing you down?" I slide my hand along the inside of her thigh, pausing before touching her pussy. She exhales.

"They filmed me in the bathroom. My bathroom, Blake. They saw everything. Inserting tampons, peeing, taking a dump. Everything that is private. Things I wouldn't share with anyone."

"Masturbating?" I stroke her ass cheek gently.

"It was private. It's my time." Her hands tug on my pant leg.

I spank her three more times. It's light and leaves her skin glowing pink but shouldn't really hurt. It's not about pain right now.

"What were you thinking when you masturbated? Do you remember?" My fingers drift closer to her pussy.

"Your voice. The four of you. It was after my interview. The conference table." Her voice is soft.

I rub my fingers between her thighs, along her slit. She sucks in a breath as I spread her wetness around her clit.

"You told me about that fantasy. That day in the conference room when I got you off."

Her breath hitches as I slide a finger into her slick channel. "Yes."

I pump my single finger in and out of her. "Can I tell you my version of your fantasy?"

"Please," she whimpers. She can't rock into my hand to get more of what she needs. She lies limply across my lap. Her breathing quickens.

I add a second finger and she moans.

"You naked on the conference table, spread out for us. Each of us takes a turn licking your wet pussy while the others take your breasts and your mouth, making you come until you're ready to take us all."

"Blake—" She cuts herself off in another moan.

I pull out, then push three fingers back into her. My thumb teases over her clit. Her wetness coats my hand.

"Coop will sit in a chair and lower your asshole onto his cock. Has he taken your ass yet, tiger?" I pause my fingers, waiting for her answer.

"Last night." Her hips try to move, but she doesn't get anywhere. My cock twitches as I stare at her puckered hole, imagining sinking my cock deep inside the tight sheath of her body.

"That's good." I thrust my fingers again. "I'll sit in another seat, and there's a way for us to sit so we both penetrate you from below."

"Fuck." Her hands tighten on my pant leg.

"You'll use your hands on Noah and Seth standing beside us and turn your head to service their cocks. One, then the other, back and forth. Sitting there stuffed full of our cocks while our hands touch you everywhere, tweak your nipples, pinch your clit."

"Blake, I need—" She groans as I press my thumb down to rub her clit.

"We'll lift you slowly up our cocks and have you sink back down on them. While Seth and Noah thrust into your hands and mouth until you are vibrating with pleasure, trembling with need. So fucking close that you can't help—"

She cries out as her pussy clutches my fingers. I keep rubbing as she gasps and wiggles to get away from my thrusting hand, rolling her into another orgasm. I could keep going. Drag another orgasm out of her, but I'm pretty sure she's here with me now.

She sags over my lap, her whole body twitching slightly as her breathing steadies. My fingers drip with her juice as I pull them out and lick them clean.

I help her stand and pull her panties up. "Look for your bracelet while I look for other cameras in this apartment."

She tips my face up. Her blue eyes are soft. She kisses me long and deep. "Thank you."

I smirk. "Anytime, tiger."

Madison

I search the room that has been my home for almost three years and come up with nothing. The guys Blake used to move me were thorough. No bracelet. I stare at the door, which thankfully Blake closed when he led me in here.

I could check Valerie's room and probably should. I turn to meet Blake's eyes. He remains seated on my bed. My pussy still flutters from the orgasms he gave me.

He lifts his gaze from his phone. "Done?"

"In here." I sigh. "I should check Valerie's room."

He nods and stands, adjusting his hard cock in his pants.

"Want me to help you with that?" I raise my eyebrow. I'd love to feel his huge, thick cock in my mouth or pussy. To forget about everything that happened here for a few minutes. My insides burst with heat.

"In a few." He lightly grips my chin and claims my mouth with his. The kiss fills me with all sorts of emotions: happiness, lust, desire, closeness, need.

He takes my hand and leads the way with his little device. It doesn't go off in the hallway or even near Valerie's room. Not that I'll be able to find anything in Valerie's room. It's a pigsty. Clothes are everywhere. A few pizza boxes lie on the floor.

My nose wrinkles. I wouldn't be surprised to find actual bugs.

Like insects. A shudder of horror ripples through me. I can take a lot, but not bugs.

When I begin to walk into her room, Blake catches my hand. "No, tiger. I'll have a crew come through and see if there is anything salvageable. You don't need to go in there."

I nod. We turn to the other door. The bathroom. My heart pounds and my hands grow slick. How long? How long did someone watch me in my private moments? How many people did they show it to? When and how did they get the camera in there?

Has it always been there?

Blake opens the door and uses his device. When he holds it near the ceiling, it lets out a sound. He pockets it. His fingers trail along the ceiling tiles, looking for a variation that would give away a camera, I suppose. He grabs the grate of the ceiling vent, and it easily comes off in his hand.

He hands it to me. I set it on the sink before wrapping my arms back around my waist. This was my home and safe space. I never thought someone would breach my privacy here. At least no one but Valerie, which is why I always locked my door.

He reaches into the opening, grabs something, and pulls it out. After taking a silver bag out of his pocket, he puts the small device in and seals it.

I want to stomp on it and pound on it until it's dust, but he might get something useful from it. My need to know outweighs the irrational part that needs to destroy what hurt me.

"Can you be brave for me?" He tips my chin, and I get lost in his green eyes. He's treating me with kid gloves, which I need for this, but he also snapped me out of my nightmares and made me come so hard.

So, if he needs me to be brave, for him I can. I nod. He touches his forehead to mine.

"Stand in the shower like you were in the video. I want to find the angle of the camera."

I tense for a second, but I move to the shower. "Are there any more devices in here?"

"None that are currently transmitting." That's not a no, but I'm not vulnerable in this situation.

I shiver as I lean against the shower wall, fully clothed and tuned in, aware of everything around me.

Blake opens something on his phone and walks around. He opens the bathroom door and his mouth turns into a grimace.

"What?" I step forward but pause.

"Someone recorded it from the door." His eyes are on his camera.

It takes my mind time to process what he said. My whole body goes cold.

"They were in the room when I was—" My hand covers my mouth and I shake my head. It's one thing to be filmed but another for someone to be right where Blake stands now, watching me pleasure myself. "I lock the door."

Blake sets his phone on the counter. "Easily picked. Not even picked. It's just a narrow emergency key."

"Valerie?" I mean, she wanted to fuck with me. She might have taken the video for her boyfriend. The thought of the two of them watching it. Watching me. My stomach turns, but there's nothing left to come up.

"How often was she here?" Blake asks.

I shrug. "Not often. Mostly when Jeff broke up with her."

Blake closes in on me and I back into the shower. He follows.

"What are you doing?" I meet his eyes.

"Giving you a new memory." He drops to his knees and ducks under my skirt, keeping me completely covered.

"Maybe not now?" I press my back to the shower wall, not exactly feeling sexy at the moment. But the minute he touches me, my insides wind up.

He slips my panties down my legs. "It's the perfect time."

His breath is hot on my bare thighs. He lifts my leg and puts it over his shoulder before his mouth closes over my pussy. I gasp at the heat of it. His tongue slides through my folds to thrust into my core.

I have nothing to hold on to as desire courses through my veins and makes my limbs weak. Blake lets out a growl against my pussy. It's so fucking hot and needy that I nearly come. His fingers hold me open as he explores every inch of me with his tongue, stopping to suck on my clit. My gaze darts to the door, closed, but I can imagine it open.

But instead of some no-face person haunting my vision, I can imagine Seth watching me, his eyes darkened and his shoulder resting on the doorframe as he tracks my hand. I slip my hand beneath my shirt and pluck at my nipple as Blake thrusts his tongue into me. My breath comes out in quick pants as the pressure builds.

His thumb rubs my clit while he continues to fuck me with his tongue. It's too much. I can't hold back. I shatter into a million pieces, crying out as wave after wave crashes over me. Blake's grip on my hips tightens as he keeps licking me through my orgasm.

He draws back and releases my leg. He flips my skirt over his head and stands before me. I grab his belt and undo it. His hands dive into my hair and cradle my head as we each stay locked in the other's gaze. I lower his pants and pull out his cock, stroking it with my hand.

"Fuck me, Blake."

He yanks me into a kiss before lifting me against the wall and thrusting deep inside me. I cry out in pleasure. He's so thick and fills me so well. Nothing is leisurely about the way he pounds into me, chasing his own demons away with a fast and hard fuck against the wall.

I wrap my legs and arms around him, clinging to him as he finds his pleasure inside of me. He captures my mouth, and I moan as the waves take me back under. I shatter on his cock, pulsing and pulling him deeper inside me.

Groaning, he comes, filling me, clinging to me, holding me tight against him, until he is spent. Pushing me against the wall and using his hips to hold me up, he brushes the hair out of my face.

Our eyes catch and hold as our breathing slows and we come back to ourselves. Back to each other.

Memories are funny things. The memory of me coming thinking of them all is now tainted by some unknown person. But this memory . . . This one will stick in my mind as the day I fell in love with Blake Wagner.

Chapter 36

A Door Closes

Madison

We step out into the hallway. When Blake locks the door to my old apartment, I release the breath I didn't even know I was holding. This part of my life is almost over.

"Madison!"

Ice creeps over my skin. I turn to see Robert rushing toward me, and my heart starts to beat again. I've been on edge, wondering if Valerie and Jeff would somehow appear. Blake steps in front of me, and Robert stumbles to a halt.

"Blake, right?" Robert grins and tries to peer around Blake to see me. "I'm good with names and faces. Aren't I, Madison?"

"Yes, you are." I move to the side a little so Robert can see me. I'm glad I put my scarf back on before we left the apartment. He would overreact to my injury and offer all sorts of things, like ice and food and a place to sleep.

It's not like he doesn't know I was injured. Blake told me Robert saw me when I was passed out that day. The picture of Blake carrying me flashes in my mind, and I take a half step away from Robert. What if he's my stalker?

"I'm glad you're okay. Did you want some chocolate cake? I have some cake. Just bought it from the grocery." He gestures as he takes a step toward his apartment.

My chest loosens. I don't think it's Robert. Yes, he had the opportunity, but how would he have gotten that video in my apartment? He was only in my apartment one time and never left my sight.

Blake takes a step forward, as if to make Robert stop talking to us, but I rest my hand against the center of his back. Robert was nice to me, even when he gave me the creeps.

"Not today." I smile wearily. "I've had a long day. I just need to go home."

Blake tenses a little beneath my hand.

"Oh, okay." Robert's sad face turns into a smile. "If you need a place to stay, I have room. I've told you before, but it would be safe."

His gaze darts to Blake. For the most part, he's been acting like Blake isn't even here, talking around him to me.

"I'm good where I am." I give him another smile. Politeness was ingrained in me from a young age. I don't see a reason to not continue to be polite to him. After all, he seems to care for me. "Thank you for your concern."

"I watched your place while Blake took you to the hospital. Nothing happened until guys from Morrigan Technology showed up. They were good guys. Secured the scene and everything. Even fixed the door."

"That's good." I scoot a little forward. Blake's hand shoots out and holds my hip to keep me from going around him and getting any closer.

"Valerie came back the next day and cussed about the locks being changed. I told her she shouldn't have hurt you." Robert shook his head. "She wasn't happy about that, but she left."

"Next time you see her, don't approach her, just call the police and tell them she's here." I glance up at Blake, but his eyes are narrowed on Robert. "The police are looking for her."

"I can do that. Are you sure you don't want cake? I can give you a slice like last time." Gesturing for me to come along, he grins at me as he steps toward his door again.

"Not tonight, Robert, but thank you. We have to go now."

Blake tucks me into his side as he maneuvers us around Robert to the stairs.

"You have my cell if you need anything or if you lost anything."

I pause to ask about the lost thing. It's an odd thing to add, but Blake keeps me moving. As he rushes us down the stairs, I pause to ask, "Where's the fire, Blake?"

He grunts and lifts me up and over his shoulder. I cover my mouth to keep from shrieking. The last thing I need is Robert following us to the car. Blake holds me steady with a hand on my ass.

I give up and relax. He'll tell me when we get to the car. I'm sure it's about Robert, but it could be about Valerie. Blake doesn't lower me until we're at the car. The driver doesn't even glance our way. I give Blake a look before climbing in.

When he joins me, I turn to him. "What was that about?"

"That guy isn't all there."

I wave him away. "He's harmless. Just lonely."

"He watches you. He knows your patterns. That's what stalkers do, Madison." Blake looks out the window as we head back to their building.

"Robert's not a stalker." He did occasionally give me the creeps, but he's fine. I'd know if he was stalking me. Wouldn't I? A shiver runs through me.

"You don't know that. And we can't know that. Not unless he's done it before." Blake takes my hand and pulls it onto his lap. His thumb brushes over the back of my hand, sending little sparks through me.

"Thank you for taking care of me." I shift closer to him on the seat, drawn to his warmth and strength.

He smirks at me. "Part of the job description."

I shake my head as I grin. "Yours or mine?"

"Both." He kisses me, and it feels like the first time. Soft. His lips linger on mine as his tongue explores the curves of my lips before I open beneath him. By the time we pull into the garage, I'm close to straddling him again in the car.

He chuckles as he lifts his head. "I have you all night, tiger."

A little thrill goes through me as we climb out and head upstairs. I can't wait for bed.

———

Dinner is, of course, wonderful, and I didn't have to cook, which makes it even better. While I'm still a little off-balance from the texts this morning, I'm doing my best to put them out of my mind and focus on the conversation around me about work.

"Tomorrow is Friday." Seth sits back and steeples his fingers against his lips while watching me.

Arousal flows through me at the thought of all of them taking me again. Blake's and Coop's words replay in full-scale color in my head. I cross my legs against the ache and longing.

"Everyone needs to make a list of what they want out of this arrangement. As detailed as possible." Seth nods at me. "Including you, princess."

"I gave you all my hard limits."

Seth sets his hands on the table. "And we need to know soft limits and what you want. Things you want to try. We want to fulfill your desires."

I'm all for that. I want to strip naked right now and beg them to take me, but maybe we should clear the dishes first.

"This is still something you want to do. Right, kitten?" Noah is sitting beside me and reaches beneath the table to trail his hand under my skirt, curling his fingers against the inside of my thigh, sending tingles straight to my center.

I meet his dark eyes. "Of course."

"Good." He squeezes my thigh and stands to collect our dishes. I miss the warmth of his touch.

"What exactly goes into this contract?" I turn to Seth and place my hands together on the table.

The others move around us, clearing the dishes. When I begin to rise to help, Coop presses his hand on my shoulder and gives me a smile, shaking his head. I settle into my chair and focus on Seth. His eyes have always held mine and now isn't an exception.

"Anything we feel we need to spell out. When we will do renegotiations. What will be allowed as an out clause. If you need a day without sex—"

"That's not going in the contract, sweetheart." Coop leans down, kissing my ear and sending tiny shivers racing through me. I agree with him. I don't think I can get enough of them.

Seth gives him an admonishing look, but Coop just shrugs it off.

"It's about what will make this arrangement comfortable for all of us." Seth leans back. "Such as knowing that none of us will have sex with someone else without talking with you first."

My insides clench at the idea of them having sex with someone other than me. I understand that I'm only one woman, but I'm willing to try to keep up with their needs. I don't even know how that conversation will go. Can I say no, you can't screw anyone else?

An unpleasant thought races through my mind. "What about dating?"

Seth contemplates me. Is he wondering if I want to date or worried I'm going to be a jealous woman? I shouldn't be jealous if this is just an arrangement and not a proper relationship. My gaze darts to the other guys who gaze at me, just as curious.

I clear my throat and pick at the napkin in my lap. "Obviously, I have no intentions of dating anyone, but I don't know what you guys have planned."

My voice is tiny by the end of my statement. This is so embarrassing, but that's what the arrangement is supposed to clarify, right? I mean, they aren't asking me to be their girlfriend.

"Madison."

My chin tips up, and I meet Seth's captivating blue eyes.

"For what it's worth, we rarely date. It's not just a time thing, but that plays into it." He takes a breath and blows it out. "This isn't a typical arrangement. We would never ask something of you that we wouldn't be willing to do ourselves. If we ask you not to date, then we would expect to do the same."

The death grip on my chest loosens.

"However, there are events which we need to attend with a date, and there is only one of you . . ."

He trails off, but I can finish that statement. They will have women who are arm candy and might not take me to these functions. It would probably be odd if I show up with four men or a different one to each event. Or show up with my boss to anything, probably. Am I going to be their dirty little secret?

Swallowing the lump in my throat, I shake off the weird feeling swirling in the pit of my stomach and smile at him. "Of course. That's understandable."

"I assure you nothing will happen between us and those women without discussing it with you first." Seth's assurance doesn't make me feel better.

If anything, it makes me shrivel up inside a little more. What if I can't be everything these guys need? What if one night a week with each of them and everyone on the weekend isn't enough? Should I be constantly servicing them to keep them satisfied and content with only me?

I'm not sure when I'd fit in actual work.

Noah sits beside me. "It doesn't happen."

I meet his eyes, having lost track of what he's saying. "What?"

"The type of woman we take to those events isn't who we're interested in." He takes my hand and squeezes it. The heat in his eyes keeps me locked in. This connection between the two of us grows each time we interact. I should shy away from it, but I can't help myself.

"This is why we need to draw up a contract, so we can all be aware of the behaviors that may cause friction among us." Seth's voice draws me back to him.

I nod, aware that they're all watching me. "I understand."

Seth cups my cheek. "We'll talk more about it on Friday when you've had time to think about what's important to you."

"I'm in the mood for dessert." Coop strolls over and leans with his hands pressed flat on the table across from me. His sky blue eyes rake over me, heating me up. "Anyone else?"

My heartbeat ratchets up as four hungry gazes fall on me.

"Are you willing to play, sweetheart?" Coop tilts his head, giving me an out if I need it.

But what I really need is these men.

"What did you have in mind?" My husky voice is the only sound in the room.

Coop lifts an eyebrow, and then his gaze falls on Seth, the ringleader.

"Princess, you can use your safe word any time to stop things completely, but tonight I want you to use green for *go*, yellow for *slow down*, and red for *stop* or *pause*." His blue eyes sparkle with mischief, making my insides tighten in anticipation. "Sound good?"

"Yes, sir."

His eyes darken. "Stand, princess."

Noah pulls my chair away from the table and I stand. Every inch of me trembles, waiting for their touch.

"Coop, give me your tie."

I turn to watch Coop's wicked smile as he removes his black silk tie and walks over to put it in Seth's hands. My panties dampen more, and I try not to press my thighs together.

"Noah." Seth holds out the tie to Noah, who takes it and steps behind me.

"You know the words, kitten. Right?"

"Green." For fuck's sake, go. I want it so badly I'm going to be leaking down my thighs. I love when they all play with me.

Noah chuckles as he draws my hair over my shoulders. Tingles scatter through me. I release my pent-up breath. He holds the tie in front of my eyes before covering them and securing the silk behind my head.

"You are ours tonight, princess. We'll do with you what we want."

"Yes, sir." My fingers tap against my thighs as I stand before them, barefoot. I removed my shoes and my scarf as soon as I walked into the apartment. Today I almost couldn't bear it around my neck, but I had to prove to them I could still work.

Someone steps behind me. I breathe in Blake's spicy cologne. I feel a slight tug on my skirt before the zipper inches down. My skirt billows to the ground around my feet.

The guys are being quiet, so all I can focus on is their quickened breaths. The scrape of a chair leg. A loud footstep. The warmth of a hand ghosting over my panties. I shiver.

"Cold, kitten?" Noah's voice is at my side.

I shake my head. "Not at all."

Someone closes in from the front, and my shirt lifts as each button is undone. I try to keep my breath even as Blake slides my shirt off slowly from the back. The silk trails along my skin like a caress. The back of a hand brushes over my stomach, and I inhale a mix of their scents.

"Beautiful." Coop stands in front of me. He takes my hands. "I'm going to lead you. I'll keep you safe."

"Okay." I step over my skirt. In my bra and panties, I let Coop lead me through the apartment. A door opens and we step into a room. It's warm in here, warmer than the open space of the living room. It doesn't smell like one of the guys, so I'm pretty sure it isn't someone's bedroom or even mine.

Fingers tickle my back as someone unhooks my bra and someone else draws it away from my body. A door shuts behind me. The rustling of clothing surrounds me. Anticipation wells within me as I stand completely still, unable to see where we are or who is where.

Every part of me waits for their touch. I'm so wet that if I weren't wearing panties, it would trickle down my thighs. My breath catches as the anticipation gets to be too much.

32

Chapter 37

Play Room

Seth

This is how it should always be. Madison in only her panties, waiting for us to fuck her. I let go of all the stress of the day. The texts, the police, the camera Blake found. None of that belongs in this room with us.

We have a range of furniture for sex that could be overwhelming to someone, like Madison, who hasn't played as much as us. We've experimented a lot over the years and found certain things we like. But we won't use most of it tonight.

We've all undressed, but no one touches Madison as she trembles, waiting. Her breathing is fast and her fingers twitch beside her thighs. Will she break the silence?

Coop reclines on a chaise and cocks his eyebrow at me. Everyone watches me, waiting for instructions, knowing this is what I do best. Fuck, I love this part.

I sit on a chair opposite Coop and nod to Blake. He steps forward and lowers Madison's panties. Her skin twitches beneath his warm breath. A shudder goes through her body, making my cock harden more.

"Madison."

Her head swivels to my voice. Her lips are parted and her cheeks flushed. Her nipples are hardened, eager. She has a dark freckle on her right hip that catches my eye. I lift my gaze to her face to watch her reaction to my words.

"I want you to fuck three of your bosses while I watch, but this time I want all of them in your body at the same time. Is that something you want to do?"

"Yes, please." Her fingers clench at her thighs. Her knees press together. Does she ache for us the way we ache for her?

"Are you still sore, sweetheart?" Coop asks, staring at her ass.

"No," she breathes out.

I nod to Noah, and he brings her over to me. I scoot to the edge of the chair. As my nose fills with the scent of her arousal, my cock twitches, wanting desperately to fuck her. Almost as much as I want to taste her.

"We need to get you ready." I take in all of her. Fuck, she's gorgeous.

Noah kneels behind her. Our breath coats her pussy and her ass. She whimpers as he nudges her legs apart.

"If you need to hold something, you can hold my shoulders, princess."

She inhales, and we both lean in. My tongue teases her clit and pussy while Noah spreads her ass cheeks and licks her puckered hole.

She gasps and her hands find my shoulders. As soon as she's stable, I lift her leg over my shoulder, opening her up to both of us. My finger tangles with Noah's as we both thrust them inside her pussy. She's dripping wet for us and moans in pleasure.

Her hips seem paralyzed by indecision as she wants to press against my tongue circling her clit and Noah's tongue thrusting into her puckered hole. Blake steps in and kisses her shoulder. Shivers course down her body.

"You need to come for us, tiger," he whispers in her ear. "Come for us so we can fuck you the way you're going to crave it from now on."

"Oh, fuck," she whispers.

My gaze drifts to Coop as he rubs his cock with lube, slowly stroking himself while watching us. Blake doesn't touch our girl with his hands, but he continues to press light kisses along her arm and shoulders.

Madison's grip tightens on my shoulders as her pussy convulses around Noah's and my fingers. She lets out a string of expletives while she continues to throb around us. When I suck on her clit, she cries out. Her fingers dig into my hair.

Precum leaks out of my tip at the taste of her slick in my mouth. Noah retreats and comes back after a moment. She tenses against my mouth as I slowly explore her sensitive pussy with my tongue, my fingers still buried inside her where she flutters around them. I thrust them occasionally.

I hold still inside when I feel Noah slide his fingers into her asshole. Sucking her clit, I feel him thrusting his fingers in and out and stopping to press along the walls to help relax her muscles. Her fingers dig into me as she pants.

Noah chuckles darkly, and I know he's going back in to rim her again as she jerks into my mouth.

"I can't—" She cuts off on a whimper, and then she comes again, her slick cunt tightening on my fingers. Noah slows his thrusting and works the muscles again.

"Do you need to slow down, princess?"

She drags in a breath. "No, sir."

I put her leg down and lean back in my chair, drawing my fingers out of her. A small shudder rolls through her body. Her breasts tempt me to lean in and taste them, but I want to watch Noah turn her pink all over with arousal.

Her hips rock against Noah's face and hand. Taking her hands, I draw her upper body down, resting her hands on my thighs. She's bent over, her mouth inches from my cock.

She would take it between her lips if I brought her a little closer. But not yet. I want to see her take three cocks before I give her mine. Besides, the view is worth it. Her breasts sway for me with every buck of her hips. She makes needy noises with her lips parted. Her silky hair dances against my thighs.

"Take her to Coop."

Noah draws his fingers out of her ass and stands behind her. I help her straighten. He's close but doesn't touch her. His eyes are dark as he leans in to say in her ear, "Next time we play, I'm burying my cock deep in your ass, kitten. It's so fucking tight and warm. I can't wait to feel how amazing this ass will be wrapped around my cock when you come."

Her breath shudders out of her, and she sways toward him, but he steps away. Blake guides her over to Coop, sitting at one end of the chaise. Noah disappears into the attached bathroom.

"Show us how you take a cock, princess."

Coop and Blake help her lower into position.

"Easy. Remember, sweetheart, how good it felt." Coop's voice is gentle. "Breathe through it. Relax."

His tip dips into her asshole.

"Coop." She moans at the feeling.

I use her slick on my hand to stroke my cock. She lowers herself slowly down onto him, her back to his front. Small gasps erupt from her lips as she buries his cock into her ass a little more with each movement. Blake stands in front of her, stroking himself as we both watch Coop's cock disappear into Madison's ass.

"She's so fucking tight," he clips out as she presses him all the way inside her.

"Show us."

He opens her legs and slouches down in the seat. The chair is low to the ground and her feet rest on the floor.

"Please," she whimpers.

"Ride him, princess." My voice is tight as I hold back the release threatening to spill over my hand. It's not time yet.

She rises, drawing in a harsh breath before she lowers.

"You are fucking beautiful, kitten." Noah stands next to Blake as we all watch her taking Coop's cock in her ass.

Blake gestures to Madison and nudges Noah. "She's still getting used to it. You should fuck her pussy, and I'll take her mouth."

Madison moans. Her hands reach up and cup her breasts. "Please."

"No touching, princess."

Her fingers glide along her nipples before she drops them to her thighs.

Blake moves to stand beside her. "I'll punish you later for touching, tiger."

"I think she likes that idea," Coop says. "You want Blake to spank your ass after you finish letting me ride it?"

"Please." Her lips part and her fingers dig into her skin as she lifts herself up and down on his cock a little faster.

"Hold still for a minute, love." Noah straddles the chaise in front of her and Coop. He drags his cock over her clit before sliding his tip inside of her. Watching her taking them so beautifully almost pushes me over the edge. I tighten my hand at the base of my cock.

"Oh, fuck," Madison whispers.

"Relax, sweetheart. You can do this," Coop whispers in her ear. His hands move up her sides and cup her breasts, massaging them. Noah kisses her shoulder as he slowly penetrates her, filling her with two cocks for the first time, one in her ass and one in her pussy.

Madison cries out when Noah thrusts in deep.

"Color, princess."

"Green. Oh, fuck, so green." Her skin is a blush from her cheeks to the tops of her breasts. She's almost where I want her. One more to add. I nod to Coop.

His blue eyes spark and he gives me a smirk. He knows what I want him to do. He draws her back to rest on his chest. His hand wraps around her hair and tilts her head to the side where Blake stands.

"Open your mouth," he whispers in her ear.

She whimpers, but not from pain. Her pink tongue darts out to wet her lips.

"Noah's going to do all the work, and I'll help Blake." Coop kisses beneath her ear. "You just lie back and let us fill you."

Blake's cock brushes against her lips, and she lets out a sigh. A small shiver goes through Blake as her breath cascades across his dick. I bet that feels fantastic.

Noah pulls back and thrusts deep inside her.

Madison's lips part in an O and Blake thrusts into her mouth.

"Such a good girl." I stroke my cock as I watch my friends use our girl. Coop stays deep in her ass while he holds her head steady for Blake to fuck her mouth. Noah's cock pistons in and out of her cunt.

It's the most beautiful thing I've ever seen.

She makes these little needy noises in the back of her throat. The kind she makes when she gets close to the edge. I stroke my cock lazily. I could get off just from this, but when they finish, I'm going to fuck her pussy and then her ass.

She can barely fit all of Blake's cock in her mouth.

"Use your hand on Blake's cock, princess."

She obeys me, stroking along his base.

"Rub your clit."

She's perfect and does as I ask. This is what we've been looking for. *She* is what we've been looking for.

Her fingers rub circles over her swollen clit. She moans deep in her throat and I can tell the minute she tightens in climax. It's her stillness even as the guys thrust deep inside her mouth, cunt, and ass. As if her body simply surrenders to the orgasm so sweetly. Deep in the back of her throat, she lets out a guttural moan that makes Blake cuss as it vibrates his cock.

Both Coop and Noah thrust a little faster before burying their dicks deep as they fill her with their cum. Her cheeks hollow out as she sucks on Blake. Groaning, he comes down her throat.

Madison swallows as she leans back against Coop. The tie

remains around her eyes. They breathe as they come down from their high. She's pressed between Noah and Coop. Still connected. Blake slumps on the bench beside them.

I stand, and Noah glances at me. He steps back and I shift into his spot. Coop grabs Madison's thighs to hold them open for me. I look at her pink, swollen pussy for a second before I thrust my cock fully into it. She gasps and shudders at my thickness. I feel Coop's cock hardening through the thin wall separating us. I hold still, deep inside her.

"Seth." Her hands come to my shoulders.

I brush her nipple and give her a moment to tell me to slow down. Her hips buck against me, and I grin. Hovering over both of them, I thrust hard into her over and over again. Her lips part as her breasts rub against my chest.

I pause buried inside her, feeling her pulse around me, so close to coming. Dragging her legs to wrap around me, sinking deeper, I grab her hips and slide her forward almost off Coop's cock before sliding her back onto it.

The mewling noise in her throat makes my cock twitch. I fuck her with Coop's cock repeatedly.

"Fuck, man." Coop closes his eyes.

Her noises fill the room as she comes loudly. I keep her riding Coop's cock until he groans his release. He collapses on the chaise as I lift her off him. She sags on me, her arms draped around my shoulders.

"Seth?"

"Shh, princess." I lay her back on a bench. Noah catches her head and claims her mouth with his.

I thrust a few more times into her cunt before I pull out and thrust into her ass. She groans into Noah's mouth as I fuck her ass, releasing all the toxicity from the day and enjoying the pulsing of her body surrounding me. She's so tight, strangling my cock.

Blake moves to one side of the bench and takes her nipple into his mouth, sucking her in. Coop joins him, taking her other nipple. She arches her body to them, whimpering into Noah's mouth.

Her skin is flushed. Cum drips out of her pussy. Coop's fingers gather it and push it back into her cunt, holding it there while his thumb works her clit. Her ass is so fucking tight around my cock that I can't hold back another minute.

Roaring my release, I drive my cock deep as it unloads. Her ass tightens as she comes again, clamping down on my cock, wringing out every last drop from me. Her body arches against the others as they continue to caress her body to drag out her orgasm.

I stroke her thighs as I wait for her to come down and relax so I can pull out.

Noah takes the tie from around her eyes, and she blinks up at me.

"Thank you." She sighs as her head falls back. Her eyes slide shut.

"You're beautiful, princess." I step back as Blake lifts her to cradle her in his arms. Her soft smile kicks me in the chest. I don't think we can remain emotionally detached from this one. I'm not sure I want to.

Chapter 38

Disciplinary Measures

Madison

I have been thoroughly fucked into oblivion. Blake has me in his arms, and it's all I can do to keep my eyes open. Before I have a chance to look around the new room with a whole lot of leather bench-like things, we are out the door, through his bedroom, and into his bathroom. He holds me cradled to his chest as he starts the shower.

I feel like a rag doll, but my whole body relaxes and buzzes with energy at the same time. I didn't know what to expect from this arrangement, but I definitely want more of that. Blake sets me on my feet and ushers me into the shower.

"How do you feel?" His hands are gentle as he sweeps my hair over my shoulder. I lean against him, his warm skin drawing me in like a beacon.

"Tired." I press my cheek to his chest as he works on shampooing my hair. If I had an ounce of energy, I would clean him in return, but I'm spent. Emotionally. Physically. Mentally. "It's been a long day."

His chest rumbles with a chuckle beneath my ear. I let go of all the tension from today, knowing I'll be safe in Blake's arms tonight.

"Anything you didn't like?" He rinses my hair and shampoos it again. His fingers massaging my scalp make me moan in pleasure.

When his cock hardens against my stomach, a pulse of heat flows through me. I'm not sure I can go any more rounds today. He doesn't act like we're going to do anything about it, though I'm sure I could rally if he needed me to. He's all about taking stock and getting clean right now. So, I just snuggle up against him.

I concentrate on his question. "The blindfold made me much more aware of where you all were." Every sensation was heightened because I couldn't anticipate who or what would touch me. Or when they would sink into me. My whole body felt like a live wire waiting to release its energy.

"It's fun to play with sensory deprivation." Blake's low voice rumbles through his chest.

"Mmm." Take away my sight and my hearing and give me these four men any day of the week. The pleasure they provide is worth it.

"What did you think of the double penetration?"

My pussy clenches as I think about the feel of two cocks inside me. "So fucking full." I tip my head to look into his eyes. "Wonderful."

His lips twitch into an almost smile. Running his fingers over my scalp, he rinses my hair and puts in some of my conditioner.

I love that they all have my products in their bathrooms. Just like I've noticed their products in my shower. It makes me feel less like I'm invading their space, rather that they've made room for me in their beds and their rooms.

Blake twists my hair and brings it over my shoulder while he soaps up his hands with my floral body wash. "Are you sore anywhere?"

His hands skate down my back to cradle my ass, then one slides between my ass cheeks. I gasp at the jolt of pleasure that thrums through me as he rubs over my puckered hole. His fingers slide inside my asshole.

My core clenches, empty.

"Are you sore here, tiger?" His voice is low and gentle as he works his fingers in and out slowly.

"No," I whisper. My breath speeds up. I reach for his cock against my stomach, wanting to feel him. I stroke him at the same pace as his fingers thrust into me.

He groans. "I won't fuck your ass tonight."

I lift my head from his chest and tip back to look at his face.

His green eyes meet mine as we tease each other with gentle touches. The pressure builds inside me, soft this time. He leans down and takes my mouth like he can't resist anymore. Like it's all too much and not enough at the same time.

I rub my thumb over the tip of his cock, feeling his precum. I draw away from his kiss and put my thumb in my mouth to taste him again.

Blake groans. He pulls his fingers from my ass. His eyes darken and he lifts me against the shower wall before thrusting his cock into my pussy. I bite my lip at the sensation of him inside me, stretching me more.

"Are you sore here?" he whispers against my ear.

"No, I'm not." I suck on his earlobe and shift my hips against his. I want him so badly. "Fuck me, Blake."

"Do you know how fucking hot you looked tonight?" He pulls out slowly and presses back into me, burying his cock deep inside. The same slow pace over and over.

"Tell me." I tip my head back against the shower wall as shivers ripple through me from his lazy thrusts.

"Watching you take Cooper in your ass was better than I imagined. And Noah, fuck. You took both of them so well." Blake thrusts a little harder into me.

"It felt so good." I moan and thread my fingers through his wet hair. "You always make it feel good."

"I can't wait until it's my cock in your pussy while someone fucks your ass." Blake's words blast over me like a tidal wave.

Crying out, I climax, clinging to him.

I'm still coming down when he says, "I'll wait to take your ass, tiger, but when I do, I'll make sure you come hard."

He thrusts into me and releases his cum inside me. My pussy convulses around his throbbing cock. He lifts his head and meets my eyes.

"I'm glad it's you, Madison." He kisses me tenderly.

Me too.

I wake up to an extra body in the bed. I'm half-draped on Blake's chest but glance over my shoulder at Coop spooning me.

His sleepy blue eyes open and meet mine.

"Hey," I say softly.

He smiles and trails his hand over my ass. "Couldn't sleep. Kept dreaming of you."

Heat rushes to my cheeks. I turn so we're face-to-face with Blake at my back. "What did you dream?"

"About your mouth." His thumb rubs over my lower lip and tugs it down slightly. "And how good it feels on my cock."

I flick the tip of my tongue over his thumb and he groans. My insides scorch with fire. After we finished our shower, Blake and I collapsed into bed naked. Coop apparently joined us in our nudity.

"Did you get punished last night, sweetheart?" He pushes his thumb between my lips, and I suck on it and shake my head.

Coop groans and grabs my hand. He clasps it around his cock and strokes himself with my hand. "I was hoping you'd say that."

I suck his thumb as I stroke his cock, my eyes never leaving his.

"Sit up against the headboard, Coop." Blake's voice in my ear makes me even wetter.

Turning, I look at Blake, sprawled behind me. His green eyes flash with heat.

"Coop's right. You earned a spanking for touching yourself

without permission, tiger." Blake runs a hand through his messy hair. "Time to pay up."

I bite my lip. They're hard and ready for me. My core clenches. "Yes, sir."

"Hands and knees. Take Coop's cock in your mouth."

I hurry to comply, knowing we need to get to work this morning. When I lower my mouth over Coop, I meet his eyes before starting back up.

Blake spanks me. "Did I tell you to suck him off?"

I release Coop's cock and say, "No, sir."

Coop grins at me and threads his hand through the back of my hair.

"Take him in your mouth."

I lower again and take his cock as deep as I'm comfortable with and wait. Blake's heat hovers between my knees. I can almost feel his eyes taking in my ass and wet pussy.

I want to tell him to take what he wants. Whatever he wants. It's his. I'm his.

My breasts hang heavy and tight. All my muscles tense, waiting for the pleasure and the pain. Needing it.

"How many should she get?" Blake asks. I swear I can feel the heat of his hand hovering over my ass cheek.

Coop's fingers tighten in my hair, and he pushes me a little farther down on his cock. "Five seems like a good number."

My mouth is full, so I can't really take part in the conversation. He's not gagging me on it, at least. I know I can stop this with a snap of my fingers. But I don't want this to stop. I want them to use me and pleasure me.

Blake's hand comes down hard on my ass, making me cry out and thrust down on Coop's cock. My eyes water at the depth. Coop pulls my head up slightly, giving me room to breathe. My head is so far down I can't even look up into Coop's eyes. All I can focus on are his abs.

Blake spanks me again. These aren't the light ones he used in the apartment yesterday. Even though I try to brace myself, they force me to take more cock down my throat with each spank. Blake massages my ass where he spanked me, and I moan at the caress, feeling my pussy lips part at the motion.

Coop curses. "If you do that again, Madison, I'm going to blow."

I slide my tongue along the underside of his cock, and he pushes my head down to take all of him. I fight the initial panic and breathe through my nose.

Blake spanks me two more times and my pussy throbs. Coop pulls me back so I can breathe normally while Blake caresses my ass. He pulls my ass cheeks apart and holds them there.

I whimper, imagining him staring at my holes and wanting to fuck me. Deciding which one he wants to fill with his thick, hard cock. I widen my legs a little and push my ass up into the air in offering.

Blake's chuckle is dark. "Trying to tempt me, tiger?"

His next slap lands on my pussy. I buck forward, and Coop lifts me off his cock. I breathe through the pain, and then Blake's hand is sliding over my pussy, lightly rubbing. Moaning, I can't help rocking into his touch.

Coop lowers me to take his cock in my mouth again, and this time he uses his hold to slowly fuck my mouth.

As Blake continues teasing my clit with his fingers, his cock nudges at my entrance, and I brace myself for his thrust. He sinks inside me and the guys find a rhythm, using my mouth and pussy while Blake teases my clit.

I come apart under their steady rhythm, moaning around Coop's cock as my orgasm drags me under its spell. Blake groans as he thrusts another time deep inside me and fills me with his warm cum. He holds my hips against his, his cock buried within me while Coop fucks my mouth a little faster.

I relax my throat as he goes deep. Blake's fingers rub on my sensitive bud and another climax works its way through me, clenching around Blake's cock. I suck on Coop's cock as he pistons into my mouth.

Coop groans and pushes himself fully inside when he comes down my throat. I swallow around him, taking everything he has to give. He groans again, then lifts my head and takes my mouth with his. Blake withdraws from my pussy and pats my sore ass.

"Good girl."

Warm fuzzies burst inside my chest at the praise. Coop pulls me into his lap and pushes his fingers into me to hold Blake's cum inside.

Coop lifts his mouth from mine to say against my lips, "Definitely a good girl."

Fuck, I love being their good girl. I'd be their good girl forever if they'd let me.

Chapter 39

Business as Usual

Madison

Friday lunch is with a new client. No surprise guests at this one. Thankfully.

"Next time I'll bring more people." Heath Duncan is a beast of a man with a broad grin and a twinkle in his eyes. As tall as any of my guys. As broad as Blake. And handsome. Brown hair with a touch of a wave and blue eyes the color of the ocean. He's a little older than my guys, I'd guess. Those eyes pause on me again. "Or you could bring more pretty women with you."

He winks at me, making me blush and look away. He's been flirting with me the entire lunch. The other guys seem fine with it, but Blake is reaching a boiling point.

Seth shakes his head. "Stop trying to poach our new assistant. There are plenty of good ones left. Find your own."

Heath's laugh is carefree and inviting. "So selfish, but I must say, you have impeccable taste. Every new one is more breathtaking than the last."

My gaze jerks up to his. *Every new one.* This guy is supposed to be a new client. How would he know—

"Enough with the compliments." Coop leans back in his chair with a grin. "You're confusing Madison."

Heath gives me a look. "That one"—he points to Coop—"and I go way back. College days. Before this lot moved him off campus."

That gives me a little context. I smile slightly, trying not to be encouraging.

"It took me years to get my business to where I could afford to hire these guys." Heath chuckles and waves at the four of them. "They have a knack for finding talent. I'm sure you're quite brilliant beneath that gorgeous exterior."

My cheeks must radiate with heat. I don't even know how to respond to this guy.

"Getting them young and teaching them right. Isn't that what I always told you?" Heath grins and hits Coop in the shoulder. Blake's fingers tighten dangerously on his fork.

Seth clears his throat. "Let's get back to business."

With the weight of Heath's stare off me, I focus on taking notes for the meeting. When we all rise to leave, Blake steps behind me and guides me out around Heath, who just laughs.

"He's a possessive one. Worried I'll slip her my card, Blake?" Heath's voice follows us out into the noisy dining room.

"Asshole," Blake mutters. He finally stops when we are outside of the restaurant, waiting for the car to pull around.

I stand beside him, always aware of his presence but also knowing we're supposed to be coworkers. His hand settles on the small of my back. I don't lean into him like I want to because that wouldn't be appropriate for his assistant to do. His thumb brushing over my ass cheek is barely appropriate, but I ignore it.

When the car finally arrives, I glance up as I step inside and swear I see Valerie across the street. My heart clatters to a stop, and my fingers go to the scarf around my neck. I rush into the car and slide over to see if I can spot her from the safety of the car.

Blake grumbles as he climbs in after me.

I grab his jacket sleeve and tug on it. He finally registers my face. His green eyes narrow on mine.

"Why are you so pale? Are you sick?" He cups my cheek.

I shake my head and force out, "Valerie. I saw her."

But when I look out the window, I don't see her at all. I gaze up and down the street, but she isn't there.

"She was right there. I didn't notice until I was getting into the car." The words tumble out of my mouth in a blur. "She was watching me. She looked right at me."

My body shakes, and Blake draws me into his side, wrapping his arm around me.

Seth opens the door and gets in on the other side. "What happened?"

"Madison thought she saw Valerie," Blake says against my hair.

"I did see her." I lift my head to meet their eyes. "It was her. She was there, and then when I looked again, she was gone."

Seth brushes his hand over my hair and meets my eyes. "We believe you."

His gaze flicks to Blake. I'm sure Blake shakes his head at Seth to tell him he didn't see her. I want to believe that they believe me, but I also know trauma does weird things to people. Makes them see and feel things that aren't there.

But this isn't that. I'd recognize her dark hair and those soulless eyes anywhere.

When the driver pulls away from the curb, I keep my gaze out the window, watching everyone on the sidewalk. It was her. I know it was. She could be watching me right now and I wouldn't know it. I can't feel her gaze on me, and I wouldn't have known she was there if I hadn't met her eyes.

After a block of me staring out the window, Seth draws me into his arms and rubs my back.

"The police are doing everything they can to find her and Jeff." His voice is reassuring, but what he's saying isn't necessarily the truth. An assault with an unlawful restraint charge isn't a high priority for the police, no matter who the victim is or who she knows. I'm well aware of this.

Those two will eventually do something that brings them in, and then they'll be charged. But until the police catch them, they're always there. Somewhere, waiting for me to slip up.

Noah

Seth filled us in about the sighting after lunch. Madison still looks a little shell-shocked an hour later. She works, but it's like she's seen a ghost. Her fingers tremble on the keyboard and she keeps looking at the elevator. I've been trying to let her be and let her adjust, but this is ridiculous.

She needs to get out of her head. I happen to enjoy getting her out of her head. Maybe a little too much.

When I clear my throat from my doorway, Madison looks up from whatever she's working on. Her blue eyes meet mine. I nod toward my office for her to join me.

When she rises, I back inside and hold the door open. She walks in with her notepad in hand.

"Sit." I nod to the couch as I close and lock the door.

Her eyebrow rises at the sound of the lock, but I don't mention it as I join her on the couch.

"You have something for me?" She opens her notepad and holds her pen ready.

"I don't have any work for you to do, but I want to talk to you." I lean back on the couch and fold my hands in my lap.

She sets the pen and pad on the coffee table and turns toward me. "What about?"

Time to get her back on track. "Limits. Hard. Soft. None."

Color rushes to her cheeks, and she barely holds back a smile. "Shouldn't that wait until later? The meeting?"

I shake my head. "I want to make sure you're okay with what I want to do to you. I don't want you to be surprised at the meeting."

Her smile grows and my pulse increases. "Okay, Noah. What do you want to do to me?"

I grin and pick up my tablet. "Did you get a good look at the room last night?"

Licking her lips, she shakes her head. "Things happened pretty quickly, and I was blindfolded for most of it."

"That's what I thought." I open some pictures on my tablet. "We have furniture that helps with certain positions."

I hand her the tablet. On the screen are photos from websites showing how the furniture can be used. If I want to bind her like the women in the photo. Which I do. Thinking of having her like this makes me hard, but I'll understand if she's uncomfortable with the idea.

It won't make me want her any less.

Her eyes widen, and her mouth opens into a small O. "You want to do this with me?"

She points to a bench that would hold every inch of her down while leaving her pussy, ass and mouth available for me—and potentially the others—to use.

"Yes." I brush her hair behind her ear.

Her heated eyes flick up to me. "I don't see anything I wouldn't be willing to try."

She hands me back the tablet, and I set it on the table.

"What do you want from us, kitten?" I take her hand and turn it over in my palm. Running a finger over her wrist, I meet her gaze.

"Anything you're willing to give to me." Her voice is breathless. Her hand trembles in mine.

"We have all explored our kinks and can't wait to try them with you, but have you been able to explore things you might want to try?" I grab the hem of her skirt and inch it up.

Her darkened eyes rise to mine. "Between your kinks, I think I'll explore everything with you guys."

I chuckle darkly. "Not necessarily. We all tend to be dominant and want control. We want you at our feet, begging for pleasure."

She bites her lip as I inch her skirt up to reveal her panties. I know she'll be wet and ready for me, but I want her to explore her own sexuality too, outside the constraints of what we desire.

"What I want to know is if you want us to kneel for you." I slide to the floor and take hold of the sides of her panties, dragging them down her legs. "If you might long for control."

Her breathing quickens. I hold her knees apart and take in her pink pussy, glistening with wetness.

"What do you want me to do, kitten?"

I rest my hands on her knees and wait for her.

Her blue eyes twinkle as she rests against the back of the couch. "Unbutton my blouse."

I rise and undo her buttons. One by one. Revealing the lacy white bra beneath. I stop when I finish her order and look at her.

"Suck my nipple."

I lean forward and suck on her nipple through the bra. Gasping, she arches her back, pushing herself more into my mouth. I keep my hands on her knees, though my fingers clench into her soft skin. I take her in, sucking, teasing. Her soft floral scent blends with the musk of her desire.

"Do the same to the other." Her eyes are barely blue when they meet mine as I latch onto her nipple and suck. Tonguing the tip. Giving it the same attention.

"Slide your hands up my thighs."

Holding myself back, I pause next to her groin, still sucking on her tit. I want to fuck her so hard right now, but she needs to know I'm willing to play by her rules too.

"Rub my clit." Her hips buck toward me as she buries a hand in my hair.

I drag my finger through her wetness, gathering it before sliding to her clit and rubbing her softly.

"Harder, Noah," she whispers, like we're sharing a secret.

I'm so fucking hard right now. My pants are almost painfully tight against my cock. I want to grab her arms and hold them above her while I fuck her.

She pulls me off her breast and pushes me back on the other one. "Fuck, Noah, put your finger inside me."

I slide my finger deep inside her, and she hums with pleasure. "More."

Another finger joins the first, but that's not enough for my kitten. "More."

I slide in a third, stretching her.

"Oh, fuck." Her eyes squeeze shut. Her lips part. "Fuck me with your fingers, please."

Slowly, I thrust in and out of her while I suck on her nipple and tease her clit. She pulls my mouth from her nipple and meets my eyes.

"Suck my clit." Her words are more a command than anything she's said so far, and I grin. She's taking charge of her own pleasure.

Pressing my lips against her clit, I tease it with my tongue before I suck it. She grabs my free hand and lifts it to her breast, moving the lace out of the way so my fingers trace her nipple.

"Faster," she says with a moan. Her heavy breaths fill the room, and her hips buck against my mouth and fingers. "I'm going to—"

She bears down on my fingers. I suck harder as she cries out. Her whole body arches against me as she comes. Slowing my pace to ease her back down, I press a kiss to her clit and feel the aftershock ripple through her. I sit back on my ass in front of the coffee table, looking up at her.

Still splayed open. Her pussy swollen and glistening wet. Her shirt unbuttoned and one hardened pink nipple exposed. Her bra damp from my lips. She looks properly ravished. She's a goddess.

"How'd that feel, kitten?"

Her smile is wobbly, and she gives a little chuckle. "So good."

"Maybe Blake and Seth's little submissive might be a switch?" I arch an eyebrow at her.

She puts her hand over her heart and inhales. Her eyes sparkle at me. "Maybe. I might need to try it out more to find out."

I grab her hand and pull her down to straddle my lap. My hand dives into the back of her hair, and I pull her mouth to mine, thrusting my tongue inside. She meets it with her own as her hips rock over me. I pull back.

"Always willing to play whichever role you desire, kitten." I lick her bottom lip.

Her lips part.

"Undo my pants."

Her hands make fast work of my belt, button, and zipper. The relief from the constraint isn't nearly all I want from her.

"Take me inside you," I say against her lips.

She rises onto her knees and pulls my cock out of my pants before sinking down over it. Her mouth opens in a gasp. I claim her lips as I thrust up into her. We surge together, fucking like we can't get enough of each other.

I break off the kiss and rest my forehead against hers. When her hungry eyes meet mine, I reach around and slide my finger, wet from her orgasm, into her ass. She convulses around my cock as she clings onto my shoulders.

"I'm taking this ass, kitten." I thrust hard into her. "In the meeting, my cock will be the one thrusting in and out of your tight ass until you come all over me."

"Noah." She shudders in my arms as I press deep one final time and explode. I can feel her all around me as I pulse within her, spilling my seed. I meet her eyes as our foreheads press together.

Maybe I'm falling too hard, too fast. Maybe I don't care. "You're mine, kitten. Every inch of you belongs to me. And every inch of me belongs to you."

Chapter 40

A Different Kind of Interview

The conference room is empty as I stroll in. We still have ten minutes before the meeting. I walk to the windows and stare down into the street. We're too high to make out people, but the sidewalks surge with tiny specks getting out of work and heading home to their loved ones.

It's a novel concept. One that I don't believe will ever work for me.

I can't imagine being so connected to someone else that I'd ever leave my friends. And having someone accept all of us for who we are doesn't seem possible. It's one thing to fuck all of us, but for a woman to love us all and to gain our trust completely, I just don't think that will happen.

Besides, I have a family. My family is right here with me. Cooper, Blake, and Noah.

A noise makes me turn. Madison.

She smiles at me. "I didn't want to disturb you. Just putting out the forms like you wanted."

Her blond hair glows in the sunlight coming in through the

windows. Her blue eyes sparkle with life. She's young. Younger than our previous assistants. But that doesn't mean she's less capable. She still has on the scarf I bought her, which makes my cock throb and makes me angry at the same time.

I love that she's wearing something I bought her but hate that she wears it to hide her bruised and battered skin beneath the soft silk.

"Come here."

With no hesitation, she sets down the papers and comes to stand before me. My cock hardens at how she accepts my commands. She never questions me. I've never had to tell her to obey me. She just does. And when she does, it's beautiful.

Her heels today make her taller, but she's still not as tall as me.

I reach out and unwind the scarf from her neck. When it's gone, her pale fingers touch the discolored skin. Her flesh is tinted shades of yellow, purple, and green.

I toss the scarf on the table and ghost my fingers down the side of her neck. "How's it healing?"

"Still a little painful," she admits. Her voice is still a little off but seems to be better every day. I trace her earlobe with my finger, and she shivers slightly.

"What's your stance on marking?" I lightly pinch her earlobe between my thumb and finger, rubbing it.

"Marking?" Her lips part, and her eyes give away her desire. She wants me and that's intoxicating.

"After you heal. Hickeys. Love bites. Possessive marks that claim you as ours."

A shiver whips through her. I drop my hand and lean back against the window.

"Do you like the thought of that? Of us possessing you?"

She bites her lip and nods. "Yes, sir."

"Take off your panties." I should wait. The others will be here soon. We should discuss the arrangement and get down the details before we play. Even though I should wait, I can't seem to make myself with her.

She reaches under her skirt and shimmies them off her hips before they glide down to the floor. She steps out of them and bends over to pick them up.

"Set them beside your scarf. Sit on the edge of the table, feet up in different chairs."

The way she follows my direction makes me hard.

"Lift your skirt and show me your pussy." Leaning against the glass, I cross my ankles as I watch her. She's not shy about it, but she doesn't draw it out either. She's impatient. Her cheeks are flushed with heat. Her lips part slightly.

"Show it all to me, princess. Spread your pussy open with your fingers."

Her breasts rise and fall with the quickness of her breath. She arranges her skirt so it won't fall between her legs and then uses her fingers to hold herself open to me.

"How do you feel today?" I keep my gaze on her pink pussy. Her cunt clenches at my words.

"Good," she breathes out.

"We didn't make you sore last night?" I raise my gaze to hers.

She shakes her head and licks her lips. "No, sir."

Coop comes in and joins me against the window. His fingers hover over his lips as he takes in Madison, spread out before us.

"You've had us one at a time and all together. Do you prefer one over the other?" I don't change my inflection. I'm honestly curious if she has a preference.

She doesn't hesitate. "I like it all."

Blake raises an eyebrow as he walks in, but he comes over and joins us at the window. She squirms on the table.

Honestly, Madison is the most captivating thing in this office. It's a wonder we don't have her like this all day long. Open like a buffet that we can come and lick and fuck whenever we want.

"Do you prefer to sleep with all of us at once or one at a time?" I tilt my head slightly.

Noah joins us and stands next to Coop. He adjusts himself as he leans against the glass.

Her cheeks are red. She cocks her head and grins at me. "Is this an interview?"

"If you'd like it to be."

She repositions herself a little. "I've liked everything this week and last. I'm open to sleeping with all of you and sleeping with just one of you at a time. I enjoy sleeping with you, period."

"The sex—"

She blows out a burst of air.

"Patience, princess."

She draws in a breath, trying so hard to be a good girl.

"Anything we've done that is a definite no?"

Her gaze flits to each of the guys, and she softens. "Not yet. I love learning what you like to do to me."

Her gaze settles on Noah. She flushes pink again.

"And what I like to do to you." Her heated eyes rise to meet mine.

I'm curious what Noah did to her this afternoon, but we can have sharing time later.

"Are we still part of the package, princess? Do you want our undivided attention and our cocks at your disposal?"

"Yes, sir." Her finger slips over her clit before going back to holding herself open.

It probably wasn't an accident, but I let it slide. This time. It's taking every ounce of control I have to stay here and not bury my cock deep in her weeping pussy.

I take in a breath. "Have you looked over the lists of things we want to do to you?"

"Yes, sir." She needs more than what I'm currently giving her. Her fingers twitch on her pussy lips, eager to dip inside and fuck herself for us.

Soon, princess.

"Have you marked any new hard limits?"

"No, sir."

That answer deserves a reward. "Put your fingers in your cunt, princess."

Sighing with relief, she thrusts three fingers inside herself and holds them there. Coop groans lightly.

"Good girl." She's learning.

"Did you add a sheet of your desires?" I try to remain unaffected, though my cock is throbbing. Her arousal drips down her fingers, glistening in the light.

"Yes, sir." Her lips part and she shifts a little. "May I move my fingers, sir?"

My lips quirk up. "You want to fuck yourself?"

"If you want me to." Her eyes meet mine and the invitation is clear. She wants a cock buried in her pussy. As many cocks buried in her as I'll allow.

"Would you prefer someone to fuck you, princess?" I rub my hand over my cock.

Her eyes flick down to our erections and she licks her lips. "Always."

"How do you want us today?" I wait for her answer. Usually I like to lead and orchestrate, but today is her chance to tell us what she wants. Her desires and needs.

"I want you all naked." She nods toward me and the others.

Without a word, we strip for her.

"May I?" She nods to her hand.

I smirk. "Please yourself, princess."

She strokes her fingers in and out of her greedy cunt while watching us strip naked. She keeps herself open to us with her other hand.

"I locked the elevator," Blake says. It's more for Madison's comfort than ours. We know his routine, but she's still new to this. New to us.

Though it feels like she's been here with us forever, it's only been two weeks. One week since she moved in. One week since we started fucking her. One week since we took her in and cared for her. Somehow, it already feels like she's always been a part of us.

She moans softly, and I meet her eyes.

Her voice is breathless as she asks, "Can we do this without all the direction? Can we just fuck and see how it turns out?"

I arch an eyebrow and consider her request. "Yes."

She gets off the table and takes off her clothes.

"Keep the heels on, sweetheart." Coop gives her a wink and a grin.

She shrugs as she ditches the bra and walks over to us. We're all naked, leaning against the window. The windows are only one way, so at least we aren't mooning the city. Our cocks are hard and ready for her.

Her hands land on Coop's and my chests. Her eyes flit to mine. "There are other things we need to discuss. Mostly logistics, right?"

"Of course, princess."

Her hands glides down our abs and grasp our cocks. She strokes us while watching our faces, smoothing our precum down over our shafts. Noah circles behind her and nips at her shoulder, running his hands over her sides and hips.

Blake grabs a bottle of lube from a drawer and rubs some on his fingers before handing it to Noah. We knew that Friday meetings were always going to end this way. Except today, we're starting with the fucking. Noah backs up and coats his cock in lube as Blake takes his place behind Madison.

"Bend over, tiger. Show them how much you like cock," Blake whispers in Madison's ear.

Her eyes light up as she lowers her mouth to my cock. She blows over the tip before she takes me into her warm, wet mouth. Blake holds her hips. His cock nudges her entrance before he surges into her pussy.

She moans around my cock. The vibration makes me take in a deep breath to steady myself. Blake's slick fingers slide between her ass cheeks and tease her asshole before he pushes his fingers inside.

She comes off my dick with a gasp. Glancing over her shoulder to watch Blake, she strokes me and Coop while her eyes follow Blake's fingers disappearing into her ass.

"Next time we fuck, we'll do it in front of a mirror so you can watch." Blake rears his hips back and slams his cock into her pussy.

Her head drops and she moans deep in her throat. She licks the underside of Coop's cock as she lifts her gaze to his. Her mouth closes over the tip, and then she slides him deep into her throat. The hunger and ache in my balls makes me want to grab her hair and move her over to suck my dick.

Her hand glides over my cock, using her spit as lube. Ignoring my urge, I palm her breast, pinching her nipple between my fingers. Holding himself deep inside her, Blake smacks her ass with his free hand before moving his fingers in and out of her ass.

When Noah walks forward, Blake slides out of Madison. She groans around Coop's cock and spreads her legs wider. She lifts off Coop and meets my eyes before deep throating me.

Fuck, she's good at everything she does. Not just the sex but work-wise too. She's the perfect assistant for us. I tug on her nipple, and she gives a little moan which vibrates through me.

Noah takes her hips and eases his dick into her ass. As she takes him in, she sucks on my cock hard, hollowing her cheeks. She moans when he bottoms out inside her. Cooper follows my lead on her other breast, and we tug at the same time as Noah slides out and then thrusts back in.

She pulls off my cock and takes a deep breath as we all move again. Her body trembles between us, so close to giving in to her pleasure.

Her mouth opens, but nothing comes out. With a shared look between Coop and Noah, Noah pulls his cock out of her. She whimpers as we take our hands from her breast. She trembles with unfulfilled desire as she looks up at us.

"Time to change things up, sweetheart." Coop helps her straighten. He draws her close and lowers his mouth to hers. She wraps her arms around his neck as he grabs her ass and pulls her tighter against him.

He lifts her and her legs wrap around his waist. They look like art. Their bodies are beautiful against each other, her skin so pale against his golden muscles. When he thrusts his cock deep inside her, she moans into his mouth. Noah steps up behind her, lines up his cock with her puckered hole, and plunges into her asshole again.

Her groan is muffled in Coop's mouth.

"So fucking tight, kitten." Noah fucks her ass while Coop holds her, his mouth claiming hers. Noah's mouth latches on to her shoulder, and she shudders beneath him.

"Come for me, kitten." His hips rock against hers.

She pulls away from Coop's mouth. As she falls apart in their arms, she cries out, "Noah!"

Biting his lip, Noah grinds out, "Good girl. Fuck."

He thrusts hard into her ass one last time and groans his release.

"Thank you, kitten," he whispers against her shoulder before he pulls out.

When he backs off, Blake steps up. His cock glistens with lube as he lines up with her asshole. She clings to Coop's shoulders as she looks at Blake's cock against her.

"Please, Blake." Her pupils are dilated, and she's ready for more. I stroke my cock, waiting for my turn. I won't be taking her ass this time, though. We want to fill her full of our cum until she's dripping with it.

Then we'll do it all over again. Watching them fuck her is so fucking beautiful. Seeing her fall apart under my direction. Hearing her moans of pleasure brought on by my friends' cocks thrusting inside her. I've always loved to watch, but with Madison, it's next-level. She's not just doing it because it's what I want. She's doing it because she wants them. Wants us. All of us.

Noah loosened her up enough that Blake shouldn't have any issue fucking her ass.

"I'll go slow, tiger." Blake presses his thick cock into her small hole. Stroking my cock, I watch her take him inch by inch. She clings to Coop, who rocks his hips lightly in and out of her pussy, rubbing against her clit to distract her.

"You're such a good girl. Fuck, Madison." Blake bottoms out in her ass, his front pressed to her back. "You were built for us."

"So good." Madison's head falls back against his shoulder.

"Ready for more?" Blake kisses her shoulder, holding her ass as she leans back against him.

Closing her eyes, she groans and nods.

"Good." Coop pulls out until his cock is almost out of her before he thrusts back into her pussy.

"Coop." She moans as he keeps up a steady pace in and out of her pussy while Blake stays deep in her ass, stretching her, filling her. Her breasts rise and fall with each caught breath.

My cock pulses in my hand. I can't wait to fuck her again, feel her wet, greedy cunt pulsing around my thrusting cock as she comes.

"Coop." Her eyes squeeze shut as she keens her release. My balls tighten at the sound.

"Her pussy is so tight. Fuck." Coop slams into her and captures her mouth as he spills his release deep inside her. She shudders in their arms. When Coop pulls out and kisses her lightly, she whimpers.

"Don't worry, princess. We aren't done with you yet."

Her gaze meets mine as the guys shift into position.

Noah and Coop move to her sides as Blake holds her on his cock. They help him support her as I claim the spot Coop left.

I cup her cheek, and she focuses her darkened eyes on me. "Blake and I are going to fuck you together, princess. Think you can handle that?"

She licks her lips. "Yes, sir. Please."

I drag my cock over her clit before sliding to her entrance. The guys support her while I thrust my dick into her tight cunt, feeling Blake's hard cock through her walls.

She moans at being filled again. I capture her mouth with mine as

Blake pulls out. When he thrusts forward, I ease out, and when I thrust forward, he draws back out, finding a rhythm. She gasps as she leans back against Blake's shoulder. Her whole body shivers around us.

Noah draws Madison's mouth to his. Their tongues meet as they deepen the kiss. Coop reaches between me and her and slides his finger over her swollen clit. Her moans grow deeper as Blake and I slowly get faster, moving together as if we've always done it this way. Totally in sync with each other as we fuck our girl.

Her muscles tense, and she breaks away from Noah as she screams her release. Blake and I slam into her as her body convulses around us. We both come, filling her, letting her milk every last drop from us.

We all stand there connected as our breathing calms down. I kiss her lips softly, and she sighs.

"Interview over?" She cracks open her blue eyes and gives me a cheeky grin.

I brush my finger over her lower lip. "Pretty sure you have the position."

She takes a deep breath in. Our eyes lock together like our bodies are. Blake eases out of her first, leaving her in my arms. Something shifts inside me as I hold her against me, skin to skin, our hearts still beating strong against one another.

She hugs me tight and whispers in my ear, "Thank you."

Coop holds out his arms to her, and she slides into them. Her fingers linger on my jaw for a moment, and I can feel the tug of a satisfied smile on my lips. Her blue eyes sparkle at me as she clings to Coop.

I'm looking forward to the rest of the weekend.

Chapter 41

Touching Base

Coop

I carry Madison into the attached bathroom and set her down while I warm the water and grab washcloths to clean us both up. She sags back against the door for a second before she gets her second wind.

"Is it always going to be like this?" She moves next to me. Her warm skin brushes against mine as she grabs a washcloth to wet.

I inhale her scent mixed with ours. Together, we smell like sultry nights tangled in a warm bed.

"It's never been like this." The words slip from my mouth. We don't like to talk about past lovers as a general rule. Especially not with our present lover.

Her brow furrows as she looks up at me. "You've shared partners before."

I release a huff of a laugh as I squeeze the water from the wash-cloth. "Pipe dreams and fantasies. Sure, we've done some things as a group before. Not really all of us at once, though."

I lift her onto the edge of the counter. When she leans back on her hands, I spread her legs. I press the washcloth against her pussy and lean in to meet her eyes. "You're an overachiever."

Her cheeks flush. With the washcloth in her hand, she wraps it around my partially erect dick and strokes it. Fuck, she's thorough as she washes me. My cock is getting the wrong idea as it hardens more and aches with need.

"But what about the lawsuit woman?" She doesn't lift her eyes to mine.

"Andrea?" I shake my head and toss the used washcloths into the basket before wetting another. After I help her stand, I turn her to the mirror and spread her ass cheeks.

"Coop?" She tries to take the washcloth, but I catch her wrists in one of mine and hold them away.

"Shh, sweetheart. Relax. Let me take care of you."

She settles but mean mugs me in the mirror, clearly not happy about me cleaning her ass. I'd fuck it if I thought I'd have time, but we still have things to discuss as a group. And while I have her to myself right now, it won't be long until someone else shows up.

"But what about Andrea? You all were with her."

I blow out a breath as I think about Andrea. About the one thing that pissed me off more than even the blackmail attempt. "She treated Noah like he was a kid, even though they were the same age. She thought she was the shit. I never liked the woman, but she worked hard and she fucked okay." I shrug.

Both Madison's eyebrows shoot up. "She fucked okay? Is that what you're going to say about me?"

Tossing the washcloth into the basket, I press my naked body against her back. When my hard cock slots between her ass cheeks, her lips part on a gasp. Her nipples harden.

She kicked off her shoes before I got her in here, so my chin rests on her head. I wrap my arms around her waist. "You just took two guys in your ass and two in your pussy, not to mention you went down on two of us before that. Much better than okay. You, babe, are a solid overachiever, and I will happily take advantage of that."

I squeeze her to me and sigh. "Andrea had issues. She was hot and a good assistant, but she wanted money. And she thought if she did everything Seth wanted her to, she'd get more money. She had a thing for Blake, and he vouched for her, but she wasn't a good person. Not like you."

Her arms fold over mine. She takes in a breath and releases it. "What about the women in college?"

"No one really fit us all." I slide my cock against her. "We don't always find the same woman attractive. Two, maybe three of us will. Honestly, I'll fuck just about anyone that will let me, but those guys" —I nod to the door—"they can be pretty particular."

Her gaze drops to the sink and she looks like she's thinking too hard.

"Madison." I squeeze her to get her attention back on me. "We're all attracted to you. We all want you. We love fucking you. We can't seem to stop fucking you. I'm sure you've been overwhelmed with cock since last Friday."

Her cheeks flush pink as a smile blooms.

"You took Blake and me this morning. Noah this afternoon from the sounds that came through my office wall, and then all of us again. And I'm sure we aren't finished with you yet for the night. Fuck, maybe Seth is right and you need a night off once in a while."

She gives me this pout in the mirror that makes my insides feel light. If I pushed it, she'd let me fuck her right now, but I'm happy just to hold her naked body against mine. She feels nice in my arms.

A knock sounds at the door. She turns her head toward the sound and rests it against my chest. She takes in a breath and I feel it inside me. This warm bubble of something I've never had before. Contentment. Happiness. Stability.

I squeeze her one more time. "Come on. Let's find some clothes."

Madison

We're all seated around the conference table in various states of undress. I have on my skirt and blouse, but Coop grabbed my panties before I could get them off the table. I didn't bother with my bra.

Coop wears only his boxers, leaving his cut chest and abs on display. His arms are impressive as he leans on the table. Heat courses through me, remembering those arms holding me up while the others fucked me.

He winks, and I just shake my head. Noah has on his pants and shirt, though the shirt isn't buttoned. Noah's just as built as Coop.

Blake just has on his slacks. His whole enormous chest is on display. While Coop has well-defined arms, Blake is ripped. I just want to stroke his muscles. A white line that I hadn't noticed before cuts along the ridge of his shoulder, a scar long past healing. Will I ever get the story behind it?

At the head of the table, Seth is dressed in slacks and his shirt, mostly buttoned.

Coop said they weren't like this with any of the other women. Not all of them were in, but they all seem to be in with me. Of course, they said they haven't done anything quite like this, where they offered this arrangement up front.

Just with me.

Would they have offered it to just anyone? Or am I special?

Seth clears his throat. I cross my legs and straighten.

"We've gone through most of the items on the agenda."

My cheeks flush with heat, remembering holding myself open as he asked me those questions. Each question made me ache a little more. When they all lined up and stripped, it was like an all-you-can-lick buffet. Abs, chest, cocks. Fuck, these men have it all and I want it.

"Expectations." Seth leans forward. His blue eyes lock with mine. "This is what burned us in the past."

He releases me from his gaze as he looks at the others.

"This is a special situation, and we don't want anyone to get hurt."

He must mean me. I can't see myself hurting any of these guys.

That doesn't mean their pride won't get bruised. But they could easily break my heart. I haven't guarded it like I should have.

Right now, I need to be a business professional. This is part of our work and our personal lives.

"We live together, work together, and fuck together," Seth continues. "At some point, it may be hard not to develop certain feelings."

My heart squeezes in my chest. Yup, if anyone is going to catch feelings, it would be me. It may be too late. But that doesn't mean I want this to end. I'll deal with the fallout when it happens. That's something for Future Madison to worry about.

Blake clears his throat, drawing my attention. "We expect you not to get involved with anyone else while you're with us. Not just physically, but emotionally. However, at any point, if you need to end this relationship, we can broach that subject."

"So, this is a relationship?" I'm proud that my voice doesn't shake at all as I meet Blake's green eyes. It's the question that's been swirling around in my head. What is this? What's my place in it? Do I get to call them mine? Or am I their dirty little secret?

"Of sorts." He smirks. "Obviously not one that would work in the real world, but for us, it is as real as any relationship."

The real world wouldn't understand, but locked up here in this building, we are free to do as we please.

"We don't just want to stick our cocks in you." Coop's voice makes me turn. "We like the things that come with a relationship too."

"Like cuddling?" I raise an eyebrow. Because that's what Coop did in the bathroom. He could have bent me over or had me on my knees—and I willingly would have done just that—but he just held me, and it felt nice. So fucking nice. I didn't want it to end.

"Cuddling. Kissing. Holding hands." Noah's dark eyes light up when I meet them. "We don't see this as transactional sex."

"Neither do I." I would never just have sex for money or a job, but this . . . I'm not even sure what this is, but I want it. I love the pleasure and the cuddling. I want it all.

"We're asking for exclusivity." Seth lets out a breath. "I know it's been a lot of forms and making sure we're on the same page sexually, but we want to know that you'll be ours for the duration of our agreement. You only fuck us, and we only fuck you."

It's not like I have other offers pouring in. And I won't need other offers if I have them. Though they said they would talk to me if they wanted to fuck someone else. "Of course."

"You understand we will need to have dates occasionally to keep up appearances." Seth taps the page in front of him. "Rachel made it clear that with the four of us not dating, the media takes notice. We've dealt with our relationships being leaked in the past and the fallout is unpleasant. We don't need people digging into our situation."

I don't have to like it to understand it. "Of course."

Seth leans back, holding my gaze steady. "Are you the type of woman who gets jealous and catty, Madison?"

Not princess. Okay, he's testing me. I raise an eyebrow at him. "Will I be jealous watching some other woman paw you like she owns you?"

"Completely clothed, most likely in a tuxedo, but yes. Probably photos online."

Shrugging, I try to appear nonchalant even as my heart races. "As long as you come home and fuck me instead of her, what do I have to be jealous of?"

Coop laughs. "Fuck, I like her."

Shaking my head at him, I lean in. "I'm here for my career and the future Morrigan Technology can offer me. I'm also here because I enjoy having sex with all of you."

I wouldn't have been surprised if Coop stood up and dropped his boxers, but he just slides his hand over his erection while his eyes hold mine.

I swallow and turn away from the temptation. "I know you've had issues with other women before. They wanted more from one or all of you. We don't know each other very well."

Coop snorts.

I shake my head and blink at him. "We haven't had a lot of conversations. Or get-to-know-you type things besides *getting to know* each other's bodies. Which is good and I love it."

My tongue trips a little on the L-word. I wish I hadn't said it, but at least I hadn't applied it to any of them. I clear my throat.

"What you've done for me just this past week . . ." I take a breath as my voice trembles a little. "You've taken me in and protected me. I haven't had anyone in my life for a long time who would do that for me."

"We'd do it all over again." Blake rocks in his chair as his green eyes meet mine.

Smiling, I say, "I grew up wanting to make my own money, my own imprint on this world. I don't want anything from you that you aren't willing to give me. Knowledge, experience, and really great sex."

Coop grins. Before anyone can interrupt me, I need to get out the next bit.

"I know we won't be going public with this at any point." That tears a little at my heart. "But that doesn't matter. As long as you are . . ." *mine.* I can't say it, so I clear my throat again and reach for the glass of water. I take a moment to drink and settle my thudding heart. "As long as you are committed to me for the duration of our agreement, I'll be committed to you."

I'll be yours.

The words tremble in my chest. Noah said it to me when we were alone, but I can't say it to all of them. I can give them my heart and body freely, but I need to keep some part of myself safe from the fallout.

Chapter 42

The Arrangement

Madison

"We want to get to know you better." Seth leans forward, his elbows on the table. "And not just sexually. You're a hard worker, and we can tell you're devoted to making this work for everyone."

I recross my legs as the guys murmur their agreement.

"We'll continue the current sleep rotation." Seth brings his hands together on the table as he meets everyone's eyes. When his dark blue eyes land on me, they hold me still. "That way, everyone gets time alone with you."

I blush as I think of Coop in Blake's bed this morning. It seems like everyone is okay sharing time. This entire week has been a whole lot of sex. And I'm definitely here for it.

"If you need time to yourself"—his lips soften at the corners—"please tell us. We don't need to monopolize all your time. It's good if you have some life besides us."

"Hope is coming over on Sunday to watch *The Witcher* with me." I want friends outside of them. I need to connect with other people, especially for when this ends. "When things get back to normal, I'd like to hang out with her more outside of the building too."

Seth takes a breath and blows it out. "There's not much new information on your assault case or the camera in your bathroom. Right now, they suspect your roommate and her boyfriend of planting it."

"Though from the tech used," Blake says, "I would assume someone else funded it even if she installed it. It's expensive. They were shaking you down for money. If they knew the camera was there, why didn't they take that and pawn it?"

My hands tremble as I reach for my water. That camera. The person watching me. It's still too raw in my chest. Someone watched me get myself off. Who knows how many times? Who's to say there wasn't a camera in my bedroom and they just didn't have it live when Blake and I were there?

At least here, I'm safe.

Noah stands. "We'll type up the details later and sign the agreement, but I want to show Madison our play room."

I straighten and warmth floods my chilled body. My curiosity is epic for this so-called play room. I remember the smell of leather and the softness of the furniture beneath me, but I can't help envisioning torture-like racks and swings and weird bondage masks. Which honestly, might freak me out.

Noah holds out his hand for mine. I don't hesitate to take it. He helps me stand as the others rise. I dip down to grab my shoes and then let Noah lead me to the elevator with the others.

"Are you sore?" Seth asks as the elevator arrives and we step on.

My cheeks flush hot as I shake my head. "No."

Blake draws me back against his front, holding my hips against his. I can feel his hard, thick length against my ass, making me wetter. When Noah squeezes my hand, I meet his heated, darkened eyes. Awareness floods me.

The mood shifts in the elevator as they all close in on me. My heart races in anticipation. My breath catches in my chest as I look at the men who are mine. For now. For as long as they want me.

Coop trails his hand down the side of my neck. "You're healing nicely, sweetheart."

His touch is light, not hard enough to reach the bruised muscles, and sends shivers down my spine. Seth captures my other hand and brings my knuckles to his lips, brushing a kiss across them.

The elevator stops way too quickly, in my opinion, and it opens into the hallway outside our apartment. As we step out, Noah draws me into his arms, separating me from the others.

Coop slides his access card into the door, and we all walk in. Noah leads me to a door that looks like it should be a closet of some sort. It gives the illusion of being insignificant, like there wouldn't be enough space for a room to be behind it.

Seth holds the door open as Noah leads me into a small corridor that opens up to a decent-sized room. My eyes flit between everything, taking in the leather-covered furniture in weird shapes. There are no racks or whips on the walls or weird rubber suits.

I don't know whether or not to be disappointed. The furniture just looks like furniture at first glance. The walls are painted a deep cerulean blue. It's nice.

Stepping into the room, I run my hand over a leather bench. Against one wall is a four-poster canopy bed without fabric draped over the top. There's a chaise-lounge-looking seat that must be where they fucked me last time.

Feeling hot all over, I walk toward a bench-like thing, and I wouldn't have known what it was for if Noah hadn't shown me a picture of it earlier. He wants to bind me to this so I won't move while he uses me. So he can do what he wants with me. I squeeze my thighs together at the achy need throbbing in my pussy.

"The sheets are silk." Coop's deep voice draws my gaze to the bed.

It's a standard king size, so not big enough for all of us to sleep on together. As I look at it, I catch details. There are metal loops and holds all around the top of the square frame and the base of the bed.

I run my hand over the fabric and turn to see the guys watching me explore. "What attaches to this?"

Reaching up, I slip a button free on my blouse and move to the next.

"A few different things. We can use the holds for ties or cuffs. The top can support a swing." Noah takes off his shirt and leaves it on a chair.

My shirt dangles in my fingers before I let it slip to the floor. The guys take in my breasts, which feel heavy as my nipples tighten under their hot gazes.

"Will you let me tie you down too?" I'm not asking anyone in particular. I find the zipper on my skirt and release it, letting it flutter to the ground around my feet. Leaving me naked as I crawl onto the bed.

Their eyes follow me as I kneel, facing them. My palms on my thighs.

"You want us to give you control?" Seth removes his shirt and pants before striding toward me. His cock is hard and thick against his stomach. I lick my lips.

"Sometimes." I raise an eyebrow.

Do I think Coop and Noah will let me have my way with them? Yes. Blake and Seth, though, are another thing. They thrive on control. Honestly, it surprised me when Noah let me take control, but that feeling . . . Gah, that feeling of power over him. Making him do what I wanted to get me there. I want more.

"Tonight?" Seth doesn't answer my question, but maybe that's an I'll-consider-it answer.

I shake my head. My blond hair spills over my shoulders. "Not tonight."

There's freedom in letting Seth direct me. I don't have to make decisions or worry about anything. I can focus on the pleasure.

Seth climbs on the bed in front of me and kneels so close I can feel his heat, but not close enough for our skin to touch. "Do you want to explore the room, princess?"

"I want to be touched." My gaze sweeps the room and all the unique pieces of furniture. We have all the time later to wander the room and play, for them to show me exactly how they want me on each piece of furniture. Right now, I just want their bodies against mine. Their heat to engulf me.

"Noah." Seth doesn't release my gaze. "Behind her."

Naked, Noah walks across the room and climbs on the bed behind me. He gathers my hair in his hands and shivers course through me.

"We'll take it slow this time, kitten." His lips brush the nape of my neck. Sparks course through me.

My eyes try to flicker shut at the soft touch. I miss neck kisses. I want to be healed so we can explore each other fully without worrying about hurting me. Noah wants to hold me down by my neck, and though the idea scared me at first, now I want to see what I can handle.

"Coop." Seth's voice is commanding and makes my pussy pulse, needy, wanting.

Coop slides onto the bed beside me. He kneels like Seth, just out of touch, to my right.

"Blake."

Blake takes my left side. They surround me like four corners. All naked. All mine. No one touches me, but we all breathe a little faster together.

"You ready, princess?" Seth's eyes twinkle with mischief.

Even though I'm not sure what exactly they have in store for me, I'm more than ready for it. Every second stretches out in anticipation of their touch.

I draw in a breath and release it. "Always."

"Put your hands on my shoulders but don't move from your spot on the bed." Seth keeps his hands on his thighs.

Rising on my knees, I lean forward and place my hands on his hard shoulders. My face is so close to his I can feel his breath on my lips. This isn't a wild ride like in the office. This is slow, methodical Seth in control of every moving part of us.

"Spread your thighs."

My knees slide on the silk, opening myself up to Noah behind me. A pulse of heat flows through me.

"Do you want Noah in your ass or your pussy, princess?"

Fuck. I almost clench my thighs together at the aching pulse racing through me. Noah said he wanted my ass, and he's already had it once tonight, but I want to feel him deep inside me. Not overwhelmed by two of them inside me at once. Just him.

"Fuck my ass."

"Blake, hand Noah the lube."

Seth's eyes hold mine as I feel Blake shift and hear the squirt of the bottle behind me. A shiver courses over my hot flesh.

Noah smooths his fingers between my ass cheeks, dragging lube over my puckered hole. My fingers clench into Seth's shoulders as Noah plays with my asshole, dipping his finger in and rubbing the entrance. My pussy throbs, empty.

"Blake, rub her clit."

Blake reaches between my legs and dips his finger into my pussy to gather some of my wetness before sliding forward to tease my clit. My breathing escalates as I stare into Seth's eyes. As the heat inside me builds.

"Coop—"

"Boobs, on it."

A giggle rushes out of me, taking some of the tension out of the room. The corner of Seth's lips quirks up. I want to lean in and kiss him. My lips part as my gaze drops to his full lips. Coop's fingers drag over my nipples as Blake rubs my clit while Noah teases my asshole, winding me up in the best way.

"Kiss me, princess."

It's exactly what I want. I press my lips to his as Blake thrusts his fingers inside my core while teasing my clit with his thumb. Noah's hand retreats, and I feel the soft head of his cock against me instead. I groan into Seth's mouth as Noah pushes his tip inside my ass.

Coop and Blake use their free hands to hold my ass cheeks apart.

"You're doing great, sweetheart," Coop murmurs in my ear.

My breath catches as Noah rocks into me slightly. Blake's fingers slip out of my core to slide over my clit as Noah eases in a little deeper before retreating. He holds my hips steady as he rocks in and out of me, getting a little deeper with every forward thrust.

Seth's tongue strokes mine, and I moan into his mouth. My fingers itch to do more than stay on his shoulders, but orders are orders. And while I enjoy punishment, I want pleasure.

The tension builds inside me, each stroke of Noah's cock is emphasized by Blake rubbing my clit and Coop brushing my hardened nipple. Seth's tongue slides against mine.

My fingers tighten on Seth as Noah fully impales me on his cock and begins to fuck my ass, pulling almost all the way out before pushing back in. Warmth surges through me at the feel of him so deep inside me.

"Your ass is so tight and hot, kitten. It's almost as good as your pussy."

I can't focus on anything anymore as I pant into Seth's mouth while the others work my body into a frenzy. They've all been inside me. They've all touched me. They've all branded me as theirs.

Now they're working together to make me come, and it's intoxicating.

Seth releases my mouth and presses his forehead against mine. "Let go, princess. We've got you."

My gaze meets Seth's and I know he means it. They've got me. They won't let me go.

Noah thrusts harder into my ass as the others tease and torture my body. It's like the moment at the top of a rollercoaster where you can see the miles of track ahead of you with so many twists and turns. For just a second, everything freezes as I crest the peak. I hold my breath as my orgasm crashes over me and I fall over the edge, safe in their arms. My body tightens and releases around Noah's cock as the world slows to a crawl around me.

My fingers dig into Seth's hard muscles. Coop's hand cradles my breast as he tugs on my nipple. Blake rubs my clit a little harder. Noah growls as my ass clamps down on his cock, but he doesn't stop fucking me.

Time rushes back in as I pulse around Noah's cock, still slamming into me. Coop's teeth sink into my hip, while Blake buries his fingers in my pussy again. I cry out as I swing back up into another orgasm. Or the same one. I can't tell as my body keeps coming, tightening and releasing, riding each wave as it hits me.

Noah slams into me one last time and roars as he comes deep inside me. I can feel his warm cum filling me as another wave crashes over me. He presses my ass cheeks open, and I blush, knowing he's looking at his cock buried in my ass.

"Beautiful, kitten." He pulls out and climbs off the bed, heading to a door. Blake shifts to the spot behind me when I hear water running. My breathing is ragged, but my body is satisfied.

"Ready for more, tiger?"

Chapter 43

———

Declaring Assets

Madison

Blake doesn't give me time to answer before he thrusts his cock into my pussy from behind.

I gasp at the tremors of aftershocks that flow over me. Seth backs up a little.

"Suck my cock while Blake fucks you, princess."

I meet Seth's darkened eyes before lowering myself down. I trace the head of his cock with my tongue, eliciting a groan from Seth before I take him into my mouth, sinking down on him when Blake sinks his thick cock into my pussy again.

We fall into a rhythm while Coop watches. Every thrust fills my pussy and my throat with cock. Blake's hands spread my ass cheeks as he fucks me. Seth's hand caresses my hair as I take him as deep as I can.

I feel the bed shift as Coop moves, then the tickle of his hair against my breast before his mouth closes over my nipple, sucking it into his mouth like the air he needs to live. His finger rubs my clit in lazy circles.

Already primed from my previous orgasm, I come around Blake's cock as I hollow my cheeks out, sucking on Seth's cock. A rush of cum fills my mouth and pussy at the same time, making me warm all over and keeping my orgasm flowing.

Blake pats my ass as he withdraws. "Good girl."

I flatten my tongue against Seth's cock as I pull off. My eyes meet his and he cups my cheek.

"Perfect."

That word twists me up inside, but I smile. He kisses me before moving away. Coop repositions himself as Noah lifts me against him on the side of the bed.

When Noah's lips find mine, I wrap my arms around his neck to hold him close. Our bodies flush against each other, warm skin to warm skin.

"Ready," Coop says.

I gaze over my shoulder. Seth and Blake sit with their backs against the headboard while Coop lies flat on his back next to them. Noah helps me straddle Coop's waist. Coop cups my breasts. His thumbs tease my sensitive nipples.

Coop spreads his legs and Noah moves between them behind me.

"Put Coop's dick inside you, princess."

My gaze rises to Seth's, but I do as he says. I scoot back and stroke Coop's cock with my hand before holding it still and sinking my pussy down on it. Fuck, I never want this to end.

"That's it, sweetheart. We're going to go nice and slow this time, okay?" Coop draws me down onto his chest and captures my mouth with his. His tongue brushes mine when I feel Noah's cock against my asshole.

I try to relax as he presses in, pushing past the ring of muscles. Their cocks rub against each other through the thin wall. It's indescribable how it feels to have both of them inside me like this. When he's deep inside, I take a breath. I'm full of cock. Sparks light across every inch of me. I lift my gaze to Blake and Seth watching us, their hands on their already hardening cocks, stroking slowly.

Noah's hands grip my hips, rocking me forward before drawing me back on both his and Coop's cocks. I moan at the sensation of both of them sliding in and out. My fingers tangle into Coop's loose hair as my nipples brush over his chest with each stroke.

"How does it feel, princess?"

"What?" I'm in a sex haze so thick I'm not sure what Seth is asking.

"Being thoroughly fucked by us?" Seth licks his lips as his thumb drags over his tip, spreading his precum over it.

I want him in my mouth again. How does it feel? "Wonderful."

Noah and Coop stay true to Coop's words. Slow and easy. We rock together, building the flames hotter with each stroke, each thrust. I can feel the orgasm closing in on me, filling me with tingles.

"Wait for us, sweetheart." Coop cups my cheek.

I'm sure I look like a well-used wreck. But his blue eyes shine at me like I'm the most beautiful thing he's ever seen. The waves of my orgasm are swelling with each rock of their hips, ready to crash over me, and I'm not sure if I can hold back.

"We're almost there, kitten." Noah kisses my shoulder. His tongue traces my shoulder blade before he sucks on my skin.

My gaze stays on Blake and Seth stroking their cocks. I want to take over. Have their cocks in my hands, make them come, but it's all too much.

"After they come, princess, you can finish us."

The pressure overwhelms me, rising inside me like a tsunami, but I fight back the urge to come, trying to stay afloat. Our bodies shimmer with sweat as we writhe against each other.

"Now, kitten." Noah and Coop thrust deep into me one last time, holding me down on their cocks as they pulse inside me. My pussy and ass tighten around them as I come, soaking them with my orgasm. The sound coming out of my mouth is a cross between a groan and a scream. Hot pulses of cum fill me, keeping my orgasm dragging me under.

I collapse against Coop. Noah kisses my shoulder tenderly. My body shakes with aftershocks.

"Almost done, sweetheart," Coop whispers. I lift my eyes to his and he smiles and glances up toward the other guys. I lick my lips and nod.

Noah pulls out first, and Coop lifts me up onto his chest so I can reach Blake and Seth. I thread my fingers with theirs as we stroke their cocks together. Coop captures the cum leaking from my pussy and shoves it back inside, holding it there with his fingers.

Lowering, I alternate sucking on Blake's and Seth's cocks until Blake grabs my hair and thrusts into my mouth, groaning his orgasm as he fills my throat with his cum. I swallow as I lift off him. Our eyes lock and the pleasure in his fills me with satisfaction.

He brushes his thumb over my lips. "Good girl, tiger. Now finish the boss."

My gaze goes to Seth, and I lower my mouth over his cock. Coop flicks his thumb over my clit as he thrusts his fingers inside me. His mouth latches onto my breast as I suck on Seth's cock, trailing my tongue along the underside.

Seth's fingers weave into my hair and hold me still until I relax my throat. "You're perfect, princess."

He takes control, fucking my mouth with his cock until he pushes in deep. I hollow out my cheeks as I suck on him, wanting everything he can give me. Coop plays my body like he knows every secret place that draws out my pleasure. When my orgasm rolls over me, Seth fills my mouth with his warm, salty cum.

I swallow it down as I lift off him and sit up on Coop's chest. Noah hands Coop a warm washcloth, and he cleans me up. His hard cock brushes against my hip. I raise an eyebrow at him, and he smirks.

"You want to do something about that, sweetheart?" He raises a dark eyebrow in return as he hands me a fresh washcloth from Noah.

I turn around to straddle him, taking the cloth and cleaning his cock before I lower my mouth over it. He groans and tugs my hips back until his mouth covers my pussy. I whimper around his cock. Everything is sensitive. He licks my swollen pussy and sucks on my clit as I take him down my throat.

Both his hands are on my thighs, so when a finger dips into my pussy, I look back. Seth drags his finger in and out, slow and steady. My body tightens. I rock into his hand and Coop's mouth as I suck on Coop's cock.

Coop growls against my pussy and comes down my throat. The vibration pushes me over the edge. I collapse on Coop, my head on his thigh as my body shakes with release. All my energy drained.

Noah lifts me into his arms. "I think that's it for tonight, kitten."

I want to disagree and rally, but I'm a limp noodle in his arms. I curl into him and release my breath.

Noah

As I walk through the apartment to Madison's room with her in my arms, a gentle snore reaches my ears. Her face is pressed against my chest as she snores softly.

"We wore her out." Coop walks beside me. His fingers brush over her hair.

Seth opens the door to her room. "Probably could skip the shower until morning."

"I can change the sheets tomorrow," Blake adds. He pulls down the covers.

Kneeling on the bed, I lay Madison in the middle before climbing in beside her. She curls into me, her cheek against my chest, her leg resting over mine. Seth lies behind her while the others lie on the outside of us.

Brushing her hair off her cheek, I say, "She's worn out."

"We should be too." Blake rests behind me, his hands behind his head.

None of us bothered to get dressed. We wiped down before getting in the bed though.

"Do you think this will work this time?" Seth's voice is quiet as he trails his hand down Madison's spine. She doesn't react. She's too deeply asleep already.

"I don't see why not." Coop's voice is solid, like he isn't afraid to wake Madison up with this conversation. "She fits us. She isn't settling for all of us because she wants one of us. She wants all of us."

"What if it's because she's young?" Blake asks. "What if it's just an experiment to her? Something to try before she gets on with her life?"

"Then it is what it is." Coop shrugs. "It's not like we're offering her a future with us."

"Why not?" The words come out of me before I can stop them. I've never felt this way about any of the other women. Dating during high school had been difficult for me since I was always a year younger than my classmates. The women the others attracted tended to be harder. Not soft like Madison.

Coop chuckles. "How's that supposed to work? It isn't legal to marry multiple guys. You think she's the kind of woman to be content shacking up with four men without a ring, without them being able to claim her outside of their apartment?"

"Coop's right." Seth sighs. "It may work in here, but it won't work out there. Just the rumor that we might have all been in a relationship with one woman lost us a few accounts."

"Fuck them." I can't help feeling it as I draw Madison tighter against me. "It shouldn't matter what we do behind closed doors."

"You're right, it shouldn't. That doesn't mean it doesn't matter to some people, though." Blake releases a breath. "We have to do what we can to protect her and our business. How are we going to handle going out with other women?"

"I don't understand the question." Seth turns his face toward Blake. "What do you mean *handle*?"

"Well, I don't particularly want to date someone else or even go out and be seen." Blake reaches over me to run a strand of Madison's hair through his fingers. "So if we have to date, we need a system.

Who has to go out and be seen. How long it has to last. The right places to go."

"There's a benefit next weekend." Seth folds his hands behind his head. "We each need to bring a date to it. Clients and vendors will be there. The press will be there. It's the perfect time to show we're single and dating."

I look down at Madison's face, peaceful in sleep. "What about Madison?"

Seth glances at her. His gaze strokes along her naked body, wrapped over mine. "She understands this has to happen. We aren't hiding anything from her."

I press my lips together, wanting to argue. I see the hurt in her eyes every time Seth brings up other women. Even though we aren't doing it to hurt her, even though we're doing it to protect her, it still twists my stomach.

Blake shuts off the light. "It still sucks."

I can't help but agree. We have a beautiful woman in our arms and have to hide her from the rest of the world. "What happens when someone asks her out?"

"That's up to her." Seth's gaze lingers on her face for a minute before returning to the ceiling. "We have an agreement. She'll let us know if she needs to change anything."

Unless one of us asks her out. I don't say it out loud, but the words buzz around my insides. Why can't my plus-one be Madison? Sure, she can't go with all of us, but if I can't bring her, I don't want to bring anyone else.

It's time for me to claim what I want.

Chapter 44

Overtime

Blake

I wake up to a warm body crawling over mine. I clutch at her waist, and she stops half on top of me.

"I need to use the bathroom," she whispers, drawing her hair over her shoulder.

Nodding, I release her. She presses a kiss to my forehead before scooting off the bed and disappearing into the bathroom. Waking up a little more, I rise up on my elbows and look over at the others. At some point, someone drew the sheet up. At least it isn't a sausage fest.

I roll out my side and pad into the bathroom, closing the door softly to not wake the others. The door to the water closet opens, and Madison walks out. She goes to the sink and washes her hands while looking at me in the mirror.

"Sorry I woke you." She dries her hands off and gives me a self-conscious smile.

I wonder if the smile is because I'm blocking the way out. Or maybe the fact we're both naked and I'm aroused. "Does it bother you that we always want you?"

Her brows furrow as she steps toward me, closing the distance. "No. I really like the way you all want me."

Her hands rest on my chest as she leans into me.

"We aren't too much for you?" Because we can be a lot. Even when it was only three of us playing with one woman, she would eventually tap out before we were finished.

I lift Madison under her arms and pull her against me. She wraps her legs around my waist. Her eyes sparkle at me as I lower my mouth to touch hers. When I try to pull away, her fingers tangle into my hair and her lips part beneath mine, letting me in.

Deepening the kiss, I press her against the wall, stroking my cock against her clit. When I lift my mouth from hers, lust darkens her eyes.

"Remember how you said next time we'd use a mirror . . ." She glances over her shoulder at the mirrors in the bathroom.

"Do you want to watch me fuck you, tiger?" I kiss the tip of her nose. Her pussy is wet against my stomach.

"Yes, Blake. Please."

I walk her over to the counter and set her down. There's a bench under the vanity and a floor-to-ceiling mirror off to the side. I drag the bench over before grabbing Madison.

Sitting on the bench facing the mirror, I hold on to Madison standing in front of me, her back to me. I make her straddle my legs as I bring her back against my chest. Her gaze is glued to mine in the mirror.

I run my hands up the insides of her thighs and stroke her pussy. We both watch my hand working her in the mirror. Her breathing quickens and a quiet moan leaves her throat.

"What does it feel like to fuck me?" Madison's words are quiet in the softened light of the bathroom.

"Your pussy?" I don't wait for her answer as I push a finger inside her wet cunt. "Hot, wet, tight. It wraps around my cock like your lips but pressed around all of my cock. And when I slide it in and out . . ."

I pull my finger out and thrust it back in. "It feels so fucking good. I'm lucky I don't come as soon as I slide deep inside you."

I watch the mirror, my finger gliding in and out of her easily. Her eyes meet mine in the mirror.

"And what about my ass?"

I slide my wet finger back to her asshole. "This? This feels like a snug sweater, hot and tight, almost constricting." I dip it into her puckered hole, and she lets out a soft moan. "When someone is fucking your cunt at the same time, it tightens everything, and I can feel them move inside you."

"Next time we do this, I want to watch two of you take me." She whimpers.

I'm tempted to get someone now, but she needs some time to recover. Last night was the first night we double penetrated her. She doesn't say she's uncomfortable, but I don't want to make her sore. I ease my finger out of her and hold her hips.

"Soon, love." I lower her down with her back against my chest. Holding her with my arm across her waist, I line my cock up with her entrance. I check the mirror to make sure our angle shows the head of my cock pressed to her cunt. My legs spread hers wide.

"Fuck me, Blake. I want to see your cock buried inside me."

I kiss her shoulder as I ease her onto me, slowly sinking my thick cock into her tight pussy inch by inch. Even though she's been thoroughly fucked tonight, it's still a tight fit around me. Her eyes widen as she watches my cock disappear inside her.

"Breathe, tiger," I whisper in her ear. She relaxes and I bottom out. "So wet and hot."

Her eyes are glazed, and her hands reach back to wrap around my neck, stretching her body against mine. I wrap my arms under her legs and raise her up before lowering her down.

"Oh." Her lips part as she watches me fuck her slowly. The muscles in my arms flex with her slight weight.

"Play with your breasts for me," I whisper in her ear.

She lowers a hand to her breast and cups it, plucking at the nipple. "I love your voice."

"Better than my cock?" I meet her gaze in the mirror for a second before she drops her gaze back to where we're joined.

"I love it all." She huffs out a breath when I lower her again. "Blake?"

Her fingers tug on my hair.

"What, love?" Our eyes meet in the mirror.

"Fuck me harder." She bites down on her lip.

I release her legs. Moving her leg with mine to straddle the bench, I press her front down onto it, not taking my dick out of her pussy. This position spreads her legs open wide. She rests her cheek on the bench as she watches me in the mirror.

Standing behind her, I use my hands to lift her hips up as I thrust my cock deeper inside her. She moans.

I kiss her and whisper, "Rub your clit like I do."

Her hand slides beneath her, and her pussy tightens around me as she touches herself.

My lips brush her ear as I whisper, "Fuck, Madison, you're so fucking tight around my cock. I need you to come so I can fill you until you overflow with my cum. I can't wait to fuck your ass again. It's so hot and tight. When you walk around in skirts in the office, all I'm going to think about is pressing you down over my desk and fucking your ass hard until you come all over me."

As I punctuate each word with a thrust, she moans, deep and throaty.

"You get so wet for us. I could finish fucking your pussy and use your wetness to fuck your ass without needing any lube. I could fuck your pussy until you come all over me and then fuck your ass until I explode in it. Filling you with my cum, knowing you'll sit at your desk with it leaking out onto your thighs, smelling like me. Like a dirty girl. Would you like that?"

"Fuck," she cries out as she comes. Her pussy tightens on me so much I can barely move. I thrust deep and let go, filling her.

I've never been with someone like Madison before. So open to trying everything we want. Begging to try new things. I kiss her ear.

She's becoming a craving I don't want to resist.

"Good girl."

Seth

Madison's mouth wrapped around my cock, sucking lightly, wakes me up. I caress her cheek and see Coop behind her, about to slip his dick into her pussy. I stretch. This is the way to wake up on a Saturday.

Madison sucks harder as Coop thrusts inside. Her darkened eyes lift to mine, and I grab her hair to ease her up and down on my cock the way I like. Not that I don't like what she does, but I want this to last.

Noah rolls over in his sleep and snores.

I meet Coop's eyes. "I want her pussy."

Coop withdraws as Madison lifts her mouth from my dick. He lifts her, moving her forward until she straddles me. I widen my legs as I slip my cock inside her wet cunt.

Coop grabs some lube off the nightstand. Tossing the lube to the side, Coop kneels on the bed between my thighs as I bring Madison down for a kiss. Her pussy tightens around me when Coop slides his cock into her ass. She pulls her mouth away from me on a gasp. He bites down on her shoulder.

Holding the back of her neck, I pull her down to kiss her again, needing to feel that connection.

"Going to fill you up for the day before my workout." Coop licks her skin where he bit.

She whimpers into my mouth as we both thrust.

I break our kiss. "Sore, princess?"

"No, sir. It feels amazing." Her forehead rests on mine as Coop and I fuck her together. Our eyes lock.

"I'm not gonna last, sweetheart. Your ass is just too fucking good." Coop shifts slightly, and all their weight presses down on me.

Her lips part as she pants with each thrust of our hips.

"Come for us, Madison." I keep her eyes on mine as Coop and I quicken our pace.

I can feel her orgasm building in her. Right as it bursts over her, I take her mouth to muffle the scream. We all hold still as Noah rolls away and his arm bumps Blake.

Madison lets out a little giggle that makes me smile. She lifts up, her gaze locked on my mouth as she traces her finger over my lower lip. "I didn't think you could smile."

I thrust up into her, and she lets out a moan as an aftershock works over her. Coop groans as he rocks against her ass. His dick slides against mine inside her, separated by the thin walls.

"You make me want to smile." I claim her mouth. Unable to hold back any longer, Coop and I fuck her, alternating our thrusts until we climax. Madison shudders through another orgasm between us. "So fucking perfect."

Coop leans over her and kisses her shoulder. "I've got to go work out. Thanks for the warm-up, sweetheart."

Her head rests on my chest as her breathing slows. "Anytime."

"I wouldn't make that promise if I were you." Coop lifts off her.

She snuggles on top of me, and I run my hands over her back.

"Do you have to go too?" Her finger draws a little circle on my chest next to her head.

"Not yet." I tighten my arms around her, not wanting to leave this moment.

"Good." She relaxes into me. Her warm skin presses against mine. Her heart beats strong against my own.

I don't want to do anything to disrupt this moment. It's not just sexual gratification with Madison. It's peaceful. She calms parts of me I didn't even know needed to calm down. She wiggled her way into our lives and keeps making new divots that she fits in perfectly.

"I'm not perfect." Her words are soft, but I can hear the strain in them. For a second, I'm confused because I just thought that, but I realize I said it after I came.

"Why do you say that?" I ask.

She raises her head and rests her chin on her hands to look down at me. "You keep saying I'm perfect, but I'm not. I'm flawed and won't ever live up to that standard."

I brush her hair behind her ear as I focus on her face entirely. She has this dark spot in her iris on her left eye, like someone spilled ink on it. It doesn't mar her beauty, just makes her more real. "You may be imperfect in a lot of ways, Madison, but to me, you fit. Your personality. Your sexuality. Your body. Yes, perfection isn't truly achievable, but for me, right now, you're perfect."

I draw her down for a soft kiss. She lets out a sigh and rests her head on my chest. I don't know if she truly heard me, but it's as close as I'll probably come to telling her how much she means to me.

Chapter 45

Work Weekend

Madison

I take a really long shower when we all finally get out of bed. I run soap over every inch of my body. Every inch they touched and caressed. My insides warm as I think about their hands on me, in me. I can't help but feel like a very lucky girl.

Even if I'm a little sore, my body is getting used to being fucked all the time. That's not a bad thing in my book. I finish cleaning myself and dress in a sundress with white panties and bra. When I enter the living area, the smells from the kitchen are divine. Cinnamon and fresh bread.

"Something smells good." I put my hands on the island and focus on the pan in Seth's hands. My stomach growls.

"Cinnamon rolls." He sets it on the counter and opens some cream cheese frosting to spread over them.

"I guess I've already had my workout for the day," I say. When he gives me a smirk, I grin. "I could use some carbs."

After he finishes icing them, he cuts one out of the center of the pan and puts it on the plate, setting it in front of me.

"The best for our girl."

My cheeks get warm.

"Sit. I'll get you some milk to go with it." Seth grabs a glass and walks to the refrigerator.

I like him pampering me. I haven't had anyone look out for me in a long time. Once I left home, it was just me. I haven't talked to anyone from home in a while. I should call my mother today.

"Here you go." He sets the milk in front of me and then gets his own cinnamon roll. When he has his plate and drink, he takes the chair next to me.

"I was serious about the jealousy bit yesterday." Seth glances at me. "I know it can tear people apart inside. I don't want that to happen to you."

Thinking, I trail my fork through the icing and lick it off the tines. I take a breath and cut into the still-warm cinnamon roll.

"I've never really been in a relationship or had anyone to get jealous over before." I purse my lips, trying to think of a time I might have liked someone who wasn't available. "In college, I focused on graduating as quickly as possible to not get too far into debt. In high school, I worked on getting into college. Guys were just something that might or might not happen along the way."

I shrug. It was what it was. I didn't have boyfriends. I had a few hookups, but nothing that stuck. More something I was curious about.

Tingles rush through me when Seth tucks my hair behind my ear. When I lift my gaze to his, his thumb traces my lower lip. My body lights a fire waiting to see if it needs to burst into flames for him or just stay on low for later.

"You keep surprising me." He turns back to his cinnamon roll and takes a bite. "Open and honest communication is essential for this to work. If you feel off about something, talk to us. Any of us. We're here to help you grow."

It's not a proclamation of undying love, but it's nice. They want me here. They care about me. I'm not alone in this anymore. I take a bite of cinnamon roll and moan at the soft gooeyness that fills my mouth.

"Oh my god, this is so good." I look at Seth in shock.

He gives me a smirk. "One thing Mom insisted was that I learn to cook. These are her famous cinnamon rolls."

"Thank her for me next time you talk to her."

His smirk falls, and he gives me a look that makes me think I over-stepped.

"My mom passed away years ago, Madison. But she would have liked you a lot." His lips curve into a sad facsimile of a smile.

My heart aches, and I don't know what to do. I haven't lost anyone like that. I put my hand over his and squeeze it. With no hesitation, he flips his hand over and holds mine. Warmth settles through me as we both eat, connected.

After finishing two glorious cinnamon rolls, Seth heads downstairs to work on a project I can't help with, so I make my way into the library with my Kindle.

I test the chairs until I find the perfect spot. Gnawing on my lip, I scroll through my to-be-read books. I added a few stories that play to my guys' kinks, but I also found a whole category of reverse harem books. One woman to as many men as an author could pack into the book, apparently.

I settle on a dom/sub book. I pluck my lip as I read. It's one about a girl learning she likes to be submissive and the dom who teaches her. I keep envisioning Blake as the dom. Giving orders, punishing her, punishing me. This scene, he's letting someone else use her while he watches.

"Madison!" Blake's voice startles me.

I drop my Kindle on my lap and take my fingers off my lip. He smirks at me.

"I said your name at least three times."

His eyes fall on the Kindle, which thankfully went black when it dropped. Because that page had a whole lot of sex on it. It feels like I should be working, not reading. Reading still feels decadent to me.

"Sorry, I was reading." I straighten. "Do you need me?"

"We could use someone to pull some files." He arches his eyebrow.

I take a deep breath and shake off the arousal from reading the book. Work. I can work. "Sure. Do I need to change?"

Standing, I hold my hands out to the side. I'm still wearing my sundress.

"What you're wearing is fine. Might want some shoes, though."

Giving him an embarrassed smile, I look down at my bare feet, then hurry to my room to grab some sandals.

When I get back to him, he takes my hand and leads me to the elevator. I follow him in. "We're looking through clients right now and need some of the work files that haven't been scanned into the system. They're from a few years ago."

The elevator stops, and I follow Blake into Seth's office.

Seth raises his eyes to me. "Sorry to call you in."

"No problem. I'm always happy to help." I straighten and smile. "Do you have a list and where are the files?"

"The files are on the main floor. Usually people don't work on the weekend, so it should be empty. Room 400. Here's the list." Seth hands it to me.

When I turn to head to the elevator, Blake steps next to me like he's going to go down with me.

"Blake, I need you to pull up the schematics on the Andersen project."

Blake's fingers flex against my back, and he looks down at me.

"I'll be fine." They really haven't let me out of their sights since the incident. "I'm sure no one is in the office. The building is secure, right?"

Blake nods, and I give a small smile to him and then Seth before heading to the elevator.

For a moment, I consider going upstairs to find my phone before heading down. This dress doesn't have pockets, so I have nowhere to keep it. Why waste the time? I'd probably put it down somewhere and forget it, anyway. If I need one of them, there are computers everywhere and phones on the desks.

The elevator ride is a little longer than between the office and apartment. I step out onto the vacant floor. It's weirdly quiet with no one here. The lights are on, so I assume one of the guys has been down here already. The paper in my hand crinkles as I walk down the carpeted hall. A slight buzz from the lights is the only other sound as I make my way around the outside hallway until I find room 400.

I slide my access card in the slot, and it flashes green. Grinning, I push open the door. I still get a little rush at being able to access rooms.

The room is huge, with rows of filing cabinets. Letting the door close behind me, I get to work. I almost wish I'd changed and grabbed my phone. Being in here alone is too quiet. Some music would be nice.

The filing cabinets emit a metallic sliding noise every time I open the drawers. The monotony of the task lulls me as I move from cabinet to cabinet to find the proper file for the client they want. I hear a door slam and I jump.

Setting the files on top of the filing cabinet, I hold my breath, waiting for some other noise. My heart pounds so loud I almost miss the footsteps. I glance around for something to defend myself with, but there's nothing in here.

"Hello?" My voice wavers as I call out. I back up against the filing cabinet nearest me and stare in the direction of the footsteps. Should I have stayed quiet rather than letting whoever is here know where I am?

"Where are you, sweetheart?"

Coop's voice makes me inhale as relief pours through my body.

"I'm over here." I laugh a little at myself. Getting worked up over nothing.

Coop rounds the corner and grins as he spots me. "I came to give you more files to pull and get what you have already. I tried calling."

"I don't really have pockets." I hold my arms out to the side and his gaze rakes over my sundress.

His blue eyes are heated when they meet mine. "If we didn't have work to get done, I could think of a few games I might like to play with you down here."

He closes in on me, and I rest my hands on his chest as I look up at him. His hair is caught back in a bun. I love running my fingers through the silky length when it's down.

"Hide-and-seek. Or maybe a darker fantasy." He sets the list behind me on the filing cabinet and cradles the back of my head in his hands, weaving his fingers through my hair.

My initial fear changes to lust as he kisses my forehead. "What kind of dark fantasy?"

That was on Coop's list. He wants to role-play with me, including consensual nonconsent. I put it as a soft limit, meaning I'd be willing to try, but we have to talk about it beforehand.

I like the idea, but with the assault still so recent, I worry it will trigger me.

Coop's eyes darken. He leans down, so his lips brush my ear with his words. "I could cut the lights in here and everything would be dark. So dark you couldn't see in front of your face."

My breath catches at the thought. A hint of fear rushes through my heart.

"You'd have to find an escape while I hunt you."

I bite my lip, not hating that thought.

"Maybe I wouldn't be alone in my chase." He licks the shell of my ear and I shiver. He presses his body against mine. "Whoever captures you can fuck you where they find you, whether you want it or not."

Fuck, that shouldn't arouse me, but it does. I rub my thighs together.

"Do you like the sound of that, sweetheart?" He drags his cheek back against mine until our lips brush.

I arch into him and seek his mouth, but he holds himself just out of reach.

"Do you want to be caught and fucked like a naughty girl?" He tips my head back. His eyes meet mine before he captures my lips. He rocks his hips into me, and I whimper at the rush of desire spreading through me.

He breaks the kiss and rests his forehead against mine. My heart is going a hundred miles a minute. I ache for him.

"Answer the question, sweetheart." Coop drags his hands from the nape of my neck down my spine, leaving sparks in his wake, until he cups my ass and thrusts my hips into his. "Do you want to be a bad girl instead of a good girl?"

"Coop," I breathe out his name. Wanting everything he can give me.

He smiles. "Did my little fantasy get you hot?"

Nodding, I squirm against him, still caught between him and the cold metal filing cabinet.

"Do you want me to help you come?" Coop lifts his head from mine as he looks down at me. His fingers massage my ass. "Say *please* like a good girl, then."

"Please, Coop," I whisper.

"I do love skirts." Coop turns me around and presses me against the cabinets. The cold metal against my cheek does little to cool the heat welling inside me. His hands slip under my skirt and drag my panties down to my knees.

"Keep them there. Don't let them fall or I'll stop playing with you," he whispers into my hair.

I spread my legs to keep the panties where they are. The sound of his zipper is loud in the quiet room. Even my breathing sounds harsh in the silence.

The slide of Coop's cock against my pussy makes me gasp as his hips press into my ass.

"I haven't decided if I want to fuck you yet." Coop draws back, dragging his cock between my pussy lips and pressing against my clit. "Maybe I'll fuck your pussy for a while before taking your ass again. You're so wet I wouldn't even need lube."

I gush at his words, and his low chuckle in my ear makes me crave him more.

"You like that thought, love." His cock slides between my thighs against my pussy, back and forth. "Maybe I'll just keep doing this until you come all over my cock and then finish in your talented little mouth."

I want to tip my hips to force him inside me. I want to draw my thighs together to press him harder against where I need his touch. But then my panties will fall and he'll stop everything.

"I know you like being a good girl for Blake and Seth, but do you want to be my dirty girl? My little slut?"

I whimper, not sure what I want besides to come. The last person who called me a slut was Valerie, but the way Coop says it doesn't fill me with fear. It turns me on.

"If we weren't in the file room, I'd cover you in my cum. Paint your skin in it and then shove it up your greedy little cunt until you came all over my fingers. Then I'd make you suck my fingers clean of both our cum."

My lips part as I get closer. The touch he's giving me is good but fleeting.

"Do you want that, sweetheart? Be my dirty little whore for me while you play the good girl for Seth and Blake. They'll think you love it sweet, but really you like it dirty and hard."

Groaning, I can't take it anymore. "Fuck me, Coop."

His dark chuckle accompanies his cock shunting through my pussy lips quicker. "How do you want me to fuck you?"

"Fuck me hard. Please, I need you inside me." Whimpering, I press my forehead against the cool metal.

"Where do you want me, sweetheart?"

"Everywhere." I can't think, I just need. I need him to push me over the edge.

"Aren't you a good little whore." His words send a shiver down my spine. He thrusts his cock deep into my pussy, and my release overwhelms me. I tremble against him. My mouth opens in a silent scream as he fucks my throbbing pussy before pulling out and sinking into my ass in one stroke.

The scream works its way out of my throat as I come harder.

"That's it, dirty girl. Milk my cock of my cum." Coop takes my ass rougher than before, but it still feels good. His hand slides over my pussy and pinches my clit, sending me spiraling all over again.

I cry out as he groans his release, filling me as he strokes in and out until he thrusts deep one last time. My panties flutter down to my ankles as my knees give way. Coop holds me up with an arm around my waist.

"Hey there, pretty girl. You okay?" His voice sends tremors through me as he pulls out.

"I'm good," I whisper. Little aftershocks work through me. "So good."

He chuckles and lifts me into his arms.

"Good and dirty." He presses a kiss to my lips and carries me out of the file room. "Just the way I like you."

Fuck, I like him too.

Chapter 46

The File Room

Madison

After Coop helps me clean up and cuddles me a little, I return to work. He took the files I already pulled and gave me a new list. It's been a while since he left, and I'm on the last one. I find the file cabinet in the back corner of the room.

Everything is well maintained and cleaned, but it still feels a little creepy all the way back here. Especially on my own. But I shove it to the side. The guys wouldn't leave me somewhere they thought might be dangerous.

I pull the file and add it to my stack on top of the cabinet.

The lights go out and everything around me is darkness. I hold my breath to listen, waiting for footsteps or the door, a voice, but nothing. I don't even have my phone to turn on my flashlight.

"Hello?" I call out and wait. A shuffling noise reaches me from far away. "Guys? Coop?"

I huddle into the corner and watch the blackness, hoping that maybe I'll adapt and be able to see a little, but there is no light coming into the room. I can't see my hands in front of my face. The shuffling sound reaches me again.

My heart trips over itself with fear. I'm here by myself. Any employee can access this floor from the lobby with their card. It's not as protected as the top floors, where only the guys and I have access.

Reasonable, I can be reasonable. The lights could have just shut off. I need to make my way to the door.

I try to make myself move, but I can't. My feet are glued to the floor.

Coop's fantasy comes back to me. I never said yes or no, but it'd definitely be something we'd need to discuss beforehand. And if he decided to play, I have a way out.

"Yellow!" I yell into the darkness.

The shuffling draws closer. I lower myself to the ground and hold my knees against my chest, trying to be as small as possible. I squeeze my useless eyes shut.

If it's the guys, they need to tell me, now. "Red! Gold! Gold! Gold!"

Flashes of that night in the apartment come at me. Valerie laughing as her boyfriend holds me by my neck. The flood of relief when Blake came to the door followed by Jeff's hand tightening around my throat.

Suffocating. Not being able to breathe. Knowing this could be my last chance to survive.

My chest is tight and I can't catch my breath. The shuffling noise sounds louder, closer, like it's right on top of me.

I cover my ears with my hands as a scream rips out of my throat.

"What the hell is going on in here?" a woman's voice shouts.

Light floods the room, and I close my eyes against the sudden brightness. My breath comes out in pants as I claw at my neck. Nothing is holding it. I'm free to breathe. I'm not trapped.

I'm fine. I'm fine.

"Hello?" My voice cracks.

A tall brunette stands at the end of the aisle with her hands on her hips. "Why are you sitting here screaming in the dark?"

I slowly rise to my feet and brush off my skirt, feeling embarrassed and ridiculous. "Someone shut the lights off."

She scoffs like I'm being a child. "They're probably on a timer over the weekend."

I shake my head. That's not right. I've been in here for a while now, and they've never gone off. What about the shuffling noises?

Did I imagine them? My hands are shaking. Grabbing the files off the cabinet, I hurry toward her. I need out of here.

As I get closer, I recognize the woman as the hater who whispered with the receptionist and gave me a disdainful look on my first day. She's gorgeous and tall and has on slacks and a sleeveless top. Her arms are crossed over her chest.

"Thank you for turning on the light." I'm not sure what else to say to her.

"Whatever. Come on. I'm not leaving you alone in here. I'm almost done with the project I came in for and don't want to waste any more of my weekend babysitting." Her gaze drags over me like I'm some poor street urchin. Her eyes linger on my neck.

I resist the urge to reach my shaking hands up and touch it, knowing I left my scarf upstairs. It's not as bad as when it first happened, but the bruises are still noticeable. The press of his fingers remains on my skin in vivid color.

"I'm finished in here, anyway." I look back over my shoulder, positive that something will be there. Following me. Stalking me.

When she opens the door, I step out into the hallway and take a deep breath. Everything is still exactly the same. I release my breath as the door closes. "I'm Madison, by the way."

"Courtney." She stops and points down the hallway. Her blue eyes linger on my throat a second time. "Your elevator is that way."

She's trying to get rid of me, but that doesn't mean I can't still be nice. I may have been acting like a child, but she did come in and turn the lights on for me. She saved me. Who knows how long I would have been trapped there in that nightmare?

"Thank you, Courtney. I'm sorry if I alarmed you." I tuck the files against my chest and head toward the elevator. Back to safety.

I don't get far when she mutters, "It's not like you're the first person I've found screaming in this place."

What the fuck does that mean? Turning back, I catch sight of her dark hair as she's walking away. I'm tempted to follow her and ask her what she means, but I also want to get to the safety of upstairs and my guys.

The elevator ride helps me calm down. I'm sure it was just my overactive imagination. Maybe I should talk to a therapist about the assault.

When I walk on to the executive floor, the guys are deep in it and spread out in the conference room. I walk in while Seth and Coop are quietly talking in one corner. Blake gestures for me to come over to him.

When I reach him, he takes the files from me. "Thank you."

He sets them on a stack and goes back to reading the file in front of him. I could tell him about it, but what really happened? I panicked because the lights went out. Maybe they go off after hours or are motion sensing. No one but employees can get into the building.

I'm safe here.

"Is there anything else I can do?" I ask quietly. I don't really want to interrupt their flow, but if there is something I can do, I want to help.

Blake shakes his head. "You can go back to reading, tiger."

Not really wanting to be alone right now, but not wanting to disturb them, makes me hesitate. Blake glances up, and his green eyes narrow on mine.

"You okay?" Blake's fingers capture my fingertips. Coop and Seth glance over at us for a moment. I can't tell them I freaked out like a child because the lights shut off. I'm fine now. I need to let them work when they need to work. They've already taken a lot of time to comfort me.

Making my smile bigger, I nod. "I'm good. I'll just go upstairs."

"Noah's up there if you need anything." He releases my hand and gives me a half smile. "If you need company, you can come down and read in here, but this is the quietest it's been."

The guys are still talking, and while I'm sure I'd be able to focus, I might distract them. "I'll go see what Noah is doing."

Noah

The apartment is blissfully empty as I read in the library. The main door opens and closes quietly, and I wait to see who's come up. Madison walks through the living room in a floral sundress, looking a little lost.

I clear my throat.

She spins, and her smile is beautiful as she finds me. My heart beats a little harder as she makes her way toward me.

"You don't have to work today?" She drops into the seat next to mine.

"Not today. Are you finished?" The problem isn't a financial one, so I took the day off after working last Saturday.

"I found all the files they needed." She shrugs and plays with the skirt of her dress. "I thought about reading . . ."

I hold up my book, but I close it and set it to the side. "We could do something together."

She brightens at my suggestion. I wish I could take her out of the apartment, but it's still too risky. Especially if she really did see Valerie the other day. But there haven't been any new texts from Valerie or the stalker.

"We could watch a movie or show." I gesture to the TV room.

Her smile falls a little. She's not big into watching things. During college, she didn't have the time. It's not really my thing either.

"We could play," I suggest. I always want to play with Madison.

Her eyebrow arches with interest. "Did you have something in mind?"

"We could explore the play room." When I stand, I offer her my hand.

She takes it, and I help her to her feet before walking to the door. I shove it open and gesture for her to precede me. As she walks in, I flick on the lights.

Glancing over her shoulder, she gives me a naughty look as she trails her fingers over the furniture she passes. My cock stands to attention, even though we may not actually have sex right now.

It isn't a matter of Madison letting me or not. If I express interest, she's usually down to do whatever, but right now is about exploring and learning. Tonight, we all have her again, and I don't want to wear her out for the grand finale.

"Can you show me something?" She leans back against the bondage horse. My cock twitches, imagining her strapped down on it with her mouth, pussy, and ass all exposed, ready to be fucked.

"What do you want me to show you?" I lift an eyebrow but don't move closer to her. That fantasy needs to be built up to.

"You could show me the ropes, maybe?" Smiling with a mischievous look, she bites her lower lip. "Knots?"

I nod and walk over to a dresser, then open the top drawer. She stayed by the horse, but I gesture her over. Different ropes fill the drawer. Her fingers reach out to touch, but she stops to look at me first for permission. Such a perfect little submissive.

"You can touch anything you like, kitten." I give her a smile.

She picks up a nice thick twist of blue-dyed hemp rope. Her gaze lingers inside the drawer. "Why are they so thick?"

"You want thicker rope so it doesn't cut into your skin. That's hemp in your hand. I have a good supplier. It was difficult to find a good quality one that didn't shed. I have some cotton and a few others." I pull out some natural-colored rope and hold it out to her. "This is silk rope. My particular favorite."

She sets down the hemp and takes the silk. The end of the rope slides through her fingers.

"Can you show me how to tie a knot?" She holds the rope out to me.

Taking it, I gesture with my head for her to follow me. I sit on the bed. She joins me, sitting cross-legged, facing me. I unravel the rope and take her wrist. As I talk, I work on tying the knot.

"This is a single column tie. The knot ends up flat and it's aesthetically pleasing." My fingers work easily around her small wrist until the rope is wrapped around her and tied tight.

She gives it a tug and the knot doesn't collapse. Her gaze lifts to mine. "Will you teach me?"

We spend the next few minutes going over how I made the knot and then having her use my ankle to tie one of her own around. That way, if she needs my hands, they're free. And my jeans keep her from tying it too tight.

When she finally gets one that looks fairly decent, she grins up at me. "I did it."

Her genuine excitement makes me long to touch her. Using my knuckle under her chin, I nudge her face up and claim her mouth. It's a gentle and exploratory kiss. When I pull back, she smiles softly.

Her gaze wanders to the bondage horse.

"Will you tie me like that picture for tonight?" Her blue eyes sparkle as she meets mine.

My cock hardens at the lust in her eyes. The woman tied onto the horse in the picture had a gag, but for Madison, I'd want us to be able to fuck her mouth. I stroke my thumb across her lip. "We can modify it slightly from the picture. You'd have to hold a bell, so if your mouth is full and you need us to stop, you could drop it."

She kisses the tip of my thumb and smiles. "Yes, please."

"Let me see when they'll be finished downstairs." I take out my phone and shoot a quick text to Coop. He responds that they should finish in time for dinner. It's only four thirty now.

"What did he say?" Madison tries to put the rope in some sort of twist.

I take it out of her hands and say, "I have time to show you one more hold before dinner."

"Okay."

"Hold your wrists out for me."

She does as I ask and I start tying.

"This is a double column tie, useful when you want to bind two columns such as arms or legs together." I finish the knot and pull the free end through a metal loop, effectively tying her to the headboard.

"You did that rather fast." She studies the knot and holds them out to me to untie.

"I just needed you ready." Smiling, I pull her legs down on the bed until the rope is tight. "We have time to play, but I only want you to come."

"What?" Her eyes meet mine right before I toss her skirt up over her face. "Noah."

I pull her panties down her legs and drop them off the side of the bed. I push her knees to her chest. "Hold them like this, kitten, or I'll tie them that way."

"Fuck, Noah." She's spread out before me. Pink and wet. I lean in and lick her sweet pussy.

She gasps at my first touch. I use my fingers to hold her open as I taste her, licking and sucking and flicking my tongue over her sensitive bud. Driving my tongue into her slick channel. She makes those needy noises in the back of her throat that drive me wild.

I'm so fucking hard, tasting her, making her squirm. Her entire body tenses, and she moans when she finds release, but I don't stop. I dip lower, spreading her cheeks, and drive my tongue into her puckered hole.

Every inch of her is a feast for me. I want to explore every freckle, every scar. Find the parts of her that are ticklish. The parts that make her moan.

I lick and fuck her asshole with my tongue. Her breath catches as she shatters, arching and tugging at the ropes. When I sit back on my knees, I lower her skirt and study her. Her face is red and she's panting.

I could keep her like this all night. Make her come over and over until her brain shuts off entirely and all she feels is pleasure.

"Noah." She lowers her legs around me. Her gaze falls to my erection. "Let me help you."

"How do you want to help me, kitten?" I undo my pants to relieve the ache and pull my cock out to stroke it.

With her eyes on my cock, she licks her lips. "Use my mouth like you did the other night."

Not needing more of an invitation, I crawl up her body until I straddle her chest. Leaning against the headboard, I feed my cock between her waiting, parted lips and let her engulf me in her warm, wet mouth.

I let her lick and suck as I rock my cock in and out of her mouth. Loving the tease almost as much as coming. She moans and her darkened eyes meet mine. Fuck, she wants me as much as I want her.

When she gags a little, I draw back, but she brushes her tongue along my length. I push in deep and she moans around my cock. So fucking good. I could go as hard as I like, but she doesn't have a way to let me know to stop. Holding her gaze for any hint of panic, I fuck her face slowly, sliding my cock deep into her throat.

When she hollows out her cheeks and sucks hard on me, I explode, groaning my release, clenching the headboard. I draw out of her mouth, and she swallows for me. My cock twitches. I can't get enough of her.

Moving off the bed, I release the knot on the headboard before untying her hands. "Come on, kitten. Let's get cleaned up for dinner, and then we can tie you up for dessert."

Chapter 47

Circle Back to That

Blake

We finish with the project in time for dinner. The need to check on Madison beat in the back of my head for the past few hours. She seemed off when she brought me the files. Even her smile had a slight edge to it. But I knew Noah was with her.

When we get to the apartment, Noah and Madison are at the island assembling pizzas for dinner. Seth, Coop, and I slip into our rooms to clean up. I take a quick shower, knowing that we're all going to fuck Madison again tonight.

The thought of her makes me hard, but I ignore the urge to jack off. Instead, I focus on the discrepancy we found. No one is stealing money from us, but someone is contacting our clients behind our backs.

After our lunch this week, Jason Harper alerted us when someone emailed him about working with Morrigan Technology.

We've always had some client turnover, so we hadn't worried when a client here and there would suddenly no longer need our services. Part of doing business. But this isn't normal attrition. Someone is poaching our clients intentionally.

After going through several files of clients who left, we have a handful of names. Employees who worked with these particular clients and are still employed by us.

Of course, Rachel works at Harper Associates now, so she may have been the leak there. She has her reasons to want us to pay for the alleged harm we did her. We made her an offer, which she turned down, and then she quit. The end.

We haven't ruled her out, but it's still likely a current employee. The meeting with Jason Harper wasn't that long ago. Madison was there, and she's only been with us for two weeks.

I stop towel drying my hair and stare at my reflection in the mirror. Only two weeks feels wrong. With all that's happened, it seems like we've had her much longer. No one before her has woven into our lives quite as seamlessly as she has.

After I dress, I return to the living area and watch Noah smiling at Madison. I've never seen him this happy before. It strikes me hard as I try to remember over the years any time that Noah was this happy. This carefree. He always had to behave more mature than his age. Being the youngest, he always felt like he had something to prove.

"Noah, stop." Madison's laughter fills the room. Noah's fingers tickle her sides. She's bent over trying to protect herself.

"Tickling wasn't a hard limit, kitten." Noah laughs as he wraps his arms around her from behind and lifts her into the air. "If you really want me to stop, you could use your safe word."

She squeals with laughter. I lean against the wall, watching them with my heart filling my chest. This is everything to me. Having my brothers with me and having them all happy. And Madison. She's smart and sexy and so open about everything.

This is what I want. This life right now with these people.

Sure, we have some issues to resolve, but I want this to work.

"Creeping?" Coop settles next to me on the wall.

"Just appreciating." I glance over at him. "You happy?"

Coop smiles as his gaze goes to Madison and Noah. "Seem to be."

"Yeah."

Madison turns her bright blue eyes on the two of us, and her beaming smile makes my heart ache. "What are you two talking about?"

Shaking my head, I walk across the room to the island. "Nothing."

She cocks her eyebrow at me suspiciously, but she doesn't lose her smile. Her neck is still bruised. The overall bruising is down, but not the finger-shaped ones. There's still so much we haven't figured out. Her roommate is still out there, and so is the mysterious stalker.

"Just dreaming of fucking your sweet ass tonight." Coop sits at the island and bats his eyes at Madison.

Her cheeks flush with color as she gives him a shy smile back.

"Dinner first." Seth's strong voice comes from behind us. He likes order. This whole ordeal with the client poaching pisses him off. It has to be an inside job, which means one of our employees, or more, is betraying us.

I've already put out background checks on the employees we suspect. It tears me up inside knowing we trusted the wrong person. Again.

Noah pulls out the pizzas and carries them to the already set table.

"Did you find what you guys were looking for?" Madison asks as she follows Noah.

Seth sits at the head of the table and leans back in his chair. "We don't know who is involved, but it seems to be less about money than strategically dismantling what we've created."

Madison's brow furrows as she takes a slice of pizza. "How so?"

"Someone is contacting potential clients and warning them off our company. The clients don't all go to the same cyber tech company afterward." Coop rests his forearms on either side of his plate. "It doesn't make any sense. If someone were trying to get in good with a new employer, you would see the clients all signing on to the same company."

"And it's been going on for a while," I point out. "Whatever employee is leaking our information has done it so slowly that, if Jason hadn't called, we wouldn't even be aware of it."

"We have to look at possible collusion as well." Seth shakes his head and sighs. "We won't find the answers today or tomorrow, but we might get some indication of who might be involved. Until then, we need trusted people on our integration teams."

Which means more work for us, but Seth doesn't say that.

"But not tonight," Coop says around a bite of pizza. He swallows before adding, "What's tonight's agenda?"

"Madison had a request which I'm going to help her with." Noah's voice is nonchalant, but I can tell he's excited about what she wants.

Madison flushes red again. "We'll set up, and then Noah will tell you when to come in."

I'm tempted to say fuck dinner, but I'll need energy.

"So, Noah's running the show tonight?" Coop glances at Seth, like he's eager for him to blow up.

Seth smirks. "It's about time someone else took charge."

We chuckle. I give Seth maybe fifteen minutes of whatever Noah has planned before he's barking orders. Usually we all enjoy his orders, so I don't fight it. Madison shifts in her chair as her gaze darts between all of us. When her gaze falls on me, I give her a slight smile.

Smiling back, she relaxes into her chair and eats. Conversation shifts to the game we missed today while working. Noah and Madison listen as we talk about what this win means to our team.

The homemade pizza is delicious, and when we finish everyone helps clean up the kitchen. Every time I pass by Madison, I let my fingers drag across her thigh, and she smiles with that needy look in her eyes. I can't wait to have my fingers drag on her bare skin.

I'm probably not the only one ready for tonight to begin. Honestly, I'd be happy to strip Madison naked and spread her out on the island for all of us to enjoy.

When Noah reaches out his hand for Madison, she takes it and gives us all an excited grin as he leads her to the play room.

Coop heads to the living room and turns on the news. Seth and I join him on the couches.

"So many scenarios." Coop relaxes into the couch and sighs. "Maybe he's going to tie her up for us on the bed. Or use the swing."

Seth makes a noncommittal noise, but his gaze strays to the play room door.

"We have the Taylor's installation next week." Seth puts his hands on his knees. "We need to be aware of who is on that project."

Hunter Adams will be there. He wanted Madison on that team, and his father did too. William Adams seems genuine in his desire to help Madison learn more, but Hunter . . . I can't forget her nightmare. The attraction between Madison and Hunter doesn't appear mutual. I'm not willing to send her into that lion's den without backup.

"They want Madison on the project. I can go with her." I won't let her out of my sight.

"That could work." Seth rubs his chin. "But should she be out yet?"

"We can't keep her locked in the tower forever," Coop says, and he's not wrong. She can't just live up here at our disposal.

"We have to assume her roommate and the boyfriend are still lying low. Besides the street, no one has seen or heard from them." I put my hands behind my head. "There haven't been any new texts from whoever sent the shower video. I've got a man monitoring the old next-door neighbor. Just in case. The only thing that will be a problem there is Hunter."

"Shit." Coop's gaze darts to mine at the mention of Hunter. "Did you see something too?"

I arch an eyebrow at Coop.

He rubs the back of his neck. "He had her cornered in the break room during their meeting here in the office."

Fuck.

"He cornered her when she went to the ladies' room at the restaurant." At the time, it was suspicious, but I wasn't just suspicious of Hunter then.

"What the fuck?" Seth draws his hand through his blond hair. "Why didn't you guys tell us about this?"

I take a breath. "I wasn't sure we could trust Madison then. It was her first day, and she's got a previous employer acting like she's his property. I figured they were possibly a thing."

Seth narrows his eyes. "That still would have been important information. Honesty, remember?"

"I didn't know if we could trust her." I shake my head. "Andrea—"

"Was a fucking bitch from day one." Coop turns off the TV.

"None of us saw her true colors," Seth says.

"But I'm the one who brought her in. I'm the one who said we should take a chance on her." I can't help feeling guilty over the whole thing. While we'd played with fucking the same girl in college, we hadn't really done much since starting our business. It made sense. We were so busy with the business. If we found someone we all were attracted to, why not have someone we could all fuck on the regular?

"And none of us blame you, Blake." Coop meets my eyes. "Fuck, maybe I should have been more clear about her when we discussed her, but what did I care as long as she fucks?"

"We all had reservations about her. She seemed too good to be true." Seth meets my eyes. Madison seems too good to be true as well. "But no one is to blame for how that turned out. We all found out we needed to be more honest with each other. And with what we want from this arrangement."

Standing, Seth stretches his back. "We learned from each woman before Madison. Not every woman can handle us. Not every woman wants to be shared by four guys who aren't offering her anything but sex and a job. Maybe Madison won't last, but maybe she will. But while we have her, I propose we enjoy her openness and willingness to try new things. And protect her from assholes."

"Like Hunter." Coop gets to his feet. "She's ours now. If he tries any of that shit with Madison—"

"I'll take care of it." I stand to join them.

"If you guys are finished stroking each other's dicks, we're ready for you." Noah stands next to the open play room door and gestures for us to enter.

Chapter 48

Test the Limits

Seth

When we walk into the play room, Madison is tied down to the bondage horse in the center of the room. The rest of the furniture is pushed back to give us space. She's naked with her knees spread wide around the bench. Her pussy glistens in the light. Already wet for us.

My cock twitches and presses against the zipper of my jeans.

"Coop," Noah says, holding out a bottle of lube. "Can you make sure our girl is ready?"

Smiling wickedly, Coop takes the lube and stands behind Madison's ass. The bench sits low, in the right position for us to stand and fuck her. Coop spreads the lube down Madison's crack and over her puckered hole.

When she gasps, I adjust the hard-on in my pants.

"She isn't allowed to speak or moan." Noah leans back against the bedpost as we all watch Coop prep her ass with his hand, teasing her asshole with his fingers. "Blake, you'll hand out punishment if she disobeys."

Blake raises an eyebrow and Noah nods to the table. There are a few basic paddles out.

"She's agreed to these. You can choose which one."

The paddles are leather, a few with fur, soft, but they'll still sting. It's a good first-time selection. Blake nods his approval.

Madison makes a muffled noise and I turn. Coop has three of his long fingers fucking her ass while his mouth sucks on her clit. Her face is red as she tries to keep from making any sound.

"Do you need something in your mouth, kitten?"

Her wide eyes meet Noah's. She nods. Noah smirks and turns back to us.

"She has a bell in her hand. If she rings it or drops it, we stop. Once she can speak, she can let us know what needs to happen with no punishment." Noah sighs as he looks her over. "I'd take pictures, but it's too risky with everything that's been going on. She looks beautiful all tied up and ready to take us."

Fuck, but she looks good enough to eat.

"Other than that, no rules. Use her how you want to. She's ours to do with as we like."

The position eliminates us fucking her ass and pussy at the same time, but we can be inventive.

I open the drawer with the toys and pull out some that I might want to play with. Setting them next to the paddles, I take a seat so Madison can see me watching, and I can see all of her luscious, pale skin on display and watch my brothers use her.

Noah walks over to watch Coop finger fuck her ass while eating her pussy. Blake stands at Madison's face, undressing in front of her. She licks her lips as she waits for him. Every now and then, she sucks in a breath to hold back a moan.

When Blake is naked, he rubs his cock against her lips. Her eyes lift to his and she licks the precum from his tip. Blake wraps her braided hair around his fist. She won't be able to move her head to take any more of his cock into her mouth than he lets her.

He taps his cock on her lips, and she opens. Coop draws his face back to watch his fingers. As Blake thrusts into her mouth, Noah slides his fingers into her cunt, following the rhythm set by Coop's fingers in her ass. Her toes curl as her body tenses. She comes with a muffled noise around Blake's cock.

Not enough sound to get punished.

"Good girl, kitten." Noah draws his fingers out of her pussy and licks them clean.

Removing his fingers, Coop straightens and undoes his pants to pull out his cock. He doesn't bother to get undressed as he slams his dick into Madison's pussy. She makes a muffled noise.

Blake continues his slow fuck of her mouth. She takes cock so well. Her wet pussy clings to Coop's cock as he draws it out and slams back into her.

I undo my pants and free my cock, stroking it while watching my friends fuck Madison, knowing how tight she feels wrapped around me.

Coop and Blake meet each other's eyes and smile. They thrust with each other, burying their dicks into Madison at the same time. Noah stands beside her and slowly fingers her asshole. His other hand trails over her arm and side.

"Fuck, man, I can feel her tightening. She's going to come again," Coop tells Blake.

Her whole body tenses as an orgasm shimmers over her muscles. Coop stops fucking her and holds his breath while still buried inside her pussy.

"Swallow, tiger." Blake thrusts deep into her mouth one last time, and her throat ripples as she swallows around him. He groans as he comes, letting her suck off every drop before he steps back. He rubs her head where he tugged on her hair.

"Good girl." Blake sits next to me while Noah moves to her mouth. He's removed his clothes and stands before her naked.

Coop strips off his shirt while his cock remains buried in her cunt. "I can feel her pulsing around me. She's so fucking sensitive."

He reaches down and pinches her clit.

She moans loudly as she comes again.

Coop smirks and steps back, gesturing for Blake.

"Open up, kitten." Noah thrusts his cock into Madison's waiting mouth.

Blake takes a minute to select a leather paddle.

She sucks on Noah as he thrusts in and out of her mouth. She's so fucking beautiful with our cocks inside her.

After choosing a paddle, Blake waits for Noah to withdraw from her mouth. I walk over to stand behind Blake, then stop next to a now-naked Coop as he strokes his cock with lube.

"If you need to cry out, kitten. You can. Five spanks this time. Next time will be ten." Noah rubs his thumb over Madison's lips and nods to Blake.

The paddle swoops through the air and smacks her ass. She lets out a startled gasp. After two more smacks to the right side, Blake switches to the left cheek. She inhales when he finishes.

"Good, kitten?" Noah asks.

She nods. Blake moves out of the way as Coop steps behind her again. His hands grab her pink ass cheeks and spread them wide. She whimpers slightly, her skin sensitive from the spanking.

"Quiet, sweetheart." He smacks her ass before thrusting his cock deep into her puckered hole.

She gasps, and Noah nudges his cock against her lips. I return to the side so I can watch them fuck her together. Her skin flushes pink as Coop takes her ass a little harder than he usually does. I brush my hand down her side and feel her muscles tremble beneath my fingertips.

Exquisite.

I go to my pile of toys and grab a bullet vibrator. I stroke her thigh, feeling the muscle beneath my fingers tighten. Turning the vibrating bullet on high, I press it against her clit. She jumps and makes a noise around Noah's cock.

Her muscles tremble as an orgasm rushes through her. Her orgasms consume her, and I can't help sliding my finger inside her cunt to feel it convulse around me. Coop growls as he pushes in deep and groans his release before staggering back.

"All yours, boss." Coop slaps me on the shoulder before going over to watch the show.

I grab a towel and clean her up a little. She's soaking wet from her orgasms. Noah stands with his cock buried in her mouth while she sucks and licks him. He waits to see what I'm going to do.

Checking out what else I've left on the table, I keep the bullet pressed firmly against her throbbing clit. A vibrating butt plug and the bullet should do the trick. I take the bullet away and her body sags in relief as much as the ropes allow.

Turning on the plug, I press my cock against her entrance and thrust deep inside her hot, dripping cunt. She makes a slight noise but keeps sucking on Noah's cock. I hold the vibrating toy against her asshole, and she tightens around me.

"Shh, kitten, you wouldn't want to get more spankings, would you?"

She obviously doesn't answer Noah's question. I press the toy inside her, letting it vibrate against the sensitive nerves of her opening. I draw out my cock and thrust into her pussy again before pressing the plug a little deeper.

"Fuck, I wish you could see this, Madison." Blake steps to my side to watch her asshole accept the toy.

She sucks a little harder on Noah, and he comes in her mouth. He wipes his cum from the corner of her lips with his thumb and slips it into her mouth. She sucks on it to clean it. "Thank you, kitten."

Madison

I breathe in deep, unable to move from my position. Seth's cock throbs inside my pussy while the vibrator pushes into my ass a little deeper. The guys all move around to the back of me to watch.

Knowing they're all watching my pussy and ass get fucked makes me even wetter. I don't know how I'll keep from moaning as the vibrator pulses against my every nerve, filling me so fucking full. Seth finishes, thrusting it in deep, and I feel the fullness of his cock in my tight pussy and the vibrator in my ass.

He slides his cock out slowly before thrusting forward, jostling the vibrator. Hands spread my ass and thighs. Someone's fingers swirl on my clit. Seth stops playing around and fucks me harder and faster.

I choke back the moan threatening to burst from me. I'm right back on the edge again, trembling, waiting to fall off. Giving in to them is so fucking easy.

The finger on my clit rubs circles. Someone pulls the vibrator out a little before sliding it back in. Then they fuck me with it while Seth fucks me hard and deep with his cock. I suck in a breath as tingles chase through every inch of me all the way to my toes. I can't focus. It's too much sensation.

A scream bursts from me as my body releases, convulsing around his cock and the plug. It's too much. Part of me wants to move away because I'm too sensitive, but I can't. My body tenses and I'm ready to come down. Someone yanks out the plug, and I moan as another release floods over me. But he's not finished with me. Fucking me hard, Seth groans as he comes inside me.

Warmth floods me and I can't quite catch my breath. I want more, but I'm not sure if I can take it.

When he steps back, another cock fills my pussy, stroking in and out slowly while fingers thrust into my asshole. I squeeze my eyes shut at the overstimulation, knowing I'm going to shatter for them all over again.

"So fucking tight, tiger." Blake's behind me, in me. He pulls out, and his thick cock slides easily into my asshole. Every inch opening me up a little more.

Someone taps me on my lips with their cock. My eyes stay closed as I open to take his cock inside. I suck on it, licking it as they thrust deep into my mouth.

A small part of my mind thinks it should disturb me that this is getting me off. They're using my body for their pleasure. Fucking me while I'm held completely still and open for them. Not able to take them deeper anywhere. Not even able to get away from them. But the thought only makes me wetter, needier. I want this.

The bullet vibrator is pressed against my clit, and I explode as I come. It's almost painful as I clench around Blake's cock. But the euphoria is worth it. I need this bliss.

"Fuck." Blake takes my ass harder as he comes. When he withdraws, the cock in my mouth spills cum into my throat.

"Good girl," Coop says, brushing his finger along my cheek.

"Ten," Seth says the number, but it doesn't register until I hear the whoosh of the paddle and the smack of my ass. I cry out.

Someone holds the vibrating bullet against my clit as Blake spanks me, and I fall over the edge. I'm still coming as someone thrusts their cock into my pussy again. My brain is almost floating on the high of so many orgasms.

It feels like I'll never come down. Nothing exists except these men and my body, falling over the edge over and over again. Pleasure and pain wrapped into one endless orgasm.

Noah

Seth is fucking Madison's pussy again after Blake finishes spanking her. I crouch down in front of her face and cup her chin. She opens her mouth.

"Kitten? You still with us?"

Her eyes open and her pupils are blown. She makes this little mewling noise in the back of her throat.

I smile at her and rub my thumb over her lower lip. "Feeling high?"

She blinks at me, and her lips part as she cries out again.

When Blake steps toward her with the paddle, I hold my hand up. "She's done."

Her tongue runs against the tip of my thumb as she tries to suck it into her mouth.

"She's out of it. So lost in the pleasure that she can't feel anything but." I lean in and kiss her softly. Her tongue tries to slip into my mouth even as I pull back. "Which means she won't be able to tell us her limits."

Coop nods and goes to start the shower. Blake and Seth clean and put away the toys while I work on untying Madison. When Blake finishes, he comes over and rubs her arms as I loosen them.

Coop returns and works on massaging her legs. When the last rope is gone, I lift her into my arms. She turns into my body and kisses my shoulder before sucking on my skin. Fuck, this is the best time to play with a submissive, but I have to be careful.

She's all high on the hormones coursing through her body.

We can't introduce anything new or anything that she might normally use a safe word for.

That doesn't mean I won't fuck her. I shift her in my arms until her legs wrap around my waist. I adjust so my cock notches against her entrance, wet and hot. My cock slides into her pussy. It feels so good to be buried deep inside her. I carry her like that through the apartment with the others following us. Her hands float over my skin as her mouth explores my shoulders and neck.

When I step into the shower, I press her against the wall, holding her up while I fuck her tight pussy. My lips capture hers as I pound into her, chasing my release. She cries out into my mouth as she comes undone. Her pussy convulses around me, drawing me into my orgasm.

My balls tighten and my cum spills into her. Holding her against me, pressed to the wall of the shower, I drag in a breath. She starts to writhe in my arms, rolling her hips against mine, craving stimulation.

When I pull out of her, Coop draws her into his arms. She kisses every inch of skin she can reach. Blake cradles her from the back, and her hips thrust back and forth between them.

Seth joins us in the shower, quickly washing himself while watching Madison. "Fuck, does she even know what she's doing?"

"Yeah, but she's high on it. Kind of like a good buzz on alcohol, but we need to watch for the crash." All those feel-good chemicals running through her brain will eventually go back down to normal, and she'll come down. It's different for every sub, but it can be dangerous if we aren't careful with her. "But while she's high, she'll crave us touching her. It's not a good idea to push any limits when she's like this because she won't want to stop even if she should."

Coop groans, lowering her feet to the tile, but supporting her. Her hand wraps around his cock, stroking him. Blake bends her forward and thrusts his cock into her pussy from behind. Her breasts sway with the rhythm of his hips thrusting into her. Moaning, she takes Coop's dick deep in her throat.

"Fuck," Coop breathes out as he grabs her braid to help control how deep she takes him. The water pours down on all of us from the multiple heads.

Watching them fuck her makes me hard again. They all groan at the same time as they come. Blake helps her straighten and then she's in Seth's arms. I grab her soap and work on cleaning her back while she kisses Seth's shoulders and strokes his cock.

When I rinse the soap from between her legs, I lower myself to kneel behind her and lick her wet pussy. She's so on the edge that when I thrust my fingers into her, she comes again. I rise to my feet and Seth turns her around. I pour some soap into his hand and lather my own as we clean the front of her body together.

Blake sucks on her nipple while Coop fondles her other breast. I finish cleaning her pussy and legs before turning to wash myself quickly.

We move as a unit. Coop turns off the water, and Blake hands everyone a towel. Seth holds Madison wrapped in a towel while we all dry off. He gives her a glass of water that she greedily drinks.

When Coop finishes drying himself, he takes her from Seth and dries her off before carrying her into the bedroom. The way we all care for her. None of us wants to let her go. Aftercare has always been a part of our play, but never like this.

I've never seen all of us so caught up in one woman. *I've* never been caught up like this in anyone.

We're all in this one hundred percent. Not just for the sex, but for Madison. Though the sex is amazing and not even close to finished.

Chapter 49

Diminishing Returns

Coop

Madison is a greedy little thing, and I'm not sure I have enough energy to take her again. We've settled on the bed, but she's not done. Fuck, how many times have I come in the last hour or so? Her ass keeps rubbing against my cock, and even my dick is getting ideas.

Her mouth is on Seth. Licking, sucking, kissing. Everywhere.

I love watching her take the others. Not as much as Seth, but it's erotic as hell to see her so into someone else while she wants me too.

When she kneels up and leans over to take his cock in her mouth, I reach for the lube. Yeah, we all got cleaned, but I like my girl a little dirty. I rub the lube over my cock before rising behind her and sliding lube over her puckered hole with my fingers before sinking them inside her hot, tight body.

She presses into my fingers, driving them deeper.

Fuck.

She whimpers when I draw my fingers out. Before I can line up my cock with her perfect little asshole, she straddles Seth and impales her pussy on his cock. Seth grabs her hips and thrusts up tighter into her. Moaning, she leans forward on Seth and turns her needy eyes on me.

I don't need a second invitation. Seth widens his legs, and I kneel between them before slowly easing my cock into her puckered hole. Little mewling noises come from Madison.

"You're doing great, princess. He's almost inside you, just a little more. Then we can fuck you." Seth takes her mouth with his as I bottom out in her ass.

Fuck, there's nothing like the tightness and feeling of another cock thrusting with me in a woman. I love a good, tight ass, and Madison's is the best I've ever felt.

She moans loudly as her body convulses around us before we even start moving.

"I think I love subspace." Kissing the back of her neck, I pull back and thrust deep into her ass again. I sit up and part her ass cheeks so I can watch my cock slide in and out of her.

Noah lies down on the bed beside us, and Madison reaches out to stroke his cock. She hasn't said much, but Noah's told me before that it's not unusual for a sub to stop communicating when they hit that high.

Seth thrusts from below while I alternate. He pushes in, I pull out. I push in, he pulls out. She's making these needy noises in the back of her throat. I can feel my balls tightening with every thrust.

"Fuck." Noah comes all over her hand.

Her eyes remain locked on Noah as she brings her hand to her mouth and licks his cum from her fingers. That's enough to push Seth over the edge. He thrusts up into her and holds her hips against his. Groaning, he fills her with his cum. I draw her upright against my chest as I piston my hips, fucking her ass while Seth remains buried in her pussy.

She rubs her skin against mine as I palm her breasts. When I trail my fingers in circles around her hardened nipples, she exhales a shaky breath. Dragging my fingers lower, I slide them over her clit and rub it lightly. It won't take much to get her off, as sensitive as her body is right now.

She leans her head back against my chest as her lips part and no sound comes out. When she comes, she tightens around me and Seth groans. Her body throbs against mine as I drive my cock into her one final time and spill my seed into her ass.

We all hold there, catching our breath. For a second, everything inside me is still and quiet as our rough breaths fill the air.

"Come here, tiger." Blake holds out his arms for her, and we pull out so she can go into them. He lies down and she cuddles against his chest. Noah returns from the bathroom with a warm cloth to clean her up.

By the time Seth and I return to the bedroom, Noah has wrapped his body around Madison's back. A small shiver ripples through her. I lie down next to Noah and draw the blankets over us, resting my hand on her back.

On the other side of Blake, Seth holds her hand. All of us are touching her. She sighs gently before closing her eyes.

Nothing is better than this moment right here.

Everyone I love is safe and accounted for. I'm on the edge of sleep as that thought tugs me awake. I'm not a fearful man. But when things seem to be going right in my life, everything falls apart.

Madison

The sun isn't even over the horizon when I wake up feeling hot and sweaty. I'm cocooned between Blake's and Noah's warm bodies with covers over us. Flashes of last night flow through my mind, and my lips tip into a smile. I don't think I've orgasmed that much in my life.

Continuously fucked. Unable to get away as they thrust their cocks deep inside me. Filling me up over and over again. My body heats at the memory. I definitely want to do that again.

I try to stretch without waking them. My body aches in the most delicious ways. Noah's hand slides up my thigh, leaving a trail of sparks in its wake. It's arousing but in an almost loving way, not the longing, needful way of last night.

Rolling toward him, I lift my gaze to his soft brown eyes. This close, I can see flecks of amber in them from the glow of the bathroom light. My chest feels like it's ready to explode.

"Good morning," I whisper, to not wake the others.

"Good morning, kitten." He tugs on my very loose braid. I'm surprised it survived during the shower and everything after. "How are you this morning?"

Heat floods me at how insatiable I was when we got back to the room. The shower. The bed. I couldn't get enough of their skin touching mine. I bury my face against Noah's chest. Everything just felt so much better.

His deep chuckle rumbles through his chest and warms me. "Don't be embarrassed you enjoyed yourself, kitten. We wouldn't want it any other way."

I peek at him, and he rubs his thumb across my lower lip. I press a kiss to the pad of it. Even my jaw is a little sore this morning.

"I really liked what we did last night." I mean those words, but part of me feels off. Yes, the whole thing was super intense. Held down, unable to move. That feeling of being a vessel for them, something to use to find their release, made it even hotter. But my mind keeps tripping over what that means.

Noah cups my cheek and presses a soft kiss to my lips. "Try to get some more sleep. You might feel a little hungover or sad. We'll take care of you when we get out of bed."

I lay my head down over Noah's heart and listen to the steady beat. His naked body presses against mine. It's comfortable and familiar. This is what I want, to be safe in someone's arms. In his arms. I let out a sigh and close my eyes, ready for more sleep.

My mind can't stop spinning, though.

I loved being used by them last night. But is that all I am to them?

Someone to try new things with or practice their kinks? Just a hole to fill to satisfy their base desires?

How long can this thing between us really last? Until the guys don't want to share a woman anymore? Before they want someone to call their own? Before I lose them because I will never be enough for them? I can't be perfect. That isn't who I am.

"Hey." Noah's arms wrap around me, and his hands stroke soothingly down my back.

His chest is wet under my cheek. Warm tears stream down my face. I didn't even realize I'm crying. I rub at the tears.

Noah props himself up on the headboard and draws me into his lap, cradling my body in his arms and between his legs. "It's okay to feel whatever you're feeling, Madison. Things got intense last night. You aren't used to that level of hormones flooding your system."

Sniffling, I meet his eyes. Tears blur my vision. I should be happy, content, satisfied.

His smile is soft as he brushes the tears from my cheek. "What's going on in your head right now, kitten?"

I glance around at the others still sleeping. The tears fall unchecked.

"This is going to end," I whisper and meet Noah's eyes, feeling so small and helpless. I should be stronger. I shouldn't tell him this, but it throbs in my chest like an ache that needs to get out. "I don't want it to, but it's inevitable. It's not like this is a real relationship."

"Why not?" Noah tilts his head and his blond hair falls over his eye.

Unable to resist, I reach out and brush it back. "We have a contract—"

"As most relationships that involve kinks should. Ours just happens to be written down." Noah tightens his arm around me. "Every relationship should start with a talk about what you expect from each other. Our relationship involves a lot of sex and a variety of different needs we want met."

I try to smile for him, but this ache in my heart keeps pounding away at me. "It's not like we are emotionally tied—"

"You don't think this is emotional for us?" He shakes his head with a small smile. "This thing between us requires a lot of trust. We trust you to be faithful to us. We trust each other to not hurt you in any way. We trust that we'll remain open and honest with each other so that no one gets hurt or jealous."

"But what about when you guys find someone else?" I draw a heart on his chest, letting myself wallow in the sadness of what's to come. I've never been anyone's. Not really. Even my previous boyfriends were convenient rather than anyone I wanted long-term.

But I want to belong to these men. To be theirs fully and completely.

"What makes you think we'll find someone else?"

"You guys have to go on dates. Those women will have expectations and hopes." I can't bring myself to say my fears out loud. *And I can't be enough for all of you. I'm just me.*

Noah glances at the others. "Can I tell you a secret?"

I nod, and he shifts me so that I'm straddling his lap. His cock is hard between my thighs, and even though I'm aroused being close to him, this isn't about sex right now for either of us.

He leans in and presses his mouth against my ear. His lips tickle me as he whispers, "The only one I want to date is you."

I draw back to meet his eyes, surprised. "What?"

"We'll talk more later. When we're awake and can focus." He gives me a tender kiss and pulls me in for a hug, which feels amazing. I don't know what he means, but my heart is pounding so hard right now.

Is it hope or fear? Maybe a little of both?

He tips my chin up and searches my eyes. "Feel better? A little?"

"Yeah, a little."

"Back to sleep, kitten. Sleep will help."

As we settle down on the bed, Blake rolls toward me and draws my back into him, surrounding me with his heat. Noah closes his eyes, and I study him. He wants to date me? Like outside of this relationship? What would that mean for the others? What would that mean for me?

Blake rubs his nose along the nape of my neck. "Sleep, tiger."

My eyes are useless to resist him, and the world around me fades. But questions still linger. Can I date one and fuck the others still? Can I give my heart to only one of them?

Chapter 50

Discovered

Madison

The guys stay near me all morning. Seth cooks me breakfast. Coop showers with me, but only cleans both of us. Blake keeps talking to me about some employees we need to monitor. They've been seriously sweet.

And Noah . . . Gah, Noah . . . He hugs and kisses me. Holds my hand and gives me soft smiles. He makes me want so much more than what they are offering me. But what if we could be more? He wants to date me, but what does that mean?

My phone buzzes.

HOPE:

I'm here.

ME:

On my way.

I push off Coop's chest where I'm half watching the movie he has on. It has aliens and action scenes. Still not my thing.

"Hope here?" Coop asks as I straighten my clothes a little. We've been cuddling on the couch for the past half hour. His hand strokes over my arm as bombs go off on the TV.

"Yeah. I'm going down to get her."

"You want the living room?" He begins to sit up but I stop him.

"No, we'll go to my room." I lean over him and press a soft kiss against his lips. "Thank you, though."

"Whatever you need, sweetheart." Coop winks at me and heat flushes through me.

The one thing we haven't done today is have sex. I'm afraid I might be addicted to them because I crave it. I like the constant attention, the orgasms, the touching, the edge of fear when they play with me.

As I enter the elevator and press the lobby button, I remember yesterday in the file room. Coop's fantasy and my nightmare of an experience. I forgot to mention it to the guys. At first, because they were all busy working, and I didn't want to sidetrack them from their project.

With Noah, I just wanted to forget about it. Forget the fear and the strange shuffling noises. Lose myself in the pleasure and fun he could provide.

I am going to tell them, but right now, I'm enjoying the snuggles and just being with the guys. Not worrying about the craziness my life has become.

After the Valerie sighting, I'm not positive they'd believe me. Not that they wouldn't check out everything for me, but I shouldn't need to be protected more than what they're already doing.

Besides, Courtney was probably right. The lights were probably on a very long timer that finally went off. It's not the lights' fault I was assaulted a week ago and Coop primed me for that little scenario.

I'm lucky if Courtney doesn't tattle on me screaming like a scaredy-cat because the lights went out. Of course, Courtney isn't aware of my attack or the messages from a stalker.

I sigh. I should bite the bullet and tell the guys, after Hope leaves and before they get me naked again.

The elevator doors open and Hope smiles. "Hiya."

"Hey." I smile back as I slide my card and press the button. The elevator starts up.

"Your neck is looking so much better." Hope's focus on my neck makes me slightly uncomfortable. It's still colorful. The thought of wearing a scarf makes me feel suffocated all over again. "Though you can definitely see fingers now. That must have been so scary."

Her eyes flick up to meet mine.

"It was." I lean against the elevator wall. "It's not like they can get to me locked away in this building, though."

Hope chuckles. "Nope, you're completely protected. And you live with four huge guys who would take out anyone who tried to get to you."

The elevator stops and I open the front door.

"Oh." Hope stops in the doorway.

I can see Coop over her head. He's fully dressed in jeans and a t-shirt that shows off his muscles, relaxing on the couch.

He holds up his hand in greeting. "Hope."

"Mr. Grah—I mean Cooper, hi. It's nice to see you."

Nodding, he returns to watching the TV. I grab her arm and pull her through the apartment to my door. Now would have been a great time to have one of the bedrooms that opens into the hallway. I'm just lucky no one was walking around without a shirt on.

When I close my door behind us, Hope blows out a breath.

"That was so weird." She chuckles. "I don't know how you cohabitate with those guys and don't burst into flames constantly."

"You get used to it." I shrug and sit on the couch. I'm still not used to it, but I like the fires they set inside me.

"I don't think that's possible." Hope shakes her head as she joins me. "I mean, having four very attractive, single men walking around my apartment. Yeah, I would definitely need to invest in rechargeable batteries."

I laugh. No batteries required here. I pick up the remote. "I thought we could order some Thai for lunch with the show?"

"That sounds delicious." Hope settles on the couch. "We need all the nourishment to get through watching the Witcher take his baths. You'll have to be careful not to attack the bosses after he gets us all worked up."

Hope giggles. She's not wrong, though. I should be completely satiated, but tonight they all sleep with me. I can't wait to see what they have in mind. I'm already anticipating my nights alone with each of them too. Not that I usually only end up fucking one guy on any given day, but maybe that will slow down.

"Can I grab a Diet Coke, please?" Hope moves to stand but stops to look at me. "That's okay, right?"

I grin. "Of course."

"You want one?" She walks over to the fridge and pulls out a bottle for herself. When I nod, she grabs another.

I successfully navigate the menu this time. Last time, Hope had to show me. She hands me my bottle, and we turn on the next episode.

Just as the episode ends, my phone buzzes. "The food is downstairs. I'll be right back."

"Sounds good." Hope pulls out her phone.

I pause at the door. I'm not supposed to leave anyone alone in the apartment, but it's fine with Hope, right? She's my friend and it's only my living space. I shake off the weirdness as I head into the main living area.

"Hey," Seth calls from the kitchen.

"I need to grab our delivery." I pass by the island, but Seth steps out to block my path.

"Why don't I go down?" Seth glances at my door. Maybe he's worried about me leaving Hope alone up here. "You can return to your show, and I'll bring it to you."

I could fight him on this, but honestly, I really want to get back to the next episode. "Okay."

I turn back and open the door to my living room. Lifting her gaze from her phone, Hope smiles from the couch.

"That was fast." She glances at my hands and frowns. "Wrong order?"

"No, Seth is going to get it for us." I return to my place on the couch, not even registering what I just said.

"The boss is getting our lunch?!?" Hope's mouth drops open like I just told her the queen herself would get our lunch.

"The guys are weird about having people left unattended in the apartment." It's the first thing I can think of that would explain why Seth, my boss, went to get our meals.

"That makes sense." Hope nods. "They're all really private guys. I'm surprised they have their assistant pretty much live with them."

"They talk about work over dinner." My brain keeps coming up with excuses that make sense. Ones that the guys use to explain their dirty little secret. My cheeks heat. "It just saves on time if I'm there too."

"Huh, yeah." Hope smiles and snaps her fingers. "See, that's why I'll never make it as an entrepreneur. I don't have that think-outside-of-the-box mentality."

I chuckle. "That's what I'm here for. To learn that."

"Well, once you figure it out, clue me in."

A knock comes from the door. I'm walking toward it when my phone buzzes. There's a message from an unknown caller. Maybe the delivery person to make sure I know they delivered.

I open the door as I open the text.

UNKNOWN:

Were you always afraid of the dark, little one?

There is a black-and-white picture of me in my sundress, standing next to the filing cabinet. My heart stops and I freeze, staring at the image of me with a Play button on it.

"Madison?" Seth's voice reaches me, but I can't move. Someone was there with me. Someone was watching me, stalking me. It was real.

Fuck, it was real. My hands tremble.

"Madison, are you all right?" Hope's voice sounds closer.

I lift my gaze to Seth. He sets the bag of food on the floor before taking my phone from me. This isn't my old phone. This is my new phone. My business phone that only a few people outside of this company would know.

"Fuck." Seth breathes out as he glances at the screen.

"What's happening?" Hope touches my arm, and I inhale deeply into my starved lungs.

Seth glances at Hope and sighs. "Come on."

He turns and heads into the kitchen. Nodding at the chairs, he says, "Sit."

We both do, and Hope puts the bag of food in front of us.

"What? I'm hungry." She pulls out the containers and sorts them for us. "We've gotta eat no matter what's going on. Is this about the roommate's boyfriend?"

Seth shakes his head and sets my phone down on the island. His eyes meet mine. "Do you trust her?"

I know he means Hope. If I say no, he'll usher her out while we deal with this. But I'm allowed friends. And I want Hope to be my friend. If I say no, I'll hurt her feelings and I don't want that. I want to trust her.

"I do."

He leans back on the counter as he studies both of us. Apparently coming to some decision, he speaks. "Madison has a stalker. We don't think it's her roommate or her roommate's boyfriend. But we don't know who it is."

Hope pauses with a plastic fork filled with noodles halfway to her mouth. "Stalker?"

Seth nods. "He first contacted her on her old cell phone. This is the first time he's contacted her on her new phone, after we turned her old phone in to the police. He had a hidden camera in Madison's old apartment."

"That's awful. So, what's this message about?" Hope glances at me but asks Seth the question.

"We're waiting for the others to watch it, but it must have been yesterday." Seth glances at the phone. "That's when she wore that dress."

"I didn't leave the building." The words fall from my lips. I'm still trying to process everything. My fear yesterday. Believing it was my imagination, but now, knowing it wasn't. I feel chilled to my bones, like no amount of warmth will ever heat me back up. Someone was hunting me in the dark. Shivers crawl down my spine.

My stalker was here. In our secure building. He cornered me, and I couldn't do anything about it. Tears flood my eyes as I jab my plastic fork in my noodles. I try to hold the tears back, I really do, but it's too much.

I'm still a little off from what Noah calls subdrop, and now this.

"Madison." Seth steps closer and puts his hands on the island across from me.

"I'm fine," I assure him. I can see the need in him because I feel it too. I want him to hold me and comfort me, keep me safe from all the things that are trying to get me. "I mean, I'm being stalked by at least two parties, but what girl isn't?"

I give a helpless shrug. Hope puts her arm around my shoulders and tugs me into a side hug.

"One stalker is more than anyone needs," she says as her forehead touches mine. I'm so grateful for her comfort right now.

The door opens and Coop, Noah, and Blake come in. Their eyes take in Hope and then fall on Seth.

They all come over to the island but no one touches me. I guess our relationship is something we're hiding from everyone, including my only friend. It shouldn't sting. I knew that when I agreed to this, but right now, I need my guys to hug me.

"What's happening?" Blake asks.

"Is everything okay?" Noah's gaze rakes over me, making sure I'm not injured.

Seth picks up my phone. "She received a new video on her work phone."

"What video?" Blake nearly snarls the words.

Hope's eyebrow rises, but she just stuffs her mouth with noodles while watching them.

"We haven't watched it yet." Seth rounds the island to stand beside me.

I stick my fork in my noodles, not having taken even a bite. If it's anything like the last video, my stomach might not be able to handle it. What if he caught Coop fucking me?

I glance at Hope. I guess that's one way to break it to her I'm fucking the bosses. Or at least one of them.

"Are you ready?" His hand brushes my shoulder for a second.

I'm never going to be ready for this, but I nod.

The guys huddle behind Hope and me. Seth presses play.

The video starts in color. I'm in the back corner, so not when Coop was in there. I pull out a file, set it on the stack, and the lights go out. All is darkness before the camera turns to night mode, showing me in black-and-white.

I back into the corner. My eyes close now. My voice is tinny when I say, "Hello? Coop? Guys?"

My breathing is ragged on the video, but that shuffling noise comes through loud and clear. Fuck. I hoped it was in my mind. That it wasn't real. I squeeze my eyes shut tighter.

I don't want to relive this, but it's impossible not to.

"Yellow!" What I thought was a yell yesterday was more of a whisper shout. Until the next shuffling. I hear the rustling of my dress as I drop to cower in the corner.

"Red! Gold! Gold! Gold!" The shuffling is right on top of me. Fear ripples down my spine as my ear-piercing scream fills the room.

"What the hell is going on in here?"

Now, I open my eyes and the video ends. No one moves. It's almost like no one is breathing. I can't look at them. I can't see the disappointment on their faces. I should have told them yesterday.

"Fuck, that's messed up." Hope sets her fork down. "Why did you yell colors? Who was the woman at the end?"

"She said her name is Courtney." My voice is barely above a whisper. I ignore the color question. Unable to explain that they're safe words because why would I need safe words in an office where I'm not fucking anyone? Besides, I'm too disappointed in myself to focus on those words.

Honesty, trust. I didn't tell them about this. I didn't trust them to believe me.

"That's weird. She rarely works on weekends." Hope glances around and clears her throat. "Should I . . . make myself scarce?"

"Please." Seth sets my phone down, but I don't dare meet their eyes.

Hope squeezes my arm, and I give her a reassuring smile. She slips off the stool and heads back to my room. The door shuts. I still haven't turned on the access code for my door. I like the guys being able to come and go as they please.

I shift in my seat, but Seth pulls me out of it and into his arms. His solid chest is against my cheek as he crushes me to him. He breathes in against my hair.

"Fuck, princess," he whispers. His voice trembles with an edge of fear.

The tears I held back flow down my cheeks, making his shirt wet.

"I wouldn't have . . ." Coop sounds fucked up. "Fuck."

I open my eyes and turn my head so I can see him. His fingers dig into his long hair like he wants to pull it out. He puts his hands down as his eyes meet mine.

"You thought I was playing?" Coop pushes out, sounding so ashamed of himself. I don't want that. It's not his fault.

I shake my head. "Not really. I mean, when the lights first went out. Maybe, I hoped. But it's a soft limit, which means we would need more discussion than a fantasy spilled out in the heat of the moment."

Coop lurches forward and tugs me into his arms, folding himself around me. He whispers against my hair, "I never want to hear you that scared again."

"I never want to be that scared again," I admit as I cling to his warmth.

"They were in our building." Blake's voice is solid and sturdy. He's the rock I need right now.

"I thought I might have imagined the shuffling noises." I draw in a deep breath of Coop's clean, crisp scent. Tears run unchecked down my cheeks. I bury my face in his shirt, trying to forget the way I felt in that moment yesterday.

Coop's hands stroke up and down my back as he makes soothing noises in my hair.

"I forgot my—" Hope's voice makes everyone freeze. She stands halfway to the kitchen with her hand over her mouth, looking at Coop holding me so close.

Fuck.

Chapter 51

Pivot

Coop

I don't release Madison from my arms. It's not like I can step away at this point and make Hope not have seen us.

Hope is practical and logical. And she's staring at me holding Madison like she just discovered the biggest secret in the world. Her cheeks are bright red.

"Sorry." She points to the food on the island. "I just wanted to grab my lunch."

No one else moves as she walks to the counter and grabs her food. Her wide eyes meet Madison's for a brief second before she scurries into the other room. As soon as the door shuts, Madison buries her face in my chest and groans.

My gaze flits from Noah's disappointment to Blake's contemplation to Seth's resignation.

"It was bound to get out." Seth shrugs. "But we can control how it spreads."

Madison lifts her face to meet my eyes. I brush the hair from her cheek and give her a small smile. I'm not sure what Seth means by that, but I'm sure he'll tell us.

Blake sighs. "Hope doesn't spread things around. This won't get out if we don't want it to."

Madison's gaze goes to Noah. He gives her a soft smile and shrugs. Wonder what that's about.

"It might be easier to just say that Coop and Madison are dating." Seth's words drive into my skull.

"Wait, what?" I grip her tighter.

Madison strokes her hand over my cheek before pulling away from me. I resist for a second before letting her go.

"Is that smart?" Madison takes a deep breath. "What if whoever is stalking me finds out? What if it makes them angry or escalates things?"

"It's possible they already know about me, sweetheart." I look up before meeting the others' gazes. "I fucked Madison in the file room. It's possible whoever was in there later could have been there then."

I'm not one for dating. Not since college and the girlfriend who tried to destroy my relationship with the guys. I'm usually happy to fuck whoever the others want to bring on board, or find my own women to fuck, but there's something about Madison that draws me.

Not having to hide my affection for her would certainly be something I wouldn't mind, and being able to fuck her in public without reprimands from the others would be a huge bonus. My heart thumps a little harder.

I'd get to call her mine.

Noah shifts and looks uncomfortable, but he hasn't said anything. He's never been close to any woman before, but he's smitten with Madison. It would make sense for him to date her. He rarely goes with a date to functions because he's shy about it.

The few times I set him up were disastrous. The type of women I date like a more gregarious guy, and Noah just isn't. But Madison likes him.

She goes to him and takes his hand. He brings her hand to his mouth and kisses it while looking into her eyes.

Even I can feel the sparks between them. The longing in Madison's eyes to step into his arms, but she can't risk it with Hope still here.

"We can talk about proper office behavior later." Seth shakes his head. "Blake, erase that part of the security tape after we review it."

"After?" I smirk at Seth.

The corners of his lips curl up as he turns to Madison. "It would be best for appearances if you and Coop date. Even if Hope wouldn't spread it around, the stalker might know the two of you had sex."

"Courtney mentioned it wasn't the first time she'd heard someone screaming in the office." Madison's cheeks burn bright red. "I didn't know what she meant, but maybe she heard us having sex too."

"Guess I have a girlfriend." I arch an eyebrow at Madison. Her blue eyes are wide as she looks back at me. It wasn't part of the deal, but I'm okay going with the flow. I just hope it doesn't upset Noah too much.

"Is this okay with you, princess?" Seth quirks an eyebrow at her. "Even if it makes sense, it isn't part of our arrangement."

Her cheeks flush. "It's fine. I'm adaptable."

Her gaze meets mine, and I give her a warm grin. I've always openly flirted with whoever I wanted, but now I get to openly flirt with Madison. Fuck, this will be fun.

"I'll review the security footage to see if I can tell who else was in the building." Blake nods to Madison. "And go over the logs."

"Coop and I can help you comb through the video," Seth says. "Noah, I need you to review Courtney's financials and check to see what exactly she was working on yesterday."

"What about me?" Madison asks.

Seth's smile is soft. "Go hang out with your friend. We'll discuss what we find over dinner and how we'll work this whole 'dating' thing into this."

She nods and squeezes Noah's hand before releasing it. Picking up her food, she heads to her bedroom. I step in front of her. Leaning down, I cup her cheek and press a kiss to her lips, knowing I'm now the only one who will be able to get away with this.

"We'll figure this out." I slide my thumb across her cheekbone. Her eyes are like a sunny sky. I want to take her and fuck her on the island. Mark her shoulders with my lips and teeth. Make her come so hard she sees stars.

She nods. "I know. I trust you."

When I step out of her way, I watch her disappear behind the door. Her words make my heart feel funny. Before I can open my mouth to say anything, Seth jerks his head toward the door. We all follow him out of the apartment, making sure the door is secure before heading up to our office level.

Blake does a quick bug check before we all sit in the conference room. Seth sets up his phone to send the video the stalker sent to the large screen. When we watched it downstairs, I could only focus on Madison and her fear.

I still want to try that scenario. To hunt her in the dark and fuck her when she can't be sure it's me, but not like that. I want that edge of fear tinged with excitement. Her terror was palpable in the video, and even just watching it, she shook with fear. Even knowing she was safe with us.

When Blake joins, Seth replays the video. This time I note the angle of the camera and the background noises and other sounds. There's a breath that isn't Madison's. We might isolate it with some of our software.

"Her fear excites the stalker," I say.

Her scream is even louder on the speakers. My heart clenches. We weren't there for her. While she was terrorized, we were working, not even aware of what was happening in our own office.

Seth stops the video. "Anything?"

"I want to go down and check out the file room to see if there's any trace of him." Blake stands. "I'll try to figure out the angle of the phone."

"I'll get started on the Courtney file." Noah rises.

"Are we sure having her 'date' me is the best course?" It's not the best idea we've come up with. I'm not like the others. I don't do long-term anything. My reputation around the office is as a player.

Blake makes a decisive noise. "It doesn't matter what's best. It matters how we cover our asses. If we have to date other women, it makes sense for someone to date Madison to keep an eye on her while the others are busy. We obviously can't leave her in the building alone. This fucker slipped in when we had everything locked tight."

"Not tight enough to keep out other employees," Seth points out.

"Fuck." We didn't have this problem when the company was smaller. Employees have access to the building to work on projects, but when we were smaller, we knew everyone who worked for us. Now we have an HR department that takes care of most of that for us.

"I would have taken Madison to the charity dinner." Noah leans back against the wall with his hands in his pockets and his shoulders drawn forward. "I planned to ask her later today. I figured I could date her."

Shit. And once again, I fuck things up for Noah. "Why can't Noah be her date?"

"Because if word gets out that you fucked her and then Noah is dating her, the rumors will start all over." Seth reclines in his chair and focuses on Noah. "We can't go through that again. Coop has to be the one, especially if whoever took this video or Courtney comes forward saying he fucked Madison."

Noah nods. "I get it. I'm not going with someone else. It's not unusual for me not to have a date."

Seth blows out a breath and turns to Blake. "That means you and I have to find dates for Saturday."

Blake doesn't look happy about it, but the guy rarely looks happy about anything.

"If you need some numbers, I'd be happy to give you a few." I try to lighten the mood with a grin. Nothing will make this okay. Someone's fucking with our girl.

"All right." Seth claps his hands. "Let's get busy."

The other two leave, and Seth pulls up the security camera footage. He pauses the footage when Madison enters the room. He then kicks it up a little faster while Madison is working alone.

The door opens and I walk in. Seth, the voyeur, puts the video on normal speed. Unfortunately, there's no sound. In the video, I close in on Madison.

"What did you tell her?" Seth asks, his gaze is locked on the video as I turn Madison around against the filing cabinet and hike up her dress.

"I wanted to shut off the lights and hunt her in the dark. Then if we caught her, we would fuck her wherever she was, whether she wanted it or not." Even though I want to play out that scenario, consensual nonconsent is a soft limit for her. And after this, she might not be as willing to play that particular game. I wouldn't blame her.

In the video, my hips rock against hers as I slide my cock against her clit. She was so fucking wet, I could have just fucked her ass.

"We should definitely play that sometime." Seth's voice is deeper as he watches me slam my cock into Madison's pussy. Of course, the security camera doesn't do it justice. It can't pick up her scream as she comes or the hot wetness of her cunt surrounding my dick. The sound of her pussy gripping my cock as I draw it out.

I pull back and thrust into her ass. It's obvious that I'm fucking her, but it's not graphic. Nothing is shown. My body blocks hers, but if anyone heard those noises, they'd draw the correct conclusion.

"I know how much she loves being a good girl for you and Blake, so I asked if she wanted to be my dirty girl." Stroking my finger over my lip, I watch the video of me coming deep in her ass. I'm already hard thinking about it.

I'd love to watch a video of me fucking Madison. My dick glistening with her wetness as I slide in and out. The little noises she makes as she gets closer to coming.

"What did she say to that?" Seth pauses the video on the image of us straightening our clothes.

I grin. "Let's just say I can't wait for my night this week."

Madison

Hope has been quiet since I joined her in the living room an episode ago. But now she releases a sigh.

"So, you have a stalker?" Hope turns to me on the couch. "Are you safe here?"

I nod. "Yeah, safer here than anywhere else."

My heartbeat is erratic, waiting for her to say the words. Ask why I was in Coop's arms. Why Seth got our food. Why they were all here.

Hope smiles wickedly. "Is something going on with you and Cooper? I mean, it's none of my business if there is, but I can't help but speculate."

"Maybe," I hedge with a small smile, trying to act shy about it. I really didn't have a friend to talk to about the guys I saw during college. I had a few friends in high school, but no one I was close to. "But we aren't spreading it around."

"Oh, my god! I knew you couldn't stand to be around all this man candy without indulging." Hope's cheeks flush and she leans forward. "Personally, I wouldn't know how to even decide among them. They are all hot, and so different."

I press my lips together to keep from blurting out that I know, and I'm glad I don't really have to decide.

"But Cooper. Holy shit, he's like the holy grail of men." Hope rocks back. "I mean, I've accidentally passed him after he's been out for a run in his shorts and a tank top. He's ripped. I bet he has that V thing that men get when they work out a lot."

I grin. "He's also really sweet."

Except when he wants to be dirty. My thighs clench thinking of what he wanted to do to me yesterday.

"I'm so happy for you. At least about Coop." Her smile falls. "You really don't have any idea who your stalker might be?"

My smile fades as I shake my head. "I've always kept to myself, mostly. I have a weird neighbor, but he also texted on my old phone to check up on me."

"Sometimes it's the person you least suspect." Hope sighs. "We should really watch some of those series on stalkers. Maybe it will give us some ideas."

"Or nightmares." I shudder. I don't need to know what other stalkers do. It's bad enough I have one who can apparently get to me wherever I am.

Hope reaches over and squeezes my hand briefly. "I'm sorry. Yeah, probably not very entertaining for someone who has a stalker."

"It's okay. Let's just finish watching *The Witcher*. I could use a nap this afternoon."

Hope grins. "We definitely need to go out for a drink sometime, so I can loosen those lips and get all the details."

There's so much I could tell her, but not about my sex life. I have an NDA and a relationship with four guys. It's not something I can go talking about with anyone but those four. "We'll get that drink soon."

I don't know if Hope is the jealous kind of girl, but she doesn't seem to be. I wish I knew how to read people better. Maybe I'll learn as I go.

Chapter 52

Stick a Pin in It

Seth

Frustration pours through me. Whoever was in there with Madison knew where the camera's blind spots are. We could clearly see Madison but not whoever tormented her. Watching that video over and over made me want to bundle her in my arms and never let her out of my sight again.

Which is completely unreasonable, but this need inside me keeps pulsing relentlessly.

We're waiting for Noah in the conference room. Blake has his hands behind his head as he leans back in the chair. Coop looks like he wants to hit something.

"Should we call Madison down for this?" Blake asks.

"I'll go get her." I can't sit here any longer. I need to see she's safe.

"Shouldn't her boyfriend go get her?" Coop gives me a sly grin.

"Fuck off."

Coop's laughter follows me to the elevator. Of everyone who could have been her 'boyfriend,' Coop is the worst choice. He's a player—everyone knows that—and taking him out of the dating pool will break a lot of hearts on the lower floors.

Not that he would date while we have Madison, except for appearances. Maybe after we figure out this stalker deal, we can have them break up. Then it won't be an issue.

It doesn't bother me that much. She's still ours, not just his. But Noah didn't take it well.

If I'd thought about it before, it would make sense for Noah to be the one to date her. They're the closest in age. And Noah doesn't really date, so it would give him someone to take to events. We should have considered that an option. But now we're backed into a corner.

Because Coop had to fuck Madison outside of the apartment and our floor.

The benefit of this situation is I get to pick a fantastic dress and shoes for Madison to wear to the charity dinner. Some subtle jewelry will finish the outfit. It's not that I like women's clothes, but I love to dress a woman in something sexy that I bought.

Growing up, I couldn't afford much. Gifts to my mom were usually handmade. I always wanted to spoil her when I made it big, but she didn't live long enough for me to do that. Madison reminds me of my mom. She doesn't expect fancy things. She's happy with what she has.

The elevator arrives on our floor, and I enter the apartment. I pause outside Madison's door and knock. It feels weird to knock when I know I'm sleeping in there tonight. I plan on taking full control of this evening because I need it. I need to watch everyone get their pleasure on my terms.

Madison answers the door. Her eyes widen when she meets mine. God, she's beautiful.

Hope shows up behind her. "I was just leaving."

"I came to get Madison to discuss what we found. We'll ride down with you to the ground floor." I step out of the way. Madison's floral scent floats over me and makes me want to back her against a wall and fuck her hard. To assure myself that she's safe and whole.

"Did you enjoy your show?" I ask instead as we leave the apartment and enter the elevator.

"I did. Even if it was a little hard to follow at points." Madison leans on the opposite side of the elevator from me. She's careful not to show too much interest in me.

"I had to watch it twice to figure out the timelines." Hope smiles at her before turning to me. "Have you seen it?"

"I don't watch a lot of TV." I tuck my hands in my pockets while the elevator takes us down, anxiously waiting until I have Madison alone. Already undressing her in my head.

"Maybe you could watch it with Madison on her second viewing." Hope smiles. "It could be a team-building exercise for the whole floor."

I chuckle softly. "We'll consider it."

Though we definitely have better ways to do team-building exercises with Madison. In fact, tonight will be a good time to make sure we're all still on board as we go into our week of sleeping with her separately.

"I'll see you tomorrow." Hope hugs Madison before stepping off the elevator. "I hope you guys figure out who's doing this to Madison."

"I do too." I give her a nod of acknowledgment and press the button.

When the doors close, I close in on Madison. She's wearing jeans and a t-shirt. Her blue eyes lock with mine and her lips part.

I'm not usually into a quickie of any kind, but fuck do I need to feel her. Right now. I capture her mouth with mine before unbuttoning her pants and pulling down her zipper.

Echoes of the fear in her trembling voice as she called out words that should only be said during pleasure fill my head. I need to replace those noises with ones of her coming around my cock.

She stretches up to explore my mouth with her tongue. Her hands go to my pants and release the button and zipper. Smelling her arousal, I yank hers down over her hips with her panties. She trembles in my arms and strokes my cock as she frees it.

"You need a new safe word, princess." Because if I hear her yell *gold*, I will hurt whoever is touching her wrong. Even if it's me.

I spin her to face the wall and pull her hips out before thrusting into her. She lets out a low moan.

"Yes, sir." Her hands go to the elevator wall as her head drops.

I fuck her slowly, pulling out and thrusting back in deep.

"Do I get to see the video of Coop fucking me?" She presses her hips back into me, trying to draw me back in. I spread her ass cheeks to watch my cock disappear into her hot, wet core.

"If you want." I groan before I give up on going slowly. I thrust hard and fast. Her jeans keep her from spreading her legs wide for me, and she feels so fucking tight around my cock. "Do you want to play his game of hide-and-seek in the dark?"

"Yes. With you, I do. Please." She sucks in a breath. Her hands fist against the side of the elevator, bracing herself as I pound into her. She whimpers. "Oh, fuck. I'm so close. Touch me, Seth."

Reaching around her hips, I rub her hard clit. She moans as she convulses around my cock, dragging me into my release. I thrust a few more times before sinking deep inside her, filling her with my cum. Marking her as mine.

Taking a deep breath, I pull out and straighten my pants while she straightens hers. The elevator is almost to the floor. I back her into the wall and claim her lips. She meets me with just as much passion. I love that my cum is dripping from her pussy, soaking her panties with a combination of us. That I couldn't wait to bury myself in her. That I want her to feel how much I need her while we work through this fucked up situation.

The elevator stops on the office floor and I lift my head. Pressing my forehead against hers, I breathe her in. In this moment, she's safe in my arms.

The doors open. "Come on, princess."

When she takes my hand, we walk to the conference room. The others are standing and turn to look at us. Coop's face spreads with a knowing grin I ignore.

"Come sit on my dick during the meeting, girlfriend." He holds his hand out to Madison.

She arches an eyebrow at him but goes and stands in front of him like the good little submissive she is. "I don't even know what that means."

"It means I'm hard and want you to keep my dick warm." He tips her chin up so she meets his eyes. "Did Seth get you warmed up for me?"

Her cheeks flush but she nods.

He grins and leans in to whisper in her ear. I barely make out the words, "Such a dirty little whore."

Her lips part on a gasp.

"I don't want to fuck you, sweetheart. Just act like a warm cozy for my cock." Coop traces her lips with his fingers.

"Is this really necessary?" Blake asks, shaking his head.

Coop gives him a grin. "Absolutely."

Blake spins his finger in the air. "Turn around."

She turns and faces the rest of us. Her breasts rise and fall with anticipation.

Coop pulls his pants and boxers down before closing in on her. He presses against her back to reach around and undo her pants. Her blue eyes are dark when she lifts her gaze to mine. Her lips, still swollen from my kiss, part as he pulls her pants down and runs his finger through my cum before shoving it back inside her.

Her hands press on the conference table. Her eyes flutter shut as she savors his touch. She whimpers as he thrusts his fingers in and out a few times, her jeans pulled tight between her knees. When he pulls his fingers out of her pussy, he holds them in front of her mouth.

"Suck them off."

My cock stirred when he first started, but now I'm hard as a rock again, watching Madison suck his fingers clean of my cum mixed with her essence. Her eyes never leave me as she tastes us.

"Good girl." Coop sits in his chair and uses her hips to guide her to sit down, pressing his cock to her entrance and helping her lower until he's all the way inside her. Once she's settled, he asks, "Comfortable?"

She blows out a breath and leans back against him. "Mm-hmm."

"Can we start now?" Noah adjusts his hard-on in his pants.

"If you aren't comfortable, use her mouth." Coop draws her hair back from her face. "You don't mind. Do you, babe?"

"Yes, please." Madison licks her lips as she meets Noah's heated gaze.

Before Noah can move, Blake stands and pulls out his cock. He taps her lips with the tip, and she gives him her beautiful eyes. Her tongue flicks out over his cock before she opens her mouth and takes him inside.

Coop speaks in her ear. "Hum a little, sweetheart."

When she does as he says, my balls tighten. Blake threads his hands through her hair and fucks her mouth slowly. We all watch her, mesmerized, as she licks and sucks when she can. Her hands stroke his cock and cup his balls.

"Can you take me deeper, tiger?" Blake asks before he pushes himself deep into her throat. Her muscles work as she swallows him. Tears well in her eyes. When he draws back, she gasps around his cock. His thumb rubs her tear away. "Again?"

He must see something in her eyes because he does it again, and this time, he unloads in her throat, groaning his release before pulling back. She sucks him clean as he draws his cock out of her mouth. After he tucks his dick back in his pants, he leans down and kisses her.

She tries to shift on Coop's lap, but he holds her hips still.

"Thanks, love," Blake whispers against her lips before returning to his seat.

I meet Noah's eyes to see if he's going to use her mouth, but he shakes his head. Coop takes a tissue and wipes Madison's tears away before drawing her back against him, still buried deep inside her warm, wet cunt.

I might have to work that way someday. Having my cock nestled inside her would definitely make going over reports much better.

Clearing my throat, I glance at everyone. "Are we ready to proceed?"

Madison's blush deepens.

"The security footage doesn't show the person filming Madison. While we have some clips of them breathing, we don't have a voice either."

Blake presses his fingers to his temples. "We had a few employees access the floor, including an employee who is no longer with the company. The card was deactivated a few weeks ago but reactivated late the night before last. I called in my team to go through the security and doublecheck the firewalls."

"Fuck." I lean back in my chair. Someone has access to our system, or an employee is in on it. Which brings us to Courtney. I turn to Noah, but his eyes are locked on Madison. I have a feeling the fucking part of this meeting isn't finished yet, if the heat in his eyes is any indication. But I'll keep trying to steer us in the right direction.

After all, if we have an issue with our employees, that means Madison might not be safe here either.

Chapter 53

Deep Dive

Madison

Coop's cock twitches inside me again as I try to focus on Blake's words. I should have told Coop that I wouldn't sit on his dick, but it also feels really great to have him buried inside me. To have that connection to ground me. To keep me from spiraling off about everything.

The only problem is I keep wanting to shift, to come, but he holds me motionless against him.

Noah lifts an eyebrow at me as I meet his eyes. I won't know how much this decision for me and Coop to appear publicly as a couple hurts Noah until I get him alone. It's no one's fault that Coop and I were seen together, possibly twice.

"We need to cross-reference the names of who accessed the floor with the names on our list of possible spies. I don't think this is a coincidence, but it could be." Seth runs a hand through his hair as his gaze drops to my lap. With my jeans still on, he can't really see much.

I can fix that. I lean forward on Coop's lap and shove my pants farther down until I can kick them off.

"Fuck, sweetheart, you're going to break my dick." Coop thrusts deeper inside me. The motion sends tremors through my body.

I roll my eyes as I finally get my pants off. "I'm getting hot."

Finally free, I spread my legs on either side of Coop's. Seth's eyes flash with heat as his gaze drops to my pussy impaled on Coop's cock. Sparks flow through me. This is something I can control.

Noah stands and moves in front of me. His hard cock presses against his fly. I meet his eyes. Noah's been mine from that first day. I would have loved to be his date or girlfriend or whatever he wanted me to be.

"Do you want me to . . . ?" I take in a breath and wait. Because I really want to. The guys seem to need the release almost more than I do. I love helping them with this and it helps me.

He grabs his pants and opens them, taking his cock out and stroking it right in front of my face. Fuck, I love all their cocks. I lick my lips and open my mouth for him, keeping my gaze locked with his darkened eyes.

Groaning, he steps forward and thrusts his cock into my waiting mouth. Coop's finger slides between my legs and over my clit, and I moan deep in my throat, taking Noah even farther in. I long to ride Coop's cock while sucking on Noah's.

I meet Noah's hooded eyes. I want to take him as deep as he can get. Feel him pressed inside me until he comes. Grabbing his hips, I shove myself forward until his cock is in my throat. My nose bumps his hard abs.

"Sweet fuck." Noah grabs my hair and drags me back until only his head is in my mouth.

Fuck, I love the way he takes control of me. I need it. My watery eyes meet his darkened ones.

"You want to play dirty, kitten? I'm going to fuck you so hard."

My pussy throbs around Coop's dick as I suck on the tip of Noah's cock.

"She likes that idea." Coop opens his legs, spreading mine open more. "Fuck her throat, Noah. She wants it. Her cunt strangles me when she chokes on your cock. She's so wet it's dripping down my balls."

Noah groans and thrusts deep into my throat, holding my nose against his skin. "Do you like that, kitten? Do you want me to be rough with you?"

Yes, I want that right now. Crave it. To give in to him. I want him to be aggressive, to take out his frustration on my body. I swallow around him before giving a low hum.

It's my fault I didn't tell anyone about the incident in the file room. I should have trusted them to listen to me. If I'd told them yesterday, Hope wouldn't have seen Coop holding me. Noah would have told me his plan.

Coop pinches my clit and my pussy squeezes around him. Noah pulls my hair back in his fist. I can breathe through my nose again. He meets my eyes. Hopefully, he sees how much I want this. Not dropping my gaze, he nods to Seth.

"Give her a pen."

Seth steps forward and puts a pen in my hand.

"You want this to stop, tap on the table." Noah narrows his eyes. "Do it now so I know you understand."

The command in his voice is so fucking hot. My pussy gushes around Coop's cock as I tap on the conference table.

"Such a horny little slut," Coop whispers for my ears only. My cheeks flush as I get even wetter at his words. I know the others can hear him. "I bet you could come right now if I flicked your clit."

He's not wrong. I want to ride his cock and suck Noah until he comes down my throat. I burn for them. Craving their touch. Aching for the pleasure they wring from my body.

Seth pulls a chair up beside us. He strokes his cock lazily while studying Coop's dick buried in my pussy. I long to help him stroke it, but he's too far away. Instead, I watch his hand slide effortlessly over his cock up to the head, where he rubs his precum on the way back down his shaft. Fuck. My pussy throbs, and I whimper at the aching need to come.

"You're so fucking distracting, kitten." Noah pulls my hair until my nose presses against him, blocking my airway with his fat cock. I meet his darkened eyes. "I can't even focus on protecting you without wanting to fuck your face."

Tears flow down my face from his cock choking me, but I don't drop my gaze from his. I want this. I need this. He wanted to be the one to date me. He wanted to show me off, not keep me like a dirty little secret.

And now that's what I am for him. What I have to be for him. If I could, I would claim them all, but that's not part of this arrangement.

He pulls out and thrusts lightly in my mouth, controlling my movement with my hair. Unable to stop myself, I rock my hips on Coop a little. Sparks surge through my system. A moan escapes my throat at the feel of Coop's cock twitching inside me.

When Noah pulls my face forward on him again, Coop's finger rubs my clit. It's the push I need, so close to the edge already that I fall over it. Moaning, I come in a gush all over Coop's cock still buried inside me. My walls pulse around him, trying to draw him in deeper. Needing his cum to fill me.

Coop hisses in my ear and bites my earlobe. An aftershock shudders through me. "Do you want me to fill you with my cum when Noah blows in your throat, sweetheart? Is that what you need, my little whore?"

Fuck, that shouldn't make me want him more. I swallow around Noah's cock, and he retreats from my throat, still deep inside my mouth, but I can pull in a breath through my nose. Coop's jeans rub against my legs.

What I want is for everyone to get naked and fuck me. Fill me so full of cum that even Coop can't push it all in. Not that I can say anything when I'm sucking on Noah's cock.

"Tap once if that's what you want." Coop licks the edge of my ear before biting my earlobe again. I whimper at the aftershock pulsing around Coop's hard cock. I rock my hips against his as I suck hard, hollowing my cheeks around Noah's cock.

I tap the pen once. Noah grins wickedly and nods at Coop.

"Dirty sluts don't get it the way they want it. Do they?" Coop's voice in my ear makes me whimper. Fuck.

Noah steps back. His cock slips from my mouth while he strokes himself. I pout at the loss of him inside me. Coop slides his arms beneath my knees. Maybe he's going to leave me wanting. He lifts me up and lets me slide back down on his cock.

Fuck. A moan escapes me at how good that feels. Just a few more times and I'll come again. Noah closes in on me and grabs me beneath my arms, lifting me from Coop's cock and into his arms before he slides his cock deep inside my pussy. Moaning at the feel of him, I wrap myself around him. Coop stands behind me and thrusts his cock hard into my ass.

"Oh, fuck," I can't help saying, stuffed so full. It's sudden, and it burns a little, but it also feels so fucking good.

My hands dig into Noah's thick blond hair and pull his mouth to mine as they thrust inside me. Our tongues tangle. My hips follow his thrusts. Coop holds my hips as he finds the rhythm with both of us as he fucks in and out of my ass, making me hum with pleasure into Noah's mouth.

The friction is too much. My body explodes around both of them, tightening both my pussy and my ass in waves, drawing them deeper. I cry out as my whole body shakes with orgasm.

"That's a good girl," Noah whispers in one ear.

"That's my dirty whore," Coop whispers in the other.

My pussy and ass convulse around their cocks still thrusting within me. They both speed up until I can't find their rhythm anymore. I'm helpless in their arms as they take me. They both press their mouths against my shoulders and suck.

It's too much, giving in to them, letting them claim me, take me. I shatter again, crying out at the overwhelming ecstasy of these men fucking me. They both thrust deep. Their groans mix with my cry as they release, filling me, pumping me full of everything they have to give.

My body shivers between their warm bodies, suddenly aware we're all still clothed except for my pants.

Noah presses his forehead to mine and breathes me in. His dark eyes meet mine. "You and me. We're good, kitten. Did I want to claim you in front of everyone? Absolutely, but as long as you're mine, I'll be yours."

I give him a smile and rub his silky hair between my fingers. "I'm all of yours. It doesn't matter who's technically my boyfriend. I belong to all of you and that won't change."

He takes my mouth, kissing me deep and sure.

"You're amazing, sweetheart," Coop says quietly, and his words fill my heart. Kissing my shoulder, he slides his cock out of me.

These guys are mine. I continue to kiss Noah as I feel someone step behind me.

"Princess," Seth says as he eases his cock into my ass.

Noah presses his forehead against mine. Our eyes meet as Seth seats himself deep inside me. I clench around both of them at the invasion. My insides buzz with need.

"We're good, kitten."

I cup Noah's cheeks and lean in to kiss him again as Seth thrusts his cock in and out of me. When I gasp, Seth holds me tight as Noah slides out of my pussy. Blake takes over Noah's spot, holding me up, and his shirt brushes against mine.

Blake's thick cock presses at my entrance before sliding inside me, stretching me. My mouth falls open as my eyes slide shut at being so full. This is what I need. All of them claiming me.

Seth and Blake have their own rhythm together. They hold me up as they fill me. Already sensitive, I can't hold back my orgasm as they fuck me hard together. A guttural sound works its way out of my throat as I tighten all around them, clinging to Blake as my world shifts on its axis.

Unable to hold myself upright, I lean against Seth's chest with my arms around Blake's neck, letting the press of their bodies hold me in place.

Blake gives me a cocky smile as he pulls almost all the way out before thrusting all the way in. My walls tighten and convulse around him in an aftershock. He grabs my hips and holds me against him while his fingers spread my ass cheeks for Seth.

"Fuck her hard, boss." Blake's words make me shudder as another orgasm flows through me. "She wants it. She needs it. Her cunt is dripping for it."

Growling, Seth doesn't hold back. He fucks my ass hard, giving me a little edge of pain along with a whole lot of pleasure. Blake whispers dirty things in my ear as I cling to him. Electricity flows through every nerve. As my orgasm overwhelms me again, I bite down on his neck. Seth groans, coming hard into me.

"So fucking good," he whispers against my hair as he pulls his cock out.

Blake turns with me and lays me down on the table. He holds my hips up, level with his pelvis, as he slowly fucks me. "You need to tell us everything, tiger. When it happens, whether or not you believe it happened. That's nonnegotiable."

"Yes, sir." I arch my body as his slow fuck builds the heat within me again. The fire they never fully put out. I'd agree to almost anything they want at this point as long as they don't stop fucking me.

From near my head on the table, Noah reaches for the hem of my shirt and drags it off me. He tugs my bra cup out of the way and lowers his mouth to my hardened nipple, teasing it with his tongue. Hot and wet. His mouth closes over it and he draws on it, making me gasp and my pussy clench around Blake's thick cock.

Fingers stroke my clit. My already overheated body burns even hotter. I gaze down and see Coop sitting next to where Blake stands, slowly fucking my mind out of my body. Coop's eyes focus on Blake's cock moving in and out of my pussy. His touch is featherlight on my clit, spinning dizzy little circles around it.

Noah moves to my other breast, sucking it hard and deep into his mouth. I can't think, all I can do is feel and give in to these powerful men. My gaze flits down to his blond hair brushing my sensitive skin.

It's almost too much for my senses. My insides are on fire, ready to explode. I want to close my eyes, but I don't want to miss a single expression on their faces.

Fingers press into my puckered hole, making me buck against Blake's cock. I'm surprised to see Seth sitting on the other side of Blake. His fingers press deep inside me, pressing his and Coop's cum deeper, holding it in while using it as lube to draw his fingers back and forth against those overstimulated nerves.

Coop's lips trail over my hip bone before he latches on, sucking my skin into his mouth. Blake picks up the pace a little. My pussy flutters helplessly against the quickening desire. I never thought about what this would actually feel like in the moment. Being overwhelmed with so many hands, all devoted to making me come.

"You are so fucking hot being fucked by four guys, tiger." Blake's deep voice flows through me like another caress.

My eyes lock with Blake's darkened green ones. My insides are an inferno swelling with heat. Every touch makes me burn even brighter. Makes me rise even higher. I writhe in their arms, feeling the impending break heading for me.

"Come for us, princess." Seth kisses my hip as he finger fucks my ass.

As if waiting for his permission, I succumb to the fire, letting it consume me. My body arches as I scream my release. Blake's cock, Noah's mouth, and Seth's and Coop's fingers rock me higher and higher until the world melts around us in a blaze of flames.

When Blake comes, his cock twitches inside me and every pulse of cum feeds my orgasm as my pussy milks him. I collapse onto the table and press my hand to my overwrought heart, trying to catch my breath.

Noah kisses his way to my lips before taking my mouth in an upside-down kiss. The embers stir within me, and aftershocks rock through me. When he lifts his head, I realize I'm naked while everyone else is fully dressed. Blake has his pants open and his cock buried inside me.

He smiles down at me as he thrusts once, making my pussy clench before he pulls out. Coop's fingers go to work, pressing their cum back into my pussy. I can't be bothered to move right now. Not to cover up. Not to clean up.

This is my new home. The conference table. They can just come and fuck me whenever they want.

The guys all take their seats like me spread naked on the table, with Coop's fingers in my slick channel holding in their cum, is a totally normal thing. He slides his fingers in and out slowly, easing me down.

With these guys, I don't think I'll ever come down.

"We need to talk about what we've found." Seth's voice makes me sigh. Pushing away the real world only works in the moment, but fuck, what a moment.

Chapter 54

Bring to the Table

"What did you discover about Courtney?" Seth asks Noah as he settles back in his chair. His gaze flows over my naked body a few times. He settles on watching Coop's fingers and their gentle slide in and out of my pussy.

"Financials all look normal. No new influx of cash. She had a project she worked on while she was here yesterday. So it seems legit." Leaning casually in his chair, Noah reaches out and teases my nipple lightly with his fingertips.

I bite my lip at the gentle arousing feeling spreading through me from them watching and touching me. My knees are bent so my feet are on the edge of the table.

"She put down exactly the time she spent here." Blake crosses his ankle over his knee, takes my ankle in his hand, and presses my foot onto his leg. "She was likely here when Coop fucked Madison. But there's no telling if she saw or heard anything. We can't exactly track her once she's in the building." His fingers stroke my ankle slowly, stirring little fluttery sparks up my leg. "I'm surprised she heard you scream the second time. Her office is on the other side of the building."

My skin tingles where the guys touch me, but I still don't have the energy to move. I blow out a breath and look at the ceiling beams. Right now, their touch is more of a comfort. An arousing comfort, but a comfort nonetheless.

"I'm just glad she showed up." I sigh as Coop moves his fingers slowly inside me. Noah keeps circling my nipple with his fingertips. Their touch keeps me from falling into the fear of that moment. "I froze in that corner, paralyzed by fear. Without my phone, I didn't have a way to find the door. And I was petrified. Could you tell what the shuffling noise was?"

Blake shakes his head as his finger trails up and down my calf. "It's hard to hear on the video. It could be the stalker's clothes. If you'd told us after it happened, the guy might have still been in the building."

I shake my head and take in a breath, trying to tame the fire raging out of control inside me. My hips rock with Coop's hand. "You guys were busy with work, and I panicked in the moment. When Courtney said the lights were automatic, she made me feel like a child for screaming."

I can't continue. She made me feel ridiculous.

Coop leans in and sucks on my clit, flooding me with heat. The thoughts clouding my mind burst into a wave of hot desire. Noah pinches my nipples at the same time. I gasp at the shockwave of lust.

"No one here thinks you're a child, princess." Seth's words draw my gaze to him. "We can't protect you if you don't trust us."

"There are other things you've held back from us." Blake squeezes my foot.

My brows furrow as I try to concentrate around Coop's tongue on my clit and his fingers pumping into me, faster, harder. My hips instinctively follow him. "What things?"

I hear a belt buckle clang. Coop's fingers pull out, and then his cock thrusts into me, filling me. My back arches at the burst of need that unleashes within me.

Coop pulls me upright, and I wrap myself around him, his cock deep inside me again. "Blake's talking about Hunter Adams harassing you."

His name makes coldness flow through me, but Coop eases out before thrusting his cock deep again, heating me back up. His shirt is under my hands and brushes my sensitive nipples. I'm still completely naked and in the middle of everyone.

"Tell us, princess." Seth uses his commanding voice.

I meet Coop's eyes. "I'm feeling a little vulnerable right now."

"You should feel vulnerable with us, sweetheart." He turns and backs me into the wall before he fucks me, slowly, firmly. "You're ours. We need you to give us your everything. Your secrets. Your desires. Your fears. Everything you are is ours now."

His mouth closes over mine, and nothing in the room matters right now except Coop and what he's doing to my body. I dig my fingers into his hair and grip it tight as he fucks me. As tired as I was, I can't help but rally as he thrusts deep, tossing kindling on an already out-of-control blaze.

I combust. So hard. My pussy milks his cock as he continues to thrust deep inside before he stills and fills me with his cum. His body crushes mine to the wall, but the weight of him on me feels so awesome, I don't want it to end.

Coop presses his forehead against mine. His light blue eyes are serious. "Tell us about Hunter Adams, sweetheart."

Swallowing, I look into Coop's intense eyes. He's still pressed up against me. His cock still hard and throbbing inside me.

At least I'm not laid out on the table, exposed.

"He was handsome and charming at first, but he doesn't take no for an answer." I tug on Coop's hair, winding the silky strands around my fingers. "He decided he wanted me at my internship last year. I did all the things you're supposed to do. Told him *no thank you* when he asked me out. Avoided him at company functions. But he still sought me out, always touching me. Sometimes inappropriately."

"Everything, sweetheart." Coop narrows his eyes.

I blow my hair out of my face. "Near the end of my internship, he cornered me in the copy room. Told me how much he enjoyed our game of cat and mouse." A shiver runs down my spine, thinking about how he trapped me. Coop's hands slide over my hips, squeezing, keeping me here. "He said he knew I wanted him and that we should just fuck and get it over with."

"And?"

"He almost had his hand up my skirt before someone came in and I got away." I drop my gaze. "It's not like I could tell the owner his son was sexually harassing me." I lift my gaze to Coop's. "And I couldn't tell my new bosses that their new client, who was my previous boss, was harassing me when they'd been blackmailed for the same thing."

"Fuck," Blake says.

He didn't trust me then. He wouldn't have believed my side of the story. But now he knows some piece of me. He protects me.

I lean my head against the wall and look over at Blake's green eyes. "At the restaurant, he was upset that I didn't take their job offer. He said I didn't have an excuse to not be with him anymore since I didn't work for him. Thank you for intervening."

Blake shakes his head. "I thought you had a thing with him."

I hold his gaze steady. "Never." I turn back to Coop. "He trapped me in the break room, startled me, and I dropped the mug. He grabbed my arm, but I kept away from him. He insisted he'd leave me alone if I gave him a kiss. I told him no, but he had me cornered against the wall when you showed up. Thank you."

"I don't want you anywhere near that fucker." Coop kisses me. His cock hardens inside me. "You're ours."

I capture his face in my hands and meet his eyes. "I'm yours and no one else's."

Coop captures my mouth and thrusts his cock in and out of me. He's fucking me hard now. It's possessive and quick, and I love every second of it as I cling to him. I thread my fingers through his hair as I moan into his mouth. They may not have known, but they saved me from Hunter. And now they know.

"We need to move this downstairs." Seth's voice penetrates my fog of desire. "Before we all fuck again. For now, Madison doesn't go anywhere alone. Not in the building. Not outside. Until we have a handle on who might be after her."

Coop reaches between us and rubs my clit. I cry out as he pushes me over the edge. My orgasm draws him into his, and he collapses against me.

Our breathing is heavy and ragged, my skin damp with sweat. I feel sticky between my legs as he settles against the wall with me.

"I could just keep fucking you like this all night." Coop trails kisses back to behind my ear. "You want more, don't you, my filthy little slut? You want so many cocks inside you that you can't even move from the pleasure."

Fuck. An aftershock ripples through me as I lay my head back against the wall. Those words shouldn't arouse me the way they do. His cock slips out of me.

"I'll talk to the boss," Coop whispers. His lips tickle my ear. "I'll get him to have all of us fuck your pussy, and then I'll feed you the mixture of all of our cum with yours."

My pussy clenches at the thought.

He lifts his head and chuckles darkly. "You'd like that, wouldn't you?"

I let my legs slide down his, and he sets me on my feet. I grab the front of his shirt and tug him down until his mouth is just above mine. His eyes darken as his hands grab my ass. A burst of power goes through me at the desire in his eyes.

"Only if you're a good boy." I lick his lips. "Otherwise, I'll have to punish you myself."

He arches an eyebrow. "Fuck, sweetheart. You're going to make me hard again and upset Seth when I bend you over that table and fuck your ass."

I glance over at the others, who eye my naked body with hungry gazes.

"To recap," I say, not releasing Coop's shirt. "We don't have any real information on the stalker yet. Courtney seems legit, even if she is a bit of a bitch. Coop and I are dating for appearances, and the rest of you have to date other women?"

"I'm not dating anyone." Noah's words make me meet his dark eyes. "I didn't before, so I won't now."

I nod to him and my heart hurts. I would have been honored to be his date. To show him off as mine.

Blake rubs the back of his neck. "We don't think the stalker is your neighbor. We've had guys on him since the first incident. He didn't leave his apartment yesterday."

I release Coop's shirt and he straightens. I step over to Blake and put my hands on my hips. "You have someone on my neighbor? Robert? I told you I didn't think he did it."

"We're being careful." His gaze dips down my naked body. "Can someone grab her clothes?"

"Why—" I squeal as Blake leans over and lifts me onto his shoulder. His hand clamps on my ass cheek to hold me in place.

"While Coop likes his girl dirty, I'm going to get this one cleaned up." Blake leaves the room with me over his shoulder and calls the elevator. Movement draws my attention. Noah follows us. But Seth and Coop remain in the conference room, where I'm sure we've left a mess.

"Shouldn't I have clothes on?" I ask when they step onto the elevator.

"They'd just get in the way of your shower." Blake's hand rubs my ass cheek. "Just be glad there aren't security cameras in this elevator like the public ones."

"Did you guys review the elevator footage?" The elevator reaches our floor, and the guys step into the apartment hallway. A door opens, and we step into Blake's bedroom.

"Our mystery guest must have used the stairs. There are fewer cameras, and they're easy to avoid if you know where they are." Blake lowers me to my feet on the tile in the bathroom. "Do you want to wash your hair?"

Noah turns the shower on and stands to the side, taking off his clothes. His eyes don't leave me. Mine take in his fit body. The conference room sex was deliciously hot, but there's something about their warm skin pressed against mine that revs me up. My gaze goes to Blake, who is also almost stripped down. Fuck, they're beautiful.

"Hair, tiger? Up or down?" Dropping his boxers to the ground, Blake steps toward me, fully naked.

"Down." I don't know how I can get turned on again, but these guys make me so fucking horny.

Blake smirks at me as he wraps his arms below my ass and lifts me straight up against him. "You'll be sparkling fresh for whatever the boss has in mind tonight."

He walks us straight into the shower and Noah follows us, closing the door behind him. They both run soapy hands over me while I try to wash them. Our wet bodies slide against each other, building that fire hotter inside me.

When I start to lower to my knees to suck their cocks, Noah holds me up. "Not now, kitten. Seth has plans for tonight."

I pout as Noah pulls me against him while Blake cleans my ass and pussy, his fingers stoking the flames ever higher. The water washes all the soap away, and Blake turns off the shower before passing out towels.

Noah wraps one around me before drying himself. After drying off, I do my best with my hair. Blake opens a drawer in his vanity.

"Yours."

I peer inside and find a brush in the style I like, some hair ties, a toothbrush, my brand of toothpaste, my facial soap and lotion, some styling supplies, and makeup wipes.

"Seth stocked all our bathrooms with your stuff. Especially since you sleep with us now." Blake kisses my shoulder before heading into his bedroom. A tingle careens through me.

With my towel wrapped around me, I brush my hair and teeth. It feels good to be clean, and a lot less sticky.

Noah kisses me before leaving the room. Blake comes back in with a men's black t-shirt and hands it to me.

"So you don't get ravished on the way to your room." He gives me a cocky grin. "If you do, I'll punish you."

"Do you know how difficult it is for a girl to not get ravished in this apartment?" I draw his shirt over my head, and it falls to midway down my thighs.

Blake cups my cheek and draws his thick thumb over my lips. "I think you can manage it, tiger. Find some panties."

Meeting his green eyes, I flick my tongue over the tip of his thumb. He groans and lifts my shirt to smack my ass.

"Ah!" I try to dance away, but he holds my shirt hostage.

"Behave, tiger, or you won't leave this room until your ass is so sore, you won't be able to sit without a constant reminder that you picked a battle and lost." Blake draws me closer and captures my lips in a searing kiss I feel all the way to my toes.

I can't wait to find out what Seth has planned for us tonight.

Chapter 55

Performance Review

Seth

The free-for-all in the conference room makes me pensive about fucking Madison more. She took us all beautifully, as she always does, but I know we can be too much. She seems to want us as much as we want her, but I need to make sure that's what she really wants.

She's so agreeable that I worry she's just going along with us. Letting us do whatever we want. Sure, she has some limits, but not many in the grand scheme of things.

She walks into her bedroom in Blake's t-shirt and smiles at me.

"Come here."

When she stops in front of me, I slide my hand up the back of her thigh to her bare ass. My thumbs stroke her smooth skin as I raise an eyebrow at her.

"I planned on finding some panties when I got here," she says.

I let my hand fall away and meet her wide blue eyes. "How are you?"

Her eyebrow shoots up, and she gives me an odd look. It's not an unreasonable thing to ask. "I'm good. How are you?"

"I figured now would be a good chance to check in with you."

Leaning back on my hands on her bed, I nod to her closet. "Put some panties on and come sit with me."

She glances over her shoulder with a quizzical look, then heads to her closet and steps inside for a moment. When she returns, she sits beside me, turned toward me with her leg up on the bed. Her red, silky panties attract my attention, and my cock gets ideas.

"So how do we do this check-in?" Madison asks.

"Are we too much? Do you want to have a quiet evening? We can play a game of some sort or watch a movie. We don't have to have sex."

She cocks her head to the side, and her lips tug toward a smile. "Be honest. Do you guys need a break?"

I chuckle. "No, princess. You want us, you've got us. But we've been fucking you a lot this weekend. This whole week. We've never had this kind of access before. If you need us to slow down and take a step back—"

She straddles my lap and runs her fingers over the nape of my neck, sending shivers of awareness through my body. My cock is hard for her. It always is.

"I'm good. Is my ass a little sore?" She gives me a small smile. "Yeah, but it's all good. I love everything you guys give me."

She bites her lip and hesitates. It happens when she uses the word *love*.

"We could leave your ass alone for tonight." I smirk, knowing how much she likes ass play.

"I don't know if I'd say we need to leave it alone, per se. Maybe just fuck it gently?" She plucks at the buttons on my shirt. "I definitely prefer you all naked. Though fucking you in the conference room while you were clothed made my blood boil."

I slide my hands over her silk-covered ass and rock my cock against her pussy. "Have we done anything you don't like?"

She bites her lip and shakes her head as she opens the top button of my shirt. Her darkened eyes lift to mine. "I like it when you're all involved."

"Do you want to take all of us at once, princess?"

Her lips part as she flicks open another button. Her eyes flash up and lock with mine. "Can we do that?"

I'm willing to try.

Dinner is leftovers. Once Coop finishes eating, he ducks into the play room to set things up for tonight. I pulled him aside before dinner to tell him what we'd need. Madison might be okay with being ridden hard, but she also needs to be taken care of. I plan to do just that.

When the last plate is loaded into the dishwasher, Madison turns to me. She's still wearing Blake's t-shirt and those red panties that I'm sure everyone has gotten a glimpse of or touched at some point this evening.

"What's on the agenda, boss?" She cocks her eyebrow as her fingers toy with the hem of her shirt.

Coop comes out of the play room in just his boxers. "All set."

Noah and Blake head into the room while Madison raises an eyebrow at me.

"Do I get to know what I'm walking into, or is this a surprise?" She closes the distance between us and plays with my belt buckle.

"Be surprised, princess." I turn and draw her toward the play room. When we enter, the other guys are in their boxers already. The lights are dim, and soft music plays on the speakers.

Madison's eyes narrow on the piece of furniture in the center of the room, and then they widen in surprise. "Is that a massage table?"

I draw her back against my chest and lean down to say in her ear. "Let us take care of you tonight, princess."

I reach for the hem of her shirt and draw it off over her head. Noah steps in front of her and eases her panties down her legs, kneeling before her to let her step out of them. Blake takes her hand and leads her to the table while I take off my clothes.

"Lie on your stomach, sweetheart." Coop has a selection of body oils that can also work as lube out on a nearby table. He hands her a clip for her hair. Smiling at him, she winds her hair into a bun and clips it in place.

Her body is a fucking work of art, all clean, curved lines. I have plans to touch every inch of her tonight.

Madison lies on the table with her face in the cradle. Blake stands at her feet and draws her legs apart. Noah rubs oil on his hands before standing beside her and running his hands up and down her back. She releases a content sigh.

Exactly what I hoped for. She needs to unwind, and yes, orgasms are relaxing, but tonight I just want her to let go and enjoy herself.

Blake rubs her feet, pressing on the pressure points, while Coop works on her other leg, massaging her calf and thigh.

I take the other side of the table from Noah and start working on her shoulder and arm. Her warm skin is soft and pliant under my hands.

"Why don't we do this every day?" Madison moans softly as we release her tight muscles.

"And spoil you?" I massage the palm of her hand as her fingers twitch.

"I'm not opposed to being spoiled." Laughter clings to her words.

Blake moves to her other foot, and Coop changes to her other calf and thigh. Noah and I switch sides as well. We're avoiding her neck because of the bruises, and also her ass and pussy because we want her to truly relax without overstimulating her.

We massage her for about a half hour, getting into a rhythm. Her muscles ease and her breathing slows as she relaxes beneath our touch. Coop and Blake work their way up to her thighs while Noah and I move down to her lower back. She sucks in a breath as our hands draw closer to her erogenous zones.

Coop draws her leg out a little, and his fingers work on her groin, drifting over her pussy. Blake follows his lead. Her breath quickens again, but she stays liquid beneath our touch. Noah and I focus on her glutes but slide our hands between her ass cheeks, brushing over her asshole in the process.

I warm up the oil in my hand before tracing her hole with my fingertip. Her harsh breath fills the air. Blake's and Coop's fingers tangle on her pussy, rubbing her clit and circling her cunt. Noah slides his finger into her asshole and draws it out again.

Her hips try to follow each of us as her little needy noises fill the room. Noah and I ease our fingers into her ass, at the same time Blake and Coop thrust theirs into her cunt. Her legs part more, and she moans. We all ease them in and out of her slowly while still massaging with our other hands.

Her breathing bursts out of her in little pants. Her hips try to follow our fingers. We each add an additional thick finger to her holes as we finger fuck her all together, stretching her. My cock is so fucking hard right now watching her take all of us. Hearing her wet cunt sucking on their fingers. Feeling her tight ass around mine.

Her muscles tense beneath our hands before she lets out a guttural cry. She soaks Blake's and Coop's hands as she comes. Her ass clenches down on Noah's and my fingers. We keep our fingers inside her as she pulses in waves around us. Slowly, we ease from her one at a time, wiping our hands on towels.

"Time to flip over." Coop helps Madison turn onto her back and puts the face cradle down. We all take off our boxers before oiling our hands again. Madison's heated gaze roams over all of us.

We all take different spots on her body. So I can watch better, I move down to her feet. Blake continues to work her legs, but his fingertips graze her clit as he reaches the top before heading back down. Her breath catches and releases. Coop sits at Madison's head and massages her scalp while Noah rubs oil over her breasts.

While Coop is an ass guy, Noah has always had a thing for breasts. He glides his hands between hers like I'm sure he wants to do with his cock. When we plan to play longer, I have an idea I want to try that will get everyone off.

Blake moves up to rub her belly and then down between her legs.

Madison's thighs fall open on a sigh. Already keyed up, she squirms more under our touch. Noah massages her breasts, running his fingers over her hardened nipples. Moaning, she bites her lip.

Coop leans over and kisses Madison upside down. Pulling her by her shoulders, he brings her head over the edge of the table and lowers it down, stretching her neck. "Open, sweetheart."

She licks her lips before parting them, and he slides his hard cock into her mouth, thrusting his hips gently while she makes wet sucking noises. Precum leaks out of my tip. Her mouth is divine when she sucks us off.

Noah climbs onto the table and straddles Madison's stomach. He rubs oil on his cock before resting it between her breasts, then squeezes them around his dick while he strokes himself back and forth between them. His fingers tease her nipples as he thrusts.

Blake leans down and licks her pussy, thrusting his tongue into her greedy cunt. Stroking my cock, I round to the side for a better view. To watch her get fucked by my brothers. Her hand joins mine on my cock, and I meet her eyes as she strokes up and down with me.

So fucking beautiful. Her other hand is buried in Blake's hair, gripping it tight as she rides his mouth. No one is in a rush to finish. Our heavy breaths fill the air.

Madison clutches me tighter as her entire body tenses with an orgasm. Blake lifts his mouth from her pussy, his chin shining with her wetness. He climbs onto the table between her legs and lifts her hips to ease his cock into her.

She arches, but Noah's body holds her down as he slowly fucks her tits. His cock shuttles back and forth. The head almost touches Madison's neck before he draws it back. She's not taking Coop as deep as before, but her cheeks hollow out as she sucks his cock.

And her hand on me, fuck. She rubs her fingers around my head and thumbs my slit before slowly pumping my cock in her fist. Madison's skin shines from the oil.

She was glorious in the conference room, but right now, everything is soft and easy. Not the rough need of before. We're worshipping her body. Not that we used it for relief before, but some of upstairs was about her trusting us.

But also us venting our frustrations and her taking it so fucking beautifully.

This is all about pleasure. Her pleasure.

She's so much more than I ever expected.

Chapter 56

Personal Time

Madison

I think they're trying to kill me by orgasms. But what a way to go. I was a little hesitant about getting a massage. This guy I saw in college swore he was the best, and he most definitely was not. Squeezing my muscles hard was not relaxing.

But my guys . . . Fuck me sideways, my guys are perfection at massages and getting me off. Their hands kneaded my muscles into submission. And the way they fuck me . . .

My body hums with energy and an aching need as Coop thrusts his cock back and forth between my lips. He's not pushing in deep. I could take more, but I'm overwhelmed with sensations.

It's hard to see the rest of what's happening with my head like this, but I can feel everything. The glide of Noah's cock between my breasts. His fingers teasing my nipples before pinching and pulling them, sending waves of heat to my pussy.

Blake keeps a slow and steady rhythm as he fucks me. His thick cock stretches me, and I can feel every inch of him as he drives me out of my mind with pleasure.

My voyeur Seth thought he'd watch and stroke himself. But when he moved close enough, I reached for his cock, feeling my hand slide on the oil and smooth skin. Up and down, exploring every inch of his cock and balls. Threading my fingers with his to help him stroke it.

I love every minute of this. All the stimulation makes my toes curl.

I can see Seth if I look out the side of my eye. The blissed-out expression on his face makes me want to sink my pussy down over his cock. I'm hopelessly addicted to sex with these guys.

I crave it even when I'm already getting fucked four ways. I want more. I want them all inside me. Even though I'm not sure how, I want to take all of them inside me at once. I want them to chain fuck me like the other night. I just want them. All the time.

Tingles race through my body as the waves of an orgasm crash over me, tossing me into an ocean of pleasure that I can't seem to surface from. Not when they keep stimulating my body with their thrusts. I can't come down as waves of pleasure keep hitting me from all angles.

I suck harder on Coop until my cheeks hollow, enjoying his cock in my mouth. His groan sounds over the soft music before my mouth fills with his salty cum. As I'm swallowing him down and licking him clean, Blake roars and thrusts deep inside my throbbing pussy. Each pulse of his cum that spills into me I can feel as my pussy takes it all from him.

Coop draws out of my mouth and lifts my head carefully, putting the face cradle up to support me. Seth wraps his fingers around mine and strokes his cock, freeing my attention a little.

Finally, I can watch Noah fucking my tits. His chest is flushed with desire as he rocks his cock between my breasts. He bites his lip as he focuses on what he's doing. No one's ever done this to me before, but it's hot as hell to watch his cock thrusting in and out.

The head of his cock, red and ready to burst, plays a game of hide-and-seek with me. Coop leans over and takes one of my nipples into his mouth. Game over for me.

Moaning so loud that if we had neighbors I'd be embarrassed, I come harder around Blake's cock still lodged deep in my pussy, causing him to groan. Noah's moan joins mine as his cum spurts out onto my neck, bathing me in his warmth. He jerks forward and back a few more times before leaning down to claim my lips in a kiss that hits me straight in my heart. His slippery cock rests against my stomach.

"Thank you, kitten," Noah whispers against my lips. I lose myself in his dark eyes for a moment and smile softly.

Blake pulls out of me with a smack on my ass that lights me up a little. Coop brushes his hand over my hair as Noah climbs off me.

After dragging his finger through Noah's cum, Coop paints my lips with it. I lick them clean and open my mouth for him. Groaning, he dips his cum-soaked fingers into my mouth, and I suck every last bit off without dropping his gaze.

"Fuck, sweetheart." Coop leans down and kisses me hard with his tongue in my mouth, tasting me and Noah and himself. An after-shock shakes through my body. Coop cups my cheek as he turns to look at Seth.

My gaze follows his to Seth and his hard cock as I stroke over his dick with his help. His eyes meet mine and he groans, coming all over our hands. I stroke him through his orgasm. I wait until he finishes, then bring my hand covered in his cum to my lips and lick it.

Seth gives me a smirk before he sits on the bench behind him. "You good?"

A laugh bursts out of me. I'm covered in cum and had maybe a good five minutes' worth of orgasm there at the end, and he wants to know if I'm good?

"No words." I shake my head at him as I smile. "Good doesn't begin to describe it. Wonderful. Chaotic. Orgasmic. Messy. Heaven."

Apparently, to keep their dicks out of me, we have to take separate showers. I put on pajamas but leave off my underwear. I swear it only gets in the way around here. I'd walk around naked, but I've been fucked enough for one day.

Not that I'd turn them down if they wanted to start something again.

I'm the last one out. When I enter the living room, the TV is on low and the guys sit around the couch with bowls in front of them. Their eyes track me like prey. A shiver works down my spine.

"Hey." I brush my hair behind my ear, a little self-conscious from all their attention on me as I round the couch. I'm not sure where that came from. These guys have explored every inch of me, been inside me every way they can, burrowed their way into my life and possibly my heart.

Noah holds up a bowl of ice cream. "For you."

Smiling, I sit next to him on the couch and take the bowl. "Thank you."

I kiss his cheek and rest my head against his shoulder as I take a bite of the creamy goodness. Noah would make an awesome boyfriend. I guess that's what all of them are, though, right? My boyfriends. Just not in front of anyone else.

When we're with other people, only Coop can claim me as his, and I can claim him as mine. But not the others. An ache forms in my chest.

The future seems so far away when I'm with them, but eventually my future won't include them. When I finally go off and do all the things I used to brag about back home—starting my own multimillion dollar company, being my own boss—I'll be leaving these guys to their next assistant.

I shove a bite of ice cream into my mouth, swallowing past the lump forming in my throat, and blink back the tears in my eyes. The only sound in the room is the clink of spoons on bowls and the low murmuring of the TV. I can't bring myself to look them in the eyes when I'm feeling like this.

Coop scoots closer to me on the couch until our shoulders and thighs touch. I push away gloomy thoughts of a far-off future and turn to meet his light blue eyes and mischievous grin. My heart tries to fill my chest.

"We were waiting to see if you wanted to pick something to watch." He licks his ice cream spoon like he would my pussy, and all sad thoughts are pushed away.

They're mine for now, and that has to be enough.

"Can it not be an action film?" I raise an eyebrow at the guys. It seems like every time we sit in front of the TV, there are explosions, guns, and car chases.

They concede, and we put on *The Lost City*. At least it has some action for the guys. When I finish with my ice cream, Blake takes my bowl to the kitchen for me. Coop's fingers brush back and forth on my thigh, gently warming my insides up again.

I'm not sure I can get enough of these guys. Noah takes my hand and holds it in his lap while my head remains on his shoulder. Halfway through the movie, Coop lifts my legs across his thighs and keeps gently stroking my calf. Whenever I catch their eye, Blake and Seth smile at me.

This feels nice. I'm safe, well fed, and on track to do big things in my career. Our arrangement doesn't account for love, which is fine. Someday I'll have to move on, but not right now. Right now, I just want to lock this moment in my memory. Yes, there are unanswered questions and still potential danger, but right now . . . This is what peace and happiness feel like.

When the movie ends, Seth gives me his hands to help me to my feet.

"Come on, princess. Time for bed." He keeps hold of my hand as he leads me back to my bedroom with the others following. He releases me and gestures. Without hesitation, I climb onto the monstrous bed. Anticipation wells in me.

They strip down to their boxers and join me. Blake draws my face to his and gives me a kiss. It's slow and exploratory. Not something to key me up. It feels nice.

When he backs away, Seth kisses me. I'm a little surprised because Seth usually waits until he's last. But his kiss is soft and almost loving. And I sigh happily when he pulls away.

Coop pulls me onto his lap and kisses me like he fucks me, gently but with an edge of roughness. He grinds his cock up against me and the fire burns a little brighter.

"It's time to sleep, Coop." Seth's voice sounds exasperated.

I giggle against Coop's lips. He sighs and presses his forehead to mine.

"You like being fucked all the time. Don't you, my little whore?" He cocks his eyebrow at me as his finger traces over my eyebrow.

I lean in and nip his lip. "Behave or you'll sleep at my feet."

"Fuck, sweetheart. I can't wait until our night together." Coop thrusts his hard cock against me, and my insides turn liquid.

A gasp leaves my lips.

"I'm going to let you do all the naughty things you want to me, and then I'm going to fuck you so hard you see stars."

I bite my lip, kind of wanting that now. "Promise?"

"You're going to get me in trouble with the boss." He smacks my ass and moves me to Noah.

"You get yourself in trouble just fine." I give him a smile before I turn to Noah.

"Come here, kitten." Noah draws me down onto the bed, facing him. He tips my chin up and claims my lips in a gentle kiss that rocks me to the core. My heart feels like it's trying to escape my chest. This bond between us feels almost like too much.

I drag my finger down his stubbled jaw and meet his dark eyes.

"I would have been the best girlfriend you ever had," I whisper as Seth turns out the lights.

"You already are." He kisses me softly and tugs me to rest with my head on his chest. The steady beat of his heart beneath my cheek soothes me. Blake snuggles up against my back, and my heart feels like it's going to explode.

It'd be so easy to fall. To let go and just let this be what it could be. But there's this little part of me that worries that if I love these men and have to leave them, I'll never be whole again.

Chapter 57

Business Dress

Madison

When morning comes, I wake up writhing in aching need with a cock driving into me. Not an unusual morning since I moved in with these guys.

"Good morning, kitten." Noah rubs his stubbly cheek against mine as he thrusts in and out of me.

My nipples are hard and my breasts tight as they rub against his chest. I'm soaking wet for him. My body's on fire and on the edge of exploding into a million pieces.

"Morning." I barely open my eyes before I'm being turned on my side. As Noah lifts my leg over his hip and continues to thrust in me, the soft head of a wet cock presses against my asshole.

"Morning, tiger." Blake kisses my shoulder before thrusting his entire dick into my ass. With the way he slides right in, they must have prepped me before I woke up, because I don't feel the burn. All I feel is the implosion of everything.

"Oh, fuck," I cry out as I come. My whole being shakes from the orgasm. Groaning as my ass tightens around him, Blake drives his thick cock in and out of me. Stretching me, filling me so full while Noah fucks my pussy.

I close my eyes and savor the feeling of being full. Instead of cooling off, the fire inside me burns hotter and brighter.

"Coop, get your dick off my ass," Noah complains.

Coop leans over him to flick my clit.

"Fuck off. It's not like I'm going to stick it in your ass. Besides, my little whore would get off on that. Wouldn't you, Madison?" He rubs circles around my clit, making it impossible to tell him anything. "If I rode Noah's ass while he fucked you, you'd come so fucking hard."

It's enough to make me shatter around them again, dragging Noah into his release. He shoves an elbow into Coop, who winks at me before retreating. Noah claims my lips in a fervent kiss while Blake keeps thrusting his hard cock into me. Blake's hand reaches around and palms my breast, teasing the nipple with his finger. My eyes close at the sensation as Noah draws away and scoots off the bed.

Coop moves into his place and lifts my leg over his hip. His cock presses against my entrance before he thrusts into my pussy, hard.

"Good morning, sweetheart."

I raise an eyebrow at him for the greeting. He smirks at me before his hand pulls my ass cheek open wider for Blake as Coop thrusts in and out of me at a fast and hard pace. Blake reaches down between Coop and me and pinches my clit firmly.

My moan fills the air as my pussy convulses in a gush around Coop's cock.

"That's my girl." Coop captures my lips and takes my mouth the way he takes my body. I don't think I'll ever come down, even when Blake and Coop groan at the same time and spill their cum inside me. They press against me, our bodies tangled, skin to skin.

Coop breaks off our kiss and flicks my clit, sending an aftershock through me. I gasp and he chuckles. Brushing his lips over mine one last time, he pulls out and leaves the bed.

Blake withdraws from my ass and turns me in his arms. "Thank you, tiger."

He claims my lips thoroughly. I don't know how I'll ever get used to sleeping alone again after this. When he lifts his head, he gives me a cocky smirk before rolling off the bed. Sighing, I fall onto my back. I'm not sure I can move yet. For morning, I'm not feeling like I have a lot of energy.

"Good morning, princess."

I turn my head to find Seth standing next to the bed, naked. He reaches out to me. That fire inside me perks up again. I take his hand, and he helps me to my feet, leading me naked into the bathroom where the shower is already running.

"How do you feel this morning?" he asks like cum isn't dripping down my thighs. His cock is solid and hard, pressing against his stomach. I glance down at the precum on the tip before meeting his eyes.

"I'd be better if you fucked me too." I arch an eyebrow.

He smirks before he opens the shower door and sweeps his arm toward it like a gentleman opening a door for a lady. My heart beats a little harder. I step into the warm water, and Seth enters behind me. His hard cock presses against my ass. I want him too. Even after being fucked and coming three times already, I haven't been fucked by Seth.

I love it when they all fuck me. To be filled by all of them. To never come down from the high of my orgasms. There's just something amazing about being theirs.

His hands run with the water down the front of my body, teasing my already hard nipples, curving over my stomach, and diving between my thighs.

"Are you tender here?" He strokes my clit while teasing the tip of his finger into my pussy, back and forth.

I try to chase his teasing finger with my hips. "No, sir."

His cock twitches against my ass and I smile.

His other hand slides between us. His fingers trace my asshole before slipping inside. "How about here?"

I gasp and shake my head. "No, sir."

"Where to fuck you?" He fills his hands with my soap and

washes me, starting with my neck. "Your neck is healing nicely. I suspect it'll be better by this weekend."

My breath comes in quick little pants, even though everything he does is slow and easy. I lean back against his chest and stroke my hands up and down his thighs. His hands slide down to my breasts, spending a lot more time on getting them clean than I ever have. Each stroke makes me ache a little more.

"How do you feel about dresses that reveal cleavage?" His tone is almost conversational. If his thick, hard dick wasn't currently cradled in my ass cheeks, I would think our naked bodies being pressed together didn't affect him.

"Planning on dressing me?" I brush my fingers over his hip bones. His cock twitches again. Liquid heat flows through me from his attention with the soap. He slides his hands lower over my stomach.

"You need something appropriate for the benefit since you'll be Coop's date." His fingers slip between my thighs and part me so he can thoroughly clean me.

My breath quickens with each stroke. My tone is breathless when I say, "I didn't think about that."

"I have."

He moves to cleaning my thighs. Nudging me under the shower head again, he sweeps his hands with the flow of water to push the soap from me.

"You want to dress me?" I didn't think that would be something any of them would be into. I've never had a guy want to dress me up or buy me clothes. Hell, those other boys wouldn't even want to go clothes shopping with me, but they were never my boyfriends.

"All the time, princess." He spins me and presses my front to the tile wall. He kicks my legs apart like a strip search before pulling my hands to the wall beside my head. "Don't move these."

"Yes, sir." My voice is breathy, but excitement flows through me. I love being vulnerable to him, letting him do whatever he wants to my body. Knowing that if I say *red*, he'll stop whatever he's doing. "Do you want to dress me today?"

"After I finish washing you." His soapy hands run down my back before sliding between my ass cheeks and cleaning me. "I want to pick out everything and watch you put it on."

I press my cheek to the tile and close my eyes as he washes my legs. He lifts the sprayer from the wall and rinses my back and legs. He changes the head to pulsing before moving it between my thighs.

"Seth?" As the water massages my clit, my fingers try to grip the wall for purchase. I don't want just the water. I don't want to just get off.

"What, princess?" His cock nudges my entrance and I suck in a breath. I want him so badly. For him to be a part of me.

"Yes, please," I whimper. I need him inside me. Fucking me. Filling me. Breaking me apart and putting me back together.

He lifts my leg up against the tile and drives his cock into my pussy while the water continues to stroke my clit. "Yes, what?"

I moan at the feel of him inside me. "Yes, sir."

He rocks in and out of my pussy as the water does what his tongue can do. With all the foreplay of him washing me, it takes only a few thrusts before I shatter around him, moaning so loud it fills the shower.

He bites my shoulder as he thrusts one last time deep inside me before exploding. My pussy throbs around his pulsating cock. We stay pressed together while we catch our breaths. Just feeling each other. Connected, like he's part of me now. He puts the sprayer back and kisses me behind my ear.

"Wash your hair, princess."

I'm going to be so late to work, but when the boss tells you to do something, you do it. He quickly washes himself before leaving the shower.

"I'll be back in ten minutes. Meet me in your closet." His heated eyes scorch over me as he adds, "Naked."

My closet is still sparse. I toweled off and dried my hair. I'll style it after Seth dresses me. Giddiness fills me as I wait for him. I'm not sure why this excites me. It's such a simple thing. A task I do every day without a lot of thought.

I dress nice for the guys, but it's just part of my morning routine. Seth is always so well put together. He's got the air of a guy who appreciates the finer things. I'm not sure if I qualify as one of those finer things, but I want to please him.

The closet door closes quietly behind me. A shiver courses down my back as his warmth surrounds me. I love when they surround me, filling me with lust and need, but there's something about just one of my guys seducing me that is sensual and perfect.

"Has anyone told you how beautiful your skin is, princess?" His fingertip trails down my arm, leaving sparks of desire in its wake.

"No, sir."

His other hand slides over my hip and pulls me back against him. My bare flesh presses against his clothed body.

"It's soft and silky. So pale that even the slightest indent makes a mark."

He touches where he bit me on my shoulder. While drying my hair, I could see the mark he left. Warmth spread through me at the thought he wanted to claim me in a visual way. Does he like the way it looks on me? Because just seeing it sent a rush through me. Every time it aches today, I'll remember his cock driving into me as his teeth sank into my shoulder.

I clench my thighs together against the beginning of an ache.

"I like to see my mark on you." His hands drop from me and he steps back. "Turn around."

Should I admit I like it too? Or would that reveal too much to him?

Anticipation wells within me as I turn to face him. His blond hair is perfectly styled. He wears a blue dress shirt with silver cuff links. His shirt is tucked into dark gray pants. Wing tip shoes complete the outfit. The blue of his shirt brings out his already intense eyes, making me want to drown in them.

"What we wear in business helps define us." His gaze flows over me before he opens the dresser and sorts through my panties. He finds a silky black thong. "What we wear under them gives us confidence."

"This is a business lesson?" I ask softly.

"Always, princess."

I love this about him. He takes the time to explain why he's doing this, but it's also erotic to be dressed by your lover.

He kneels before me and holds the panties out for me to step into. When I do, he draws them up to my hips and steps back with a critical eye.

"Turn."

I do as he says, helpless to resist his every command. Giving in to him is so easy.

He steps forward and grabs my ass cheeks. "Perfection."

I'm not. I don't argue with him, but my face heats.

"Wait there." He retreats, and a drawer opens and shuts. He stands behind me and holds a silky black bra out in front of me.

I slide my arms into the straps. He fits it on my breasts before clasping the back. It feels weird to have someone dress me. I've had plenty of guys undress me, but Seth is the first to put me in more clothes.

He lifts my hair to let it flow down my back. A shiver courses through me as he says, "Turn around."

I turn to face him and bite my lip at the concentrated look on his face. The panties he put on are already damp from his closeness.

"Stockings or no?" He's not asking me, I don't think, so I don't answer. He gestures to the padded bench. "Sit."

Something inside me settles as I realize this is part of his control. And this is something I can willingly give up to him. I don't need to dress myself. And if it gives him satisfaction to do this for me, then I'm more than willing to be his living doll to dress for his pleasure.

He pulls out a pair of black, sheer thigh highs. They're more like something I would wear out than to work, but I let that thought go. This isn't my choice. This isn't my concern. He'll dress me and take that decision out of my hands.

Gathering one stocking in his hands, he kneels before me. "Foot on my knee."

I do as he asks. He slips the stocking on over my foot and up my calf to my thigh, brushing the inside of my thigh with his fingers. Another ripple of pleasure surges through me.

"Your other foot." Over the foot, up the calf, over the thigh.

I bite my lip when he offers me his hand. When I stand, he holds my hand out of the way so he can see my body. He nods thoughtfully before turning to my sorry collection of shoes: four pairs of high heels, three pairs of flats, and a few sandals and sneakers.

He picks up the fancy shoes I wore the first day of work. "Are you comfortable wearing these?"

"Yes, sir."

He gestures with his head to the bench again. When I sit, he kneels before me and meets my eyes. "Good. Because I want to fuck you with these on. At the end of the day, I'll call you into my office."

He traces the arch of my foot firmly with his finger before he slides one shoe on.

"I want you to disrobe for me while I finish working, until you are just like this." He slides on the other shoe and stands, pulling me up with him.

His finger sweeps down my bra strap to follow the line of the cup across my breast. My breath catches, and I want to sway into him, close the distance between us and feel him pressed up against me. My eyes lift to his, and he smirks down at me like he knows what he's doing turns me on.

"Then I want you to lean down on the desk opposite me, your face pressed against the wood and your ass in the air." He steps away from me and looks over my skirts before pulling a black pencil skirt off the hanger. He unzips it and holds it out for me to step into.

I blow out an impatient breath and step into it. He lifts it over my hips and fastens it before looking at my tops.

"And then?" I ask, unable to resist.

He pulls out a silky red sleeveless top and gestures for me to lift my arms. I do it, trying to be patient for him to finish his story.

The shirt flutters over me, the silk smooth against my skin like a caress. He takes a moment to straighten it. It doesn't have to be tucked in. He steps back and looks me over. I wish I could see myself through his eyes.

After adding one of the silk scarves he bought me, he nods and then lifts his blue eyes to mine. The heat in them stains my cheeks, keying me up even more.

"And then, princess, I'll decide how well you worked for the day and either reward you or punish you."

Chapter 58

Tardiness

Blake

Seth kept Madison at the apartment this morning, insisting she eat breakfast before coming up to work. She tried to protest that she didn't want to be late, but I already knew she'd give in to him. She can't seem to help herself.

I stand in my doorway as she hurries off the elevator, almost skidding in the heels Seth dressed her in. She heads toward the break room, but I clear my throat in the quiet outer office.

She stops like I've caught her doing something naughty and looks at me. I've been hard and waiting for her for the past half hour. I tried to work, but just thinking of how I could punish her for being late made me lose focus. Which made me want to punish her more.

"Madison, come here."

She smooths her hands down her skirt before walking calmly toward me. "Is there something I can do for you, Blake?"

"In my office, now." I step back to allow her to come in.

She opens her mouth and points to the break room before she closes her mouth on whatever protest she was about to make. As soon as she's in my office, I close and lock the door. No need for inter-ruptions.

Turning slightly, she glances over her shoulder at me while she wrings her hands in front of her.

"You're late." I walk around her to lean against the edge of my desk.

Her cheeks flush pink. She opens her mouth, and I wait for the excuses to pour out. How Seth wanted to dress her, which I can't deny he did a good job of. How he forced her to stop and eat some-thing, which I completely agreed with.

"Yes, sir." She bows her head to me, and a rush of pleasure trickles down my spine. So obedient.

"Take off your skirt."

She raises her eyes to me but undoes the fastening and lowers it to the ground. She steps out of it and lays it over the back of a chair. She's wearing a thong, and her perfectly round, pale ass cheeks are on full display.

Fuck. I almost adjust my erection as she turns to face me. I'm confident Seth dressed her like this on purpose, knowing I wouldn't let the opportunity to punish her slide by me.

I stand to my full height and gesture to where I was sitting. "Brace yourself on the desk."

Her curious gaze lifts to mine before she does it. She bends over so her hands are pressed down on the surface. Her heels hold her higher than normal, and her ass is perfectly positioned for what I want to do to her.

Fuck me. I rub my hands together, anticipating the smack of my palm against her ass.

"Why are you being punished?" I close in on her from behind. Her breath catches at my closeness.

"I was late to work." The words are nearly breathless.

"Coop made the coffee and put away the dishes this morning. Whose job is that?"

"Mine."

As soon as the word leaves her mouth, I spank her ass. She gives a startled cry, but she doesn't move from her position. I didn't tell her she couldn't cry out. I like the idea that Cooper and Seth can hear her in their offices.

"Count them, tiger. Out loud. You need to remember, when you're late you waste someone else's time. Not just your own." I smack her ass again.

"One."

"After your spanking, you'll apologize to Cooper for making him start his day late." The sound of the spank fills my office.

"Two. Yes, sir."

"In the future, I expect you to be on time or early. You can't expect us to behave if you can't control yourself."

She counts as my hand falls on her ass cheeks eight more times. Both our breathing is heavy.

"Do you understand?" I want to fuck her. Slide that thong to the side and sink my cock into her sweet pussy until she shatters beneath me.

"Yes, sir." Her voice sounds a little weepy.

I brush my hands over her pink skin. She hisses, making me want to do it again. I stroke my finger under her panties and find her soaking wet. She lets out a shaky breath as I run my finger along her pussy.

I stop and grab a tissue from the box on my desk to wipe my finger. "If you hadn't wasted time, I could fuck you right now, but I need to get back to work."

"Yes, sir." She doesn't move from the desk. Such an obedient tiger.

I walk around to my chair. Her eyelashes sparkle with tears as her big blue eyes look up at me.

"Come over here."

She walks around my desk and stands in front of my legs as I let my gaze drag over her.

I open my pants and pull out my aching cock. "I can't get any work done when you make me like this. Kneel and suck me off while I work."

"Yes, sir." She presses her thighs together before kneeling in front of me. Taking my cock in her hand, she wraps her luscious lips around my head before sucking.

Pulling the keyboard closer, I work while she takes me deeper into her mouth. I could hold back my release and make her stay under my desk for a while, but she does have work to do. I let her mouth do its job to drive my cock into a frenzy until I come down her throat. When she swallows around me, my cock aches as it empties inside her.

Pausing my typing, I hand her a tissue, and she wipes my cock and then her lips. She tucks me back into my pants and zips me up.

"Do you need anything else, sir?" She gazes up at me from kneeling. Her face is flushed and her breathing is chaotic. She needs release. I could withhold it, make her sit and squirm while she works this morning.

"Sit in the chair over there. Pull your panties to the side so I can watch you fuck yourself."

Her eyes flare with heat as she hurries to do my bidding.

"Make it quick, tiger. You still have to apologize to Coop and get the morning reports done. Lots of work to be done today." I raise an eyebrow.

She sits.

"Spread your legs over the arms of the chair. I want to see everything."

Always obedient, she does as I ask. When she pulls her panties to the side, her wet pussy glistens in the office light. My cock begins to harden again.

She plunges three fingers of one hand into her greedy cunt while her other fingers work her clit, fast. I don't know how Seth does it. Watches her and doesn't take her. I want to fuck her right now.

I want to stand, kick my chair out of the way, round my desk, and thrust my cock into her sweet, hot cunt until we both find oblivion. But I don't.

Her eyes lock on mine as she pushes herself over the edge. Her mouth opens as her eyes squeeze shut. She tries to fold in on herself. The temptation is almost too much, but I remain seated.

Her blue eyes open and fix on mine as she drags in a breath.

"May I use your bathroom?" She draws her fingers out of her pussy and adjusts her panties.

"Make it quick." My voice is a little deeper than normal. She scurries into the bathroom, and the water runs while she washes her hands and maybe even brushes her teeth.

She would let me push her down on my desk and fuck her, but it's Monday morning and I've had two orgasms. That should be enough. But with her, nothing seems like enough. I always want more.

When she walks out of the bathroom, she gives me a shy smile as she puts on her skirt. "I'll get you that report right away."

Madison

"Come in," Coop says.

I open the door and step inside.

He glances up from his computer screen and grins. "What's up, sweetheart?"

I blush at his pet name for me. I guess he can use it all the time now, while the others tone it down at work. At least he isn't calling me *his little whore* up here. That nickname makes me warm in other places, but I'm not sure how I'd feel if he said it in front of others.

"I need to apologize for being late." I clasp my hands together in front of me.

Smiling mischievously, he rocks back in his chair. "Close the door and lock it. Then come over here and I'll let you apologize."

Heat flows through me as I do as he says. I'm never going to start my workday. Hopefully, they won't punish me when I work late tonight.

After the door is locked, I walk around his desk to stand in front of him. Will he make me suck him off too? My tongue flicks out to wet my lips. My lips aren't the only thing wet.

"I'm sorry you had to make coffee and put away the dishes this morning. That's my job." I swear this is just making me later. But if the guys need to blow off some steam, I'm more than willing to help.

"Seth dressed you?" Coop leans forward and wraps his hands around the back of my thighs before hooking his thumbs under the hem of my skirt.

"Yes." My voice wavers as he slowly lifts it.

"And Blake punished you for being late?" He pushes my skirt up over my hips.

I almost protest about wrinkles, but if I have to, I can go back to the apartment and change. "Yes."

"Turn around, sweetheart. Let me see what he did to your ass."

Fire rushes through me. Will he just tease me or will he make me come? At this point, I never know what the guys will do. He might just leave me aching with need all morning. No one's said I can't take care of it myself, but it's so much more satisfying when at least one of them is involved.

I turn around and he cups my ass cheeks. A whimper escapes me at the flash of pain.

"Do you want me to cool it down?" He licks my thong over my entrance.

My breath catches. "No. It's fine."

His tongue delves under my panties and presses inside my pussy. My whole body shakes with need as he fucks me with his tongue. I gasp and my legs widen.

"Lean on my desk, sweetheart." Coop's voice is soft and smooth.

I do as he asks, and he tugs my panties down until they flutter to my ankles.

His foot widens my stance a little as I press my chest to his desk. The papers crinkle beneath me.

"I don't think you should be punished for being late because of Seth. But I can understand why Blake did this. Your cheeks are so fucking red. It makes me want to fuck you hard."

He squeezes them, and I whimper from the pain and need building inside me. I want him to fuck me hard. Need him to. He pulls them apart and flicks his tongue over my asshole. A moan works its way out of my mouth.

"Did Seth fuck you when he dressed you?" He leans in and flicks his tongue over my clit.

"No," I say on a gasp.

"Did Blake fuck you when he punished you?" He pushes his tongue inside my pussy again, thrusting in and out while his fingers spread me open.

"No, he had me go down on him and then made me get myself off."

"Mmm," he hums against my pussy, and I instinctively press back into him with a moan.

For a few minutes the only sounds in the room are the low hum of his computer, his licking and sucking noises as he eats my pussy, and my breaths in all sorts of tones.

"So he sent you to me after making you horny?" Coop pulls back. "Is that what you want me to do, sweetheart? Make you horny and then send you to work?"

I shake my head, not ashamed to tell him what I want. "I want you to fuck me."

His fingers part my pussy lips, and he leans in to suck my clit. I cry out. I can feel my release just out of reach. It's so close. Standing, he removes his hands from me. I blow out an exasperated breath.

"You make me break all my rules. The office is supposed to be for work."

If he stops now, I'll finish myself in the bathroom if I have to. I can't imagine sitting at my desk with this aching need pulsing between my thighs, destroying my concentration.

His belt buckle clangs, followed by his zipper. My legs tremble in anticipation. The tension releases from my muscles as he draws the head of his cock against my clit. I push back against him, needing more. Needing him to slip inside me and bring us both relief.

"You're aching for dick, aren't you, my little whore? You got fucked by four men this morning and you're still writhing on my desk, needing my cock to fuck you into oblivion again."

"Yes, please." I'm beyond caring, so close to the edge but needing that shove to fall over.

"Maybe Blake is right. Maybe you're a naughty girl who needs to be punished. Maybe you shouldn't get to come until you're properly contrite for what you did."

Whimpering, I press my forehead against the desk. My pussy is on fire, pulsing, aching with need. I can feel him close to me. I just need a little push to go over the edge.

His finger slips inside me and I moan.

"More," I beg. My legs tremble.

"You want my dick?"

"Yes, please, Coop, give me your dick."

His cell phone buzzes on the desk beside my head, and I almost shout *fuck*. The universe and these men are suddenly conspiring against me getting fucked.

"Be quiet and I'll fuck you while I work."

My brow furrows as he clicks the phone on speaker next to my face. Heat engulfs my cheeks as I realize what he's about to do.

"Heath, how are you?" Coop slides his cock along my clit before pressing against my entrance.

I bite my lip. I don't know if I can be quiet. But I definitely don't want to alert Heath that I'm getting fucked.

"Doing well. Thought we might go out sometime this week. Have dinner. Maybe some drinks. Find some willing women." Heath still sounds just as jovial as he did the other day.

"Sorry, old man, I'm off the market." Coop slides his cock deep inside me, and my walls quiver around him. I hold my breath, trying not to make a noise as my insides go off like fireworks.

"Off the market?" Heath exclaims like it's unthinkable that Coop might have one lady in his life. "It's not Becca, is it?"

Who the fuck is Becca?

Chapter 59

One for the Road

Coop

"Which one was Becca?" It's a dick move to ask in front of Madison, but the way she tightens around my cock feels fantastic. How long can I keep her in here before Seth calls to make her go to work?

"The one with the big breasts and tight ass." Heath chuckles. "You couldn't stop talking about how you almost couldn't get your cock into her ass."

Fuck. I almost reach for the phone to take it off speaker, but Madison shifts against me, pressing me deeper again. Her pink ass cheeks are parted, and her asshole is right there. There's only one ass I want now. Tight and hot like an oven.

"It obviously wasn't that good if I can't remember it." I open my top drawer and pull out a small bottle of lube. I usually don't keep any in my office. But if anyone could make me break my rules, it would be Madison. I wanted to be prepared.

"So who's the lucky woman if it isn't Becca?" Heath asks.

I rock my hips against Madison's, drawing out a little before going in deep again a few times, slow and easy so we don't alert Heath to our fucking. "We're keeping it on the down-low until Saturday's fundraiser. Can you hold on for a moment, Heath?"

"Yeah."

I push the Mute button before sliding my other fingers into Madison's puckered hole.

She lets out a breath as her pussy gets wetter around me as I rub the sensitive nerves inside her asshole.

"Remember, be quiet." I press to unmute. "Sorry about that."

"No problem. I'm surprised you aren't fucking that assistant of yours. Now that looks like a tight ass. Don't tell Wagner I said that. I think he's sweet on her."

Madison's face is red from Heath talking about her ass, likely. Or the fact I'm balls deep inside her with my fingers fucking her ass while on the phone with a client. It's hot as hell, and I wouldn't do it with just any client. But if she makes a noise, Heath would be cool with it.

I really haven't given her much choice, and unless she wants Heath to realize what I'm doing to her, she can't really say a safe word, but she knows a snap will stop me.

"Now Heath, what kind of gentleman would I be if I spilled all my lady's secrets to you?" I draw my cock and fingers out of her before pressing my cock against her ass. I give her a moment to protest if she wants to, sliding just the tip inside. She grabs the opposite side of my desk.

"Like you're a gentleman." Heath chuckles. "If you won't go out with me, then maybe we can talk some business so I don't feel guilty for calling."

"Did you want to discuss the IT crew I'm sending over later this week?" I press into Madison's asshole, and she relaxes and rocks back against me, driving me farther in. I almost groan at her heat engulfing my throbbing cock.

Heath says, "I've got the current schematics being drawn up, and my team is ready for them. What day are they coming?"

"Let me check my schedule." I press Mute again. I shove my cock deep inside Madison, and she holds back a moan. "Did you look at my schedule before you came in?"

She blows out a breath. "Thursday morning around ten."

"Good girl." I squeeze her ass cheeks and thrust a few times.

"Coop," she whimpers.

"Just a minute, sweetheart. I need to finish business." I press to unmute. "Thursday at ten. That still work for you?"

I slowly pull out of Madison before pushing in again, keeping the sound to a minimum.

"Yeah, that will work. I don't suppose you have some hot IT women to send on the team?" Heath sounds hopeful.

"There will be one, but she doesn't like to be hit on while she works," I warn him before pressing on Madison's clit with my thumb. She squirms beneath me.

"That's my kind of woman."

"Something has come up, Heath." I'm getting close to coming. "Can I call you back later this week?" I squeeze her clit and she tightens around me. She's going to come any second too. And when Madison comes, it's rarely quiet.

"Sure thing. Talk to you later." The call ends.

"Good job, sweetheart. What do you want?" I thrust my cock in and out, watching her take me inside her body.

"Fuck, Coop. Make me come." Her voice trembles as she presses her forehead against my desk. "Fuck me hard."

I tease her clit with my finger before I give the lady what she wants. Grabbing her hips, I fuck her ass hard. My cock almost comes all the way out before I slam it back into her. All those noises she had to hold back flow out of her now, filling my office with moans and gasps.

"Coop," she cries out as she comes.

I thrust into her tight ass and groan as I spill inside her. Leaning over her, I rub her clit with my thumb and slide my fingers into her cunt, working her fast. She bears down on my fingers and cock as she shatters around me with a scream.

Madison

After cleaning up in Coop's bathroom, I go to the break room and pour a cup of coffee. I take a sip and lean against the counter to catch my breath for a moment. Maybe Seth is right. I should designate some time off from my busy sex schedule.

But I don't really want to. Sure, I'll need to work late to make up for this morning, but damn, was it fun.

When I get to my desk, I sit gingerly. My ass cheeks still sting from the spanking. When I told Coop to go hard, he did. It was fantastic, but now, I'm a little sore. I quickly run the reports and email them. Then I pull up everyone's schedule and verify everything is the way I remember it from Friday.

My mind focuses on work until my phone buzzes with the reminder that we have lunch out with a client. A wave of arousal flows through me as I wonder who I'm riding with and what will happen this time. I really need to get my mind off sex, but these guys . . .

"Lost in thought?" Noah's deep voice rolls over me.

I turn in my chair, and he's leaning against his doorframe, watching me. His blond hair falls into his dark eyes. My insides stir a little hotter. It's not my fault they're all gorgeous and make me feel so damn needy all the time.

He raises an eyebrow, and I remember he asked a question.

I laugh lightly. "Apparently. Who am I riding with for lunch today?"

My breath catches as I wait for the answer.

"Who do you want to ride with, kitten?" His voice takes on that tone he gets when he has me tied up. It sends shivers coursing through me. I can't wait to play with Noah again.

"I could never choose," I admit. I want them all. If I had my way, I would fuck all of them all the time. Of course, that would make getting any work completed impossible.

His smile is soft. "Good thing you don't have to, then."

My heart flutters. No, I don't have to choose. But Noah would have asked me out and that could have changed things. Would being his girlfriend by choice have made the others feel less than equal to him?

"You ride with me today." Seth walks out of his office, straightening his cuff links and putting his suit jacket on. His dark blue eyes flow over me.

I stand and straighten my skirt, which didn't wrinkle from Coop's manhandling, before grabbing my purse and phone. Blake steps out of his office, and his gaze goes to my ass. I can still feel the sting of his hand on my cheeks. Coop joins us and puts his arm around my waist.

He tugs me to his side. "Might as well make it official. Right, sweetheart?"

He kisses me before I can respond. I can't help falling into his kiss.

"She's riding with Blake and me." Seth walks to the elevator and hits the button. "During work hours, she's all of our assistant. Yes, she will be seen out with you, but that's the extent of your relationship outside of all of us."

"Of course." Coop wraps his hand around my hip, still holding me close. "But I can hug and kiss her in public, and you can't."

Seth's eyes narrow on him as the elevator arrives. Seth holds his hand out to me, and I wiggle away from Coop and take it.

"We aren't in public," Seth says before claiming my lips. My fingers grab his lapel as he drags me into the elevator while kissing me. The others get on, and I can feel the heat of them surrounding me, but my focus is on this kiss with Seth.

He strokes his tongue along mine like we have all day. When he grabs my ass to drag me closer, I whimper slightly from the sting. He lifts his head and raises his eyebrow, searching my eyes.

Smoothing a hand over my ass, he asks, "What happened?"

My cheeks heat as I glance at Blake and then Coop before

returning my gaze to Seth's. "I was late to work, so Blake punished me and made me apologize to Coop."

The elevator reaches the garage, and Seth leads me to the car. He opens the door and I climb in. After he gets in, he raises the privacy glass. Blake gets in on my other side.

"Tell me everything." Seth's hand rests on the inside of my knee. His thumb rubs circles over my stockings.

"When I arrived, Blake called me into his office. He spanked me ten times for being late. Since I made him hard, I sucked his cock while he worked."

Seth's fingers press into my thigh, and I gasp at the sparks flooding my system. "And then?"

"He let me masturbate for him." My gaze flicks to Blake, who sits patiently beside me.

"Did you get off?"

"Yes, sir."

"And then?" Seth's hand moves a little higher as the car rolls forward.

"Then I had to go apologize to Coop for being late and for him having to do my work."

Seth's hand inches farther up my skirt, and I let my legs fall a little more open, wanting him to touch me. His fingers brush my bare thigh above my stockings, and I breathe in.

"Coop lifted my skirt to my hips and pulled my panties down before licking my clit."

Seth's finger brushes my panties, and I close my eyes for a second at the wave of desire that crashes over me. "Keep going," he says.

"When he thrust his cock into my pussy, he got a phone call, told me to be quiet, and put it on speaker."

"With who?" Blake asks.

I turn my gaze to his green eyes. "Heath Duncan."

Blake's lips tighten. I haven't forgotten that he didn't like Heath flirting with me. Is there some underlying reason? Seth's fingers toy with the edge of my panties, bringing my attention back to him.

"Princess," Seth says lightly.

I return my gaze to him.

"Finish your story."

"Coop fucked me while on the phone with Heath. He put his fingers in my ass to work me open. And then he took my ass with his cock, pushing deep inside me while I had to stay quiet." I swallow as Seth's finger curls under my panties. "He ended the call, and then he fucked my ass hard like I asked him to."

Seth's finger parts my lower lips and strokes over my clit. His eyes hold mine hostage as he teases me with a light touch.

I let out a needy whine at how wet I already am for him.

"Did you get your work done?" He dips the tip of his finger inside my pussy, swirling it in my wetness.

"Yes, sir. Everything I scheduled to work on before lunch is complete."

He presses his finger into me and I sigh, welcoming the sensation. "Close your eyes, princess."

I do as he asks, and he strokes inside me a few times before he pulls his finger out. I don't open my eyes as I wait. Something cold touches against my entrance, and he presses it inside me.

"We have five minutes to the restaurant. If you don't come on my fingers, I'll wait for the ride home to turn this on."

Something vibrates softly inside me, but then he ramps it up, and I'm twisting in the seat at the overwhelming need to come. It halts.

"Open your eyes."

I meet his gaze. "If you come on my fingers, then I'll play with you during the meeting. Do you understand, princess?"

My mouth opens and closes. "Don't come and you'll play with me on the way home. Come and you'll turn it on during the meeting."

I swallow because I'm not sure I can sit still with this thing inside me. And I'm really afraid the second he touches me, I'm going to shatter. It was hard enough to stay quiet while Coop fucked me this morning, but to control my expressions and breathing and noises during a business lunch sounds impossible.

"Good." Seth's finger rubs my clit and I bite my lip.

I can't come. Blake's hand rests on my thigh, and I turn my gaze to meet his.

"He didn't say I couldn't help. I love to watch you squirm." Blake's finger tips my chin up, and he takes my mouth. His tongue presses inside at the same time Seth slides his fingers into me, curling inside to hit that spot that makes my toes curl and breathing difficult.

Blake holds my leg open as I shake, trying to hold back the orgasm that's hurtling toward me. Seth circles his thumb around my clit while thrusting his fingers inside me. His other hand slides under my shirt to pinch my nipple.

Fuck. I just have to hold out a little longer. Their hands make it impossible. I cry out into Blake's mouth as I shatter. My core pulses around the toy and Seth's fingers as wave after wave crashes over me.

Blake rests his forehead against mine. "Good girl."

I meet his green eyes and try to calm my breathing. It was only a few minutes. I swallow. How am I going to last a whole meeting with this toy going off inside me?

Chapter 60

Conflict of Interest

Blake

Seth passes me the remote for the toy inside Madison when we get out of the car at the restaurant. I smirk. He needs to focus on the new client, but I can focus on Madison. While toys aren't my thing, punishment is. And watching her hold back her orgasm will be enjoyable.

Though making her come in front of this particular client might not be the best idea. I'll have to wait and read the room.

Stiner Enterprises. Our history with their family is tangled.

"What did you learn this morning about the client?" I ask Madison in a low voice as I lead her to the dining room we've reserved. The restaurant has white tablecloths draped over the tables, and the waitstaff is dressed in black slacks with white shirts and ties.

"Stiner Enterprises was the brainchild of William Hartfield and his wife Emily Stiner. It's still a family-owned business. When they retired ten years ago, they left it in the hands of their eldest, Gloria Hartfield. Gloria and her daughter Elizabeth Hartfield are meeting with us today. They have multiple subsidiaries. Their headquarters are here in New York." She turns her gaze to me. "Do you want their financial data, or perhaps the current number of employees in each division?"

I chuck her under her chin. She always impresses me with how quick her mind is. "That will do for now. What isn't in the file is that Elizabeth and Seth dated in college. Long before we decided to be with the same girl. She's only his baggage. However, Gloria hoped Elizabeth would snag Cooper."

"Why?" Her eyes are confused. "Seth is amazing."

"New money." I make a low grunt because it doesn't matter to me. Back then we didn't have much, but Noah kept making it grow. "Cooper is from old money. It would have been a coup for Gloria to have the power that comes with the Graham name and fortune."

Madison stops walking for a moment, but I give her a slight tug to keep moving. "But if she really loved Seth—"

"Love wasn't a factor in her decision." I scoff. Most women interested in us rarely want love. Our power, our money, they crave it. "It was probably a move to get closer to Cooper. The apple doesn't fall far from the tree. Neither woman is very . . . romantic about alliances, especially when it comes to business. Besides, Coop was with Leighton and didn't even look at another woman during that time."

"Leighton?" Madison says softly.

I pull out a chair for Madison. "College girlfriend. Picked out by Mommy and Daddy Graham. Rich as Midas and way too full of herself. But Coop fell for her."

She looks down at her lap and seems lost in thought. Maybe I shouldn't have said anything about Elizabeth or Leighton. Most women don't like to hear about previous lovers. We try to make it a rule not to talk about our past partners.

But those two almost tore us apart, and I have no idea how Elizabeth will react to Madison, especially if Coop decides to act like her boyfriend. Fucker. I don't want Madison caught off guard.

Before I can say anything, not that I know what to say, Seth walks in with Gloria and Elizabeth.

"You remember Blake Wagner." Seth gestures to me.

"Pleasure to see you again." I step forward and shake Gloria's hand before turning and taking Elizabeth's. She's just as petite and pretty as she was in college. Her dark brown hair and huge brown eyes make her seem like a lost soul in need of rescue. That's an illusion that getting to know her shatters.

"This is our assistant, Madison Harris." Seth holds his hand out to Madison. Both women nod in her direction.

Gloria is in her fifties but still looks young. Her dark hair is pulled back in a bun, and her dark eyes don't miss a thing. She's taller than her daughter and holds herself like royalty.

"A pleasure to meet you." Madison gives them a smile.

"We're just waiting for Noah and Cooper to join us, but why don't we all have a seat?" Seth gestures to the round table where Madison is already seated.

I sit next to her and Seth sits on my other side. Gloria sits on the opposite side of Seth, leaving a chair on either side of her. Elizabeth takes the seat between her mother and Seth. I was leery of taking this meeting.

Elizabeth was the reason Leighton tried to tear us apart. Or at least, part of the reason. Leighton was a spoiled, rich girl and didn't understand why Cooper would choose to be friends with people like us.

"How have you been, Seth?" Gloria sits up straight in her chair.

"Busy with work. Building a company takes a lot of time, as you well know." Seth gives her an acknowledging nod. Her parents may have started Stiner, but Gloria is the one with the vision who took it to the next level. She never took her late husband's name and never remarried. As far as I can tell, she got what she wanted from him. A child to take over her company.

"Elizabeth has been taking on more responsibility at work lately." Gloria unfolds the cloth napkin and lays it across her lap. "It seems like young people like yourselves don't have time to find dates these days."

"Mother," Elizabeth whispers harshly before self-consciously smiling at Seth.

"I don't see why it would be a secret you haven't found time to acquire a partner for the benefit this weekend." Gloria rubs her huge gemmed ring on her right hand as her sharp gaze meets Seth's. "I saw that Morrigan Technology Group has a table. I assume, unlike Elizabeth, you already have dates?"

I stiffen in my seat. Is this why they were so eager to meet with us now?

"Not yet," Seth says with a slight wince that only I would notice. It's barely a twitch of his eye, but I've known him forever.

"You and Elizabeth should go together. Save yourself the stress of finding someone to bring. And the two of you can catch up on old times." Gloria smiles like she's made everything better.

Seth inhales before he turns to Elizabeth. "Of course, it would be lovely to catch up if you want to attend with me."

"I'd like that." Elizabeth gives him a smile that seems soft. It's all fake. My money is on Elizabeth and her mother concocting this entire conversation before coming to lunch.

Madison's hand slides into mine under the table. I squeeze hers. This isn't easy for either of us to watch. But Madison doesn't know all the history here.

While she seems like a blushing, sweet woman, Elizabeth is a manipulative bitch when she sets her sights on something, or rather, someone. Seth was up-and-coming when they were dating. Now, he's made it. We all have. He's worth a lot more to Gloria and Elizabeth now than when he was in college.

"Wonderful." Gloria clasps her hands together. "Now we have that settled."

Maybe that makes it okay in Gloria's book to be with new money. If that new money is still connected to old money like Cooper's family.

"Sorry we're late." Noah walks into the room and glances at all of us. His brows furrow when he meets my gaze and then looks at Madison. Her face is pale and her smile is fixed. I squeeze her hand under the table again to reassure her. We're still hers. All of us.

Seth stands. "You remember Elizabeth, and this is her mother Gloria."

Noah's smile tightens and he nods. "Of course, lovely to see both of you."

When Coop steps into the room, Elizabeth blushes. He nods at Elizabeth before taking Gloria's hand and brushing his lips over her knuckles. "Gloria, a pleasure, as always."

"How are your parents, Cooper?" Gloria gives him a smile as he rounds the table and takes the seat next to Madison.

"Vacationing in some far-off destination this time of year." His hand takes Madison's other hand beneath the table. "But we're not here to talk about my parents. We're here to discuss your business and what our company can do for yours."

He purposely looks to Seth to get the ball rolling. I don't blame him. These women used Seth to get to him before. Coop was against this meeting. It doesn't matter how much the project could bring in. To him, dealing with these women isn't worth it.

The rest of us disagreed, but what if they're after more than a solid cybersecurity company? What if they're still after Cooper, or even Seth?

The connections we could make if we won them as a client would be invaluable. Where Stiner goes, a lot of companies will follow.

Seth nods, and the server comes in with drinks for everyone. "We were surprised when Stiner contacted us. We thought you were happy with Addison Group."

Gloria waves in front of her face delicately, like she's getting rid of a foul smell. "They've been decent, but Stiner prefers to work with the best. And everyone says *you* are the best."

That must eat away at the woman. The fact that Seth and

Cooper rejected her daughter and still made it big. Bigger than anyone could imagine back then. They didn't realize that the four of us together were unstoppable.

Seth talks about what we can do for them as a business, drawing their attention. When the salads arrive, I squeeze Madison's hand before releasing it. Every now and then, I need to interject some information, especially when Gloria has a question.

Our lunch follows, and by the time we finish our meals, we've laid the groundwork for what we can do for Stiner.

"I have to admit, I'm impressed with how far you gentlemen have come." Gloria doesn't really relax, but she lets herself smile a little. "When Elizabeth told me who she was dating in college, I was opposed to the match. It seems I underestimated you."

Seth makes a noncommittal noise. "Water under the bridge."

Is it? I definitely want to dig into Seth's thought process on this whole thing, but not here, and definitely not now.

"Excuse me, gentlemen." Gloria's eyes flit to Madison, who she's largely ignored for the past hour. "And lady. Elizabeth, will you join me? We'll be back in a moment."

The two women stand, and Elizabeth gives us all that somewhat-shy smile before they leave. I refrain from rolling my eyes. Nothing about that woman is shy. It's all conniving and scheming.

"Thoughts?" Seth asks when the door closes behind them.

"You know my feelings about it." Coop leans back and toys with Madison's hair, making a shiver work through her.

"Did you have to agree to take Elizabeth to the benefit?" I ask, watching Madison wince.

"You did what?" Coop leans forward to meet Seth's eyes. "She tried to fuck us all up, and you want to reward that bitch?"

Madison's eyes grow wide as she looks between Seth and Coop and their stare down.

"Financially speaking, this is a good business move. Winning Stiner will bring in some of the other big names in the industry."

Noah leans back as if all this means nothing. His focus during college was on his studies. The drama the women brought made him uncomfortable, but he stayed out of it.

"We need dates." Seth shrugs, but his gaze moves to meet Madison's. "Elizabeth is nothing more than a means to an end. It pleases Gloria for me to take her, but she means absolutely nothing to me."

Madison's cheeks flush with color. That leaves me to find a date for this stupid benefit. The benefit isn't stupid. It's for a great cause, but having to find a date makes me feel ill.

"She's a fucking snake." Coop's fingers play with the silk scarf around Madison's neck. "Business is one thing. Fine, taking on Stiner as a client is a good thing, but dating her fucking daughter again? That's messed up, Seth."

"I'm not dating her." Seth raises an eyebrow. "It's one benefit."

"Where she'll do everything in her power to dig her hooks into you." Coop shakes his head. "You know this. She nearly destroyed you before. Nearly destroyed us."

Madison's face pales. Noah's lips tighten. Before Seth can say anything, the door opens, and the ladies return. We all stand.

"Thank you for lunch." Gloria walks to Seth with her hand extended. "It was a pleasure to see you again. I hope to see more of you in the future."

We all shake hands with Gloria and Elizabeth. Elizabeth stops in front of Seth last.

"I still have your number. I can text you about Saturday." She's practically batting her lashes at him.

He doesn't smile but nods his head in acknowledgment. "That sounds good. Since all of us are attending, it might be better if we meet there."

Elizabeth's eyes widen and she glances at her mother, who gives her a slight nod. "Or you could pick me up on the way? I'd hate to arrive alone. Mother can't attend. She's out of town on business."

A snake wiggling into our lives. Fuck.

"Of course." Seth almost reaches for Madison, but he stops himself.

Coop wraps his arm around Madison's waist. "We can't wait."

Gloria sweeps her discerning gaze over Madison now that Coop has claimed her. "I'm sorry I'll miss it."

Chapter 61

Distraction

Madison

Lunch was uncomfortable not just because of the company, but also because I still have the toy inside me. I flinched every time Seth went for his pocket. Would he really turn it on for a client meeting with his ex and his ex's mother?

Fortunately, it stayed still as I sat horrified while Elizabeth batted her lashes at Seth. My insides churned with brimstone and hellfire at this beautiful petite pixie of a woman with her doe-like eyes and sleek hair.

At one time, she had Seth. All to herself. He loved her. This was the type of woman he could love. Not someone like me. If he wanted perfection, he'd already had it. The woman was truly flawless.

It dug at something deep inside me, twisting me up into knots. When he hesitated to reach for me, it pierced my heart like a knife.

I know it's all for show. I know I shouldn't be jealous. He's mine. And he'll be all mine when I sleep in his bed tonight. I have him for as long as this arrangement lasts.

When we parted ways, she held his hand a little longer than necessary. His hand that made me come on the way here.

But it's all behind closed doors. I can never claim all of them. I can never tell another woman to back off my men. Except with Coop.

Coop pulls me into his side as we wind our way out of the restaurant to the cars.

"Coop," Seth says as we reach the sidewalk.

Coop stops and looks down at me. "See you in the office, sweetheart."

He tips my chin up and presses a sweet kiss against my lips. His gaze meets Seth's as he straightens. His grin is smug. He possessively caresses my hip as he gently urges me toward the other car. Tingles spark under his touch.

Shit, is this going to be a new game for him? To flaunt his newfound ability to touch me whenever he wants? To claim me in public?

Seth's lips tighten as he opens the car door for me. I slide in beside Blake. The partition is already up. Seth joins us and holds out his hand to Blake.

Blake reaches into his pocket and pulls out the remote. When did he get the remote? He presses a button. A low buzz starts deep inside me. I gasp at the liquid desire flowing through me.

"Didn't seem appropriate to tease the poor woman while another woman hit on you." Blake doesn't hand Seth the remote but kicks it a notch higher. I press my thighs together, but it doesn't help. The throbbing is relentless.

"We weren't flirting, and she wasn't hitting on me. Elizabeth and I were together in college. It was a long time ago." Seth drops his hand to his lap. He meets my eyes. The honesty would have been better before the meeting instead of letting me walk in there blind.

"Blake told me." My voice is wobbly as Blake turns up the vibration. I clamp my hand on Blake's solid thigh as I try to shift away from the object inside me, pressing myself against the back of the seat. "Oh, fuck."

I press my head back and close my eyes. The toy feels like it's rolling inside me, touching all the spots.

"She used me to get to Cooper." Seth pulls my knee against his, opening my legs.

I bite my lip as a moan works its way from deep inside me. I don't want to talk about his ex while Blake makes me so fucking horny. The toy stops, and I swing my gaze to Blake. He smirks. I take a few deep breaths as things calm down. My pussy still throbs with unfulfilled need.

"You guys have history. I understand you had lives before me." I meet Seth's deep blue eyes. It sucks to meet that history and see how perfect she is, but I keep that part to myself. They don't want to hear about my insecurities. I don't need to be that honest with them.

The car stops as it hits traffic.

Seth tips my chin up again and searches my eyes. "I promise I feel nothing for her now. Whatever I felt for her back then broke when she came on to Coop."

I swallow and nod. How is that different from what we're doing now? I have all of them. She only wanted two. Maybe she didn't want both of them? "Why didn't you just share?"

"She's not the kind of woman that would take on two men." Seth shakes his head.

But I am. Does that make me less than her or more?

The buzz starts low in me, and I draw in a breath. My fingers clench into Blake's thigh.

"You're worth ten of her." Seth lowers his mouth to mine.

Seth's and Blake's fingers slip beneath my skirt. They brush against my panties. Need races through my veins, hot and heavy.

Blake removes his hand. The slide of a zipper is loud in the quiet car. I can't see what he's doing as Seth keeps my mouth occupied with his. Seth's fingers move higher. The anticipation of his touch is overwhelming.

He draws a hair's breadth away from my lips. "Lift your hips, princess."

I lick his lips as I raise my hips. He slips my panties down off my legs while teasing my mouth with his. The toy continues to spin drunkenly inside me, spinning me even higher.

He lifts his mouth from mine and waits until I open my eyes to meet his. "On your knees on the seat."

My pussy weeps at his words. I never take my gaze off Seth's, even though I know Blake is stroking his cock beside me. I do as Seth orders.

"Hands on my thighs."

I lean over and brace my hands on his thighs. Blake eases my skirt up over my hips as he turns the vibrator up. My head hangs between my arms right above Seth's hard cock straining against his pants. My body pulses in time with the vibrations. My pussy aches. I can almost feel Blake staring at my pussy, seeing it dripping with longing. I need his cock in me so badly.

"Lay your head in my lap."

I turn my head to face his cock and rest my ear against his thigh.

"Spread your legs apart, tiger." Blake's voice makes me tighten in anticipation, knowing he's watching my pussy open for him.

Seth reaches down, unbuckles his belt, and lowers his zipper. I lick my lips as he takes out his thick, hard cock. "I want you to suck on it while Blake fucks your cunt."

Beyond caring about any other woman, I whimper, needing it, wanting it. Aching for it.

He guides his cock to my lips, and I open for him. He slides in at the same time Blake presses against my entrance. The toy buzzes inside me and he's not drawing it out.

I didn't get a chance to look at the toy when Seth put it in, but it rubs against my G-spot as Blake's thick cock eases inside with it. A moan escapes me. So much pressure, so fucking full.

My lips close around the head of Seth's cock, and I suck on it like a lollipop, running my tongue through his slit. Blake pushes in until I feel his balls against my pussy. He holds himself there while I get used to the feeling of him and the vibrator inside me together.

Seth brushes my hair away from my cheek. His finger strokes my lips around his cock. "Blake's going to fuck you, but you're just going to suck my cock. Don't move from this position. Do you understand me, princess? Tap my leg twice."

Whimpering in need, I tap twice. I love when he tells me what to do. I burn for it. Seth's hand takes hold of the hem of my shirt and pulls it up over my breasts. His fingers work under my bra, and he tugs on my tight nipple. Blake grips my hips firmly as he turns up the vibration and eases out of me before thrusting back in.

My body aches with the need to come, so fucking full and over-stimulated. Every time Blake pulls out, the vibrator rolls inside me and I can barely think to suck on Seth's cock. Seth's fingers work my nipple, sending pings of pleasure straight to my pussy.

The vibrator shifts and hits something inside me that lights me up like a slot machine. I suck on Seth's cock as I explode into a million pieces. White spots fill my vision like fireworks. Blake groans as my already full pussy tightens around him and the toy.

Seth's hand travels lower and presses against my clit, shattering me again. Or still. Blake keeps thrusting into me, and my world narrows down to these two men fucking me, filling me with their cocks, bringing me pleasure.

Blake thrusts one last time, and his cock pulses his release deep inside me. Seth's groan warns me before his cock jerks and spills into my mouth. I suck and swallow as I come down from my high.

When the toy stops buzzing, I can breathe again.

"Your ass is still pink from my hand." Blake caresses my ass cheek. It stings a little.

Seth removes his cock from my mouth and rights his clothes. His hand caresses my jaw, and his thumb strokes my lower lip. "You're amazing, princess."

When Blake draws his cock out of me, I lift so I'm on all fours. The toy is still inside me. Blake presses his fingers into my pussy, and I rock back against them.

"Leave it." Seth turns my face to his. "When we get back, clean it off and put it back in. I want to play with you this afternoon."

I whimper, knowing work is going to be more difficult than normal. Blake keeps teasing me with his fingers on the way to the office. Seth draws my lips to his, exploring my mouth with his tongue like we have all the time in the world. When Blake leans in and sucks on my clit, I explode one more time with a loud moan.

As the car pulls into the garage, the guys help me back into my underwear and straighten my clothes. Blake hands Seth the remote. Seth's smirk is a little evil as we step onto the elevator. Blake backs me against the wall and kisses me. His hands cradle my ass and press me against him tight.

The vibrator pulses on and off as Blake devours my mouth. I can taste myself on his tongue. I get right to the edge of an orgasm, and the vibrator shuts off as the elevator dings our arrival.

Blake gives me a half smile as he pulls away. "Next time, tiger."

I blow out a breath. This will be a long day.

***

Seth

Seeing Elizabeth gave me echoes of past feelings. I remembered how we used to be when we spent time together, especially at first. Those warm feelings that accompany falling in love, followed by the blistering sense of betrayal when Coop showed me who she really was.

Fuck. It's ruining my focus this afternoon.

Playing with Madison in the car helped to calm things down for a while, but it's been an hour now. I pick up the remote and glance at my open door. I can see the edge of her desk and hear her typing away.

I click the vibrator on low, and she lets out a startled gasp. The typing stops. My lips curve into a smile. I let it go for a few seconds and then turn it off. The typing resumes.

After reading a report for a few minutes, I press the button again and ramp it up to high. A soft *oh fuck* sounds from the outer office.

Fuck, it's fun to tease her. Leaning back in my chair, I change the mode to oscillating and wait for her response.

She tries to type. But it isn't the consistent strike of keys from before. She might have to retype whatever she's writing. I stop it again and leave it alone while I work on a new report. A sense of calm flows over me, knowing I have the power to control Madison's every move. That she lets me. It's almost two thirty when I stand and walk to my doorway.

She makes this whole situation easier.

I lean against the doorjamb and watch her working to get ready to go get the grocery order. Reaching into my pocket, I click on the vibrator. She freezes and closes her eyes, biting down on that luscious lower lip of hers.

My cock jerks, already hard and aching for release.

"Madison."

She turns toward me with wide blue eyes.

"Come here."

She draws in a breath and stands on shaky legs. She follows me into my office, and I close the door behind us, engaging the lock.

"What can I do for you?" she asks.

Chuckling, I brush past her to sit at my desk. My cock throbs. Hearing her little noises has been a test of my control. "I've been having trouble concentrating this afternoon. You?"

She arches an eyebrow. "Just every now and then."

"Stand in front of me."

She walks around my desk to do as I ask.

"Hike your skirt up and lean back against my desk, spreading your legs."

She bites her lip as she follows my commands. I reach forward and press my hand against her panties.

"So fucking wet, princess."

She nods. I hook my fingers into the sides of her panties and drop them to her ankles.

"Do you mind if I remove the toy?" I sit back in my chair.

"No, sir."

"Remember the first time I made you strip in my office?"

"Yes, sir." She gives a small tremble. She looked so beautiful splayed before me, bringing herself to orgasm.

"Sit on my desk, feet on my knees."

She slips out of her heels and her panties before sitting on my desk in front of me and putting her stocking feet on my knees. I spread my legs wide and open her up to me.

Fuck, she's got a pretty pussy. I want to devour her, fuck her, feel her come around me. The vibrator makes a small humming noise.

"Lie back."

She lowers herself to my desk. Such an obedient submissive. She gives me complete control over her body without a second thought. This is what I need. It helps center me and makes me feel calm.

No woman has ever been like this with me. No woman has given me full control. The illusion of it? Yes. They would follow my orders after I explained what I wanted, but they always hesitated. It's subtle. But with Madison, she puts herself in my hands completely.

I lift her feet as I stand and press her knees to her chest. "Hold your legs, princess."

Her blond hair spreads beneath her on the dark wood of my desk. Her sky blue eyes meet mine with such trust. Fuck, it's powerful. An amazing aphrodisiac that makes me so hard I feel like I'll explode in my pants if I can't get inside her.

I part her knees and slide my fingers inside her soaking wet cunt. Fuck me.

"Seth," she whimpers.

"Do you ache, princess?" I draw my fingers out and thrust in again. The small cord on the toy is right there to help me pull it out, but I'm not quite ready for that.

"Yes, sir." She catches her breath.

My fingers slide against the vibrator. I lift it and press it against her G-spot.

"Oh, fuck, Seth." She arches against the desk, pressing my fingers deeper inside.

"Come for me, princess."

She cries out as she gushes her release. So fucking beautiful. Her cunt convulses around my fingers as I draw the vibrator out of her. She trembles on the desk before me as I press the vibrator to her clit while opening my pants with my other hand.

I stroke my cock once before pressing the tip to her entrance. Her eyes are closed as she bites her lip. I roll the vibrator over her clit.

"Open your eyes and watch me take you, princess."

She opens her lust-blown eyes, and our gazes lock as I thrust inside her. Her walls convulse around me, still coming down from her orgasm. Being inside her is unlike anything I've felt before. Tight, wet, snug, and so fucking willing to let me do whatever I want.

Willing to let me watch her take my friends' cocks and still wanting mine. Begging for it. Pleading for it. Craving it. Needing it.

I tease the toy over her clit while I fuck her. I watch her cunt take my cock, bathing it in her wetness with every stroke. Her legs tremble against her chest. Her lips part as she tries to keep her eyes open as she shatters all around me.

Her pulsing drags me into my release. Spilling it all inside her, I understand Coop's need to press it back into her, to make her take every drop we give her and hold it inside. She's ours. Ours to pleasure. Ours to tease. Ours to fill.

I pull her legs around my waist and lift her off the desk to press my lips against hers as I hold her against me, my cock still buried deep inside her. She meets my lips with her own aggression. Claiming me. Marking me as hers. Taking whatever I have to give her.

She's amazing, and she's mine. I won't let anything change that. Not even the past.

Chapter 62

Hands on Demonstration

Madison

My panties are damp as I ride down to let Fox up to the apartment with the weekly groceries. Seth didn't want me to clean up after. I try to keep my thighs together as I step out of the elevator to see if he's on his way.

My skirt is definitely rumpled, but hopefully it just looks like I've been sitting too much. Fortunately, the receptionist is busy and by herself today. Courtney is nowhere in sight. After this weekend, I don't want to run into her again.

Sure, there really was someone in there with me, but I can't tell her that. What if she's working with whoever is stalking me? I can't risk it. Besides, the guys want me to keep it to our group for now. And Hope.

The outside door opens, and Fox grins at me as he makes his way to the receptionist. He pauses, and she's so busy she just waves him on.

"Good afternoon, Madison." He gives me his cocky grin.

"Fox." I hold the elevator doors open while he puts the first load in.

"Give me one sec." He hurries back out and I take a breath. He's a nice enough guy. If I were free, I might have been interested in him. Maybe he'd like Hope.

Are Hope and I close enough for me to suggest guys to date? I don't know the protocol of friendships. I pull out my phone.

ME:

If I knew a cute guy who might be single, would you be interested?

HOPE:

Maybe. Is he Coop hot?

No one is Coop hot. But Fox has a carefree attitude and is cute.

ME:

Maybe not Coop-level hot, but he's good-looking. I don't know much about him. He delivers the groceries.

HOPE:

??

ME:

I'll text you when we head back down to the lobby, so you can sneak a peek at him on his way out.

HOPE:

Ok

Fox returns with the second load, and I slip my phone into my pocket.

"You made it another week," he exclaims as I push the button for the apartment level.

"So have you." I raise my eyebrow.

He grins and leans into the corner with his hands in his pockets. "You liking the job?"

"It suits me." Warmth creeps up my neck. This morning and afternoon have been busy, and I still have work to do, but my bosses like to fuck me. And often. And I definitely enjoy being fucked by them.

"You definitely aren't like the others." He chuckles.

I don't even want to know what that means. The elevator reaches our floor, and I hold the door open while he unloads. I hurry to the apartment door to open it for him as he carries a couple of bags inside.

Helping him bring in the bags, I set them on the counter. When we finish, I take out my phone and text Hope the word *Now*.

"You sure you don't want me to help put these away?" Fox blows his hair out of his eyes as he looks me over. He's asked that every week so far. It's kind of sweet, but also not allowed.

"I've got it from here." I lead him to the door and call the elevator. "Thank you for the offer."

Fox shrugs as he enters the elevator. "If I thought you'd say yes, I'd ask you to coffee sometime."

"I'm not really available." I press the ground floor and take a breath. Thank goodness I now have an excuse. "I'm seeing someone."

"Knew I should have asked weeks ago."

Smiling softly to let him down easy, I shake my head. "Not sure the answer would have been yes then, either."

"That's a shame." Fox leans into the corner.

The elevator is mercifully quick, and when the doors open, Fox flashes me a grin. "See you next week."

My gaze darts around, looking for Hope. "Yeah, see you."

He heads out with his hands in his pockets, whistling. I pull out my phone and check to see if Hope read my text.

"Hold the elevator."

The receptionist looks at who called out. I turn to see Coop heading toward me. He gives me a huge grin and pulls me into his arms. I don't have time to react as his lips take mine. This isn't a light peck but a we're-definitely-fucking type of kiss. For a moment, everything around us fades away as I fall into his kiss.

"Thanks, sweetheart." Coop raises his gaze to look over my shoulder and winks at the receptionist, who I imagine caught this whole thing. My cheeks flush with heat as he straightens.

"Really, Coop?" I whisper as I head into the elevator.

He joins me with an arched eyebrow as he hits the apartment level button. He closes in on me, taking my hands in his. With our hands locked next to my head, he presses me against the wall. My breath catches and my knees get weak. The hold these guys have over me is powerful and intoxicating.

"Have to lay my claim wherever I can. Before word of you and me in the file room makes its rounds. Can't let people think I'm just fucking you." His nose rubs against mine, and my eyelids lower as butterflies fly through my veins.

"I need to put away the groceries," I whisper as he closes in on my lips again. His crisp cologne flows over me. I crave everything he can give me.

"We have an elevator ride." He skims over my lips before his chin brushes the top of my scarf. His scruff rasps against my jaw as he tugs my scarf out of the way, sending ripples of desire through me. "Have I told you how much I want to just sit and appreciate your beautiful neck with my lips and teeth?"

He kisses my neck gently. His tongue flicks out to taste my skin. The only thing holding me up is the elevator wall behind me. Reaching up, he unwinds my scarf, then lets it fall to the floor. My eyes open to find him studying my neck.

His fingers reach out to trace the marks Jeff's assault left behind. "Still hurt, sweetheart?"

My heart is firmly lodged in my throat, making it impossible to speak, so I shake my head. The purple faded into green and yellowish brown, and now that's fading into light brown. He gently traces over my bruises, making me shiver.

His fingers linger at the spot where my neck and shoulder meet.

Teasing, stroking, lighting a fire we won't have time for him to put out. His eyes meet mine. "Can I kiss you here?"

"Yes, please," I whisper.

His silky hair brushes my jaw as he kisses, sucks, and nibbles at the spot, turning me into a pile of mush. The elevator dings its arrival.

Coop captures my lips in a hard kiss before resting his head against mine. "If I didn't have so much work to do, I'd follow you in and fuck you on the counter until you screamed my name."

I bite my lip at how much I want that.

"You cause me nothing but trouble, my little whore." He smacks my ass. "Out before I ravish you."

I linger for a second. His laughter follows me to the door.

Without the toy buzzing inside me randomly, I actually get work done in the late afternoon. I changed my skirt and panties but picked a similar thong for when Seth calls me into his office.

The guys are all still working. It's a little past six before Seth asks me to come in. Focused on his computer, he doesn't say a word as I walk in. I close the door but don't engage the lock.

I take my time taking off my shirt and skirt. His gaze flicks to me briefly before focusing on the computer screen again. There's a space cleared for me across from him. I lean over and rest my chest and cheek against the cool wood, my hands flat on the surface next to me.

Seth reaches over to his phone and dials it. "I need to see you in my office."

My panties are already damp. I don't know who he's calling in or what he'll have them do. Maybe he's decided I was naughty and called Blake in to hand out more punishment. My insides churn with want. With the heels on, my ass is tipped up, and whoever enters the office is going to get an eyeful.

The door opens and closes. Seth nods his head toward me before he returns to typing.

Heat closes in on me from behind, and the soft scent of the outdoors on a sunny day washes over me.

Noah.

His hands brush over my hips, and I shudder under his touch.

"Did you get all your work done today, kitten?"

"Yes." I worked diligently the last few hours and cleaned the slate because I didn't want to miss whatever Seth had planned. Punishment is fun but rewards are better.

Noah's finger slips between my thong and my skin at the base of my spine, trailing down between my ass cheeks to brush over my pussy. I suck in a breath and close my eyes at the sparks lighting me up. I began my day fucking Noah. Ending my workday with him fucking me seems like a nice bookend.

His fingers slide inside my pussy. "Who did you fuck today, after this morning?"

"Coop, Blake, and Seth," I bite out as he pumps his fingers in and out of me, tugging on the thong, making it rub against my asshole. Tingles chase through me.

"Fuck, kitten, that's a lot of cocks. You sure you want more?" Noah's low, scratchy voice makes my pussy pulse around his fingers.

"Yes, Noah. I want you to fuck me."

When the typing suddenly stops, I glance up at Seth. He's leaning back in his chair, watching the two of us. Always watching. Liquid desire flows through me.

Noah draws his fingers out of me. The sound of him sucking them clean makes my core clench. He parts my ass cheeks, and the thong teases my asshole more.

Seth opens a drawer and pulls out a beaded toy, passing it and a bottle of lube to Noah in front of my face. I'd clench my thighs together against the ache, but I don't. Anticipation wells in me, remembering when Seth used beads on me before.

"Thank you," Noah says, making me wetter.

I don't move from my spot. Noah tugs my panties down over my ass, exposing me but not taking them off. The squirt of the lube is the only sound over the hum of the computer and their breaths. Noah parts my cheeks with one hand while his cool finger prods my puckered hole.

My body tenses in eagerness, but I will myself to relax into his touch.

"Good girl." He slides his finger inside and presses the walls, coating my insides with lube.

A belt buckle clinks, drawing my attention to Seth. He undoes his belt and then lowers his zipper. He pulls out his hard cock, and my pussy weeps with need. I lick my lips as he strokes his hand down his cock. I should be embarrassed by how much I need what these men give me. My pussy is soaking wet, so fucking ready.

Noah pulls his fingers out and feeds the beads into my ass one at a time. Filling me up. Stretching me, pushing me higher. Each one is a little bigger than the last until the base touches my ass. When he pulls out the last thick bead and then sinks it back inside me, my pussy gushes.

He walks away and opens a door. I breathe through the feeling of being full while Seth strokes his cock before me. I ache between my thighs. Water turns on and, after a minute, shuts off.

Returning, Noah puts his hands on my ass cheeks, pulling them apart again. The clink of his belt makes my insides buzz with anticipation. The slow draw of his zipper makes me shift on my heels. Everything they do right now is achingly slow.

His cock nudges at my entrance before he thrusts all the way inside. I gasp at the sudden fullness. My fingers clench on the desk next to my head. My pussy pulses around his hard length.

"Such a good kitten." Noah's fingers wrap around the base of the beads. He lifts out three beads before sinking in two of them and then drawing out three more. Then he feeds all of them in again. My pussy throbs around his cock as I pant. I need to come.

Seth's hand moves, drawing my attention. A little black box is between his fingers, and he presses down. The beads in my ass vibrate and I lose it. I come so hard, black edges my vision. My pussy tightens around Noah. Dragging his cock along every firing nerve, he thrusts in and out of me like a piston as the beads knock against each other and shift in my ass with the vibration.

I squeeze my eyes shut as Noah's fingers dig into my hips, his cock pushing me higher and higher in orgasmic bliss. The beads come out of me one at a time. Too lost in the feeling, I can't count them. They push back in, and I convulse again, strangling Noah's cock with the force of my orgasm.

"Now, Seth." Noah's voice is strained as he thrusts deep inside and roars as he comes. The beads all come out quickly, making me scream as the pleasure is too much.

If Noah wasn't holding me up, I would crumple to the ground.

"What the fuck—" Blake's and Coop's voices chorus as the door hits the wall.

Noah smooths his hands over my hips as aftershocks ripple through me. "Just Madison coming so fucking hard she strangled my dick."

Taking a deep breath in, I release it. I sense more than feel them all behind me, looking at Noah's cock buried in my pussy and my worked-over asshole.

"All of them?" Coop asks. "Fuck me."

I can only assume he's talking about the beads. Blake's hand trails down my spine, and an aftershock ripples through me.

"She's so fucking sensitive right now." Noah pumps his still-hard cock in me, and another aftershock goes through me. I whimper at the overwhelming feeling.

I open my eyes and meet Seth's as he leans against the wall, stroking himself while staring at my face. I lick my lips as my eyes follow his hand's motion.

His gaze goes behind me. "Fuck her pussy, but her ass is mine tonight."

Chapter 63

Market Penetration

Noah

Playing with Madison is too much fun. I pull out my cock before I go soft. Coop already has his cock in his hand, waiting his turn. He lines up with her entrance and thrusts inside.

Madison whimpers.

"Color?" I ask.

"Green," she breathes out.

We haven't discussed a new safe word, but the colors might be enough. I pick up the beads and feed them back into her ass. Seth has turned off the vibrations, but she still shakes a little at each intrusion.

"I'm going to need to get some of those." Coop thrusts hard and deep inside Madison. Her eyes close and her breath hitches with each thrust. Her fingers clench and unclench on the desk.

I draw out a few beads before pushing them back in. Her face is flushed with color, and she shivers with each bead.

"She fucking tightens with each one." Coop makes it sound like she's a toy. "When Blake fucks her, I'm playing with the beads."

I shake my head at his eagerness and toy with the final, largest bead, drawing it out and sinking it in over and over. The base shakes in my hand and Madison keens. I glance over at Blake, smirking with the remote in his hand.

"Fuck." Coop pistons in and out of her, probably feeling her tighten around him until it feels like she's never giving up his cock.

I yank all the beads out the way Seth did, and she screams her release.

Coop cusses like a sailor as he comes, filling her up. Her body sags on the desk and her eyes close.

Coop pulls out and takes the beads from my hand. Blake lines up his cock and sinks into her. She moans, deep and low.

"Still with us, kitten?" Even if she slips into subspace, we can keep doing this over and over, but I need to check in with her. I need to make sure we don't push her too far.

"Green—" She breaks off on a moan as Coop stuffs her full of the beads, popping them inside her quickly.

Blake grunts as he keeps his cock moving inside her. Coop draws them out and presses them in over and over again. Crying out, she shakes on the desk.

My cock is already hard again. I stroke it with one hand while helping Coop part her ass cheeks with the other. When they are all inside her again, the soft vibration sounds, and she shudders beneath my palm.

"That's it, tiger. Come all over my thick cock." Blake fucks her faster and harder. Coop pulls out all the beads at once, and she goes off, screaming her release.

"So fucking tight," Blake says through gritted teeth as he pumps a few more times before coming. He staggers back, and I slot my cock against her entrance.

As I press in, her cunt convulses around me, squeezing and massaging my cock. She's warm and sloppy wet with our cum and hers. She mewls softly as aftershocks rack through her.

Coop feeds the beads into her ass again. Pressing one in and tugging it out, then two in and tugging one out. Her pussy has a stranglehold on my cock as he does the last bead.

"Color, kitten."

The vibrator clicks on, Coop yanks out the beads and she screams, "Green!"

"That's enthusiastic consent," Blake murmurs as he watches her asshole clench just like her pussy is on my cock.

I thrust hard and deep. Her body is slack beneath mine as her pussy ripples with aftershocks. I play with her clit and she moans and comes, drawing me into spilling inside her. I squeeze her ass cheeks and lean over to kiss her lower back. She quivers beneath me.

That's it for me. I draw my cock out and head to the bathroom as Coop lines up to fuck her again. I wash my hands and cock before straightening my clothes. Leaning against the wall with Seth, I nod to the remote.

"You should do it now," I say.

Coop grits his teeth as he's trying to hold back his release. Madison's face is blissed-out on orgasms. Blake has the beads in her ass and is toying with that final thick bead, sliding it in and tugging it out.

Seth hits the button while slowly stroking himself. Madison keens as the beads rock against each other inside her.

"One more time, tiger. Come for Coop, and I'll fuck you into oblivion." Blake jerks out the beads all at once and she screams hoarsely. Her body bucks against Coop's, and he growls as he thrusts into her one last time, giving her every drop of his cum.

He staggers back as soon as he's done and drops into a chair. "Fuck, man. Her pussy is like next-level shit."

Blake slides inside her and she gasps. He feeds the beads into her ass. "One more and then Seth will fuck your ass until you can barely sit tomorrow without thinking about all our cum filling you full. Tonight, we can eat dinner while your cunt drips our cum in your seat."

"Blake," she cries, her legs tightening to hold her upright on her heels. Her panties are still tugged just below her ass cheeks.

I step forward and take hold of the beads. Giving me a half smile, Blake grabs her hips and fucks her hard while I toy with the beads. When the vibration comes on, I leave them inside her as she tightens around them. Her breathing is ragged.

"Now, Noah," Blake grits out. I yank them out as he thrusts deep inside her and roars. Her hoarse scream blends with his as they come together.

Blake leans over and kisses her shoulder. "Thank you, tiger."

"Color, kitten?"

She has one more to take, but if she needs a break, I'll make sure she gets it.

Madison

My pussy throbs, and I feel like I'm on a rollercoaster I can never get off. My body shakes through the last orgasm, and my throat feels almost raw from the screaming. But I want more. Need more. I never want to get off this rollercoaster.

"Green." I want Seth so badly.

I feel him step behind me like a heat wave. The soft tip of his cock presses against my asshole and pushes inside. I groan at the thick, solid feel of him filling me as he bottoms out inside me. His arms wrap around me and draw me up against his chest.

His dress shirt is soft against my bare back.

Coop steps in front of me and slides two fingers into my pussy. I'm so sensitive it tips me into a small orgasm. The buzzing never seems to end. Instead of coming down between climaxes, I just hover in this space of near bliss.

"Fuck, princess." Seth slides out and pushes back in deep. I shudder at his thickness inside me.

Coop draws his fingers out and holds them to my lips. "Taste."

Meeting his eyes, I lick his fingers before sucking them into my mouth. I taste them all and me. All except Seth. Keeping his fingers in my mouth, Coop sinks the fingers of his other hand into my pussy.

Seth bends me over the chair beside his desk, while Coop keeps his fingers in my pussy and my mouth. I love the feel of them all in me. I grab the back of the chair and hold on while Seth fucks my ass slowly. His cock drags over every nerve, and then Coop starts finger fucking my pussy and mouth.

When he pulls his fingers out of my mouth, I whimper in need.

"I've got you, kitten." Noah's cock presses against my lips, and I take him into my mouth. Seth grabs my hair and pushes my face forward on Noah's cock until my nose touches his abs. I swallow against my gag reflex and breathe through my nose. My eyes water.

Seth controls how deep I take Noah's cock. He draws me back and then slowly fucks my mouth with Noah's cock, guiding me as he keeps slowly pumping in and out of my ass. I've never given control to any man in my life, but with them, it seems natural. I want it with them. I love the way Seth dominates me. There's a part of me that wants to give them everything I have. To please them anyway I can.

Coop sinks to his knees before me and thrusts his long fingers into my hot, dripping cunt, filling me with so many fingers.

When his mouth latches on to my clit and sucks, I rocket into another plane of existence as my whole body comes, drawing them deeper inside me. Groaning, Noah comes down my throat. Seth keeps ahold of my hair as he pounds into my ass, keeping me under the waves of bliss.

Coop growls against my pussy as he sucks on my clit. His fingers press deep as Seth rides me hard. It's too much and not enough. I scream my release again. My throat aches, but I can't stop as I feel Seth's hot cum fill my ass. The feeling is intense and never-ending.

Noah's mouth takes mine and all the things stimulating me slip away until it's just me and Noah's mouth. Gentle, coaxing, loving. He presses his forehead against mine.

Someone lifts my panties back into place.

"Color, kitten?"

I breathe out, "Green."

Seth drags me into his arms and lifts me against his chest. My head rests against his shoulder, completely worn out. My eyes close as I fall into blackness.

I wake disoriented on the couch in the apartment. My pussy and ass ache, but not in need. I sit up, realizing I'm in someone's dress shirt. I sniff the collar. Outdoors. Noah.

My heart fills my chest as I snuggle deeper into his shirt. Protected and safe. The sound of dishes makes me turn to the kitchen. The guys are setting the table and getting ready for dinner.

"Hey there, tiger." Blake's words cause everyone to turn to look at me.

I stretch. "How long was I out?"

"Thirty minutes." Coop winks at me as he heads to the table to put the plates out. "Seth was afraid he fucked you into oblivion."

Not far from the truth, but it was all of them. My body tingles. Fuck. I can't want them all again so soon. I'll end up with a UTI if I'm not careful.

"We'll shower after food." Seth gestures for me to come join him at the table.

Blake brings over a basket of bread, and Noah brings over the beef stew. I sit next to Seth, aware that I'm dripping and wearing only Noah's dress shirt. The food gets passed around, and soon everyone is eating.

"Blake still needs a date for the benefit." Coop lifts his eyebrow at Blake. "Need a number?"

Blake shakes his head before lifting his gaze to mine. "I have someone I can call."

My heart feels like it's on fire. I don't like that it's that easy for them to find a date. So easy to find someone to replace me.

"My sister is in town. She'd be happy to go as my plus-one." Blake takes a bite of beef from his stew.

My heart returns to pre-nuclear levels. I stir my spoon in my soup before turning to Seth. "Why didn't you warn me about your ex?"

Seth takes a deep breath and blows it out. "Because I honestly didn't think it would matter. Not just to you, but to me. And it doesn't. She doesn't matter. It was almost a decade ago. And not a relationship I would ever consider good."

"I can't believe she's stupid enough to think she might have a second chance with you." Coop leans back in his chair. "She tried to fuck me while she was dating you. Pretty sure the bitch was trying to get pregnant and make me believe it was mine."

My mouth drops open. If I'd known that, I wouldn't have lasted five minutes at the same table without launching myself at her.

Noah reaches over and presses on my chin to close my mouth. "She's just a means to an end. Especially with Blake taking his sister." Noah rolls his eyes. "The whole point is to draw the press away from believing Madison is with all of us."

"Then you find a fucking date," Blake mutters.

Noah sighs, and he glances at me with determined eyes. "I'll find someone to bring. It's not fair to Madison if the press crucifies her."

My eyebrows rise. "What do I care about the press?"

"It's not just now, princess." Seth leans back. "If the press gets wind of our arrangement, it will get dragged out every time something good or bad happens to you. They'll label you as a wild child or some less flattering term."

"You want a future in the business world." Noah takes my hand. "We want to help you achieve that, and part of that is staying on the good side of the press. Your reputation is everything. Every story, no matter how small, can come back to bite you the higher you get."

I blow out a breath. As a future business owner, my image is everything if I want to build a brand. The guys took a hit when it was just rumors. What would happen to me if it came out that I'm in a contract to have sex with my bosses? What kind of woman would they paint me as?

Independent? Self-sufficient? Sexually confident? Whore?

"I want to say I don't care, but I've got a lot of career ahead of me." I lean my head against the back of the chair. "I trust all of you, especially with this and my future. Just don't fuck anyone else."

I push my mostly untouched bowl away and stand. Thinking about them with other women was one thing, but having to go and watch them have someone else in their arms . . . My heart squeezes. "I'm going to take a shower."

Chapter 64

In Sync

Seth

We finish dinner in silence, each lost in our own thoughts. What we told her is the truth. Our reputations reflect on our business. She's still young, and earning that type of reputation could damage everything she hopes to achieve in the future.

As much as I'd love to claim her as ours, it would be detrimental to what we all hope to achieve. I leave the table first and head into Madison's room. The shower is still running. I step into the bathroom and shed my clothes on the floor.

When I open the shower door, she lifts her head to look at me. Her eyes are red rimmed and her lower lip trembles. My heart aches to see her like this. I close the distance between us and take her into my arms.

She wraps her arms around me and gives a little sigh. "Why does everything have to be so hard?"

I brush her wet hair out of her face. "Anything worth having is worth fighting for."

Including her. If I thought this could work in the real world, I would risk everything, including my business. But this thing between all of us is fragile and new. The whims of the press would tear us to shreds.

"I don't want Elizabeth or any other woman. All I want is you. I promise to let you know everything that happens at the benefit." I press my lips against the top of her head. "Not that anything will. Even when I dated Elizabeth, we weren't a hot and heavy kind of couple."

"Are we?" She lifts her face toward mine.

The absurdity of that question makes me laugh. "I fucked you three times today. That qualifies as hot and heavy. I'm hard for you all the time, princess."

She shrugs as she snuggles against me. My hard cock rests against her stomach, but there's no urgency to fuck her. Right now she needs reassurance, and I'm grateful to be the one to give it to her. I rub my hands down her back.

"For now, we're in this bubble of our own invention. You, me, and the guys. We can't stay in here forever. The real world will continue to intrude, and at some point, someone might put two and two together. We can delay that by dating other people. By having Coop be the one you date." I swallow against the ache that brings inside. That one of us can claim her but not all of us. "By keeping up appearances. As long as no one digs too deep."

She leans back to meet my eyes. "But someone is already looking. I have a stalker and you have a corporate spy."

I press my lips against her forehead and hold her close for a few more minutes. She's not wrong. We have things we need to take care of. She also has her roommate doing who knows what to get to her, and we don't know why she and her boyfriend want Madison. While we have to rely on the police to find them, we're doing what we can to try to locate them. Our resources are limited, but almost everything is linked to computers now.

They'll fuck up and we'll find them.

"Let's get you washed and ready for bed."

Her soft blue eyes meet mine. "I don't want to lose any of you."

"You won't." I press my forehead to hers. "We'll take care of you."

I hug her close, hoping I can keep my promise.

After we shower, I lead her to her closet, both of us still wrapped in towels. Earlier today, I had a surprise delivered, and I want to see her face when she sees what I've done.

"We need to get you into some clothes."

Her lips press together, and she drops her chin a little as she meets my eyes.

"If you dress me for bed, I'm expecting you to fuck me. Not like this morning." She gives me a stern look.

I draw her against me and kiss her softly. "I prefer you to be naked in my bed, but we'll dress you in something to walk around the apartment."

Satisfied, she turns and opens her closet door. Her eyes widen, and she gasps as she steps inside. Her hand covers her mouth. Instead of her one little section of clothes, the closet is stuffed full.

"I might have gone a little overboard." I rub the back of my neck. Seeing all the things I ordered spread out like this, it's a lot. It started with just a few items, some lingerie, some panties and bras. Then some skirts. Blouses. Of course, dresses.

"You bought all this for me?" Her fingertips trail over the fabric as her wide eyes take everything in.

"Shoes, clothes, dresses, panties, bras, slips, nightgowns, lingerie, pajamas, t-shirts, jeans." The list goes on. "If you think of it, I'm sure I bought it."

"Why?" She finally turns those baby blues on me.

I close in on her and take the towel from her body. "Every inch of you should be wrapped in the best money has to offer. You're gorgeous and kind and intelligent. I want to dress you in clothes I chose for you. It's a small way to claim you, even if I can't do it publicly."

Her blush covers her from the tops of her breasts to her cheeks. Her brow furrows as her gaze runs the length of the closet. "This must have cost a fortune."

"Not even close." I draw her into my arms. The towel wrapped around my waist is the only thing between our bodies. Her breasts crush against my chest as I look down at her. "This brings me pleasure. I love seeing you wear the scarves that I gave you. I can't wait to see you in the clothes I bought for you."

She heads to the back of the closet and pulls out one of the evening gowns. "And these?"

"You can't go to the benefit in your sundress, princess. Not on the arm of a Graham."

She frowns at that last part. We've been isolated here. But we're about to step into another world on Saturday. A world Coop grew up in. One that the rest of us are tolerated in as wealthy businessmen. One we hoped to shelter her from.

I hold out my hand. She releases the dress and it slides back into place. When her hand tucks into mine, I lead her to the bench.

"Stay here."

I go to the dresser with her panties and new lingerie. Silks and satins in all colors fill the drawers. A dark pink camisole set with tap pants catches my eyes.

Setting the camisole top on the bench, I kneel before her with the pants. She steps into them. Her hands rest on my shoulders. I raise the pants, but when I look up at her, I realize I can't wait. I slip them down, and she gives me a quizzical look.

"Turn around and kneel in front of me." I loosen my towel and set it to the side.

Even though she appears confused, she does as I ask, placing her hands on the bench in front of her. Power rushes through me.

I lie down on the rug beside her legs, face up. "Straddle my face."

Catching her lower lip in her teeth, she moves over me. Her pussy hovers above me, spread open like a flower. I grab her hips and draw her down so I can take her pussy in my mouth and thrust my tongue into her cunt.

"Seth, you don't have to—"

She tries to pull up, but I hold her tight, fucking her with my tongue. Moaning low in her throat, she stops resisting and settles on me. Her arms rest on the bench. I reach my hands up to stroke her breasts, pinching and tugging on her nipples. The taste of her is exquisite and I need more. Precum leaks out of me.

Her breath comes out in little whining pants as I suck on her clit before diving back into her wet core. She presses against me, riding my face until she shatters. Her throat must be sore because she releases a hoarse cry.

Fucking perfect. I lift her and move her down my body before lowering her pussy onto my cock. Soft, hot, and wet, her tight cunt throbs all around me.

My eyes find hers blown with desire. "Ride me, princess."

Her hands rest on my chest as she raises her hips and lowers her pussy on me. She breathes out. I cup her jaw and draw her down to kiss her while punching my hips up into hers. I swallow her moans as I fuck up into her.

When she goes to straighten, I follow her until I'm sitting and she's straddling my lap. Her hands cup my jaw, and she grinds down on me sensually as our eyes lock. My breath catches in my chest at the desire reflected back at me. I take hold of her hips and guide her over me. Slow and easy. Her nipples scrape my chest with every rise and fall of her hips. Leaning in, I take her breast into my mouth, teasing her hardened nipple with my tongue before sucking firmly. Her hands dig into my hair.

"Seth," she sighs, riding my cock like this means more than just a fuck. Like it's about this connection we feel growing between us. Our bodies are fluid as we writhe together, chasing a goal that's just out of reach but not rushing to get there.

We've already burned through all the physical need we had. I pull off her breast with a pop before taking her other nipple into my mouth and sucking it. Moaning, she rocks over my cock, sliding me out a little before sinking back down.

"What do you need, princess?" I meet her lust-blown eyes,

wanting to make her come again. Needing to watch her shatter. To make her mine.

"You." Her blue eyes focus on mine. Her lips part. "You're all I need, Seth."

I capture her lips and take her down onto her back, kissing her while my cock glides in and out of her pussy, slow and easy. Tasting each catch of her breath. Feeling her every moan rush through me. She moves in sync with me as we surge together.

I lift my mouth from hers so I can watch her fall apart under me. "Open your eyes, princess."

Her blue eyes open and focus on mine. She threads her fingers into my hair.

When she comes, she groans as her body arches against me. Her already tight pussy squeezes around my cock, pulsing, drawing me deeper. The pressure is too much and my release follows hers. I pump into her a few more times and fill her with my cum.

Shifting to the side a little so all my weight isn't on her, I collapse. Her fingers tangle in my hair, playing with it as we lie there catching our breath. I turn my face to hers, and she gives me this smile that makes my heart feel ten times bigger. Too large for my chest to hold in.

"That was amazing," she whispers, like talking too loud will break this spell we're under.

I take her hand from my hair and thread my fingers through it. "Yeah."

"I don't want to move." She groans and ducks her face against my chest.

"I guarantee my bed is more comfortable than this floor." I kiss the top of her head and blow out a breath. Not moving an inch. Unsure how to process what we just did. It wasn't just about sex.

And that should terrify me. This is an arrangement. A convenience. Getting too close could make this blow up in our faces.

"I like the floor." Her legs curl around mine, drawing me deeper inside again. My spent cock hardens inside her. I could fuck her like this all night. But we have work in the morning.

Her face turns up to mine. I lean down and kiss her like it's the most natural thing to do. With Madison, it is. I like winding her up and fucking her until she screams, but I also like this.

Her gentleness and softness surrounding me as I take her. It's like those early-morning fucks. When she first wakes up, we move together completely in sync until we come. Nothing rushed or anxious.

I lift my mouth from hers and really look at this gorgeous creature beneath me. Her blond hair spreads around her head like a halo. Her lips quirk up into a soft smile as her blue eyes soften. Her fingers tighten on mine. I draw in her soft floral scent and let it flow through me.

It's too fast to feel like this, but I'm not sure I could stop falling if I tried. She's mine and nothing will change that. At least for now. She's given us her trust, but can I fully trust my judgment after everything that's happened? Can I trust her with all of us?

Chapter 65

Friction

Madison

We leave my room, hand in hand. My heart feels so light and bursting that I'm almost floating on my feet. The clothes were unexpected, but what happened on the floor of the closet was even more so. It didn't feel like just fucking, but something more. Something that made my heart full.

"Nice PJs." Coop leans against the counter. His gaze is heated as he looks me up and down. I stop.

"Thank you." Grinning, I glance down at the pink camisole and shorts. I've never owned anything so decadent in my life. The satin feels fantastic against my skin.

Seth's hand tightens in mine. I lift my gaze to find his blue eyes locked on me. My heartbeat triples in time. What happened on the floor of my closet was so much more intimate and connected than fucking. A shiver ripples through me at the heat in his gaze.

Coop pushes off the counter and circles around to me, drawing my attention. As he traces the strap of my camisole to tease the top of my breast, my nipples harden. His darkened eyes meet mine with a side glance at Seth.

"You know, I'm always up to play." His fingers clasp the back of my neck, tipping my head back. My lips part, begging for his kiss.

"Playtime is over." Seth tugs me against his side.

Possessively? Almost jealously? That can't be right. There's nothing to be jealous of since we aren't in an actual relationship. Sure, we're exclusive, but that includes Coop.

"It's time for bed."

Coop shrugs and steps back. "See you in the morning, sweetheart."

"Good night, Coop."

He gives me a wink as Seth leads me into his room. Seth closes the door and locks it behind us. I guess Coop won't be joining us in bed like he did with Blake. Even as heat wells within me, anticipation ripples through me at the thought of Seth wanting me all to himself.

"Strip, princess." Seth leans against the door with no expression on his face. He sets his clothes on the chair. Looking intimidating even in a towel hanging low on his hips, he crosses his arms over his bare chest.

Standing before him, I take off the clothes I just put on. The satin glides over my skin and flutters to the floor beside me. Hooking my thumbs in the sides of the tap pants, I lower them to the ground while bending over. His eyes dip to take me all in and he licks his lips. A flush of warmth flows through me. When I straighten, the cool air rushes over me, making me shiver as I wait for Seth's next command.

"Go to the drawer and pick out a toy to play with." He nods toward his nightstand.

I draw in a breath before I walk to his bedside. He usually draws out multiple items from this drawer when he plays with me. I'm curious to find out what else is in it.

The drawer is full of different toys of various sizes and shapes. Some dildos and vibrators look like cocks while others are stylized. I bite my lip as I look them over. Definitely a vibrator.

Lifting one, I turn it on and hold my hand over it to feel the strength of the vibration. Too strong. The next one hardly has any vibration at all. Feeling like Goldilocks, I pick up another, hoping it will be just right.

"That one is my favorite."

I look over my shoulder at Seth. That's all the confirmation I need. I slide the drawer closed and turn with the purple LELO rabbit vibrator in my hand. This one doesn't look like a cock, and the exterior is smooth silicone.

"Kneel on the bed." Seth's voice is deeper.

A rush of desire spirals through me. Today has been a lot of fucking, followed by what I can only call making love with Seth, but I'm still turned on and ready for another orgasm. One he's guaranteed to give me.

I wait for his command. Instead, he goes into the bathroom to hang up the towel. The clothes he carried from my bathroom he sorts for laundry while I kneel on the bed, holding the vibrator, waiting on him.

The anticipation wells inside me like a wave heading for the shore. All this energy shimmers through my veins. What will he make me do for him? Will he fuck me or make me use just the toy? My pussy pulses as I wait.

He steps out of the bathroom with nothing on. His hard cock is swollen and red against his stomach. My insides tense in anticipation. But he doesn't come to the bed.

Pulling a chair over, he sits on it, his legs spread. Leaning back like he doesn't have a care in the world.

I inhale, then hold my breath for a second before releasing it and hoping some of the tension eases in me, but I'm wound tight.

"You won't come until I tell you to." He strokes his hand over his cock, and I lick my lips.

I ache between my thighs but I nod.

"Turn the vibrator on low and tease the tip of your nipple with it."

Pressing it against my nipple, I suck in my breath as the vibration flows through me. I want to cup my breast and move the toy around my nipple, but I follow his commands, knowing that's what he likes.

"Does that feel good, princess?" His dark blue eyes are hooded as he watches me. His hand slowly strokes his cock, and my pussy aches with need.

"Yes, sir."

The corner of his lip twitches up toward a smile before flattening again. The longer the vibration stimulates my nipple, the more desire wells within me. I need more than this to get off, but he's also not allowing me to come. The craving just increases with every pulsation.

"Draw the tip down your stomach before sliding it between your pussy lips, but don't press it inside."

Biting my lip, I do as he commands. My pussy weeps for more as I hold the tip right before my entrance. It dances along my sensitive, wet skin.

"Flatten the head against your clit, princess."

My breath catches at the extra stimulation.

"Turn it up a notch."

My eyes focus on his hand on his cock as I increase the intensity. He would feel so much better sliding his hard cock between my pussy lips and then thrusting inside.

"Slide it back and forth."

Matching the strokes of his hand, I rub the vibrator along my slit. The need to come bears down on me, but I hold back. Wanting his praise almost as much as the orgasm. Some precum appears on his tip, and I moan at the want raging within, the need to lick his cock and take his cum inside me. All of it.

"Does that feel good?" His deep voice vibrates through me.

"Yes, sir." I'm so wet it slides easily back and forth.

"Push it inside your needy cunt, princess." His eyes hold me enthralled as I press the tip to my opening and slide it inside. "All the way."

I push it in until the rabbit slides into place against my clit. A shiver works its way over me as I hold it there.

"Turn up the vibration. Keep going. Don't stop. There."

Each word ratchets up my need as does the throbbing the vibration causes. My breathing is chaotic as it winds me up so much that if I don't let go soon, I think I'll explode.

"Sir?" I huff out.

"What do you need, princess?" He doesn't move except that hand on his cock. I need him inside me. I want his warm body to be fucking mine instead of this toy.

"Please." Words won't form in my mind as desire takes over. I'm sitting on the edge of oblivion, so close to tipping over that the only thing inside me is need.

"Do you want to come?"

"Yes, sir." My pussy tightens around the toy, anticipating the release. I hold back, hoping he'll give me permission.

"Do you need Coop to get off?"

My lips part at the question. For a second, it startles me enough to think, *What kind of question is that?*

"No, sir."

"What about Blake? Do you need him to get you off?"

I meet his eyes with a puzzled look. "No, sir."

"What about Noah?"

I draw in a frustrated breath. "No, Seth. I can get off without any of you if I have to, but I like when you guys make me come. I like when *you* get me off."

He rises from the chair. "Don't remove the toy. Turn around and hold on to the headboard."

My pussy flutters, so close to release I'm not sure I can hold it back. I don't know what he'll do if I come without permission. Blake would spank me but Seth is a mystery. The drawer opens and closes, and a cap opens. The squirt of lube makes me drip in anticipation. Is he just going to prep me or is he going to fuck my ass?

"We don't get jealous about this, princess." The bed shifts beneath my knees, and his warmth comes up behind me. "But we're still men. We want to be the one our woman comes for. Who are you thinking about right now, princess?"

"You, sir."

His presence is all I can think about. His hard cock and what it will feel like inside me, moving, filling me full until I explode all around him.

His hands spread my ass cheeks apart. My mind is a tangled mess, waiting for the chemicals it knows he can provide.

The soft head of his cock pushes against my asshole. "Only me?"

"Only you, Seth. Fuck. Please let me come."

He slides his tip inside my ass and I moan.

"When I fuck you, who do you think about?"

"You, sir."

He presses in a little farther, and I gasp in air, fighting against the need to come. So tight, so full. Every nerve ending sparking. He pushes right up to the ring of muscles.

"You're being such a good girl, Madison. Not coming until you're told." He slides all the way inside me, and I shudder beneath him. Drawing my hair over my shoulders, he grips it in one hand, tipping my head back, making my body arch, sinking him deeper inside. "How much of me can you take before you explode?"

I whimper at the need throbbing inside me. It won't take much. I could come right now just from his breath against my neck and his cock in my ass.

He slides almost all the way out before punching back in. I moan, ready to let go. He grabs my hand with the vibrator and turns it off. "Wait for it, princess."

I shiver. He holds it there as my body unwinds slightly, even being filled with his cock and the toy. My pussy flutters, so close to release. He draws his cock out of my ass and takes the vibrator out of me, leaving me empty and unfulfilled.

"Both hands on the headboard."

I do as he says, even as anticipation thrums through me. His body is close, and all I want is for him to stop toying with me and let me come. Every breath feels like torture as he waits. His breath caresses the back of my neck. His heat is so close that I can feel him but not close enough to do anything more than fill me with more aching need.

"Could you sleep like this? All pent-up, waiting to come?" His words are whispered against my neck, sending chills cascading down my spine. I pant, knowing he could stop right now. Leave me aching, throbbing, needing.

"Maybe." I don't want to though. "Please let me come, Seth. Please fuck me until I can't think straight anymore. Until you fill me so full of your cum that it drips from me. I want it. I need it."

His finger trails down my spine as he tugs my hair back gently. "Do you want me in your ass and the toy inside you again? Is that how you want to take it, princess?"

At this point, I'll take anything. "Yes, sir. Please."

The vibrator slides inside me again, not filling me the way Seth does, but it's good. I moan as everything ramps back up. His cock presses against my puckered hole.

"Come for me, princess." He thrusts inside my ass as he ramps the vibrator up in speed.

A hoarse cry leaves me as my whole body convulses with release. I cling to the headboard and ride the waves while Seth thrusts in and out of my ass, drawing every ounce of pleasure out of me. I whimper as the vibrator and his cock trigger aftershocks so hard that I can't seem to come down.

He pumps the vibrator in and out of me in time with his thrusts until I come again. My muscles try to give under the weight of my release. My head hangs between my arms as tremors race over every inch of me, like my own personal earthquake.

My lips part, but no sound comes out. He thrusts in deep a final time as he explodes inside me. The vibrator is on high and pressed to my clit and G-spot, making me come all over his hand that holds the toy against me.

He jerks the vibrator out and thrusts his fingers inside. My pussy flutters around him as he drags his cock out of me. My breath releases as he moves off the bed behind me.

I can't move. My fingers feel glued to the headboard as I focus on breathing. A warm cloth presses between my legs as Seth cleans me up.

"You did a good job, princess. Such a good girl to let me fuck your ass."

A ripple shudders through me, loving his praise and his dirty words. He steps away again before returning to the bed and prying my hands from the headboard. I sigh slightly at losing my hold. My one grip on reality.

"It's okay. It's time to sleep now." He cradles me against his front, surrounding me in his warmth. "I'll fuck you again in the morning."

My pussy pulses like I have any energy to fuck at this point. I close my eyes and slip into darkness.

Chapter 66

Run With It

Noah

Sighing, I pick up the phone to call the one person I know will blow this out of proportion. It's Tuesday morning. Tonight is my night with Madison, and I want to do something special, but first I have to take care of acquiring a date for the benefit.

My chest aches like I'm betraying Madison, but I'm doing this to protect her.

"Noah, darling." My mom's way of greeting me always makes my teeth clench. "To what do I owe an unscheduled call?"

We have a deal. I call once a week, and she stays out of my personal life otherwise. My relationship with my mother is not a normal one. She wanted to raise a genius, which she did, but she hoped I would be more than a CFO at a start-up with my friends. She aspired to bigger and questionably better things for her only son.

My stepfather is who she hoped I would become, and she keeps trying to fit me into his shoes. Wealthy, expensive shoes with the perfect rich girl on my arm to increase our *position* in life.

"I need to find someone to attend a benefit with me on Friday." As soon as the words leave my mouth, I wish I could take them back.

She's pestered me for years about letting her set me up. It's a hot topic of conversation for our weekly call.

"I have just the woman for you. She's sweet and knows when to talk and when to keep quiet. She'll be perfect for you." I can almost imagine my mother's hands rubbing together.

"It's just for the night, Mom. That's it. It's not a first date or the start of a relationship. I don't have time for that." I rub my forehead at the headache forming. For the next month, all my mom will want to talk about is how this went with her choice and why haven't I contacted the woman and we should all have dinner together.

"You'll never have time with an attitude like that. Besides the right woman could change your mind. Especially someone as special as Sara Morris. She's perfect for you."

For a moment, I consider telling my mom to forget it, but then Madison steps into my open doorway and pauses before knocking. Her bright blue eyes meet mine with a question in them.

That sigh works its way back up. I'm doing this to protect her. To keep the reporters from digging into why none of us are dating other people.

"Send her my number. Tell her it's formal. Text is best." I blow out a breath, and Madison's eyebrow rises. I wave her inside.

"You're going to love her. Just wait and see." Mom sounds all glowy. I just shake my head.

"I'll talk to you Saturday morning."

Madison stands uncertain before my desk.

"I can't wait." Mom is way too pleased with herself and hangs up before I can tell her to forget it.

"You okay?" Madison asks.

Setting my phone on the desk, I look at her. A flowing black skirt sways around her knees, and a creamy silk button-down shirt hides her breasts. "Better now that you're here. Close the door."

Without hesitation, she does as I ask.

"Come here." I need to work off this tension tying me in knots and only have a little time before lunch to do it. The phone call was necessary, but every part of me aches at having to concede to this.

She walks around my desk to stand beside me. She's beautiful in her submission and fierce when she takes control. Next time we play, I'll hand her the reins again, but not today. This boiling cauldron in my gut needs an outlet.

"May I take control?" I meet her blue eyes and something softens in them.

"Always," she says quietly.

"Take off your underwear." I reach into my desk drawer and pull out a length of rope.

She drops her panties on the edge of my desk and looks at me expectantly.

"Turn around and put your hands behind your back."

"I take it the 'her' you were referring to is your date to the benefit." She turns and puts her hands together.

"My mother has found me a date." I quickly tie them in a double column knot. Spinning her to face me, I run my fingers over the hem of her skirt. "I wouldn't take someone else if I didn't feel like it's necessary."

She bites her lip and nods.

"Down on your knees."

She sinks to her knees on the carpet before me as I undo my belt and pants. As I pull my hard cock out, she licks her lips, like she can't wait to get it in her mouth. Fuck, she's perfect for us.

I grab the bun she's wearing today. "I'm going to go hard and fast. You need me to stop"—I pick up a small paperweight off my desk—"drop this."

"Okay." She swallows as I put the paperweight in her hand. Her bright eyes search mine. "Use me, Noah."

When I straighten, I aim my cock toward her mouth and push inside, dragging her head all the way forward by her bun. Her throat tightens around my tip as her nose presses against my abs. "Fuck. Your mouth is so fucking good."

I pull her back, and she curls her tongue around me as she sucks. I don't want it nice. Giving this opportunity to my mother will have repercussions for weeks. She'll want to know if I've thought about calling Sara. If I've asked her out again. If she's reached out to me and why haven't I gotten back to her.

It will be hell, but this woman on her knees before me, sucking my cock like it's her favorite flavor, makes it worth it.

But right now, I need to use her to get through this. I pull her all the way forward again. Her throat swallows around me, and I hold her there for a few seconds before pulling back.

She inhales around my cock. I look down and meet her watery eyes. She gazes up at me with so much longing and trust. Fuck.

I don't deserve her trust. I wanted to be the one to take her to the benefit. I wanted to be the one to dine her and make her feel like my fucking girlfriend, not just a woman I like to fuck.

Never lifting my gaze from hers, I fuck her face, going hard into the back of her throat before pulling off and going right back in. She gasps and tears stream down her cheeks. She's powerless to stop me in this position with her hands tied. But she doesn't drop the weight.

She can't press against my thighs to slow down every hard thrust. She can barely balance herself as I take her throat brutally. And she takes everything I have to give her and more. So much more.

My balls tighten as I get close to coming, but I don't want her to swallow me down.

I jerk her off my cock and kneel before her. Her breathing is as chaotic as my own. Meeting her eyes, I shove my hand under her skirt and thrust three fingers into her weeping cunt. She gasps at the intrusion, but she's soaking wet and ready for me to fuck her.

"Noah," she whispers harshly, longing in her eyes. "Fuck me."

I pull my fingers out, turn her around, and push her head down to the ground. Her breath hitches as I toss her skirt up. She spreads her legs open for me.

"Good girl." I line my cock up with her entrance and thrust in hard.

She lets out a strangled cry as I fuck her savagely, pulling her hips against me with every thrust until I'm buried so deep inside I can't tell where she ends and I begin. We're one.

"Fuck me harder, Noah. Faster."

Her words egg me on as I take her roughly. Every thrust nudges her forward on the carpet. She presses back into me like I'm not already pounding into her. The slapping of our bodies smacking together fills the room.

Her cunt tightens around me as she keens her release, drawing me into filling her with my cum. I thrust wildly a few more times as cum jets out of my cock to coat her walls. She lets out a little whimper as I thrust in hard and hold her against my hips.

"Color, kitten." I take a breath and check her hips for bruises where my fingers dug into her.

"Green," she sighs.

"Tonight I'm going to tie you and blindfold you." I draw my cock out of her and stand, leaving her in a pile on my office floor. Her pussy drips with my cum, and I lean down to press it back inside her.

She moans as I thrust my fingers into her, keeping my cum from slipping out.

"Maybe a gag too." My fingers rock in and out of her as her hips follow the movements. I drag my thumb in circles around her clit. "I want you to fight against it. While I like you soft and willing, I crave a challenge tonight."

She cries out softly as she comes on my fingers.

"Would you like that, kitten?"

"Yes, Noah."

My cock twitches in anticipation. "Good."

***

Madison

Noah keeps frowning at his phone throughout dinner. His date contacted him earlier this afternoon. He came and told me by pinning me to the wall in the break room and kissing me until my knees barely held me up.

My thighs clench as I think about what he wants from me tonight. Complete control over me, but not without a fight.

My gaze flicks over to his brown eyes as he regards me. There's heat in his eyes and this predatory gleam that makes my insides churn in anticipation. We've all fucked, but we haven't really played games yet.

Tonight, we'll be playing a game where I don't want what Noah is looking to give me. I don't know how good of an actress I'll be, but I really want him to be rough with me like he was earlier.

I cross my legs against the ache, thinking of him fucking my mouth and then taking me hard on the floor, my cheek dragging against the carpet, unable to stop him if I wanted to. I scrape my fork on the plate through my food, so turned on I just want to get started now.

Change into something you don't mind getting ripped.

His whispered words before dinner made me so fucking wet. It tempted me to leave off my panties, but that's part of the fun. So I changed into an old sundress that I loved so much it's now faded and thin.

I lift my gaze to Coop's across the table. He's watching me like I'm the one for dinner. A shiver races down my back, thinking of them overwhelming me. Coop's fantasy about hunting me in the dark creeps into my mind.

It's been a few days since I was terrorized in the file room, but if I knew it was them, maybe it wouldn't have been so bad. I recross my legs.

"I need to go finish some work." Seth stands and leans down to kiss me before grabbing his plate. "Come on, Blake."

Blake gives me a smirk before he rises, grabs his plate, then leans down and kisses me. I sigh as he lifts his lips. I can't seem to get enough of these guys.

He taps my nose before he and Seth load their dishes and head out the door.

"Plans tonight?" Coop lifts an eyebrow at me.

Noah's hand brushes my knee under my skirt, and I jump at the contact. He arches an eyebrow at my reaction and then gives me a grin that on most men would creep me out, but this is Noah. I don't relax though. I use that bundle of anticipation energy and shoot to my feet.

"Just going to bed. Maybe reading a book." I take my plate into the kitchen. Noah rises and follows me. His heat closing in on my back.

He traps me against the counter, and I press against his chest to move him away. He leans in and I hold my breath, but he moves away again. I'm not naive enough to believe I could move him. If he wants me, he can take me. That thought excites me. Knowing he could, but he wouldn't. But tonight, we'll be pretending.

I bend over to load the dishes, swaying my hips slightly.

Coop crosses to the kitchen and grabs my hips, drawing my ass against his hard cock. "Do we have a cocktease?"

I straighten, but before I can answer, Noah grabs my jaw and presses me between the two of them. "She's been a naughty girl. Spending nights in other men's beds but not wanting to give it up to me when I treat her so nice."

My eyes widen. I jerk away from Noah's hold. Hmm, maybe I don't want to pretend this. But I'll go with it for now.

"Maybe I want someone who will treat me better than a whore." I'm not sure where that came from, but the glint in Noah's eyes tells me he likes it.

Tsking at me, he trails his finger down my neck to the top of my dress. I yank away from both of them and back around the island.

"If you act like a whore, sweetheart, that's what you'll be treated like." Coop and Noah move together. One rounds the island to the left and the other to the right.

I back away from them as they stalk me. My heart flutters in my chest, desperate to get free. My panties are damp in anticipation of being caught. "Maybe you should find someone who's willing to fuck you."

"Oh, you're willing." Noah closes in as I stumble against the couch. He grabs my hair to keep me there. Tight enough to hold me, but not tight enough to hurt.

"Always so willing with everyone else. What's two more cocks, sweetheart?" Coop closes in, and I'm trapped between them.

"I'm not a whore." I jerk a little to free myself but Noah laughs.

"Maybe not yet, but by the end of tonight, you'll be our whore."

My hand whips out and I smack him. I gasp, and he looks a little surprised before he turns menacing. What did I just do? Coop grabs my arms.

I shake my head, dropping the act. "I didn't mean—"

"To slap me?" Noah rubs his cheek. A cruel smile curves his lips. "It certainly felt like you meant it." His laugh is dark, and when Coop's laugh joins his, a rush of fear flows through me.

"Don't worry, kitten, when we're done with you, your ass will be as red as my cheek." Noah jerks his head toward his bedroom, and Coop lifts me off my feet.

Suddenly, Noah's bedroom is the last place I want to be. I struggle against Coop's hold and then remember to go limp. It must surprise him because I fall to the ground and scurry away, running on my bare feet to my bedroom where I can lock them out. I can't let them catch me that fast.

Chapter 67

Captive Audience

Madison

My hand is on the doorknob. I hesitate for just a second, then I'm lifted off my feet.

"No!" I yell. "Wait!"

Some of the panic in my voice is real, but I know that I just have to call out *yellow* and they'll give me a time-out. If I want this to end, I only need to yell *red*. But once I'm in that room, there isn't a way to tap out if Noah has me gagged and tied up. Will he even give me an out?

Noah isn't checking in with me like he normally does, but this isn't Noah. This is a persona who doesn't give a shit what I want as long as he can take me any way he wants. I struggle in his arms.

Coop closes in on my front and lifts my feet, holding my ankles tight as I try to kick at him. "Now, sweetheart, is that any way to treat two guys who are going to give you the time of your life?"

"Let me go." I twist and turn, but they hold fast to me.

Noah kicks open his door, and they toss me on the bed. I land in a tangle with my dress's skirt around my legs. Before I can scramble up, the lock clicks into place. Warily, I slide off the edge of the bed as they contemplate me.

"She's a feisty little whore." Coop relaxes against the door, crossing his arms and ankles like he has all the time in the world. His blue eyes flow over my body like it's already his. A shiver works down my spine. My gaze drops to the large bulge in his pants. My pussy throbs in response, and I draw in a breath.

Fuck, I want them. I want everything they're going to do to me, but this time I'm not giving in easily.

Now that they have me trapped, there's little chance to escape.

My gaze flicks to the open bathroom door. If I get in there, I can lock it and potentially wait them out. It would be a shame, but if I were really in this situation, that's what I'd do. The overachiever in me still wants to win.

Noah watches me closely. His dark eyes never leave me, even though he appears relaxed beside Coop.

He's the hunter and I'm the prey. Tingles chase down my spine.

Maybe I can reason with them. I don't know the rules of the game. The end goal is to get fucked, but how much fight do I need to put up before I give in? Do they want me to cry or would that ruin things? The guys aren't really cruel. So maybe reason is the way to go.

"Look, we can still just leave. No one's done anything they can't apologize for or forget." I edge slightly toward the bathroom like I'm swaying a little.

"Why would we want to forget about you, kitten?" Noah pushes off the door, triggering my flight instinct.

I lunge for the bathroom. If I make a run for it, I might make it. But my feet never land back on the floor as Noah lifts me against him.

"Now, now, kitten." His voice sets my insides on fire with want.

"Let me go." I struggle in Noah's arms. My elbow sinks into soft flesh. Suddenly I'm airborne again, but I land with my back on the bed and Noah's weight pressing down on me. His hands tighten on my wrists and hold them next to my head. His legs straddle mine, locking them down.

He leans close to my ear and whispers, "Color?"

Still my Noah. Something settles deep inside me. My chest rises and falls as he lifts. His dark eyes find mine and hold them.

"Green," I respond quietly. "You okay?"

He grins before taking my mouth. His tongue thrusts between my lips, claiming me as his. His cock grinds against my pussy through our clothes. For a second, I forget to fight, drowning in the taste of him and the feel of him against me. Wanting to give him all of me.

He pushes up, grabs the front of my dress, and rips it down the center. I gasp, suddenly back in character as I try to scramble away from him, holding my torn dress together against his hungry eyes.

Coop circles behind me and grabs my wrists, pulling them above my head.

"Please don't." I bite my lip, waiting, anticipating Noah's brutal wreckage of my dress. I try to hide how much I want him to destroy it, to ravage me.

Grinning, Noah reaches for the rip and tears it all the way down. His gaze takes in my white bra and panties. Licking his lips, he grabs my ankles. My panties dampen more. His gaze focuses on that spot. Can he see how wet I am for him? For both of them?

With a nod of his head, Noah and Coop arrange me on the bed, even as I pull weakly at their grips.

I didn't notice the ropes on the bed before, but Noah loops one over my ankle to hold it in place before spreading my legs wide and hooking the other ankle to another rope. I tug against the restraint, but it doesn't go anywhere.

Coop settles behind me on the bed and holds me up with my arms in front of me. His hardness presses into my ass. I barely keep from pressing back against him.

"Please." I lift my pleading eyes to Noah. I'm not sure what I'm pleading for. I don't really want them to let me go.

"Please what?" He gives me a considering look as he pulls a length of rope through his hand. "You're getting fucked tonight, kitten. Beg all you want. Beg for my hard cock in your mouth. Beg for me to fuck your pretty pussy. Tell me, *Please stuff me full of cock. Fuck, I love it when you beg.*"

He wraps the rope around my wrists like he did earlier today. My pussy throbs when I remember the way he took me. Hard and rough. Not the gentle Noah of morning, but a wild side with an edge that makes my breath catch and my panties melt.

Coop runs his hands up my arms. Sparks light beneath his touch and scatter through me. "You want to tell me something, sweetheart, or is this happening? No turning back. I'm going to ride this hot little body until you can't walk straight."

Noah finishes binding my wrists and hands the rope to Coop. He moves out from behind me and lays me back on the bed. Our eyes meet and he holds there for a second, giving me the out. I press my lips together and he grins. Stretching my arms, he ties the rope to the bedpost.

"That's better." He slides off the edge next to Noah and they both look down over me. My dress hangs in tatters beneath me, clinging to my shoulders. My white panties are drenched with the thought of what these two can do now that they have me helpless. My breasts swell and my nipples harden, longing to be touched.

Remembering Noah's promise of a blindfold and gag, I spout off, "Let me go or I'll scream."

Coop laughs darkly, making my pussy ache, but Noah turns to grab two scarves off the top of the dresser.

"Last chance, sweetheart. One word." Coop gives me a look that says all this will all stop if I say *red,* but I don't want it to stop.

Please don't stop. Take me. Use me. Fuck me.

Noah pulls the scarf between my teeth and ties it behind my head. It isn't too tight and I can still close my mouth. Then he wraps the second one around my eyes. It's not completely black, so some light bleeds through the fabric. But then someone dims the light in the room.

The coldness of metal touches my skin and the scraps of my dress release from me.

"Did you wear these pretty panties for me, sweetheart?" Coop's fingers trail along the line of my panties, making me shiver. "I could just come all over these pretty panties, leaving you to soak in my cum."

I try to protest, but it comes out a jumbled mess. I shake my head from side to side. The straps of my bra release after the slide of the metal against my shoulders.

"These tits need fucked." Noah grabs my breasts with his hands and squeezes them together tight. I groan at the slight pain. But the memory of his thick cock between my breasts makes me wet. "That sounds like a *yes, please* to me."

Coop chuckles while his fingers run under the edge of my panties. My stomach twitches beneath his touch, needing so much more. Would it ruin the illusion if I come as soon as they touch me? The cold touch of a metal edge slides across my hip. One then the other, and Coop peels away my panties.

I'm completely naked, spread out before them on the bed, unable to see or say a thing. I can't move. The ropes hold me tight.

I've never been so helpless and turned on before. The bed shifts, and their warmth and touch move away. The rustle of fabric tells me they're removing their clothes. Anticipation wells in my belly. My pussy pulses with aching need.

Hopefully this game includes me coming, because it won't take much to push me over the edge.

Coop

When Noah told me of his plan for Madison, I couldn't wait to participate. While we undress and stare at her naked body spread out for us to use as we like, my cock aches with how hard I am. I could've come all over those white panties and still been hard enough to fuck her pretty cunt.

Consent is a huge must for both of us. But when Madison

pretends she doesn't want it while her eyes beg me to take her, my cock throbs with need. As long as it's just pretend and she knows at any minute we'll stop, it's good. I don't long for her fear, but sometimes a little challenge can be fun.

She would have let us tie her up and use her, but this way we are dominating her. Making her take us how we want.

I stroke my cock. Her nipples harden to points. Her breasts are full. Her pussy glistens with her wetness.

I could slide into her right now and fuck her until she begged for more. If she wasn't gagged.

But this is Noah's night and his show. He stares at her spread out before us with lust in his eyes.

"She looks so perfect tied up, ready for us to use." Noah lazily strokes his cock. "In a perfect world, I would take pictures and capture this moment forever. Record my cock thrusting into her pussy until she shatters into a million pieces."

She groans against the gag. Her leg tries to shift, but Noah retied her legs to hold her tight. So many ways to use her beautiful body.

"Shame we had to gag her." I nod toward her mouth. "Her mouth would feel great wrapped around my cock."

Noah chuckles. "She got me in the ribs with her sharp little elbow. If you stick your cock in her mouth, she might bite it off."

"Worth it."

She jerks on the ropes, mostly for show. She doesn't really want to get away. We gave her every option to stop. Speaking of . . . I grab a ball from the dresser. It's small and metal, like the knife Noah used to cut away her clothes.

The back of the blade brushing against her pale skin was erotic in its own right. But we don't get off on making her bleed. And actual pain and damage is one of her hard limits. Something we would never tread past.

I kneel on the bed next to her head and lean over her face, making sure my cock brushes her cheek as I place the ball in her hand. "Don't drop this, my dirty little whore."

Her fingers curl around it. We've done this before when her mouth was occupied. She drops it, we stop. I slide my cock across her parted lips. Her tongue flicks the underside as I thrust it back and forth over her lips.

"Fuck. Maybe we don't need her mouth to be open." I grin at Noah as he moves between her legs on the bed. She shifts slightly at his movements. I gaze down at my cock between her lips. I pinch her nipple. "Drag your tongue against my cock again like a good slut."

She whimpers but does it. Precum flows out my tip. I rub it against the scarf in her mouth.

"A little present for you to suck on," I whisper before backing off the bed.

Noah runs his fingers up her parted legs. His large hands against her captured thighs make my cock twitch. She trembles beneath his touch as he reaches her inner thighs. "So many options."

He spreads her pussy open with his fingers, and she moans. His thumb teases the edge of her opening.

"We could fuck you separately or together. We could just keep you open for us while we jerked off all over your body and then rubbed our cum into your skin." Noah presses the tip of his thumb into her cunt. "You'd like that, wouldn't you? Being covered in our cum while we fucked you over and over again."

She moans as her hips push against his finger.

"You want that, don't you, my little whore?" I slide my finger up the arch of her foot, and she jerks.

Noah pushes his thumb inside her. She moans. "If she wants it, then we should make sure she's hot for it."

He pulls out and she whimpers. His gaze meets mine, and he nods up her body as he lowers himself to the bed between her legs. I sit next to her on the bed.

"Do you want us to make you come, slut?" I pinch her nipple and she inhales sharply.

"I think that's a yes." Noah laughs as he presses his tongue against her clit before licking her pussy. Her hips rock with the motion.

"How does she taste?" I roll her nipple between my fingers gently. She sucks in a breath.

"Sweet." Noah sucks on her clit, and her body arches as much as it can. A moan escapes her mouth. "I could spend hours sucking on her little clit."

Her moans grow as he returns to sucking. I pinch her other nipple before lowering my mouth over her breast and suckling her.

"She likes that," Noah says. I lift my head to watch him thrust three fingers inside her. "Her cunt is dripping for us."

She moans and mumbles something against the scarf.

"What's that? More?" I lean toward her mouth like I'm trying to listen to her. "Pretty sure she wants more."

Noah smirks before lowering his mouth to her pussy. I take her nipple into my mouth and suck, making her skin redden. I tease the other nipple with my fingers, pulling, pinching, rolling.

Her breathing is uneven. Her hips sway with every move of Noah's tongue and fingers on her, in her. I lift my mouth from her breast and stare down at the redness I've left behind. I kiss it one more time before moving to her other nipple and sucking it hard.

She moans as her body arches against me.

"Her cunt is so fucking hot and tight. I can't wait to put my cock in it."

I shift to watch Noah fuck her with his fingers. They glisten with her wetness as she moans and whimpers with every thrust. I ease my fingers down her stomach and toy with her clit, rubbing her pussy in circles while he finger fucks her cunt.

The scarf muffles her cry as she arches against us again. I slip a finger inside with his, stretching her, to feel her pulse around us.

"You like that? Our fingers inside your cunt, fucking you until you come like a good little whore?" I lean down and suck on her clit.

"Fuuuu," is all that gets past the scarf as her pussy gushes its release around our hands.

Noah meets my eyes. "Trade."

I nod and he straddles her stomach. He grabs the lube from the bedside table and squirts it between her breasts.

She makes an indignant noise as he rubs it around her breasts and over his cock before passing it to me.

"Fuck her ass. Save her pussy for last. We'll have a grand finale." Noah winks before he rubs his fingers around her nipples, red and sensitive from my attention.

"I bet I'm going to love fucking your ass, my little whore. Pushing my fat cock inside your tight little hole until you can't stop coming." I lube up my cock before sliding my hands beneath her and between her ass cheeks. There's enough give in the rope that her legs can bend slightly. I slide my fingers into her ass and lower my mouth to her clit, sucking, licking, teasing.

She twists beneath me as much as she can as she releases a muffled cry.

Noah has his cock in between her breasts. I stop to watch him glide in and out of them while I fuck her ass with my fingers. I pull my fingers out when she tightens around them and thrust my cock into her puckered hole.

She moans. I match Noah's hips as I fuck her ass while he fucks her tits.

"We really should record this so she can watch it. So she can see how well she takes cock." I part her ass cheeks as I watch my cock shuttle in and out of her.

She whimpers as her breath quickens.

"Ball check," I say.

Noah chuckles darkly. "Clutched so hard, like she never wants to let it go. Like she wants us to fuck her until she can't stop coming."

Noah increases his pace and I match him. She tightens all around me, her hot, tight ass forming a fist around my cock. I drive in one last time and explode, filling her with my cum, shuddering through my release and watching her pussy clutch at the air while she comes.

I withdraw and step away to wash my cock. When she moans, I

turn to watch Noah come all over her neck. His cum drips down over her and covers her from her chin to the tops of her breasts. She looks so fucking pretty covered in cum. My cock twitches as it begins to harden again.

Noah walks over to me where he grabs a washcloth. "Time to untie her feet. You want her mouth or her ass again?"

He's not being quiet. She can hear us, but this shit turns her on too. Listening to how we want to take her.

"I want to fuck her mouth."

Noah nods and walks over to wipe his cum off her neck. "You know, I think we can do this without untying her feet just yet. Make her take it until she's begging for more."

She whimpers, and he unties the scarf from around her mouth. She licks her lips.

Straddling her chest, I lean over, using the headboard to hold myself up as I thrust my cock down into her mouth. I glance over my shoulder and watch Noah slide into her ass. She swallows around me.

"Maybe we'll fuck her pussy together." He winks at me and thrusts inside her hard. She swallows around me. "You want to take two dicks in your tight cunt, kitten? At the same time?"

She groans around my cock, sending vibrations through me. Fuck, we've never done that before, two cocks one hole. But with Madison, fuck, just the idea of her squeezing the two of us so fucking tight with her pussy as we stretch her out makes me almost nut.

"Sounds like she's game." I stroke my thumb over her cheek. "Aren't you a good slut for us."

Her tongue strokes over me as I lift out of her mouth and then press down, hitting her throat with the head of my cock. She swallows around me, sending a rush of need flowing through me.

I pull out of her throat so she can breathe easier. "Suck my cock, sweetheart."

As she sucks on me, the sounds of Noah's flesh slapping against hers fill the room. I rock in her sweet, talented mouth until she moans hard. Her body arches below me as she comes.

Noah curses as he slams into her ass until he groans. She sucks on me again, and I can't hold back my release, coating her mouth and throat with my cum.

"Such a naughty slut," I whisper as I come down, stroking her cheek as she swallows my cum. "Drink it all, my little whore. Because the next time I come it's going to be with Noah in your tight pussy."

Chapter 68

Double Entry

Madison

The air in the room chills my body as Noah and Coop move off me. The sound of water running and them moving around draws my focus. I shiver waiting for what comes next.

Both of their cocks in my pussy? Together? I'm not sure whether to be terrified or excited. It was on the list of kinks and I marked it as *willing to try*. A warm, wet cloth touches me, and I flinch away.

"Gotta clean you up, my little whore." Coop strokes the cloth between my ass cheeks. The bed dips between my knees, and the tip of his cock presses against my entrance. "You ready to fuck both of us like a good slut?"

Fuck, the combination of praise and humiliation makes my pussy so fucking wet.

A fist grabs my hair and yanks my head back. Even though it's startling, he doesn't tug so hard as to hurt, just sting.

"He asked you a question," Noah says. His fingers tweak my nipple, making me cry out a little. "Are you ready to be our fuck toy, or are you going to fight more?"

His hand leaves my nipple to skate down my stomach.

Coop eases his cock into my pussy while Noah teases my clit before pinching it. A moan escapes my throat. I'm still sensitive from my orgasm. Noah tugs my hair again, and a bolt of lust settles in my gut.

"Want a sneak preview?" Noah's deep voice sets sparks dancing across my skin. His finger slides lower until he meets Coop's cock slowly pumping in and out of me. Noah's finger slides in with Coop's cock on the next thrust.

I suck in a breath as he curls it to press against my G-spot. Waves of pleasure roll over me as I squirm against the invasion.

"My cock will slide inside your tight cunt and stretch you out." He adds a second finger.

My breath catches and then trips over itself as they thrust together. My release is fast and sudden, drenching them both in wetness.

Noah withdraws his fingers and slips them into my open mouth. "Suck them."

I do as he asks, tasting myself on his fingers, greedy for all the pleasure they can give me. He leans over me and presses his lips over mine with his fingers still in my mouth. Our tongues tangle, searching for the taste of me and each other.

Coop withdraws from my pussy, and I whimper in disappointment. He chuckles as he moves off the bed. "Soon, my little whore."

Noah keeps up the kiss, drawing his fingers out of our mouths. The kiss is dark and claiming, like he wants all of me. My right foot is released and then my left. Coop's hands massage my ankles.

Tugging my hair back, Noah releases my mouth to hover over me. I can't see him but I can feel him staring at my face, at my open mouth.

"Are you going to be a good slut?" he whispers darkly, his hot breath against my lips.

I nod.

When he tugs my hair again, I give a startled cry. "Words, kitten.

Coop and I are going to ruin your tight little pussy, and you're going to let us do it because that's what good sluts do."

I swallow and inhale. "Yes, Noah. Ruin my pussy. Use me. Fuck me. Never let me go."

Jerking my head back, he kisses me. His bare chest teases my tight nipples and his stomach brushes mine, sending bolts of aching need to my pussy. With one thrust, his cock is buried deep inside me while his mouth takes mine.

Fingers ease in beside his cock, stretching me.

"Fuck, sweetheart, you're so fucking wet." Coop thrusts his fingers in with Noah's cock, making me so fucking full.

The tension on my hands falls away. They're still bound together, but not to the headboard. Noah's hand burrows into mine to take the ball. I never once thought to drop it. He doesn't take away the scarf around my eyes yet. But he releases his hold on my hair.

Just like Coop, he fucks me a little before pulling out and moving off the bed. I whine at the loss, so close to coming again. My release was right there. I crave it.

Coop grabs my bound hands by the rope and tugs me upright.

"Off the bed, my little whore."

Following his tugs, I scoot down and stand unsteadily on my feet. Coop draws me against him, and I take in his clean and crisp scent mixed with the musk of sex. His hard body presses hot against mine. Noah closes in from behind me. They both kiss beside my neck. Noah's hands slide between Coop's and my chests to cup my breasts while Coop grabs my ass.

I sway between them, burning with desire. When Coop draws away, Noah pulls me back against his body. One hand holds my breast and the other dips between my thighs. He thrusts his fingers inside me.

"We're going to fuck your pussy until you scream, kitten." His breath teases the hair around my ear as he pumps his fingers roughly in and out of my pussy. "Then I'm fucking your ass again while Coop fucks your pussy."

I whimper at how much I want that. The scarf around my eyes lifts. I blink at the low light of the room. Noah bites my shoulder, fucking me with his fingers. Crying out, I shudder as an orgasm floods me. He pulls his fingers out of my pussy and sucks them into his mouth.

"You taste so fucking sweet, like a good little whore should." He licks the side of my neck, and if he wasn't still holding me up, I would crumple to the ground.

"Noah." I lift my bound hands but then drop them, realizing I can't wrap my arms around him.

"Come on, kitten, time to get fucked." He takes me to where Coop lies on the bed with his legs dangling off.

While I'm not sure how this is going to work, I want them both inside me now. Any way I can get them. Noah turns me to face him. He grabs a fistful of my hair and tugs it back. His dark eyes hold mine captive.

"You're going to straddle Coop in a crouch, facing me, and take his cock into that soaking wet pussy."

My pussy shouldn't be able to get any wetter. But it does as I clench. Coop passes Noah a bottle of lube. I swallow at the sight.

"It's going to be a tight fit, kitten, but believe me, it'll be worth it when you feel both our cocks inside you." He jerks my head back and captures my mouth in a brutal kiss that makes me moan deep into his mouth. "Be a good slut and take our cocks."

"Yes, please," I whisper.

Smirking, Noah helps me move into position. Coop's hands grip my hips as I hover over him. My eyes meet Noah's as I lower onto Coop's cock, feeling him fill me. My lips part as my pussy flutters around him.

"Tuck your feet, sweetheart."

As soon as I do, Coop pounds up into me, holding my hips steady. I lean back against Coop's chest as each thrust pushes out a sound from deep inside me.

Noah winks before he drops to his knees. His mouth covers my clit and sucks as Coop thrusts in and out of my pussy. I can't think. I can't move. Everything inside me churns into a never-ending swirl of desire as I come so hard, squeezing around Coop's cock.

Noah chuckles as he stands, wiping his mouth and coating his cock in lube. My gaze tracks his hand as he strokes from the tip to the base. I swallow hard, even as aftershocks tremble through me. That's going inside my already full pussy. He tosses the lube on the bed next to Coop. His eyes hold mine as he strokes his cock.

"Ready to be ruined, kitten?"

My head falls in a nod even as my mind tries to catch up. Coop holds me still as I watch Noah line his cock up with my stuffed pussy. He rubs his tip against my clit, dragging it back and forth, making the ache swell inside me again.

As he slides back, he pushes in beside Coop's cock. I gasp at the sensation. For a second, I press against Coop's hold like I'm trying to get away from Noah's invasion.

"Shh, be a good little whore and take it, Madison. Take another thick cock into your needy cunt." Coop's voice weaves all around me. One of his hands lifts to my breast and draws circles around my nipple.

"I can't," I whisper, shaking my head.

Noah presses in farther, stretching me impossibly wide. He pinches my clit, startling me, before grazing it back and forth. "You can, kitten. You can take all of us inside that fabulous body of yours. We'll fuck you at the same time. Coop and me in your greedy wet cunt. Seth in your tight ass. Blake riding your sweet mouth. All of us deep inside you, filling you full of our cum."

He shoves in deeper and holds there. Taking a steady breath, I glance down. His cock is about halfway inside me. I've never felt so stuffed full of cock. It's amazing and euphoric. The thought of his cock rubbing against Coop's as they both fuck me fills me with desire.

Taking my mouth with his, Noah thrusts his tongue into my mouth while rocking his cock in and out with short strokes, pressing a little farther in with each slide until his abs settle against mine.

Lifting his mouth, he presses his forehead to mine. "What a good slut you are, taking two cocks in your pussy."

I breathe harshly at how completely packed my pussy is right now with two cocks buried deep inside, stretching me.

"Fuck, man. I can feel your cock against mine inside her." Coop tightens his grip on my hips. "You feel amazing, sweetheart."

My pussy pulses around them, stretched so far.

"Any pain, kitten?" Noah's dark eyes search deep into mine.

"No." It's tight and there's pressure, but no pain.

He withdraws and pushes back in, sinking in deep.

"Fuck," Coop whispers. "I'm going to blow like a newbie."

He's not the only one. It's overwhelming. But my insides are wound so fucking tight, they're ready to burst.

"You can hold it until our whore comes." Noah keeps fucking me slow and steady. His fingers capture my jaw and tip my face up toward his. My eyes lock with his. "You're going to come for us so fucking hard."

He ducks his head beneath my arm, and my arms wrap around his shoulders with my bound hands behind his head. "Move with me, kitten."

Tentatively, I lift my hips and sink down on both of them. Ripples of pleasure spread through me. "Oh, fuck."

"Feels good, doesn't it?" Noah's dark eyes smile. "You're going to be begging for us to double dick you all the time."

Our bodies move in sync as I work to slide off Coop while Noah draws out a little. When he presses forward, I take them both back inside. My brain shuts off, a slave to the motion and the stroking and the fire burning through me, filling me, setting me aflame.

"Come like a good slut." Noah reaches between us and presses down on my clit.

I shatter, clenching around their cocks and barely registering the scream coming out of me. Their groans mingle with my scream as they fill me with their cum. My body convulses as my orgasm keeps shuddering through me, tightening around them almost painfully.

Noah's mouth comes down over mine as his cock keeps jerking inside me. I can't breathe. I can't think. All I can do is feel this sense of completeness and aching stretching. This amazing euphoria of orgasmic pleasure.

I've never felt anything like this before. Their cocks twitch inside me, and I can feel every movement. My arms drape around Noah's neck, holding me up as I meet his dark eyes.

"You did wonderful, kitten, but we're not done with you yet."

Chapter 69

Sixty-Nine

Noah

I lift my head and press kisses to Madison's nose, eyes, and lips. Fuck, she's amazing. As I pull out, she whimpers a little, but Coop curses.

I meet his eyes as he meets mine. We've never done that before. We've done a lot of things together, but never something as intimate. Group sex means sometimes I'm going to rub up against someone else's cock. It's inevitable. But being squeezed together while my cock slid along his was something else.

Having his cock brushing against mine inside Madison's tight cunt made the whole experience ten times better. He smirks at me, probably thinking the same thing.

We're going to fuck Madison like that again and again.

I take Madison's hands as she looks up at me. "Turn around on Coop's cock, kitten. We'll take a little break, and then we're going to fuck you again."

Her eyes widen. "I don't think—"

Pressing my finger to her lips, I say, "I'm going to take your ass, and Coop's going to take your pussy."

Her blue eyes are bright and relieved. "Okay."

I help her pivot over Coop with him still buried inside her. When she's turned, she lowers her knees to the bed, and Coop draws her down on his chest.

Lying down beside Coop, I stroke my hand over her back and side. She sighs softly as she burrows into Coop. I could love her. I might already be in love with her.

The thoughts fill me as she opens her soft blue eyes to look at me. She trusts me. It hits me with all the softness of a fully loaded truck. My chest fills.

I love her.

It's so simple and wondrous. I've never loved anyone before, but I've never met anyone like Madison. "Color, kitten?"

"Green," she whispers as my fingers float down her back.

I want to give her everything she could ever desire. I want to fulfill her every need. I want her to love me in return, just a little bit.

"Did you like your night?" I ask.

Her eyebrow perks up and she smiles. "Yes."

"Anything too much?"

She shakes her head.

Coop reaches up and strokes his hand over her hair, drawing it away from her face.

"What about what we said?" he asks. "Was it too much? Not enough?"

She props her bound hands on his chest and looks into his eyes. "It was perfect. You reminded me to use my safe words, and you gave me something to get out of it if it got to be too much."

She rests her cheek against his heart as she meets my eyes again. My heart swells too much, making it hard to breathe.

"I liked the adrenaline of fighting back, but I like submitting too. I wasn't sure what your expectations were." She reaches out with her bound hands and cups my cheek. "Sorry I smacked you. I got carried away."

I put my hand over hers, loving her soft touch. "It was a good and honest reaction."

"I'm not opposed to playing this again." Her eyes widen and she glances down at Coop. "Already?"

He gives her a wink. "You make me horny, sweetheart."

Touching Madison, talking about what we've done to her, makes my cock rise as well. Standing, I grab the lube and spread it on my cock. It hardens even more as she licks her lips, watching my hand like she wants to be the one touching me.

She presses her bound hands against Coop's chest and sits upright on him. Sliding my arm beneath her breasts, I hold her tight against my body.

"Are you going to be a good whore?" I slip my hand between our bodies and thrust my lube-covered fingers into her asshole.

She moans. "Yes, use me. Make me your whore."

Kissing her neck, I press my cock's head against her puckered hole. "Good kitten."

In one thrust of my hips, I'm fully inside her. She sucks in a breath and tightens at the intrusion. Coop reaches forward and teases her clit, making her relax again.

"I'm curious, slut. Which do you like better? Us both in your slick cunt or one in your pussy and one in your ass?"

"Oh, fuck. All of it. I'll take it however you give it to me." She moans as I draw out and punch back in roughly. "Use me however you want. I'm yours."

"Good answer," I murmur against her ear as I kiss down her neck softly. I want to suck and bite a trail down her neck, letting everyone know she's mine, but she's still healing. The bruises fade a little more with every passing day. "Friday night, don't wear panties to the benefit. Coop and I want to use you. Take you into corners and fill you with our cum until it's running down your thighs."

"Fuck me. Anytime, anywhere. I'm yours." She leans back against me as Coop punches up into her while I thrust into her ass. We move together, fucking her as one, as she pants between us. Her bound hands rest on his chest.

I take her breasts into my hands and torment her nipples with my fingers while Coop teases her clit with his thumb. Her ass convulses around me as she cries out her release. We don't let up, keeping her in that heightened state as we work her body between us.

Every shift of our cocks, Coop's dick rubs against mine through the wall. It isn't the same as being buried in her tight pussy together, but it's enough with Madison coming around us to throw me over the edge into oblivion.

I thrust into her ass and explode. My vision darkens for a moment as the waves of my release take me under. I pull out of her and collapse on the bed next to Coop. He turns her between us, and she lies on her back, taking in short quick breaths.

I take her hand in mine and realize she's still bound. Lifting her hands in front of me, I untie my knot, letting the rope slide to the floor. I hold her hand against my settling heart.

I love this woman, but I'm not sure I can hold on to her if the others let her go. She's mine, but she's also theirs, and they're my brothers. I couldn't give them up to be with her, but would she be with just me if it came down to that decision?

She snuggles against me. "Thank you."

Suddenly, she makes a startled noise, and I glance down to see Coop thrusting his fingers into her cunt.

"Keep that cum inside you, sweetheart." Coop chuckles softly. "We worked hard to put it in there."

I don't have to worry about the future right now. Even though part of me wants to plan for it, I know it's not something I can work out anytime soon. I press Madison's head against my chest and draw in a deep breath.

Another day, I'll worry about what the future holds.

Madison

My dreams are steeped in erotic images and touches. Slowly my brain wakes to actual hands touching all over my body. Coop's mouth is on my pussy, sucking on my clit. Noah's fingers are buried inside my slick channel, thrusting in and out. Their other hands caress my breasts. The raging inferno inside me bursts.

I arch my back and cry out as my orgasm pounds through me. I'm awake now. Mostly.

Coop lifts his head and his blue eyes meet mine. His lips and chin glisten from my wetness as he gives me a satisfied grin. "Good morning, sweetheart."

Noah rises over me. "You ready for more, kitten?"

I bite my lip as he caresses my nipple with his thumb. His lips capture mine, leaving me aching with want.

When he lifts his head, he smiles. "I want to taste you when you come."

Noah draws me down into the center of the bed and turns me on my side, lying down in front of me with his head in front of my pussy and his hard, thick cock in my face. He lifts my leg over him as he rests his head against my thigh. His tongue slides over my sensitive clit.

Inhaling sharply at the tingles swarming my body, I lick the tip of his cock and his salty precum beading on it. I love the taste of him. Noah groans against my pussy, causing shivers to rush through me. Fully awake now, I shift until I can draw him deeper into my mouth and work his cock while his tongue flicks over my clit before pressing into my core.

Behind me, Coop draws his hand down my spine until his hand cups my ass cheek. He lifts it, and the head of his cock presses against my asshole. I pause my sucking as I wait in anticipation. Noah grabs my hips to hold me still as he keeps fucking my pussy with his tongue.

Trying to focus on what I'm doing and not what's being done to me, I suck on the head of Noah's cock. Coop grabs my hair and holds me in place.

"Wait for it, sweetheart." His cock presses into my ass slowly until he's all the way inside. "Take Noah deeper."

He guides my head, pushing me down on Noah's cock until I'm breathing through my nose to get air.

"Yeah, like that, my little whore. Suck his fat cock, and I'll fuck your ass so good you'll beg me for more." Coop's words fill my ears. The fire inside me rages with need.

Noah shifts to suck on my clit. I swallow and suck him harder. His fingers slip inside my pussy, making me moan around his cock.

Coop pulls almost all the way out of my ass, taking me off Noah's cock at the same time. Every inch makes me tremble and crave more. His cock fills me again as he pushes my head down to take Noah deep into my throat. I'm so fucking close. My pussy flutters around Noah's fingers. Noah groans against my pussy, pushing me closer to another orgasm.

"We should just fuck all day." Coop uses my mouth to fuck Noah while he remains buried in my ass.

Noah's mouth works my pussy, licking, sucking, biting, and his fingers move achingly slow in and out of me. I'm right there. So close to falling over. So close to burning up into ashes.

Coop drops his mouth to my shoulder and sucks on the skin where my neck and shoulder meet. I'd cry out but Noah's cock is still in my mouth. Coop keeps me working Noah's cock, but he fucks his cock in and out of my ass in short bursts. I'm crushed between these two men as they work my body over, and it's too much.

When I come, I release a moan. My ass tightens around Coop's cock as Noah sucks on my clit. When I swallow around his cock, it jerks in my mouth and shoots his cum deep into my throat. I swallow every drop. Coop groans his release as he spills inside my ass.

We're a sweaty, panting pile of limbs. Little aftershocks hit me as I try to slow my breathing.

"Group shower?" Coop suggests, squeezing my ass.

"Yeah." Noah licks my clit, sending a rush of tiny spasms through me. "Our girl is dirty."

Coop chuckles. "That's the way I like her."

"I can't be late for work," I warn them as they slide off the bed, tugging me with them.

"It's early, kitten." Noah turns the shower on and draws me in with him, pressing me against the tile and kissing me like we haven't seen each other in years. He claims every inch of my mouth as his hot body clings to mine. My fingers dig into his hair to hold him close.

Coop steps in with us and takes a minute to clean himself. "My turn."

Noah lifts his lips and his dark eyes hold mine, making me throb with need before he steps away. Coop moves into Noah's place.

Coop is more sensual in how he takes my mouth, like it's a seduction for the two of us. He lifts my leg and thrusts his cock between my pussy lips. "Do you like taking two cocks, my little whore?"

I almost come all over his cock, but Noah grabs my hair and draws me away gently.

"Bend over, kitten."

I bend at the waist.

"Such an obedient little fuck toy." Coop grabs my hips and thrusts his cock into my pussy.

I gasp and Noah pushes my mouth over his cock, using my hair to fuck my face. Coop slaps my ass as he fucks me. I spread my legs for him to help balance myself.

"We should start every morning like this," Noah says conversationally, like he isn't using my mouth.

Coop spreads my ass cheeks and thrusts his fingers inside. A moan rises out of me around Noah's cock. "She's a dirty little whore who needs to be fucked on the regular."

He's not wrong. I love being fucked by all of them.

They sync up their thrusting into my mouth, pussy, and ass until I can't focus on one. I suck down on Noah as my body reaches the breaking point, and I shatter, falling into so many pieces as they fuck me. I convulse around Coop, causing him to groan as he fills me with his cum.

Noah pumps a few more times before releasing deep in my mouth. I swallow him again, greedy for all of it. He lifts my head and takes my mouth with his. Coop slides out of me and washes himself before lathering up my body.

Cupping my face, Noah leans his forehead against mine. "Wonderful."

The word fills me as they both work to thoroughly clean every inch of me. Noah dries me off after the shower, and I'm sure he can tell how turned on their touch made me. He lifts me onto the counter.

"Coop." Noah brushes my hair out of my face and puts his hands on my knees.

"Yeah, man?" Coop towel dries his hair and then looks over at Noah and me. "Ah, I've got just the thing."

Coop drops to his knees between my legs as Noah holds my knees out to the sides, spreading me open obscenely wide. Leaning forward, Coop sucks my clit and thrusts his fingers deep inside me. It takes a ridiculously short time for him to make me come again.

Coop stands and grins at me. "Thanks for the fun. Can't wait for tonight."

Noah and Coop bump fists. Coop kisses my forehead and walks out of the bathroom. The bedroom door opens and closes.

Noah steps between my thighs and thrusts his cock deep inside me.

I gasp at the intrusion and cling to his shoulders.

"Next time, I'm not going to share, kitten." He fucks me like a man on a mission as his fingers flick over my nipples. "Next time you and I are alone, I'm going to fuck you all night long until you don't want to fuck anymore."

My lips part as my orgasm washes over me.

"You'll be so full of my cum, no one else's will fit." He jerks forward into me and slams his mouth down on mine. His cock spasms, coating my walls with his cum, marking me as his.

His mouth slowly turns tender as he continues to kiss me. His hands cup my face like I'm delicate and precious. When his touch gentles, I lean into him, wanting more. Everything about Noah is brittle and vulnerable. He's hard and soft. Shy and confident.

Everything about him is mine. I love him.

It's easy and wrong. I'm not supposed to fall for any of them, but Noah feels like the other half of my soul. A piece that I've been missing.

But even together we aren't complete.

He lifts his head and his soft brown eyes meet mine. "You'd better hurry or you'll be late to work."

The words tremble on my lips. I want to spill them but I'm afraid. He steps away and helps me off the counter, wrapping a towel around me. The moment is gone, and I make my way out of his room and into the apartment.

Blake leans against the counter in the kitchen and watches me walk in just a towel to my bedroom. "Better hurry, tiger. Wouldn't want to be late for work."

He smirks at me, and I go slightly slower just to taunt him. He shakes his head as he chuckles.

"Dress nice. We're going on assignment."

His words follow me into my room. My heartbeat spikes a little. On assignment?

Chapter 70

Table the Conversation

Blake

Madison shifts on the seat next to me as the car takes us to Taylor's.

"Sore?" Fortunately the walls in the apartment are soundproof, but I saw Coop come out of Noah's room this morning with a huge grin on his face. And the hickeys on Madison's shoulders didn't happen on their own.

Her face flushes pink as she looks at me through her eyelashes. "Maybe a little."

I tuck a strand of her hair behind her ear. She's still fragile, but strong. She'll need that for today.

"You don't leave my side when we get there." Seth and I discussed it at length last night. I don't want her anywhere near Hunter Adams, but we need someone on the team to figure out who might be the spy. Plus, the owner wanted her there and he's the client. "You go to the ladies' room, I go with you."

"Don't you think people will find that strange?" She arches an eyebrow. "After all, I'm supposed to be dating Coop and you're following me to the bathroom?"

I shrug. "I don't care what people think. I'm not letting him get you alone again."

I'm still kicking myself for not recognizing the signs when I first saw them together, but I saw what I wanted to see. I wanted to confirm she was just like every other woman, out to use us for our money or power.

She takes my hand in hers. "I'll be careful, Blake."

I thread my fingers through hers and release my breath. She's not like the others, and she proves it every day. My brain keeps looking for flaws, searching for what I might have missed. I've let the guys down before. I let a snake into our lives and didn't realize it in time.

Andrea cost us a pretty penny and almost ruined our business reputation. Tried to blackmail us until we were forced to settle. Even though she signed an NDA, and we couldn't prove she started the rumors, but the timing was definitely suspicious.

I squeeze Madison's hand and press my lips to her knuckles. "I don't want you out of my sight today."

Her smile softens. "Wherever you go, I'll go."

I inhale her soft floral scent and release it. When the car stops, I get out before reaching in to help her out.

She's wearing dark brown slacks today. The wide legs sway and make it seem like a skirt as she walks. The red heels she wears bring her to a height perfect for me to back her against a wall and fuck her. Her cream blouse is flowing with a wide neck that shows off the possessive marks on her shoulders from last night. Her pink floral scarf covers some of them and the fading marks of her assault.

Seth knows how to dress our girl. Her blond hair drifts around her shoulders, and her blue eyes stand out with the shadowy eye makeup she wears. Her lips are a soft, kissable pink. She looks professional and fuckable at the same time.

"Do I look okay?" She glances down over her outfit like something might be out of place.

"You look gorgeous, tiger." I release her hand, even though I really want to draw her tight into my side and keep her there. We're at work. That means hands off. We don't need any new rumors to start. We have enough to deal with currently.

I open the door and gesture for her to lead the way. My heart pounds and my fists clench as I follow her in. My body is preparing for a physical fight, but that won't happen here. Even if I hate Hunter Adams, he's still the client.

"Good morning, Madison," William Adams greets her. He takes Madison's hand and pulls her into a hug.

"Good morning, Mr. Adams." Her tone is light and sweet.

My fingers twitch with the need to pull her back against me.

"You look lovely, dear. I'm so glad you landed on your feet." He gives her a friendly smile as he steps away before his gaze lifts to mine. "Blake, we have you set up in a conference room on the second floor. Hunter will be your liaison for the project. I believe the rest of your team arrived earlier this morning."

"Thank you." I step forward and shake his hand. "We needed to make sure all the files were ready in the office before heading over."

"I'm glad they're keeping you busy over there," he says, speaking to Madison again. "You remember where the meeting room is."

"Of course. Thank you, Mr. Adams." Madison smiles.

He returns it and shakes his head. "We definitely missed out on hiring you. I'll see you both at lunch? One?"

Our eyes meet and I nod. "Yes."

He leaves us then and Madison leads me to the elevator. I resist the urge to put my hand on the small of her back and claim her in front of all the people that smile and nod at Madison in recognition.

"Hey, Madison." A guy around her age steps onto the elevator with us. He's not as tall as I am. His dark eyes flow over her with a hint of familiarity.

Her cheeks flush pink. "Derek."

His smile widens as he steps closer when the doors close. He gives me an acknowledging nod before returning his attention to her.

"You never called me after that last . . ." He pauses and glances at me before smirking. "Date. I was hoping we could find some time to catch up."

Madison's cheeks brighten more. "I've been busy with work."

"We always found time—"

"I'm seeing someone." She smiles to soften the blow.

His eyebrow rises and he takes me in again, this time looking me over to see how I compare to him. My fist clenches, and his eyes widen on that before lifting to my face.

"Sorry, my man. Didn't know."

I keep my expression blank.

Madison shakes her head. "Not him, someone at work."

Derek shrugs and gives her a wink. "You still have my number if that ever stops."

The elevator doors open and Derek walks out.

"This way." Madison looks flustered as she leads me down the hallway. She keeps glancing at me over her shoulder. I check out every room we pass, looking for what I need.

"It's just around this corner," she says.

Bingo. After a quick glance around to see that we're alone, I grab her arm, drag her into an unoccupied office, and shut the door behind us.

"Blake?" Her blue eyes blink up at me. "What are you doing?"

I lock the door and take a breath. "You fucked that guy?"

Her cheeks flush pink again. "We were both interns together over a year ago."

"That guy." I close in on her, crowding her against the door. "You let *that* guy fuck you."

Her lips pinch, and she crosses her arms over her chest. "Yes, Blake. I had sex with people before you guys. I'm not sure what the issue is. You guys had sex before me too. All of you with the same woman, as well."

Her chest puffs up as the embarrassment changes to something hotter.

"Do you have his number?" I press my chest against hers, towering over her like a predator, staking my claim.

"If I do?" She gives me a challenging look. My submissive little pet has a stubborn side.

"Delete it," I growl out.

Her lips press together as she studies me. Her eyes fix on mine when she says, "No."

I grab her between her legs and press my fingers against her cunt.

She sucks in a breath and grabs my arms.

"This belongs to me. If I have to go through your phone and delete the existence of every other man from your life, I will."

"You can't erase my history any more than I can erase yours." Her breath comes out in quick little gasps. Her hands clutch my shoulders as I rub her through her pants.

"I can ruin you for any other man but us."

"What makes you think you haven't already?" Her eyes flash with heat and need, and her hips grind against my hand.

My mouth captures hers as I dig the heel of my palm into her clit. Her lips part beneath mine in a moan. While her body trembles from her climax, I claim her mouth. She wraps her arms around my neck and holds me close.

I press my forehead against hers and rock my hard cock against her pussy. "We have unfinished business, tiger. I'm going to fuck this pussy hard, so you remember your place, and spank your ass for every guy's number in your phone."

Her blue eyes spark up at me. A hint of defiance still simmers in them.

Fuck. I want to teach her a lesson right now. Spank her until her ass is too sore to sit still and then fuck her until her pussy aches. But we need to get to work.

"Let's go."

Madison

My pussy still throbs empty as we find our way to the conference room.

"Maddy!" Hunter's voice cuts through the fantasies my mind wove on the way.

I almost forgot about him, so caught up in Blake's jealous possession. Hunter is an effective lady boner killer.

Blake steps in front of me as Hunter approaches with a huge grin. That grin fades into a smile as Blake holds out his hand. "Hunter."

Hunter takes it but his gaze flows over me. I step farther behind Blake to block his view. I'm cowering and I don't care. Blake will protect me and run interference.

"Good of you to come." Hunter shifts his attention to Blake. "Glad you could bring Maddy as well. We've missed her around here."

Yeah, he misses cornering me and trying to make me kiss or fuck him. Asshole.

"We try to accommodate client requests when we can. It seemed important to William." Blake backs into me slightly. Taking a deep breath of his spicy cologne, I let it settle me.

He'll protect me. He won't leave me. I'm not alone.

The conference room has three other people working in it. One is Courtney. She lifts her eyebrow at me and shakes her head before returning her gaze to her work. The other two are a couple of guys, maybe Blake's age. They don't even bother looking up as they continue to work.

"Maddy's important to all of us here at Taylor's." Hunter tries to catch my eye, but I work on setting up my workstation at the conference table.

I choose a seat that will only allow Blake to sit next to me. Not that Hunter will remain in here long. He has work to attend to.

"Will you be joining us for lunch?" Blake asks. No warmth in his voice.

"Of course." Hunter shifts back and gives me a cocky grin before heading to the door. "I'll let you guys get set up. If you need anything else, my office is right around the corner. You remember where it is, right, Maddy?"

I cringe but force a smile and nod. "Of course."

"Right next to the copy room," he adds.

A shiver of apprehension races through me. Wait. Hunter calls me *little bird*, and the texter called me *little one*. Not that far off. I raise my gaze to contemplate Hunter as Blake asks him a few questions about the job.

He could have easily charmed Valerie into letting him into our apartment to place the cameras. He has the funds to afford that kind of setup. His obsession with me was obvious here to everyone except his father.

Could he be my stalker? The texts seem sexual and possessive. But if he'd seen that video of me getting off in the shower, why didn't he mention it? Hunter is cocky and self-assured. He wouldn't hide that he saw me naked, fucking myself.

He'd use it to intimidate me. Probably blackmail me into his bed with the threat of releasing it to the public. That doesn't mean he just hasn't had the opportunity to use it as leverage.

My lips purse as I study Hunter. If Blake is always with me while we're here, I might not get a chance to prove Hunter's the stalker. If he is.

Maybe I should mention my thoughts to Blake and see how he wants to proceed. His jaw ticks as he listens to Hunter. His fist clenches and releases a few times before he shakes it out. Maybe Blake is too jealous right now. Maybe I can talk to him on the way to the restaurant, and we can figure out a strategy together.

They finish talking and Hunter's blue eyes find me. He gives me a cocky grin, like he's already got me trapped and I don't know it yet. But if I have my way, I'll trap him.

Chapter 71

Punishment

Blake

After Hunter finally leaves, I settle at the conference table and check in with Courtney, Theo, and Peter. It's a small team, but Taylor's isn't as big as some of our customers. We aren't sure who the mole is, but Courtney is frequently on our implementation teams.

Given her Saturday work coinciding with Madison's attack, she seems like a likely suspect. But I'm not ruling out Peter. They're teamed together often, and both their names show up on the files of clients who were contacted and left.

"Any issues?" I ask them.

Courtney raises her blue eyes to me and shakes her head. She was friends with Andrea when the whole thing went down. Though she's never said anything, we can't be sure Andrea didn't tell her everything. I can't tell if they're still in contact.

"Nothing yet. Everything is going smoothly." Theo nods as he leans back in his chair. His dark skin contrasts with his white dress shirt. His hair is in cornrows, and his dark eyes spark with intelligence. He's one of my top programmers.

Peter turns to look at Courtney before looking at me. His dirty blond hair falls into his eyes. As soon as his brown eyes meet mine, he looks down at his computer. "Everything's good so far."

He's an introvert who works best on his own. But he focuses on his work when the others might get distracted, so even in a team he's effective.

I grunt as I open my laptop. Madison quietly works next to me. When I called her on that guy, she was a firecracker, ready to burst. My fingers still itch with the need to punish her smart little mouth.

Fuck. I adjust my cock. Thinking about her mouth has me at half-mast. It's bad enough having her in our office within reach with a lockable office door. But with her right next to me, her soft floral scent invades my thoughts, and the musky smell of her arousal makes me want to drag her back to that empty office and make good use of her mouth.

I shake off my thoughts and focus on the work in front of me, and not how much more effective my work would be if she slid under the table and sucked me off like she did in the apartment. Lunch can't come soon enough.

Eventually, we all fall into a rhythm. The work slowly takes my mind off the punishment Madison deserves. The clacking of keys is the only sound in the conference room. My phone vibrates and I check out the text.

SETH:

Still on for lunch?

I scan the room and stand to stretch. Courtney glances up with her mouth pinched before returning to work.

ME:

Yes, leaving soon.

SETH:

Good. Anything?

ME:

No.

I wish I had more to tell him. Whoever is scaring away clients is sneaky as fuck about it. If Jason Harper hadn't told us, we'd still be standing around with our flies open not even realizing someone was costing us customers and profit.

"Madison." My tone is thick.

She raises her eyes from her screen, still typing while she looks at me.

"Lunch." Fuck it. I need to get out of here.

Her brows furrow and she glances at her screen, probably noticing we have ten minutes before we're supposed to leave. Her lips part like she's going to argue.

"Now." I let the command slip into my voice and note Courtney's smug little grin. She probably thinks Madison is in trouble.

Madison doesn't question me in front of her coworkers. After closing her laptop, she grabs her purse and phone. She doesn't hesitate to follow me as we wind our way back to the elevator.

Standing slightly behind me as we wait, she shifts on her feet and glances down the hallway a few times. Is she worried about Hunter or someone else? Maybe she's afraid Derek will join us again. Maybe she's worried another past lover will want to get back with her.

My fist clenches and I release it. Everyone has a past. I just don't want hers shoved in my face. When the elevator arrives, I put my hand on the small of her back to guide her inside. I press the button. The doors close before anyone else can get on.

I tip her chin up. "Do everything I say without question. Do you understand me, tiger?"

She licks her lips nervously. "Yes, sir."

Even though that's more Seth's kink, I appreciate the *sir* from her lips. I've toyed with other terms in the past, but *master* always seemed too formal. While I want someone to serve me and let me use them, I don't want a mindless consort.

"How many, Madison?" My mind is on the numbers in her phone. Of course, she doesn't have her old phone anymore. At least not on her.

"How many what?" A little wrinkle forms between her brows.

"Numbers, tiger. The numbers of men you've fucked that are in your phone." My fist clenches again, straining my fingers.

Her eyes narrow. That burst of defiance comes back. The elevator dings its arrival and I step away before the doors open.

We move through the downstairs, and I hold open the door to the outside. The car is waiting for us. Opening the back door, I gesture for her to get in.

She gnaws at her lip for a moment before sliding in. As soon as I get in, I raise the divider. I already texted the driver to take an extra ten minutes to get to the restaurant, preferably stopping at a park and idling.

"Ten." She sets her purse and phone down on the seat next to her and folds her hands in her lap.

"Undo your pants." I rub my hands together.

She swallows but unfastens her pants. The car stops, and I can tell the driver put it in park.

"Seat belt off."

She releases it and turns toward me. "What about your number, Blake?"

I shake my head. "That's an extra spanking, tiger." I grip her chin. "Are you going to be a good girl?"

She blows out a breath and her eyes narrow at me. Her soft lips press together in a line.

"Pull your pants down and lie across my lap."

Her gaze darts around us, suddenly aware of where we are. No one can see in, but there are people walking around the park, especially since it's almost lunchtime.

"Now." I snap my fingers.

She jerks her pants off and drapes them on the seat, leaving her thong panties on, and lies across my lap.

I tsk her as my fingers trail over her bare ass cheeks. "Such a defiant little mood you're having today. Did Noah let you have control, love? Did you ride him until he came inside your greedy little cunt?"

"No, they took what they wanted. They fucked my pussy together. Both of them deep inside my pussy, filling me so full."

Fuck. My dick hardens painfully at the thought. I'll need to ask them to repeat that for our viewing pleasure.

"Did it feel thicker than me?" I tease my finger along the thong riding down between her legs.

"It felt . . . different." She struggles to find the words.

I slide my finger beneath her panties. She's already soaking wet for me. I sink my finger into her slick cunt. She gasps.

"Are you sore?"

"No, sir."

"Good, because I want to make you ache." I slip my finger out of her and bring my hand down on her round ass. "Count."

"One."

"Did you enjoy fucking those other men?" I shove my fingers beneath her panties and thrust them inside her.

She cries out softly. "At the time—"

I spank her with my other hand, cutting her off.

"Two."

"What's the answer, love?"

I thrust my fingers in and out of her. She tenses on my lap as her breathing becomes erratic and her pussy begins to pulse. I pause.

"Did you enjoy fucking those other men?"

Her pussy tightens around my fingers. I bring my hand down on her other ass cheek twice.

"Three. Four."

"Answer me." I shove my fingers deeper inside her, holding them still. She draws in a breath.

"I didn't know anything different," she bites out.

I bring my hand down and spank her two more times.

"Five. Six." Her words are breathless.

I fuck her hard and fast with my fingers, shuttling in and out of her cunt. The wet noises as her pussy clings to my fingers fill the car. She tenses around me, about to come. I jerk them out of her, denying her her orgasm.

I swat her three more times, and she lets out a groan of aching need.

"Seven. Eight. Nine."

"And now, love?" I bite out. I'm so fucking hard I'm going to come in my pants if I can't get inside her soon.

"Fuck me, please," she cries as she squirms on my lap, searching for friction. "I need you to fuck me, Blake."

I bring my hand down on her ass two more times.

"Ten. Eleven," she whimpers.

"Answer me." I undo my belt and pull my cock out, stroking it while staring at her reddened ass.

"They're nothing compared to you guys. They were never more than stress relief." She whimpers as I stroke her red, hot flesh. "Please. I need you."

I pull her upright to straddle my lap, slide her panties to the side, and bring her wet, needy cunt down on my cock.

"Oh, fuck," she cries out as she takes me in fully.

"You belong to us now, love." I grab her hips and punch up into her tight cunt. "We're the only ones who can fuck you."

"Yes, please fuck me." Her fingers dig into my hair as she lifts and falls over me. I punctuate each fall with a thrust of my hips.

"Who owns you?" I ask, trying to hold back my orgasm, needing her to come first. Her darkened eyes meet mine as she rides me.

"You do." She pants as she fucks my cock.

"Who gets to fuck you?"

"You. Fuck me, Blake."

I press on her clit and she shatters all around me. She cries out. I bite off the groan that fills me as her cunt tightens and convulses around my cock, trying to draw me in. I lift her off me, set her on the seat beside me, and grab her hair to drag her mouth down. I thrust my cock into her mouth and she sucks on me eagerly.

"Do you taste that, tiger? Do you taste your cum all over my cock?"

She makes an affirmative noise that vibrates through my tight balls.

"Take it all. Take me deep."

She pushes down as far as she can go on me and swallows. It's all I need. I come hard down her throat, groaning at the release. I lean over her as she swallows my cum and fuck her pussy hard and fast with my fingers.

She moans as she comes all over my hand. Lifting her head off my cock, I take her mouth, tasting both of us mixed together on her tongue. Resting my forehead against hers, I take in her blue eyes as her harsh breaths mingle with mine.

"Never forget who you belong to."

Chapter 72

Aggressive Timeline

Madison

I had enough time in the car to clean up with some wet wipes. I also fixed my hair and lipstick. Blake's hand settles on my lower back as we walk through the dining room. My heart does little flips from his touch. The restaurant has cloth napkins and tablecloths. The waiters wear white dress shirts with black slacks.

His hands are finally at ease instead of clenching. I'm glad I could help relieve some of his tension.

Seth stands as we enter the private room. "They're arriving."

Blake nods and puts me in the chair between him and Seth. I didn't have time to discuss my plan with him. Maybe on the way back. Tingles shoot through me, remembering his anger and aggression as he spanked me, took my pussy, and fucked my face.

Blake doesn't like the idea of me with other guys. Fuck, the feeling is mutual. I don't like the idea of them with other women. Even in the past tense. If I ever met Andrea, I might need Noah to tie me down and restrain me from going after her for what she put them through.

"Smaller room this time?" Hunter asks as he struts in like he owns the place. His handsomeness can't outshine his shit personality. Or the way his eyes linger on my breasts before he grins.

"Fewer people expected." Seth smiles but there's a flatness to it. "We don't like to waste resources."

"I enjoy a good meal." William walks in, completely unaware of his son's inappropriate behavior, and sits at the table next to Seth. Not that Hunter has done much yet, and he wouldn't dare to in front of his father. William turns to Seth with a smile. "It's a pleasure to see you again. Your team is hard at work."

"We like to make sure we're in and out so you don't have to worry about accommodating us for too long." Seth glances my way briefly before returning his attention to William.

Hunter sits next to Blake and throws me a smile like he knows something I don't. I don't like that look.

We all settle in and order our food. Blake and Seth discuss the current status of the project while William asks questions. Hunter just watches me. It's creeping me out enough that I almost want to yell, *What!*

He's doing it on purpose to put me on edge. To let me know he has a plan and is confident he'll get what he wants from me.

I'd rather die than give in to him.

"So I know this isn't business as usual," William starts. He smiles and looks at me for a moment.

The hair on the back of my neck rises as Hunter's grin becomes more certain.

"What is it?" Seth asks.

"We were wondering if it might be possible to hire Madison for a special project." William's words cut into me. This has Hunter written all over it. "Not long-term, of course."

My insides churn and solidify into a lump in my stomach. My chest tightens like a fist is wrapped around it.

Hunter smiles charmingly at the guys. "She was pretty integral to this project when she interned with us. It would be so much easier on our timeline if we could just borrow her for a few days."

Blake stiffens beside me. Seth's mouth tightens.

"I know it's a lot to ask," William says, "but we wouldn't do it if we didn't think she'd be perfect for the job."

No. No, no, no, no, no. My breath catches in my throat. I try to swallow around the lump blocking it. My chest tightens. I can't. I can't. Oh, fuck, I can't breathe. I can't think. I can't.

"Are you okay, Madison?" William asks.

Blake stands abruptly and hauls me to my feet. "Excuse us."

He leads me through a back door in the room. We're in a hallway with waitstaff hustling through it.

"For fuck's sake. Breathe, Madison." He tips my chin up, and his worried green eyes search mine. He brushes my hair out of my face. "Breathe, love."

I take a gasping breath in. He pulls me in tight against him.

"It's not happening," Blake says into my hair. His hands stroke my back. "There's no way we could give you that time off. There's too much to do at the office. And I would never let you."

My chest eases and my breathing slows. My arms wrap around Blake like he's my lifeline. Just the idea of working for Hunter again made me panic.

The door opens and I flinch, worried it's Hunter and he'll pry me away. I don't release Blake. Fuck the fact that I'm supposed to be dating just Coop. Coop isn't here.

"Are you okay?" Seth steps behind me and runs his hand over my hair.

"I'm sorry about the meeting," I say quietly as I turn my face to look at him.

"Fuck the meeting." Seth draws me into his arms and tucks my head beneath his chin. "You're more important."

That startles me. That's not right. I'm not more important than the business. Not more important than the customer. I lift my head to search Seth's eyes.

His finger traces over my lower lip. "Taylor's couldn't begin to offer what you're worth. It doesn't make good business sense. Besides, we're not willing to let our assistant go for even one day."

My insides warm again as his blue eyes hold me captive. His soft scent of sandalwood helps calm me. Resting my head against his chest, I take a deep breath. I'm fine.

"We need to finish out this meeting. Then I want you two to gather your stuff and come back to the office." Seth presses his lips to mine. When he lifts them, I smile up at him. My heart slows slightly from its rapid pace.

If we're leaving, then I might not get a chance to figure out—

"Wait. I have an idea." I turn to look at Blake. "What if Hunter is my stalker?"

Blake's lips press into a thin line. "He *is* obsessed with you."

"What are you thinking, princess?" Seth asks.

"You won't like it," I tell Blake.

"Let's hear it," Blake grumbles.

I'm so nervous my hands shake. We pack up our computers and put away our things. Courtney gives me a few glares at the noise we're making. Theo gives me a smile. Peter just looks constipated.

"I'll be right back." As the words fall from my lips, I think of every horror movie I've seen with that exact line. It's not really reassuring.

Blake waves me off and finishes a text he's sending. I draw in a deep breath. It shouldn't take long for Hunter to realize I'm not being guarded. I go into the bathroom but just wash my hands, staring at my pale reflection above the sink.

I just have to evade him long enough for Blake to come. It's simple really. Hunter is a bragger. If he's behind the stalking, he'll tell me everything. I think about the shower and the file room. Whoever did it had the opportunity to do more to me, which doesn't seem like something Hunter would pass up. Unless he was trying to make me quit and come work for Taylor's.

I shake my head. I just need to eliminate someone or figure out who my stalker is. Now or never.

Taking a deep breath, I pull open the bathroom door and stroll down the hallway to the copy room. As soon as I step through the door, my breath catches. It's the same as the last time I was in here, when Hunter had me cornered. The feeling of being trapped overwhelms me, and I almost bolt back through the door to freedom.

"You're pretty slippery, little bird."

My breath catches at his voice.

This door doesn't have a lock on it. As long as I can reach the door, I'm safe. I take a deep breath. "What are you doing, Hunter?"

"What we should have done a year ago." He closes the distance between us, and I retreat to keep the space.

"I already told you no. I don't want you. Why can't you accept that?" The presence of the wall closes in on me. He'll have me trapped again if I'm not careful.

"That Courtney chick doesn't like you much. She says you're fucking your boss." His eyes darken as he stops right before touching me, just as my back hits the wall.

"I'm dating Cooper," I toss out, knowing it's not enough to stop him.

He laughs. "I knew we should have hired you. Didn't know you were the kind to slut it up for rich guys. You know, I'm worth a lot of money if that's what gets you wet."

"Fuck off, Hunter." I go to brush by him, but he shoves my shoulder into the wall. His gaze trails over my open neckline.

"Did he leave all these marks on you?" His fingers dig into my shoulder next to one of the marks Coop left. "You could have had me gentle, little bird. But now I have to get rough with you because apparently you like it that way."

His hand draws closer to my neck. For a second, I freeze, not knowing which way to go, but then I remember. "What about the recordings you sent me?"

His brow pinches together. "What the fuck are you talking about?"

His confusion seems so genuine that it might be real. Fuck, this was a bad idea.

"The texts with the videos of the bathroom and the file room." I duck under his arm and hurry toward the door. Just as I get it open his hand slams it shut, and he traps me against the door, pressing his front against my back.

"You want to make a film, little bird? We could record right here in the copy room. I'll fuck you so hard that guy won't want your sorry pussy back." His words fill me with dread. He draws my hair over my shoulder, sending a chill down my spine. "But I'll still want you."

I jerk my elbow into his stomach, surprising him more than hurting him. But it's enough for me to get away from the door. "If you don't stop this right now, I'll scream."

Laughing, he straightens. "Scream all you want, little bird. I made sure I'd get enough time with you after being interrupted the last time."

I back behind a chair. "What do you mean?"

The door is the only way out, and Hunter stands between me and it. I swallow down my fear. Blake is coming.

"I made sure my dad would keep Blake occupied while my friend watches the door, so no one saves you this time." His grin is as evil as my nightmare version of him. For a minute, I get trapped in that dream where Blake never shows up.

I know Blake won't let me down.

"You haven't been texting me and sending pictures?" I straighten my spine and look in his eyes, needing a direct answer.

"Fuck, no. Why would I waste any more time on you than I have to? I knew you'd walk in here begging for it. Looking for any excuse to get me alone so you can choke on my dick." He grabs his bulge. My stomach turns at the thought.

"I don't want anything from you, Hunter." I glance at the door. Where is Blake?

"Fuck, Maddy." Hunter closes in on me again. "I'm going to get a taste of you today before you slip out of my hands for good. You're going to love it and want me so badly you'll be begging me to let you come work for me. So I can fuck that pretty pussy every fucking day."

"What is going on here?" William asks.

The door opened right when Hunter started his little speech. William stands with Blake behind him. The tightness in my chest eases.

Hunter swallows and smiles before he turns to his father. "Maddy and I were just messing around. Isn't that right, Maddy?"

He glares at me when he turns back around.

I look Hunter dead in the eyes when I say, "I'm sorry, Mr. Adams, but Hunter has been sexually harassing me since I worked here. I didn't tell you because he's your son. In fact, none of the women tell you. I'm not the first he's cornered in the copy room, and I won't be the last if you don't do something about him."

Hunter's face turns red and his fists clench at his sides. He jerks forward like he's going to grab me. I don't dare cower from him. Not this time.

William blows out a breath. "Hunter, go to my office."

He glares at me. "But—"

"But nothing. Go." William steps out of the way and Hunter stomps past the men. William takes a deep breath in, and as he releases it, some of that happy energy he always carries leaves him too. "Madison, I'm so sorry you didn't feel you could come forward and tell me. We've lost a lot of really excellent employees that I thought had better offers. Now I need to review what really happened."

"I should have told you." Just because I got away doesn't mean some other woman did too. "I didn't want you to think less of me."

He gives me a partial smile. "Never, my dear. I'm just sorry you thought you had to endure that."

I give him a smile as my gaze meets Blake's. One thing is certain: Hunter isn't the stalker, but that doesn't mean I didn't just create an even more potent enemy.

Chapter 73

Recoop

Coop

Dinner was quiet. Everyone seemed lost in their own thoughts. Afterward, Seth and Blake returned to the office to work on our employee problem. Noah and Madison are curled up on the couch in the library, reading together.

It's an odd visual after how rough we got with Madison last night. The two of them look like the picture of domestic bliss. While I felt welcome in the depravity of last night, this moment seems sacred, like I'm disrupting something special.

I lean in the doorway, creeping on them. They haven't noticed me yet. Noah's hand trails over Madison's hair. Her head rests in his lap. He has a book open in front of his face, and she's got her tablet. As she reads, she plucks at her lower lip.

She's wearing a pink tank top and a pair of pink-and-gray plaid pajama pants. The apartment is quiet. The TV would disrupt their moment. I don't really want to watch anything, anyway. I sigh softly.

I can continue to creep on their time, or I can insert myself in their moment. Deciding on the latter, I stroll over to the couch.

Madison lifts her feet with a smile. I sit, and she rests her feet on me before returning her focus to the book.

I've never been great at sitting still and entertaining myself. But I pull out my phone and scroll through some emails. Madison shifts against me. She's still reading her tablet and plucking at her lower lip. She lets out a little sigh.

Noah glances down at her almost absentmindedly but then returns his gaze to his book.

"What are you reading, sweetheart?" I trail my hand up her calf under her pajama pants.

She bites her lip and looks over the top of the tablet at me. "An erotic romance."

That draws my focus. I tuck my phone in my pocket and rub her foot. Noah's eyebrow cocks up but he keeps reading. His interest is as piqued as mine.

"What's it about?" I keep my hands moving on her calves and feet. She shifts beneath my touch like she needs more.

"A game of dare between two friends." She meets my eyes. Her pupils are blown and her lips glisten.

"Are you enjoying it?"

She nods. "Very much."

"Tell me about it."

She glances up at Noah like she doesn't want to disturb his reading time.

"Go ahead, kitten." He sets his book on the table next to him and teases the neckline of her top with his fingertip. "Your story is likely more entertaining than mine at this point."

She sucks in a breath and once again focuses on me. "These two friends who secretly have the hots for each other get stuck in a cabin with a bottle of alcohol."

"Are we talking two women? Two men? A man and woman?" Trying to picture it in my mind, but all I can see is Madison naked before a fire in a rustic cabin, spread before me like a buffet of delectable sin.

"A man and a woman." She releases her breath as Noah's hand slips beneath her shirt, flirting with touching her breasts.

"So they're getting drunk. Please continue." I stroke my fingers along her bare calves. The muscles twitch beneath my touch.

"They agree to play truth or dare. It starts out innocently enough. The usual questions, simple answers, but then the woman asks if he's ever thought about having sex with her."

"Mmm, what happens next?" My gaze meets Noah's. He let me intrude on his night. I'm more than willing to share mine with him.

He cocks his eyebrow and I give a slight nod. It's odd how we gravitate toward each other. Me being the oldest and him the youngest. It probably has more to do with Seth and Blake being best friends from grade school. Neither of us is quite as serious as the others. Our play styles also work well together.

"Well, they ask more revealing questions, and the heroine refuses to answer. So she has to take the dare." Madison's cheeks are flushed pink. She stretches between the two of us, like a sensuous cat.

"What kind of dares, kitten?" Noah plucks her nipple and she gives a little moan.

"They start with kissing or licking, then move to sucking and stroking." Her breath shortens with each word.

I trail my hands up the outside of her pants until I reach her waistband. "Do they get naked?"

She nods, watching me. "He strips her pants off her."

"Like this?" I drag her pants down her legs, revealing her lacy pink panties.

"Just like that," she whispers. She glances up at Noah. "And her top."

Noah draws her tank top up and over her head, leaving her in only her panties. Her breasts are full and nipples already tight as she reclines over our laps.

"What next, sweetheart?" My fingers trail up the inside of her thigh, stopping before reaching her panties and dragging back down.

"She dares him to get naked too."

I take off my shirt and so does Noah. I have on sweats and nothing else, so I move her legs off me for a second while I chuck those off as well. When I sit back down, Noah sits Madison up to take off his pants and boxers before everyone returns to their previous positions.

"Of course, she's not all the way naked yet." Madison raises her eyebrow at me.

I give her a smirk before reaching for her panties and drawing them slowly down her legs. She bites her lip as she watches me. Both Noah and I are hard and ready for anything our dirty girl has in mind.

Dropping her panties on the floor with our clothes, I stretch briefly before settling. "What happens when they get naked?"

"He dares her to masturbate in front of him." Madison looks up at Noah. "So she goes to the table and sits on it."

"Show us, kitten." Noah helps her sit upright. She stands and walks over to the library table, her hips rolling with the motion. She's divine.

"Can I get a hand?" Glancing over her shoulder, she looks at me through her lashes and my cock twitches in anticipation. I'm more than willing to offer my hand, lips, cock, whatever she needs.

Standing, I walk over to her and set her on the table with her feet dangling over the side. She reaches for her breasts but I stop her, taking her hands and flattening them down on the table.

"You asked for a hand, sweetheart." I trail my hand over her breast, circling her nipple with my fingertip. "I get to be your hand."

"Sit behind her, Coop, so I can enjoy the show." Noah leans back with his arms on the couch. His cock stands at attention.

Giving him a smirk, I sit on the library table and settle Madison between my legs. My cock nestles between her ass cheeks. "Lean back against me, sweetheart."

With a sigh, she does as I ask.

"What does she do?" I whisper in her ear, placing my hands on her thighs.

She releases a breath. "She touches her breasts, holding them, rubbing her nipples."

"I bet that gets him excited. What does he do?" I whisper as I explore her breasts with my hands.

A shiver courses through her as her attention focuses on Noah. "He watches, craving her, longing for her, wanting her hands to be replaced with his."

Noah smiles. When my fingers tweak her nipples, she sighs, arching into my palms. Her heavy breasts fill my hands. My cock grows painfully hard.

"She trails her hand down her stomach."

I cup her breast with one hand while dragging the other down her stomach.

"She slides her fingers along her pussy until she meets her entrance."

My finger dips between her legs into her wet pussy, waiting for her next command.

"She presses her finger inside." Her breathing hitches. As I press my finger inside her snug, warm pussy, Madison arches against me. "Then she spreads her legs and plays with her pussy for him."

She brings her feet up on the table edge, opening herself to Noah's view and my fingers. I spread her wetness over her pussy and play with her clit. My other hand still works her breast. Little sounds get caught in the back of her throat as she grows so wet beneath my touch.

"What's he doing now?" I whisper in her ear, caressing the edge of her ear with my lips.

Opening her eyes, she says, "He just watches until she comes."

"Mmm," I acknowledge, still stroking her.

"Oh, fuck." She whimpers as I flick her nipple and rub her clit. "She pushes her fingers inside and uses her other hand to play with her clit."

I chuckle darkly against her ear and do as she wants. Sliding my fingers inside her slick channel and working her clit at the same time.

She rocks against me. Her fingers thread through my hair, clutching it, pulling it loose of its restraint.

"Coop."

It's not hard and fast like last night but slow and methodical. Her hips follow my fingers as they thrust in and out of her. I hook my fingers and press inside her, hitting that spot that makes her toes curl.

"Oh, fuck," she cries out as she comes, tensing all around me. Her cunt squeezes rhythmically around my fingers and releases. She sags against me, rubbing her head against my shoulder.

My cock throbs, wanting more than the touch of her smooth skin against it. She's all I want and everything I need.

"What do you want us to do next, sweetheart?"

Her eyes open and she tips her head to meet my gaze. "Let's go back to your room." Her eyes meet Noah's. "All of us."

Madison

Noah helps me off the table, and we quickly gather our clothes before we head to Coop's room. Coop opens the door and pins me with his blue eyes. The heat inside them makes my insides churn with need.

"Let us please you, kitten." Noah steps behind me and presses his cock against my ass.

I lean into his warmth and close my eyes as his outdoor scent fills me.

They're giving me control tonight. After today, I really need some control. I don't want to dwell on it, so I take Noah's hand and bring him into Coop's room.

"Sit on the bed. Both of you." I lean back against the door as they both do as I say. Their muscles coiled to do my bidding. Their cocks stand proudly. Fuck, it's intoxicating.

They really are well matched for size and girth. My pussy throbs thinking of last night, both of them inside my core, filling me to the point of ache. Ruining me.

I shove off the door and kneel before Coop. Leaning forward, I lick his cock from the base to the tip and swipe at the drop of precum waiting for me there. Coop groans. My hands move up both of their thighs before I circle their cocks with my hands. I look up at them as I stroke them in the same rhythm.

"Fuck, kitten." Noah leans back on his hands, watching my hand work his cock. "I don't know how I like you most. Tied up, helpless, taking us every dirty way we can imagine. Or you taking control."

Still stroking both their cocks, I take the head of Noah's cock into my mouth and suck on him like a lollipop.

He groans as his dark eyes meet mine. "You're amazing."

I lick around his head before moving back to Coop's cock and doing the same to him.

"What can we do for you, sweetheart?" Coop's blue eyes find mine.

I sit back on my heels and stroke them while thinking of exactly what I want. I want oblivion. To not think about anything but this moment. To feel their touch on me while they fill me with their cum.

"Lie back on the bed next to each other." I release their cocks and stand.

They both lie down on the bed with a little space between them. I crawl up and straddle Coop's waist. My pussy teases the head of his cock. I slide against the edge of his cock, feeling his hard ridge against my clit.

Fuck, I just want to fuck them all night long.

My eyes meet Noah's as I position Coop's cock against my entrance. "I'm going to fuck Coop until he comes and then I'm going to fuck you. I want to keep fucking. I don't want to stop until we pass out."

Noah strokes his cock. "Whatever you want, kitten."

I take Coop into my pussy, sliding down his cock until he's deep inside me. "Touch me. Both of you."

As I rise and lower over his cock, Coop takes my breasts in his hands, stroking the nipples in achingly slow circles. Noah sucks on his finger before he teases it against my clit. We all move together as I ride Coop's cock.

As I feel my orgasm draw closer, I reach behind me and stroke Coop's tight balls. "Come with me."

I moan as the wave crashes over me, taking me under. Coop groans his release, thrusting up into my pussy before pressing in deep and filling me with his cum.

Not waiting to come down, I lift off Coop and straddle Noah's waist, lowering my pussy onto his cock. He pushes up to sitting and helps me rise and fall over him. Coop kisses my arm, trailing kisses up to my shoulder. His lips leave tingles in their wake as Noah fucks my already sensitive pussy.

Coop lifts my hair and kisses my neck. It's gentle, like when he finger fucked me. So different from last night. His front brushes my back. I suck in a breath at the heat of his skin stroking against mine.

"Soon, I'm going to mark up this neck. I'm going to claim this part of you."

A moan rips from me as I come on Noah's cock, but Noah keeps thrusting into me. Our chests rub together, and his lips find mine, exploring my mouth with his tongue as he pumps up into me.

Coop's hands stroke down my back, stopping on my waist. He helps me lift and fall on Noah's cock as his lips and tongue explore the nape of my neck. I'm hitting sensory overload from all our skin brushing and sliding together.

I tip over into another orgasm, this time dragging Noah with me. His kiss turns savage as he bucks up into me and pumps me full of his cum. As soon as Noah relaxes, Coop lifts me and pulls me back against him, lining his cock up with my entrance before lowering me down on him, filling me before I even stop coming.

"We could go all night like this, sweetheart." Coop presses his lips against the back of my ear. "Passing you back and forth, filling you so full of our cum you'll be leaking for days."

Gah, I want that. I want everything they can give me. I want them to take me until the only thing I feel is wave after wave of pleasure.

Noah captures my nipple in his mouth and suckles it. I cry out, already so sensitive. Aftershocks ripple through me as Coop pushes me up to kneeling. He grinds up into my pussy as he fucks me.

My hands fall on Noah's shoulders as his mouth alternates between my breasts. Taking his time to explore both while they tighten and grow heavy with the attention from his lips and tongue.

Reaching around my hip, Coop strokes my clit with firm fingers. I cry out as an orgasm rips through me. He grunts as he continues to fuck me. Noah's mouth finds mine and kisses me.

His cock brushes against my stomach, already hard again. Coop thrusts in and out, still tormenting my clit with his finger. "Come for me again, my little whore."

I can't help falling off the edge. I cry out as I lean into Noah. He strokes my hair as Coop bellows his release, his hot cum filling me.

Noah pulls me from Coop's arms and lays me down on my back before his cock pushes inside me. "Color, kitten?"

I brush his blond hair out of his dark eyes and smile up at him. "Green, Noah. It's always green for you."

We move together slowly, pressing together before withdrawing. My legs wrap around his waist, drawing him deeper inside. His dark eyes hold me captive as we rock against each other. He's inside me and all around me, and I've never felt closer to him.

"Do you want to keep doing this?" Coop lies down beside me, trailing his finger down my side. "Because we might need to hydrate at some point, but we can still fuck while we do that."

I turn my head to Coop and reach out to cup his cheek, drawing his face to mine. Drowning in his pale blue eyes. Pressing my lips to his full soft lips, I whisper, "All night, Coop. All night."

Chapter 74

Wake-Up Call

Madison

We passed out at some point because I wake up tangled in their embrace, Coop and Noah on either side of me, our naked bodies pressed together. I think I officially need a day off from fucking. My thighs are sticky with cum and I need to pee.

I wiggle my way out from between the two of them and into the bathroom. After using the toilet, I turn on the shower. I'm coated in way too much sweat and cum to comfortably return to bed.

When the water is hot, I slip into the shower and let the warm water soothe my sore muscles. My shampoo, conditioner, and soap are all here in Coop's shower waiting for me. I've never felt more at home than here with these guys.

My bosses. My lovers.

I shake my head as I rinse. It's insane. I interviewed for a job, and now, I'm living with and fucking four men. Plus working the job of my dreams. The shower door opens and Coop steps in with me.

"Good morning, sweetheart." He kisses me briefly before stepping under the water. "I don't think I can fuck you until I replenish with food and water."

I laugh, feeling twinges in my pussy, and not the good kind. "Trust me. I think I'm good for a while."

He gives me a smoldering look that makes my pussy clench in need, like I've lost my mind. Water trails down his beautifully built body. His six-pack abs lead to that V of muscles that engulfs my insides in flames. He reaches a hand out to me with a smirk.

"You can join me in the water, sweetheart."

"You aren't safe to be naked around." I quickly rinse off and grab a towel. He chuckles as his fingers trail over my ass cheek, sending tingles throughout me.

"Go let Seth dress you for the day." He gestures toward the door. "Tell him to make you less of a temptation so I won't feel the need to fuck you."

He throws me that smoldering look again.

I shake my head. "I'll pass along your message."

Grabbing my pajamas from the pile of clothes, I remain quiet to avoid waking Noah, still passed out in Coop's bed. He's naked and face down, spread-eagle on the mattress.

I can't help admiring every inch of his naked body. He's leaner than Coop in build but still cut. He has the best ass. I leave the room, wrapped in just a towel tucked securely under my arms.

"Your outfit is hanging in the closet." Seth's voice comes from the kitchen. He stands at the counter and pushes a cup of coffee across the island my way.

Oh, coffee. For a moment, I hesitate. I should just go finish getting ready for work, but I also slept very little. The nutty, caramelized scent of coffee hits my nose. Just like these men, coffee doesn't play fair.

And my resistance isn't that strong.

I set my clothes on the counter and grab the coffee with both hands. "Thank you."

He nods and drinks his coffee before opening the oven and pulling out a breakfast casserole. The delicious smell fills the room.

My stomach growls angrily at the reminder of how many calories we burned last night.

Images of naked bodies twisted together fill my head. Want curls through me at how it felt to be filled over and over again. Passed between the two of them. Fuck, after a break, I definitely want to do that again.

"Breakfast?" Seth's voice draws me out of the memory.

Nodding, I sit at the table as he cuts a couple of pieces and plates them. "I definitely could get used to this."

"I think we could all get used to this." The corner of Seth's mouth curls. He sets a plate in front of me with a fork and takes the chair next to me with his own plate.

Inhaling the savory scent, I take a bite of the egg, sausage, and cheese masterpiece. I moan at the goodness.

"Lose the towel, princess."

Lifting my gaze to his, I turn in my chair. Pulling the tucked corner out, I let the towel fall around me. A shiver ripples through me at the cool apartment air. I sip my coffee to help warm me up and eat another bite of eggs.

"We have a long day ahead of us." Seth continues to eat his breakfast while his eyes remain on me, taking in my naked body.

My libido sparks to life under his appraisal. I'm helpless against my need for these guys. They fill me with desire and longing, and I can't deny I want them too.

"I'm going to need you in my office for the better part of the morning."

Facing him, I ask, "What project are we working on?"

"A few things that should have been taken care of earlier this year but were put aside since we didn't have an assistant who could tackle them." His gaze warms. "But you have all the right qualifications. We'll get through it quickly."

As his gaze rakes over me like a physical caress, I purse my lips. "Will I be clothed for this project?"

"Of course." Seth smirks. "Mostly. I might have left out some essentials from your outfit today."

Taking a bite, I'm pretty sure I know what Seth decided not to put on me today, but I'll find out soon enough. We sit and finish breakfast. His gaze is drawn to my body, but he never touches me.

Control.

He told me he likes to test his control. This must be part of it. After I finish my coffee and breakfast, I stand and kiss Seth on the cheek.

"Thank you for breakfast."

As I reach for my towel and clothes, Seth drags me back between his legs. He turns me and tips down my chin. His eyes lock on mine. "You can thank me nicer than that, princess."

Smiling, I reach for his belt and zipper. He cups my face and draws me in for a kiss while I work on freeing his cock. His mouth takes mine gently, like we have all the time to explore each other.

When his cock is out, I stroke my hand over the hard length of him. He lifts his mouth from mine slightly.

"On your knees, princess." His blue eyes hold me as I lower to my knees beside his chair, waiting eagerly for his next command. He says, "Good morning, Blake."

I don't dare look away from Seth.

"Morning." Blake walks into the kitchen and pours himself a cup of coffee in the corner of my vision. He leans against the counter, bringing the cup to his lips.

My hand strokes Seth's length because he never told me to stop.

"Suck my cock like a good girl," Seth commands. My insides tumble over themselves, wanting everything he has to give me. I draw my hair over my shoulder and lean over him to take his thick, red cock into my mouth.

"We need to work on the Taylor's project today." Blake's voice is nonchalant, like he isn't watching me, naked, giving Seth a blowjob at the table.

"Everything smoothed over with William?" Seth's voice doesn't even hitch as I take him deeper, sucking, licking, teasing. Trying to break his control and make him come.

"He's apologized so many times for Hunter's behavior."

Blake's words make me stiffen. William felt horrible for what happened. Blake told him about both the restaurant and the incident in the break room while I gripped my hands together almost painfully.

My hand tenses on Seth's thighs.

Seth's hand slips into my hair and he draws me off his cock, tipping my head back to meet his eyes. "You did nothing wrong, princess. This is on Hunter. Not you. Never you. You were clear with him about what you wanted, and he didn't respect that."

I blink away the sudden barrage of tears fighting to make their way out. Swallowing the lump in my throat, I couldn't say anything if I tried right now.

Seth smooths his thumb across the wrinkle between my eyes. His blue eyes grow concerned as a tear slips down my cheek. "Do you want to continue?"

Licking my lips, I nod. I want his cock in my mouth. There's something soothing about sucking on the hard length of him. He searches my eyes.

"Please." The word is guttural and aching.

He lowers my mouth back to his cock. I take him inside and hum with appreciation. I get to work again, focusing on pleasuring Seth.

"The team should finish up there today. I can't be positive if any of them are the corporate spy." Blake's voice is closer. The chair behind me scrapes on the floor, and his heat is next to me. "Courtney is bitter and definitely doesn't like Madison. Theo did his job without complaint or much talking. Peter was nervous, but I'm not sure if that's because he has a thing for Courtney or because I was observing."

Seth keeps his hand in my hair, gently massaging my scalp as I bob up and down on his cock. Blake's hand trails down my spine, making tingles dance in its wake.

I'm between two of the men who drive my body crazy with need. Even though I should be satiated. Even though I should be too sore. Everything in me wants both of them to take me. I squirm on my knees as desire throbs between my thighs.

"Good girl." Seth's whispered praise makes me moan around his cock, taking him deeper.

"Have Coop and Noah been riding you hard, tiger?" Blake's hand wraps in my hair, drawing it away from my face, making my movements more visible.

I can't answer him with Seth's cock in my mouth. Blake's other hand smooths down my back, making a pleasurable shudder shake through me.

"She's a naughty little whore." Coop's voice rings out, and the sound of him pouring his coffee fills my ears over the sound I make sucking on Seth's cock.

"Care to share?" Blake asks, still stroking with his fingers down my spine to my waist and back up.

"The night before, we played rough, didn't we sweetheart?" A hint of laughter tinges his words.

I hum around Seth's cock and he sucks in a breath.

"Noah and I caught her and tied her up to his bed. Like a good little slut."

I'm already wet, but the memories of the other night make me soaked.

"We gagged her mouth and teased her fuckable body until she came for us. Then Noah fucked her delectable breasts while I rode that tight ass, making her squirm until she came all over us."

Seth's breathing grows harsher, and I increase the speed of my bobbing, taking him deep and swallowing around him.

"I removed the gag and fucked her mouth while she was still spread-eagle and helpless on the bed. Noah fucked her ass. We saved her pussy for last."

My pussy pulses hard and I moan around Seth's cock. Need crawls inside me, craving release. Seth's hand tightens in my hair as he holds me down while his release pulses into my throat and mouth. I swallow him down, taking him into my body.

When he lifts me off his cock, he looks into my eyes with something more than lust.

My heart flips over.

"Continue your story, Coop." Blake's hand remains in my hair.

Seth trails his hand along my jawline before nodding to Blake. "Suck off Blake, princess."

I turn. Blake has his cock out and ready for me. His hand smooths over his thick, hard length. My pussy throbs before I lean down and take him into my mouth.

"We decided to fuck her pussy together." Coop's voice rings out in the room. "We got her nice and wet. Both of us fucked her a little to loosen her up."

Every word he says ripples over me like a caress. I moan, tightening my thighs together against my aching pussy while sucking on Blake's huge cock and taking as much of him into my mouth as I can.

"She wanted it so bad. Both our cocks sliding into her tight little cunt, stretching her so fucking wide and using her like the whore she is."

Seth's fingers stroke over my swollen clit. I moan around Blake's cock as my pussy throbs empty. "Did she like it?"

Fuck, did I like it? I lift my hips so Seth can have all the access he wants.

"She fucking loved it. She came so hard, tightening around Noah's and my cocks, squeezing us together, making us fill her with our cum."

Seth's fingers rub circles around my pussy but they never penetrate me, just tease and torture me. "And last night?"

Coop chuckles darkly, and my hips push against Seth's fingers while I take Blake as deep as I can, blocking my breath for a second.

"We chain fucked her pussy. As soon as Noah came, I slid inside her. After I filled her, he took over fucking her. We kept going until we all passed out. Pretty sure my cock was the last one inside her, and she was so sloppy wet with our cum and hers."

Fuck. His words, Blake's cock in my mouth, and Seth teasing my clit cause me to shatter. I suck on Blake's cock while I come. My hips jerk against Seth's touch. My pussy convulses, empty. Blake groans as he comes down my throat. I keep suckling him and swallowing him down until he lifts my head.

Licking my lips, I look up at Blake in an orgasmic daze.

"Good girl," Blake says. His thumb rubs the corner of my lips tenderly. His green eyes are darkened.

"Fuck, kitten." Noah's voice breaks the stare down. "I'd fuck you if I had a lick of energy left after last night."

He stands in only his boxers, staring at me hungrily.

My pussy aches with the need to be filled, but it also just aches a little.

"Time to get ready for work, princess." Seth helps me to my feet and wraps the towel around my body. He draws me into his arms for a hug, and I sigh as sandalwood fills my senses. "We have a full day ahead of us."

Chapter 75

Cold Calling

Seth

I turn on the lights to the offices and stroll into mine. Breakfast took a little longer than I thought it would, but Madison naked on her knees before me is worth being a little late. I shake my head as I turn on my computer and pull up my email.

She's a distraction even when she doesn't mean to be. I need to stiffen my resolve to keep my hands to myself during the workday. The elevator dings its arrival, and her heels click on the marble floor.

Her routine is familiar to me already. She goes to her desk first, then heads to the break room to start the coffee and unload the dishwasher. When she's done, she returns to her desk.

And today, she'll come into my office after.

The image of her on my desk intrudes. For a second, I let the memories play. Her first day, sitting in front of me, finger fucking herself to orgasm while I watched her wet fingers dive in and out of her slick pussy.

Then she's bent over my desk, stripped to her heels, thigh highs, panties, and bra, being fucked by the others as they play with vibrating beads in her ass while she looks at me and screams her orgasms. Leaving me her tight asshole to fuck until we both shattered.

Fuck.

I'm already hard again and she hasn't even walked into my office. We've all been relentless the past few days. As much as we've fucked her, she has to be sore.

She needs a break and I plan to give it to her. Will I still use her mouth? Absolutely. Probably her ass too.

But after work, not during. During, I'll behave and we'll get shit done.

I immerse myself in the emails I need to respond to and barely notice the clicking on her way back to her desk. After fifteen minutes, she appears at my door.

"Are you ready for me?"

My cock jerks, always ready for her. After I nod, I lean back in my chair and watch her as she closes the door. Her skirt flows down her legs, swirling around them as she walks toward me. Her shirt is stiff cotton that shouldn't reveal her tight nipples. I didn't provide panties or a bra today.

We don't have an outside meeting at lunch, and I plan to use that to my advantage.

She settles in the chair across from me and crosses her legs. I rub my chin as I watch her, looking to see if she's uncomfortable with not wearing panties.

"What do you want me to work on first?" She came prepared with her tablet and a pen. Her blond hair is pulled up into a bun with little tendrils falling around her neck. She didn't wear a scarf today. Her neck is almost completely healed.

"Did you put makeup on to cover it up?" I touch my neck as a mirror to the spots on hers where her bruises have faded.

She reaches for her own neck. "No."

"Good." I worried about dressing her for the benefit and having to find something to hide her neck, but with a little makeup, she should look flawless. She'll need that level of perfection to deal with being on the arm of Cooper Graham. She doesn't realize the scrutiny that comes from being his, but she will.

I'll give her as much armor as I can.

I pull up the files and turn my screen toward her so we both can see.

We lose ourselves in the work. She picks up things quickly and always has some insight to help with the process. After an hour or so, she's working quietly on the other side of my desk while I deal with a vendor on the phone.

I'm on hold as the buttons on her shirt draw my gaze. She's naked beneath that shirt because I commanded it. I clear my throat to get her attention.

She raises her gaze to me, obviously focused on her work. I tap my finger on my button and nod to hers. With a questioning gaze, she reaches and starts to undo her button. When I nod, she releases it.

"I'm sorry for your wait," a voice says on the phone. "Mr. Smith should be available shortly. Would you like for me to take a message, or would you like to continue to hold?"

"I can hold. Thank you." I gesture to Madison and she releases another button.

The swells of her breasts are visible now in the opening. She is temptation embodied and she makes me weak. But I can control my urges. This is just another test.

I mouth the word *more* to her.

Setting her work to the side, she focuses on releasing one button at a time, each time checking with me to see if I want more. Of course I do.

Her shirt gapes open, and her dusty pink nipples play hide-and-seek with the material. Her chest rises and falls with her every sharp breath.

"Good morning, Seth." Jack Smith's voice comes through the phone loud and clear.

I adjust my hard-on. "Good morning. How are things over at Fantase Technology?"

Madison waits patiently for my next direction.

"We're doing good. Sorry about the wait."

"No worries." I drop my gaze to her skirt and make a raising motion with my pen.

She gathers her skirt in her hands slowly, revealing her legs inch by intoxicating inch.

"What can I help you with today?"

When her skirt is at her hips, I motion for her to open her legs.

"We're hoping to get a first look at the new technology you'll be showing at the conference next month," I say into the phone. Madison opens her legs so I can see her glistening pink pussy. Already so wet for me. My cock twitches and I swear it grows harder. Fuck.

"We could arrange that." Jack's voice becomes a little more thoughtful, and I'm ready for his next ask. "You'll be using Fantase on the Harper Associates installation?"

"Of course, who else would we use?" We already quoted Jason Harper with Fantase equipment. I gesture for Madison to open her shirt more.

She does as I ask and shows me her magnificent breasts. This woman seems built to our specifications. It's almost eerie how she fits all of our needs and wants. Almost too perfect.

"There are a lot of products on the market." Jack pauses. "We'd really be interested in getting our new product line into Harper Associates' businesses."

"When we see what you have, we'll make that call."

"Sounds good. I'll put you down for next week and email you the details."

"Excellent. Talk to you later, Jack."

"Great. See you next week."

I end the call and take in the siren across from me. She lifts her leg onto the arm of the chair, spreading herself farther for my viewing pleasure.

"Are you wet, princess?"

"Yes, sir." Her blue eyes latch on to mine.

"Are you sore from playing with everyone else?" I stand and walk around my desk. My erection is obvious, and she licks her lips before raising her eyes to mine.

"A little," she admits, which probably means she's more sore than she says. She downplays a lot in her eagerness to please us.

Nodding, I go to my office refrigerator. Earlier, I put a glass dildo in the freezer. I pull it out now and check the temperature against my wrist. It's not all the way frozen but nicely chilled. Perfect.

Madison's gaze tracks me as I make my way back over to her.

"Stay like that." I drag a chair over and sit facing her. The dildo is cool in my hand. "Don't make a sound, princess, or I'll stop."

Her eyes meet mine, and she takes in a deep breath before nodding. I like to push the limits of her control, almost as much as I do my own.

Using the tip of the cold dildo, I trace it down her neck to her nipple. Her breathing quickens but she doesn't make a noise. Her nipple tightens more as I trace the tip around and around. I lift it from her and lean in to take her cold nipple into my warm mouth.

She makes a little noise before she cuts herself off. I suck and tease her nipple with my tongue until it's warm again before leaning back. Her face is flushed with desire and her eyes have darkened.

I tease her other nipple with the icy dildo, rubbing the side of it along her peaked tip.

"Did you enjoy being fucked until you're sore, princess? Having a cock constantly inside you? Fucking you?"

She bites her lip as I lean in again with a smirk. She won't answer because she doesn't want me to stop. My mouth closes over her cold nipple, drawing her deep into my mouth. She arches into me slightly, like she's trying to hold herself back and can't.

A breath releases from her but no sound. Her breathing is more erratic than before as I lift my head.

Dragging the tip down her abdomen, I shift to relieve some of the tension on my cock. Sliding the icy edge down between her pussy lips, I tease her clit with the chilled dildo. It's slender, definitely not as thick as any of us. Even sore, she should take it easily.

I press the tip against her entrance and ease it slowly inside while watching her face.

"The cold should help any inflammation, princess." I stroke it in and out of her, pressing a little deeper every time. Her mouth falls open, but she still doesn't make a sound.

"How does it feel?" I lift my gaze from her cunt clinging to the dildo to her flushed face. I wait for her to answer.

"Cold, different, good." She bites back a moan as I push it all the way inside and hold it there, letting her cunt work to warm the dildo.

"You want me to warm you up?" I slide the dildo almost all the way out and then thrust it back inside.

"Yes, sir."

I shove the chair I'm sitting on away and lower to my knees between her legs. Keeping the cold dildo inside her, I close my mouth over her pussy.

She inhales sharply but doesn't make a sound. Her flesh is a little cold when my tongue flicks over her, but she quickly warms up. Her hips press against my mouth, seeking my touch and warmth.

I shift the dildo inside her again, fucking her slowly with the icy toy. Her jagged breathing fills the room. She stills beneath me as a rush of wetness coats my hand and lips. I suck her gently as she fights against moving and making any sound during her release.

Drawing the dildo out, I stand before her, my erection painful but still in my pants. Her satisfied eyes glow up at me as I press the dildo to her lips.

"Suck it clean."

She parts her lips and I push it inside her mouth, watching her work it like she did my cock this morning. I slide it out of her mouth and back away.

"Good girl. Get cleaned up and then continue to work on the files." I go to the bathroom and wash my hands, face, and the dildo quickly. I pass her on the way out of the bathroom.

She stops and looks up at me. My heart stalls before thudding loudly in my ears.

"Thank you." The words float behind her as she vanishes into the bathroom.

My cock urges me to follow her in there and fuck her hard against the counter. I inhale and let it go. I don't let my cock control me. I'll get some relief soon enough. I already have plans for our lunch break.

Chapter 76

Afternoon Delight

Madison

My body is both satiated and needy as I finish up the projects Seth has for me in his office. The only thing hard is Seth, but apparently, he can ignore his erection. While I work, a shiver rushes through me as I remember the chilled dildo on me, inside me, followed by his hot mouth warming me up, setting me on fire.

"I'm finished." I stand and collect my things, waiting for acknowledgment.

"Lunch will be in fifteen. Downstairs in the apartment." He doesn't even lift his head from his work, like I'm an afterthought.

I make my way out to my desk. I shouldn't be surprised. It's a workday. I don't expect to be mauled or fucked all the time, but . . . I sink into my seat and turn to look at Seth's door. It's not like he didn't satisfy me. I got an amazing orgasm, so I should be happy, complete.

But leaving him unsatisfied makes me feel weird. Like, if I'm going to get cookies, he should get cookies too. I know it doesn't have to be like that, but I could see the tension in the way he held his body. He needs release, he just didn't want it then.

After I finish up a few things at my desk, I make my way to the elevator. I'm the first to head down, which isn't surprising. But no one joins me as I step into the elevator. It's not like I need constant attention, but it's odd having it and then having a quiet moment to myself. I step out and slide my access card into the door to let myself in.

The apartment is quiet and a little cold. In the kitchen, I preheat the oven to warm up lunch. Still alone, I head into my apartment and grab a sweater from my couch.

As I leave my room, I shrug it on. Still no one. I check the time on my phone and pull out the already prepared meal from the fridge to slide into the oven. It's actually been a while since I've been totally alone. Before I started working here, I was alone all the time. Even in a crowd of people, I was by myself. But with the guys, it seems I'm never alone.

They've been especially attentive since the file room incident. The quiet is suddenly overwhelming. I never knew someone was with me until they wanted me to know. They had all the power, watching, waiting for their moment.

My heart skips, and I glance around looking for anything odd or out of place. Like something could be tampered with here. No one can access this level except the guys and me, so I don't have any cause to be alarmed. But I remember that day, the feeling of being stalked, hunted, so alone.

The door to the apartment opens, and I take a step back. My body tenses and prepares to flee. My heart pounds in my ears as I strain to listen to every noise, any sign of whether I should stay or run.

Noah rounds the corner, his head is tilted down looking at his phone. My breath releases in a rush, and all that pent-up energy deserts me. My knees give a little, and I grab the counter to hold myself up.

Walking around the island to stand next to me, he finally lifts his head and leans in to give me a distracted kiss before his attention returns to his phone. "Kitten."

Sitting at the island, he keeps doing whatever with his phone while I work on controlling my breathing and bringing my pulse back down from terrified victim to normal.

I'm safe. I'm protected. It's fine.

The door opens and voices come down the hallway. Blake, Coop, and Seth. My chest fills with warmth. They're here. I'm safe.

I turn to pull the food out of the oven and get rid of the remaining panic clinging to me.

"Sweetheart." Resting his chin on my shoulder, Coop wraps his arms around my waist and pulls me back into his body. "I'm exhausted today, but last night was totally worth it."

I push my lips into a smile and clasp my hands over his arms. "Me too."

Last night was worth the lack of sleep. They chased away all my demons until it was just me and them, our bodies flowing together, chasing orgasm after orgasm. I can't keep up that level of sex, but it definitely gave me a night off from worrying.

Worrying about stalkers and how William is dealing with his son. I care about William. He tried to give me every opportunity. It isn't his fault his son is a woman-harassing pig.

Coop kisses my shoulder and then steps over to join Noah at the island. Blake turns me in his arms and tips my chin up. His green eyes search mine closely, looking for cracks. I'm pretty sure I spackled them all up before he came over. So, I give him a careful smile.

"We're being too rough with you." He shakes his head as his finger trails over my lower lip.

"No, you aren't," I assure him.

His lips press together. "You need a break. Your pussy needs a break." He hesitates and almost flinches when he says, "Maybe you should sleep in your own room tonight."

That's not happening.

I cup his cheeks and make him look at me. "Am I tired? Yes. A little sore? Yes. Do I want to sleep alone? Hell no. I don't want to miss my night with you."

His eyes soften as he presses a gentle kiss against my lips. "I don't want to wear you out, love."

I meet his fierce green eyes and give him a snarky smile. "You couldn't if you tried."

His lips spread into a grin that fills my heart. "You'll regret those words, tiger."

A little flutter goes through my belly at the promise in his eyes. *I sure hope so.*

We all grab our lunch and head to the table to eat.

"Everything going according to plan?" Seth asks.

Coop yawns. "All my tasks are handled. I just need to get a decent night's sleep."

He winks at me to let me know he's teasing. I can't help but feel guilty for keeping them up all night. We played two nights in a row, and it was fantastic, but at the cost of being half-awake at work. I'm supposed to be convenient, not distracting.

"Make sure you look up the Haverside account this afternoon. We don't want to drop the ball." Seth eats while he watches me.

His attention makes my pulse thrum with giddy anticipation. I'm still not wearing panties or a bra. He and I are the only ones who know.

It's like this kinky little secret between us while they continue to discuss business. What would the others do if they knew? My pussy clenches. I may be a little sore but I'm also horny. Just one day without intercourse shouldn't be that difficult to do.

Lunch doesn't take long, and soon the others are heading upstairs.

"Help me clean up, princess." Seth's voice draws me back.

I return to the kitchen in confusion. "I loaded the dishwasher already."

The exterior door shuts as the others leave for the office. Seth has his sleeves rolled up. There's a bowl on the island. He waves me over.

"Come here."

I walk around the island to stand beside him. He lifts me to sit on the counter and releases me.

"What are we doing?" I keep my eyes on his.

That shadow of a smile lights his lips. "Making you feel good."

I glance toward all the things he's gathered. A towel sits next to the bowl of water with steam rising off the surface, and inside the bowl is another glass dildo. My insides clench in anticipation.

"Lie back on the island," he says and helps me lie down. "Unbutton your blouse and lift your skirt for me."

My fingers tremble as I work the buttons open. Apparently, I'm not working fast enough for him as his hands gather my skirt up around my waist.

"Good girl." He spreads my legs wide and I inhale.

I want him deep inside me, not another dildo. His warmer-than-usual hand cups my pussy, and I sigh.

"Blake is right. We need to give you some recovery time."

I want to protest but I can see their point. Not that last night was rough, but the night before—taking both Coop and Noah inside me—and Blake was rough with me in the car yesterday . . . All of that followed by last night's marathon might have been a little much.

"How long are we talking?" I raise my eyebrow as our eyes meet. I don't want them to think I can't handle all of them.

Seth smirks as he lifts the dildo out of the water and onto a towel, drying it off. My gaze falls on it, noticing it has two ends. One end is long, smooth, and curled slightly. The other end is thicker, shorter, and bumpy. My insides blaze hotter.

He holds it against his wrist and then looks down at me. "Close your eyes, princess, and relax."

I inhale, close my eyes, and exhale. Warmth rolls across my nipple, one then the other. I bite my lips at the low moans rising in my throat.

"Make noise, Madison. Let me hear you release that tension."

My eyes open and find his before dropping to the erection he's had since I entered his office this morning. "You'll let me relieve your tension too, right?"

His smirk makes my insides tumble over each other as he rubs the warm tip against my nipple. "After I ease your sore pussy, I'm going to take your ass. Slowly."

I bite my lip at the desire on his face. He lifts the dildo off me.

"Close your eyes."

I shut my eyes, and warmth touches my clit as he slides the dildo between my legs. His cool breath against my nipple is my only warning before he closes over me with his surprisingly cold mouth.

I cry out at the contact as he slides an ice cube around my nipple with his tongue before drawing it back into his mouth. The warm dildo rubs on my clit, spreading my wetness around.

His mouth captures my other breast as the dildo eases into my pussy.

"Seth." His name shudders out of me at the contrast of cold and hot. He doesn't shift the dildo, just lets the warmth flood my insides. Meanwhile, a shiver rushes through me from the ice and his tongue against my nipple.

He draws away from me and I whimper.

"You need to take care not to let us overuse this cunt, princess." His cold tongue sweeps over my clit, making my muscles tighten around the dildo. "You don't know how hard it is to deny ourselves the pleasure of you now that we've found you."

"I promise." The words fall from my lips as his tongue traces my clit before he latches on and sucks with the ice still in his mouth. "Ah, fuck."

I arch against the stone island as an orgasm rips through me.

"Shh," Seth whispers as he licks me softly. He smooths his hand over my thigh. "Easy."

He draws the warm dildo out and eases it back in. An aftershock ripples through me.

"Touch your breasts. Show me what you like." His voice is low as he stands between my legs.

I don't open my eyes as I cup my breasts and thumb my aching nipples. Tingles shoot through me.

He keeps up the slow pace of the warm dildo. "How does your cunt feel?"

My breathing hitches as he changes the angle and that curve in the dildo hits me in the right spot. "Seth . . . fuck."

Words escape me as my hips mindlessly follow his stroking. I tweak my nipples and pinch them, sending bolts of fire down to combine with the blaze already wreaking havoc on my core. The sound of Seth's belt clinking makes my breath hitch.

"Answer me, princess. How does your cunt feel?"

"Good. Ah." I catch my breath at the change in angle as Seth shifts the dildo.

Taking hold of my ankle, he lifts it to his shoulder and then does the same to the other one. He slides my ass off the edge of the island.

"We're going to go slow."

I tip my head back at the first touch of his slick cock head to my asshole. We didn't play at all with my ass last night. Now I can't wait to feel Seth's cock inside me.

He presses in smoothly, keeping a constant pressure as my muscles relax to let him in. Buried inside my ass, his cock twitches as he moves the dildo slightly inside me.

My fingers grasp at the slick stone beneath me, needing something to hang on to. Seth draws the dildo out of my pussy and rubs it over my clit. It's still warm.

"How do you feel?" Seth asks, pulling back slightly before sinking in a little deeper.

Everything in me is tingling with need and want, so close to the edge.

Cupping my breasts, I press my legs on his shoulders as the dildo rubs circles on my clit. I'm beyond thought right now. I just want to be fucked any way I can get it. The way only Seth can fuck me.

"Please," I beg, shifting my hips against him, rubbing my sensitive nerves with his cock.

"Look at me while I fuck you, princess." Seth's words call something deep inside of me.

I meet his darkened gaze as he gently pulls out and eases back in. My breath shudders out of me.

"What do you need?" He's asking what I need to get off, even as he's slowly winding me up with each slow thrust of his cock in my ass. I love when they take me hard, but right now, this is all I can take. All I want.

"Suck my breast." I offer him one.

He leans down over me and takes my nipple into his mouth, sucking fiercely while our eyes remain locked. The dildo thuds as he puts it on the towel. Then his fingers are against my clit and sliding inside my pussy, filling me so full with his cock thrusting in and out of my ass.

He fucks my pussy and ass in time with the draws on my breast until we meld into one writhing being, striving for one more orgasm.

The wave crashes over me first, and I drag Seth under with me. He roars his release as he fills my ass with his cum. Each jerk of his cock sends an aftershock ripping through me. Even though I tighten around his fingers with my release, it doesn't hurt. Maybe the heat did help.

His fingers slow to gentle strokes as he eases me down. His cock slides out of me, and his belt clinks as he straightens his clothes.

He lowers my legs down off his shoulders and lifts me to sit on the island. His hands cradle the back of my head as he draws me in for a kiss, not to stir more desire, but to rejoice in the craving we just fulfilled. It's tender and warm and so fucking beautiful.

"You're a bigger distraction than I thought you'd be." He rests his forehead against mine and gives me a smile to let me know that fact doesn't upset him.

"Maybe I should shower and put on panties before returning to work." I return his smile, feeling light and happy inside. Basking in the afterglow.

He glances at his phone. "Fuck, I have a call in five minutes."

"Go." I press my lips to his briefly and push on his chest. "I'll be up in ten."

His gaze darts around the apartment.

"Seth." I tug on his tie to return his focus to me. "I'm safe here. I'll be locked in my room, locked in this apartment. Only accessible by the four of you. I'll be fine."

My words are meant to reassure him, but they're a little for me too.

He dips his head down so our lips meet again. This time there's a gentle longing in the kiss as he savors me. He presses his lips to mine one last time before washing his hands in the sink.

"Ten minutes." He points at me.

"Right, boss."

He hesitates, like he wants to come back and kiss me again. I grin as my chest fills with bubbles of delight.

"Go." I slide off the island and shoo him away.

Finally, he makes his way out of the apartment. The door shuts behind him. I clean up our mess in the kitchen and then hurry to my shower. By the time I'm dressed, I have two minutes to spare. My phone buzzes with an alert.

RECEPTION:

Package arrived for you at the front desk.

Weird. I grab my card and head out to the elevator. My fingers automatically go to my neck, but I didn't wear a scarf today. The bruises have faded to a light brownish yellow and only in a few spots. It doesn't look like someone tried to choke me to death anymore.

When I step into the lobby, it's almost like another world. The rush and buzz of the business day swirls around me. Everyone is in a hurry.

It's so easy to sink into the fantasy that it's just me and the guys. But there's this whole world outside our doors that wouldn't appreciate what we've found together. The appeal of keeping to ourselves isn't hard to accept.

A little happy sigh works through me. This is the part I love about working in a huge company. I pass the normal elevator banks and reach the receptionist desk.

The receptionist is on the phone while a person waits for her on the other side of the card-accessible area. She notices me and, with a roll of her eyes, points to a white box wrapped with a silver ribbon.

I lift what seems like a garment box and return to the elevator. Did Seth get me another outfit? I already have more clothes than I could wear over the next year. Even so, my heart pounds with excitement as the elevator climbs to the top floor.

Presents aren't something I'm used to. Growing up, we didn't have extra money for things that weren't useful. I'm not used to feeling spoiled, but I love that they want to spoil me. That Seth wants to spoil me.

When the elevator arrives, I walk to my desk and set the box down. My gaze goes to Seth's closed door. Should I ask first? He's on a call. He didn't give it to me directly, so I should just open it.

I unwrap the ribbon and take the lid off. Cold sweeps through me as I stare at the contents. A scream fills my ears.

Find out what happens next in PRIVATE LISTING: BOSS ME

Meet C.S. Berry

C.S. Berry is a combination of my love for writing and my love for reading. She began as an experiment and took off into something I absolutely adore. It's not often you can do what you love and it works as a career. As for me, I love reading and romance and heroines seriously getting railed. I assume since you've read my books that you do too.

If you want to discuss books or anything with me, come join my Facebook group, C.S. Berry's Spicy Executive Suite. And you can always catch me on Instagram @csberry.

Oh and me, I have a lovely family who aren't allowed to read my books. But are so proud, they keep leaking my pen name. My dog and cats don't care about my writing as long as I sit still long enough for them to snuggle. For more of my books and to join my newsletter, visit my website csberry.com.

XOXOXO,
C.S. Berry

For more stories and updates:
csberry.com
Join my Newsletter